A Certain Age

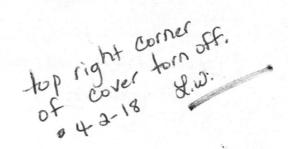

ALSO BY BEATRIZ WILLIAMS

Along the Infinite Sea

Tiny Little Thing

The Secret Life of Violet Grant

A Hundred Summers

Overseas

A Certain Age

Beatriz Williams

An Imprint of HarperCollinsPublishers

A CERTAIN AGE. Copyright © 2016 by Beatriz Williams. All rights reserved. Printed in the United States of America. No part of this book may be used or reproduced in any manner whatsoever without written permission except in the case of brief quotations embodied in critical articles and reviews. For information address HarperCollins Publishers, 195 Broadway, New York, NY 10007.

HarperCollins books may be purchased for educational, business, or sales promotional use. For information please e-mail the Special Markets Department at SPsales@harpercollins.com.

FIRST HARPERLUXE EDITION

ISBN: 978-0-06-244028-0

HarperLuxe™ is a trademark of HarperCollins Publishers.

Library of Congress Cataloging-in-Publication Data is available upon request.

16 17 18 19 20   ID/RRD   10 9 8 7 6 5 4 3 2 1

To Greenwich, Connecticut, and its marvelous
cast of characters for sheltering our dreams
for ten years (and keeping us stuck in
traffic for at least one of them) . . .

Keep striving.

The New York Herald-Times, May 29, 1922

TIT AND TATTLE, BY PATTY CAKE

At last! It's the day we've all been waiting for, dear readers: the opening of the latest and greatest Trial of the Century, and I don't mind telling you it's as hot as blazes inside this undersized Connecticut courtroom. You're much better off reading about it from the comfort of your own armchair, believe me. Oh, the suffering I endure on the sacred altar of journalism.

And now, after all these months of fuss and hysteria and delectable details—the Patent King, his beautiful heiress daughters, the downstairs tenant, the kitchen-maid-cum-tearful-Scarsdale-housewife and her munificent husband, the turret window, the missing gardener, the exact length and serration of the blade used to murder the victim—here we all sit, waving our makeshift fans before our perspiring faces, and it turns out these mythical figures are human after all! The Patent King is smaller than you'd think. He doesn't say a word, sitting stiff as a wire by the side of the defense counsel, and the daughters huddle next to each other in the front row, so pale and haggard that their much-ballyhooed beauty is, I'm afraid, purely conjecture.

A number of well-known society figures populate the benches around me. Chief among them is that perennial mainstay of the social calendar—and this column, naturally—the iridescent Mrs. Theresa Marshall of Fifth Avenue and Southampton, Long Island, as exquisitely dressed (and as exquisitely fashioned) as ever. I've had the privilege of visiting Windermere, the Marshall family estate down there by the shore, and I admire Mrs. Marshall's fortitude in enduring this untoward inferno when she might be reclining among the dunes, or riding her famous jumper, Tiptoe, around the ring at Lake Agawam.

The reason for Mrs. Marshall's sacrifice is quite clear, however. He sits by her side, and he's a fine specimen of manhood, as judged by the expert eye of yours truly. Mr. Octavian Rofrano will soon figure as one of the key witnesses in this case, and given his newfound fame and undoubted allurements, I don't blame Mrs. Marshall in the least for her vigilant oversight of his person, though I can't help wondering what poor old Mr. Marshall thinks of all this devotion.

So much for the man on Mrs. Marshall's left side. To her right sits another well-known Manhattan Thoroughbred: none other than the lady's brother, Mr. Edmund

Jay Ochsner, famed bachelor-about-town and not so far past his considerable prime to lay claim—so rumor has it, anyway—to the lesser of the two Patent Princesses. As to whether rumor has their engagement right, neither principal is talking, and I certainly don't see a ring glittering on the telltale finger. So, as always, I'll let you decide the truth for yourselves, dear ones.

As for me? Hold on to your hats. I've got the Trial of the Century to watch, if I don't melt away into the benches by the end of the morning.

Chapter 1

In olden times, sacrifices were made at the altar—
a practice which is still continued.

—HELEN ROWLAND

THERESA

Long Island, New York, on the second day of 1922

During the night, I dream that my husband arrives unexpectedly from Manhattan, in a plume of sultry exhaust from the engine of his Buick Battistini speedster, and let me tell you, the intrusion is most unwelcome.

To be sure, outside of feverish dreams, the possibility's remote. I have no doubt that, at the instant my dream-husband's wheels disturb the dream-gravel outside, the genuine Mr. Marshall lies in cetacean slumber on the bed of that jewel-box apartment on Sutton

Place he's bought for his mistress, this being the second night of the New Year and one conveniently placed on the calendar for adulterous pursuits. In any case, he's not the sort of man to storm down a frozen highway at dawn. Mr. Marshall's manners are impeccable.

Still, the very suggestion is enough to awaken me, lathered and breathless, from a state of abandoned repose. The room is heavy with that charcoal light that arrives just before dawn, and since it's a small room, unheated, unpainted, perched above the dusty remains of a pair of carriages made redundant by the ilk of Mr. Ford, I can't quite decide where I am, except that the place feels like home.

A mattress sags beneath my hips, and the sheet is flannel, musty, like an Adirondack cabin. I'm borne down by the weight of a thousand wool blankets, and someone is smoking a cigarette.

I roll on my side. "Boyo?"

The Boy stands by the window, matched in color to the smoke that trails from his hand. His shoulders are the exact width of the sash, and just as level, from clavicle to humerus. I have forgotten the substance of my dream, or why it terrified me; my breathing returns to normal at this indisputable proof of a male companion. Without turning, without even twitching—he is absolutely the stillest man I've ever known—he says:

"I keep wondering, are you going to call me that when I'm sixty?"

Yes, the room is dark and cold, and the blankets are heavy, and underneath those blankets I'm as naked as an innocent babe, though the resemblance to both babes and innocence ends there. I sit up anyway and hold out my arms. "You'll always be my Boyo. My lovely laddie."

He steps to the bed and sits down on the edge, entering obediently into my embrace. His skin is icy, the flesh underneath as hot as blazes. "There's a car outside," he says, after kissing me, as if this piece of information is of no consequence whatever.

I sort of startle. The Boy's arms, which are planted on either side of my hips, prevent me from startling too much.

"A car?"

"Yes."

"What make?"

"Can't tell. It's too dark." He picks up my arm and kisses the skin of my inner elbow.

"Saloon or coupé?"

"Coupé. Sit still, will you?"

I struggle to drag my arm away from his lips, and he won't let me. "For God's sake, Boyo, have you gone loony in the night? Where are my clothes?"

"Why? He's not getting out."

I swear. The Boy, who doesn't like me to take the name of his Lord in vain, applies the pad of his thumb to the center of my lips. I open my mouth and bite him.

"Ouch!"

"It's Sylvo. It's got to be Sylvo."

"So what?"

"So *what*? My husband's at the door, and you have to ask?"

"He's not at the door, Theresa. He's sitting in the car. Smoking a cigarette. Probably lit."

"But he's going to come out eventually."

"Maybe." The Boy shrugs. "No need to rush him, though."

There is little purpose to stirring up the Boy when he won't be stirred. His cold nerves kept him alive in France, and I guess they'll keep him alive now. It's Sylvester I'm worried about now. I sink back into the pillows. The Boy follows me. "You have to hide in the cupboard when he makes up his mind," I tell him.

"I'm not hiding in any cupboard."

"Yes, you are. I don't want a scene, Boyo."

The Boy finishes the cigarette at his leisure, exhaling the smoke directly from his mouth into mine, and crushes out the stub in the sardine tin on the floor next to the bed. (The Boy is awfully clever at improvising ashtrays from the raw materials at hand.) He knows exactly where the target lies, and his gaze remains on my face throughout this little operation. I think that's one of the little tricks that drew me in, all those months ago: his concentration. His refusal to be hurried. "There's only one reason your husband's here," he says, "and that's because he knows *I'm* here. So there's no point hiding in cupboards, even if we had a cupboard, and even if I were inclined to hide. Which I'm not."

"Why do you want to make things difficult for me?"

"Why do you make things hard for *me*?" He takes a piece of my hair between his thumb and forefinger, rubs it once or twice, and curls it tidily behind my ear. "I play by your rules, don't I? I do what you want."

"Most of the time."

"All right, then. So let me handle this one."

He lowers his head to my neck. I place my two hands on his shoulders and push, without much result. "How can you kiss me at a time like this?"

"Because I'm your Boy, aren't I? You're my baby. Kissing you is what I do, after a hard day's work. It's what makes me tick. It's who I am."

The Boy is built like a reed, or maybe a rope—that's it—coiled neat and tight into a knot you can't break. If he wants to sit here kissing me, I'm not going to stop him, at least not by force. You can't force the Boy into anything, you have to uncoil him first. Only his lips are soft.

It's who I am, he says. But who *are* you, Boyo? I've been puzzling that for a year and a half, and I could go on forever, at this rate.

So I think of something. "I'm no baby. When you're sixty, I'll be eighty-two."

"Well, now. Here's what I figure. As long as I'm your Boy, you're my baby."

As long as he's my Boy. But then who am *I*, Boyo? What am I doing here, puzzling over you? How did I— Mrs. Theresa Marshall of Fifth Avenue, Manhattan— become one half of you-and-me?

I don't think I know the answer. Something is lost. Something has gone missing inside that you-and-me, and I suspect it's me.

He is twenty-two years old, my Boy, and therefore a man, in the eyes of his almighty Lord God and of the law. He *looks* like a man, all the more now than when I first saw him. That was the summer of 1920, a year and a half ago, and he was a man in a boy's skin, let me tell you, a perfect pink-cheeked Boyo, young lips and old eyes. How he fastened on me. It's a heady thing, you know. And it was July, a late-night Long Island Fourth of July party, warm and slow and syncopated, dark and dreamlike, the sweat melting off the highball glasses and entering your palms. Someone told me he flew airplanes in France, had only just returned, the sole man in his squadron to survive, but then they always say that, don't they? *The only man in his squadron to come home alive!* He's never one of three survivors, or ten. All the other poor sons of bitches have to die, in order to render the cocktail conversation more breathless, the chitchat tip-top, the midsummer ennui less oppressive.

He was standing near the swimming pool. I thought he was much too young for me, but maybe that was why I was interested. As I waded through the air in his general direction, I became conscious of his puncturing gaze, and the wavelets glimmering on the skin of his face, the exact size and shape of a leopard's spots. This general impression—the Boy as predatory cat— aroused all my early interaction with him, and it was not until much later that I realized just how wrong I was.

By then, of course, it was far too late.

He does have a way of making me forget things, important things, like the fact that a man sits in an automobile outside our window, smoking a cigarette, possibly drunk, and that this man is very likely my husband. Or maybe it's part of the thrill, this terror of imminent discovery? Maybe I've been wanting a showdown like this all along, ever since I transformed that boy by the swimming pool into a fully grown lover, and I stopped sleeping with anyone else, including my own husband.

When my baby smiles at me, he croons.

"You're a terrible singer."

"That's why I only sing for you."

"Sweet boy, I want you to be *serious.*"

"I *am* serious. I only sing for you, Theresa, and you only sing for me. I think maybe it's time Mr. Marshall understands that."

Oh yes. He'll say things like that, my Boy, from time to time: statements of permanence that no civilized lover is supposed to make. Permanence is not what lovers are for, is it? But the Boy never does anything the way the others do. He packs more intention into a single word than the president drizzles into an entire inaugural address, and that's what snaps my bones when he enters a room, or a bed, or a car headed across the Queensboro Bridge at midnight. I stare a moment into those steady eyes and think about all those airplanes he must've shot down, the ones he never talks about. I think about a pile of lumber and shredded white fabric, smoking softly atop a frozen brown field, and the Boy's eyes looking down, circling, taking the whole mess in.

"I won't have you making scenes, Boyo, do you hear me? No scenes."

"I'm not going to hurt him. I'm just going to explain things."

"Explain what, exactly? He's my husband. He's got a right."

The Boy seizes my face in his hands. "He's got no right. How does a man keep a mistress, from the day he's married, and still call himself a husband? He's got no right at all." A soft bang rattles the window sash, but the Boy doesn't stop. He's got something to say to me. His thumbs make dents in the apples of my cheeks. "*I'm* the one who sleeps with you. *I'm* the one who dies in your bed at night."

"Did you hear that?"

"It was nothing."

I push the Boy away from my breast and leap out of bed. "He's coming in!"

"Let him come."

My dress lies on the floor by the door, my slip by the bed, my brassiere draped over a bedpost. I gather up these items while the Boy sits on the edge of the bed, hands braced on either side of his naked thighs, watching me like a Sopwith watches a Fokker. "What do you want me to do, Boyo? Get a divorce?"

"You know what I want."

"I'm not divorcing Sylvester."

"Why not?"

"There's no need."

"If we have a baby, there is."

My trembling hands will not operate the fastenings of my dress. I present my back to the Boy and say, "We are not having a baby."

"We might."

"I'm too old. Too old for a baby, too old for you."

He finishes fastening the dress and slides his hands around my middle. "Not true."

The Boy wants me to have his baby. He thinks a baby will solve all our problems. I don't happen to think we have any problems, other than the fact that I've got a desperate, bone-snapping crush on a boy two and a quarter decades younger than me, but the Boy has something against adultery and wants us to get married. He wants us to get married and live together in some rinky-dink apartment on Second Avenue (he doesn't come into his trifling inheritance until he's twenty-five, poor thing, and I'm afraid a junior bond salesman is paid at the mercy of the partners he serves) and then somehow make miraculous new babies, one after another, while the snow sifts down like sugar outside our window. Like one of those O. Henry stories. Love and candlelight. Except I'm forty-four years old and have already borne three healthy, legitimate, bawling children, the last of whom departed for Philips Exeter just as the war was staggering to its sepia end, and I'm about as suited to caring for a newborn now as I am for tending a rinky-dink apartment on Second Avenue.

No, our present arrangement suits me just fine: trysts every Monday and Thursday, when I'm supposed to be playing bridge, at the Boy's shabbily immaculate place in the Village, perched on the fourth floor of a building smack between an aromatic Italian grocery and a well-stocked speakeasy, so that a lady and a boy can enjoy a little hooch and a dance on the sly, before retiring upstairs to bed. During the summer months, we shack up here in the old carriage house, because while Sylvester and I have always occupied separate bedrooms here at the estate on Long Island, we do maintain a certain informal code about receiving lovers directly under the matrimonial roof. Mutual respect is the foundation of a solid marriage, after all.

Sometimes, for a special treat, the Boy and I will meet out of town at this lovely grand hotel by the sea, one that won't blink an eye at a boy and a well-preserved lady of a certain age checking into the honeymoon suite as a married couple. (The Boy always writes our names in large, neat letters in the register—*Mr. and Mrs. Octavian Rofrano, Junior*—and insists on paying the bill from his own pocket, the dear.) We stay for two or three nights, ordering room service and drinking poisonous gin and skinny-dipping in the ocean at two o'clock in the morning, sleeping and waking and sleeping, and most of all fucking. Sweaty, glorious, tireless, honeymoon fucking. Fucking two or three times a day, sometimes even four or five when the Boy is fresh and hasn't drunk too much gin. We haven't done that in a while, not since the end of summer. Autumn's such a busy time, after all. But my God, when we do, I feel like a new woman. I feel irresistible. As we drive back to the city, my skin glows like a debutante's.

So really, taken all together, Village and carriage house and naughty hotels, it's been most satisfactory, this past year and a half: the Year of the Boy, and then some.

Until now. I don't know what possessed us to jump into the Boy's Model T and head out into the tundra last night. Maybe it was the endless racket of Christmas parties and New Year dos, maybe it was the champagne. Maybe our little affair has settled too comfortably into routine, and we need a taste of excitement. "Let's go somewhere we can be alone," said the Boy, leaning back against the headboard, and I lifted my head and said that we *were* alone, silly, and he said he wanted to be *more* alone: he wanted to go out to Long Island and breathe in a little clean air, you know, just make a little New Year whoopee without all the lights and people and sirens and smoke, just sunshine and frozen air and me. So what am I supposed to say to that? I said all right.

And now look. Mr. Marshall has gone and followed us all the way here, has taken the trouble to track down Mrs. Marshall and her Boyo to a little love nest above a carriage house a hundred miles from the city, an act of jealous possession that was entirely out of character, made no sense at all, unless—

"The children!" I exclaim, and run to the window.

The Boy's eyes must be better than mine, or maybe it's youth. Under the trees below, I can just discern a shadow that might or might not be a car, and when I press my fingertips against the old glass and narrow my eyes to a painful focus, I see something more: a masculine figure leaning against the hood, possibly smoking a cigarette.

Behind me, the Boy is making noises. "Can you see him?" he asks.

"He's out of the car now. I think he's smoking. Oh God." I turn around. "Where's my coat?"

The Boy is dressing himself, rapid and efficient. "You're not going out there. It's too cold."

"Oh yes I am."

"The kids are fine, Theresa."

"How do you know?"

He takes my shoulders. "Because he would have gone straight in if something was wrong, wouldn't he? Let me handle this."

"No, please. Please. Go in the cupboard."

"There *is* no cupboard, remember?"

"Under the bed. Let me—"

A knock sounds on the wood below.

The Boy's eyebrows lift a little. "That's polite of him."

It has taken me decades of marriage to learn the sangfroid the Boy acquired in his paltry few months in France—or maybe he always had sangfroid, maybe he came out of the womb a cool, collected infant—and I'm still not as serene as I'd have you believe. My insides are all flighty, all riddled with fear and instinct. *The children!* Once you bring forth a baby into this world, God help you, the terror instinct takes up residence in your blood, like a chronic disease, and never leaves. When my Tommy quit Princeton to join the army in the spring of 1917 and had the nerve to turn up on Fifth Avenue a fait accompli in his second lieutenant's uniform, I nearly vomited into a Ming vase. Nearly. But I didn't! I held out my hand and shook his, and said he had better get a valet to look after those shiny buttons, and he laughed and promised to maintain his buttons as the shiniest in the service. Which was all our fond little Fifth Avenue way of saying how much we adored each other.

So I am more than capable, despite my shredded interior, of maintaining a purposeful calm as I pluck my lover's hands from my shoulders while my husband pounds and pounds on the door downstairs. "Get under the bed, Boyo," I say. "Now. And stay there."

His eyebrows are still up, and the brain behind them turns furiously, like an engine running fast under a placid hood. You can't see the color of his eyes, the air is too dark, but let me assure you they are a most engaging shade of pale blue-green, equally capable— depending on the light and his mood—of Mediterranean warmth or arctic frigidity. I can imagine which climate prevails now.

The pounding stops, the doorknob rattles—it isn't locked—and the hinges release a long and cantankerous squeak.

I point to the bed. "*Now,* Boyo." Or we're through. (I don't actually say those last three words, of course—no one likes an ultimatum, least of all the Boy—but you can feel them there, sharp-edged, dangling off the end of the sentence.)

The Boy shrugs his long, ropy shoulders and turns away. "If that's what you want," he says.

And that sound you hear, beneath the ponderous rhythm of a man climbing a set of high wooden stairs, is the hairline cracking of my heart, straight through the calcified left ventricle.

But the man standing in the doorway isn't Theodore Sylvester Marshall, after all, enraged or otherwise.

"*Ox*?" I exclaim. "What on earth are *you* doing here?"

My brother strides up to me, takes me by the shoulders, and kisses both cheeks. "Happy New Year, Sisser! Look at you. Haven't aged a minute."

"Oh, stop." I shove him away. "You gave me such a fright."

He steps back obediently, casts his eyes along the walls, and sends forth a slow whistle. "Sylvo said I might find you here."

"He did, did he?"

"I thought he was crazy. What are you, hibernating?"

"Well. Perhaps it's time for a little chat with my husband."

"Something like that."

"This place have a lamp or something? I can't see a thing. And boy, is it frosty."

I turn to the sole piece of furniture in the room, other than the bed: a beaten-up pine dresser wedged between the window and a diagonal roof beam. The matchbook lies next to the base of the kerosene lamp. "I thought you said I hadn't aged a minute."

"What's that?"

"Well, how could you tell a thing like that if you can't see?" I set the dome back on the lamp, and the room illuminates slowly, chasing out the frozen dawn by concentric degrees. The smell of burning kerosene enters the air, and it makes me yearn for the Boy's nakedness, his coiled-rope muscle under my hands, lit by an oil lamp.

"All right, now, Theresa. Lay off a fella. How are you? What the devil are you doing in this old shack? You gone crackers or something?" He frowns. "Say, you're not here with some sheik, are you?"

"Of course not."

"Yeah, I guess not. Old Sylvo wouldn't stand for it."

He's such a dunce, my brother. A sleek, good-looking, bachelor dunce.

"Of course he wouldn't. I'm just hibernating, as you say. Taking the edge off the New Year with a little simple living."

"Simple's right." He cast another look, shivered, and burrowed deeper into his overcoat. "Think of lighting that old stove, maybe?"

"It *is* lit." I push away from the dresser and make my way to the ancient cast-iron stove in the room's final corner, the relic of some long-gone coachman. A few small lumps lie overlooked in the scuttle, and I lift the stove's lid and drop them in. "I just forgot to bring in more coal, that's all."

Ox doesn't reply, and I rub my hands inside the feeble bubble of heat rising from the top of the stove, until his silence begins to unnerve me. I turn my head. "What is it?"

"You," he says. "You've been acting strange for a while now. Haven't seen you out much. When I do, you're not yourself. And now here you are, freezing to death in a shack in the wilderness—"

"Hardly that. I just wanted a little peace and quiet."

"You can have peace and quiet and central heating, too. What are you doing for food?"

"I've got a little something tucked away."

He shakes his head. "Sisser, Sisser. Let's drive into town and have breakfast. Ham and eggs and hot coffee."

"No, I'll stay here, thank you. I'm not hungry."

"But I've got something to tell you, and I don't want to do it on an empty stomach."

"Yours or mine?"

He grins a wolfish, ecru-toothed grin. "Both."

We are not entirely unprepared, the Boy and I, despite appearances. In the picnic basket next to the dresser, there are a dozen dinner rolls tied up in a napkin, a large flask of gin, a hunk of cheddar cheese, half an apple pie, two oranges, and a sandwich made of thick slices of left-over Christmas ham. Everything you need to shack up for the night in a Long Island attic, except the coal to keep you warm, and really, who needs coal when you have a magnificent self-heating Boy occupying your bed? I bend over and untie the napkin and toss my brother a dinner roll, which he catches adroitly. "Bon appetit. Try not to drop any crumbs on my nice clean floor, will you?"

"This is stale."

There's also a shawl in the basket, the lovely thick crimson shawl of India cashmere that the Boy gave me for Christmas. I settle it over my shoulders and step back to the stove, missing the roof beam by a slim quarter inch. "Tell me why you're here, Ox, and it had better be good."

My brother bites his roll, chews, swallows, and smiles, and when he parts his lips to speak, he says the last thing I'd ever expect to hear from the mouth of

Mr. Edmund Jay Ochsner, confirmed and eminently successful bachelor.

"I'm getting married, sis."

"Really?" I fold my arms. "Who's the lucky brood-mare?"

"Not *mare,* sis. Filly. Such a gorgeous, fine-limbed, Thoroughbred filly. The prettiest girl you ever saw. I'm in love, Theresa. I am one hundred percent, head over heels, goofy in love."

"I see." A craving for tobacco strikes my brain, but the cigarettes lie on the floor next to the bed, an inch or two from the sardine-tin ashtray and from the Boy's head resting on the floorboards, and I can't risk drawing Ox's attention in that direction. "Can I assume the poor child feels the same way about you?"

"I hope so. I've asked her father for permission, and he said yes."

"But the *girl,* Ox. What does the girl say? It's more or less the crux of the whole business, isn't it?"

"Well, I haven't asked her yet. But I think she'll agree." He gnaws another chunk from his bread. "I'm *sure* she'll agree. She's the sweetest thing, sis."

"And blind, obviously."

"Now, sis—"

"And rich. She's got to be rich."

"Sis."

From the downcasting of his eyelashes, I can see I've hit the nail straight on its bent old head. I say tenderly, "She's got to be rich, hasn't she, or you'd just do what you always do, when the love beetle nibbles."

"No, no. This time I really mean it."

"Of course you do. I'm sure she's a sweet, lovely girl, and her money has nothing to do with it." I pause. "How much has she got?"

"I don't know, exactly." He leans against the wall, on the other side of the roof beam that slopes away from the dresser.

"Oh yes you do. Down to the plug nickel, I'll bet."

The coals have begun to catch on, and the stove is getting hot, though not so much that my icy bones are inclined to step away. Ox is examining the floor now, and his arms are folded, the way he used to look when we were children and he'd been caught in some kind of mischief. The slope of his shoulders suggests confession. "Her father's got a patent on something or other, something that speeds up the manufacture of industrial . . . industrial . . ." He screws up his eyes.

"Don't hurt yourself. I've got the general idea. How much are we talking about? Thousands?"

He looks up, and his eyes are a little sparky. "Millions."

"*What?*"

"He licenses the design out, you know, and the revenue from that alone is one and a half million dollars a year, give or take a hundred thousand—"

I clutch the roof beam.

"—which is pure profit, you know, because he doesn't have to make the—the thingamajig himself. They just pay him for the design. It's *patented*." He pronounces the word *patented* with triumphant emphasis, as he might say *gold-plated*.

"Yes, Ox, darling. I understand what a patent is." In the midst of my beam-clutching shock, the shawl has sagged away from my shoulders. I resume both balance and composure and tuck myself back in while these extraordinary numbers harden into round marbles and roll, glimmering, back and forth across the surface of my mind. How could a man invent a single object and then vault—vault with such marvelous, casual ease!—over the accumulated wealth of no less than Mr. Thomas Sylvester Marshall of Fifth Avenue, whose father once supplied the entire Union Army with canned ham? A wealth that had dazzled me at seventeen. The company had naturally been sold in the seventies—canned ham being incompatible with the social aspirations of so keenly ambitious a woman as Mrs. Thomas Sylvester Marshall, my mother-in-law—and the proceeds invested in such a manner that a passive two hundred thousand dollars—give or take ten thousand—still drift gently into the Marshall coffers each year, enough to keep us all in silks and horses and ennui. But two hundred thousand is not one million five hundred thousand. A patent: well, that's a different kind of capital altogether. A patent suggests activity. Suggests having actually *earned* something.

I take the soft fringe of the shawl and rub it between my thumb and forefinger, in much the same way that the Boy caresses my hair. "Gracious me. She's quite a catch, then. Pretty and sweet and loaded. Does she have anyone to share all this lovely money with?"

"An older sister. Virginia. She's already married."

"I see. And how old is your little darling?"

He hesitates. "Nineteen."

"Oh, Ox. She's just a girl!"

"She's a very *old* nineteen," he says. "And you were married at eighteen."

"So I was."

"And Sylvo was thirty-six at the time, wasn't he?"

"So he was."

"Well, there you are." He nods and pulls a pack of cigarettes out of the pocket of his overcoat. "Smoke?"

"Thanks."

I accept the cigarette gratefully and allow him to light me up. He starts his own smoke from the same match, shakes out the flame just as it reaches the intersection of his finger and thumb. Like me, he closes his eyes as the virgin draft fills his lungs, and I am reminded of the first time we shared a smoke together, after the bon voyage party (if that's the term) that Sylvo and I threw for Tommy. *You look like you could use a smoke,* he said, upon finding me alone on the terrace, staring across the dark wilderness of Central Park, and I agreed that I did, and we stood there smoking together at three o'clock in the morning, not saying a word, until I tossed my stub over the ledge onto Fifth Avenue and turned to him. *This is our little secret, Ox,* I warned him, and bless the idiot, he's kept it ever since.

"It's not just the lettuce, though," he says now. "I was falling for her already, before I found out about that."

I reflect for an instant on my brother's extraordinary capability for self-delusion. "No doubt," I say.

"Wait until you meet her, sis."

"Oh, I can't wait. When are you proposing? I'll have to consult my calendar and throw you two lovebirds a smashing little engagement party."

"But, sis, that's why I came. Don't you remember?"

"Remember what?"

He looks around for an ashtray, and his gaze finally alights on the little oblong tin on the floor. I watch him step confidently to the bed and bend over. He's not quite the agile young sportsman he was in earlier days—everything takes its toll, and Ox has imbibed plenty of what constitutes everything—but he's still bendable enough, under that fat Chesterfield overcoat, and his glossy blond hair picks up flashes of light as he moves.

"Well, *well.*" As if he's just discovered a second Sphinx hidden between the floorboards. "Hel*lo*, Sisser. Looks as if someone's been a little naughty."

I choke back a cough. "What's that?"

Ox straightens and holds out the sardine tin in my direction. "Eight smokes already? That's some hibernation."

"Give me that." I snatch the tin and set it on the dresser, under the shelter of the lamp. "Now, then. You were talking about asking your young filly to marry you."

Ox follows the ashtray and leans against the edge of the dresser, nice and close, so I can examine the dark smudges under his eyes and the chapped skin of his lips, which are bent into a familiar self-assured smile. Underneath the Chesterfield, he's wearing evening dress, which shouldn't really surprise me. Nor, for that matter, that he stinks of moonshine.

"*I'm* not the one who asks her," he says. "Don't you remember?"

"I don't remember a thing. I hope you don't think *I'm* going to pop the question for you. I wrote all your college papers; isn't that enough?"

"The *ring,* Sisser. Don't you remember?"

"What ring? I haven't the slightest—oh!" I spit out the cigarette. "*Mama's* ring? The *rose* ring?"

Ox pats my hand on the dresser. "That's right. The old family tradition. I had it sent to the jeweler for a good polish, and now all that *remains,* all I *need,* which is why, of course, I came to *you,* Sisser—"

"Oh, for God's sake, Ox. You can't be serious."

"Why not?"

"Why not? Because it's a farce. A medieval farce. Who sends a proxy to propose for him these days? Chivalry went out with the Armistice, Ox, didn't you know? Chivalry went out when the Lewis gun and the chlorine gas and Picasso came in. This shiny modern world hasn't got any knights left in it."

"It's not a farce, sis. It's a fine old family tradition. A cavalier presents the august family ring to the lady of one's choice, the lady who will one day become the next Mrs. Ochsner, ruler of all New York—"

"Darling, the Ochsners haven't ruled anything for years, not since Mamie Fish took over from Lina Astor. And now it's just anarchy. Actresses and artists and writers, God help us. The present Mrs. Ochsner commands a crumbling house on Thirty-Fourth Street and nothing else to speak of."

"Not true. Mama has *pedigree*, Theresa, she has *history*, which is more than you can say of some ink-stained penny novelist." He pauses grandly, flicks his ash into the tin. "Anyway, I need a cavalier. A ring bearer."

I laugh. "Oh, Ox. Only you."

"I'm serious, sis. How about one of your boys?"

"Absolutely not. They haven't got a knightly bone in their bodies. Unless it's a football you want delivered, they're not interested." I stub out the cigarette.

"One of their friends?"

"What about *your* friends?"

"My friends are all married. Or else lecherous old bachelors like me."

"You know what it is, Ox? You don't give a fig for family tradition. You just want someone to do your dirty work for you. You don't want to face the girl herself and ask her to marry you. After all, what if she does the sensible thing and says no?"

He drops his cigarette in the tin and turns to the bed. "She won't say no."

"You don't sound very confident."

"She won't say no. I'm sure of it. Her father's on my side, and she—well, she's a good girl, Sisser."

"Does as she's told?"

"Exactly. And she likes me, she really does. I pulled out all the stops for her, sis. Charmed her silly. She likes horses, I took her riding. She likes books, I . . . well, I—"

"Pretended to like books?"

"You know what I mean. I dazzled her! I took her into our library on Thirty-Fourth Street, Papa's old library, and you should have seen the lust in her face."

"So she's marrying you for your strapping great *library*?"

He turns back, smiling, and flourishes an illustrative hand along his body, from brilliantine helmet to bunion toes. "And my own irresistible figure, of course."

As I said. Delusional.

I reach inside his overcoat pocket and draw out the cigarette case. There's only one left. I rattle it around and consult my conscience. "Of course, Ox. You're just as perfectly handsome as you were at twenty-two. In fact, I can hardly tell the difference."

Ox picks the gasper out of the case and hands it to me. "Go ahead. Take it. And in return, you're going to find me my ring bearer, aren't you?"

"Maybe."

"Sweet old sis. Always count on you to help a fellow out in a pinch."

"Indeed you do." I strike a match and hold it to the end of the cigarette. My brother watches me anxiously. The light's a little better now, the sun is rising, and the lines around his eyes grow deeper as the reality of daylight takes hold of them. The slack quality of his skin becomes more evident. And I think, *Is this how I look, too?* Despite the creams and unguents, the potions and elixirs with which I drench myself daily, has my face grown as shopworn as his?

When we'd been married a year or two, and Tommy was still a baby, my husband commissioned Sargent to paint my portrait. It's a gorgeous old thing, full-length, framed in thick gilt wood. It hangs in the middle of the gallery of our apartment on Fifth Avenue, the place of honor, where it's illuminated by a pair of electrified sconces and gazes down from the heights to a certain point in the marble center of the hall, the exact position where any human being would naturally come to a halt and gaze upward to pay worship.

Because—forgive me, let's be honest—the creature depicted in that portrait is a goddess. She is as beautiful and self-assured as they come. She's wearing a dress of pale pink gossamer that hugs her tiny waist—giving birth at eighteen has its advantages—and a diamond necklace arranged like a chandelier upon her sculpted white bosom. Her dark hair is piled in loose curls on her head; her eyebrows soar confidently above her opaque almond eyes. The smile that curls the perfect bow of her mouth proclaims such an extraordinary volume of youthful self-satisfaction you're inclined to smack her.

In fact, go ahead. I wouldn't blame you, really.

On the other hand, who can blame *her* for her satisfaction? My God, the world's at her feet. At the age of twenty, she's succeeded brilliantly in the one great career open to her. She married one of the wealthiest and most eligible bachelors in New York; she has already given him a son and heir. She's rich and beautiful and clever. The newspapers adore her. In fact, not a single genuine setback has ever dared to obstruct the ascendant path of her life.

And on the face of that young woman there hangs not the slightest doubt that she will remain ascendant forever. A world doesn't exist in which she will have to fight for her beauty, to guard against the slow thievery of time.

She doesn't know, poor thing, that in less than a year, she will discover that her husband keeps a mistress, and that this mistress has also borne him a child—a small and perfect daughter—only two months after the birth of the Marshalls' own firstborn son. By then, of course, the portrait's subject will be several months into her second pregnancy, and she will face an important decision, the most vital choice of her life, and one on which all her future happiness depends.

Did she make the right one?

Well, I'm here, aren't I? I stand right here in the shabby attic of an old carriage house, as rich as ever, mother of three cherished sons, wife of a generous and well-respected husband, passionately in love with a young and brilliant man—a man to whom I have no earthly right, a man who returns my passion with bone-snapping physical ardor—who at this very moment has flattened himself into the dust beneath the bed for my sake.

What more could a woman ask for, at my age?

I'm halfway through the cigarette before I address the question warping the eyebrows of the brother who stands before me. I wave away a curl of smoke, which has been illuminated into a kind of celestial spirit by the sunshine that now refracts through the window's ancient glass. The luminous new morning of the second of January. Remember that.

"Do you happen to know the young lady's name?" I ask.

My brother says eagerly, "Sophie. Sophie Fortescue. She's a good girl, Theresa. Quiet as a mouse. The sweetest girl in the world. Wouldn't say boo to a goose."

I hand him the cigarette—he looks as if he needs a smoke more than I do—and he sucks it in like oxygen.

I look past his elbow at the bed in the corner, and the dozen or so mildewed horse blankets that the Boy gathered up to cover me last night. I objected to the smell, and he said a little mustiness was better than freezing to death, and anyway I'd get used to it. Human beings can get used to anything, he told me. It's how we survive.

And he was right. All I remember of last night, other than the terror of my dream, is the smell of the Boy's warm skin.

I return my gaze to the pasty and anxious ruins of my brother's face. "In that case, I can't begin to imagine what she sees in you, Ox, though I frankly *can* imagine why your courage failed you, in the face of all that virtue."

He begins to object, and I hold up my hand.

"Nonetheless, and to your great and undeserved fortune," I continue, "I happen to know *just* the boy to get the job done."

Chapter 2

A fool and her money are soon courted.

—HELEN ROWLAND

SOPHIE

New York City, nine days later

Like all good girls, Sophie hates to disappoint her father, so she takes heroic measures to ensure he doesn't hear a thing when she sneaks out on Wednesday night with Julie Schuyler to visit a jazz joint in Harlem.

The trouble is sneaking back in.

"I think it's stuck," she whispers, rattling the knob of the service door. Her words form clouds in the frozen air.

Behind her shoulder, Julie swears. "You're such a bunny. Let me try."

Sophie steps back and allows Julie to give the knob a rattle. The service door is set down below the street, in a discreet little well reached by a stairway to the left of the six worn stone steps that lead to the front door. Two years ago, the door belonged to the downstairs tenant, a middle-aged woman who quietly occupied the lower ground floor and sent up affectionate baskets of soda bread (she was Irish) with her monthly rent. But then she had moved out—out of the blue, just as quietly as she had lived, leaving only a last farewell basket on the square table in the front room—and they had opened up the staircase and turned her apartment into a proper kitchen and scullery and maid's room, and now the door was a service entrance.

Prosperity has arrived to the Fortescue family, you see, and prosperity at least requires a house entirely your own. Even if you're hardly ever allowed to leave it.

"Damn." Julie swears again without a thought. "I thought you said your sister had unlocked it before she went to bed."

"She *said* she'd unlock it. And she always keeps her word."

"Well, it's locked now." Julie steps back and gazes through the murky glow of the streetlamps to the windows layered along the brown facade: the exact shade of a dirt road turned to mud by a week's worth of rain.

The heel of her shoe crackles against a small pile of slush, refrozen during the night. "Which room is hers?"

"We can't *climb!*"

"Of course not, darling. *What* an idea." Julie pats her pockets and turns for the stairs. "Have you got a good throwing arm?"

Sophie follows her up the steps to the sidewalk. The taxicab is rumbling by the curb, waiting to whisk Julie back to her own place on Sixty-Ninth Street, twenty-seven blocks and a world away. Soon the sunrise will be spearing between the buildings and down the long channels of the side streets, turning the brownstone pink and the windows gold. Waking the virtuous inhabitants. Next to her, Julie opens up a small beaded pocketbook and rummages through the tissue.

"Not very good," Sophie admits, "but I'll give it a try. What have you got?"

Julie hands her a tube of lipstick. "Be careful, now. It's my favorite."

Sophie's head is bleary, and that buzzing ring in her ears makes her balance unsteady. Also, the windows have an unnerving tendency to fidget whenever she tries to count them.

The taxi honks.

"Take your time," says Julie.

"Tell him to clam up, before he wakes Father." Sophie closes one eye, which seems to help. Virginia's room is on the third floor, overlooking the street, a good twenty-five vertical feet above the top of Sophie's close-fitting hat. She has two windows, both of them draped in thick swags of green damask, suitable for her dignity as a married woman. Sophie chooses the window positioned nearest the bed and waits until the panes stop jumping before she draws back her arm and throws.

The lipstick hardly reaches the upper ledge of the parlor window when its trajectory starts to slow. Tilts. Hovers for an instant at the peak, and then falls back to the pavement in a metallic smack.

Julie bends over and picks it up. "Try again. And put a little more mustard on it, will you? I'm not getting any warmer out here."

Sophie throws again, piling on the mustard thick and high, and this time the lipstick nearly achieves the third floor.

But not quite.

"Amateur," Julie says.

"And you can do any better?"

"No." Julie turns and raps on the taxi window. "Ty? Come out here. We need you."

The door opens, and Julie's date pours himself swearing onto the sidewalk. He's bundled up in a dark coat and a gray muffler and a thick wool hat, and while his eyes are bright, the pouches beneath them are thick and bruised. He wants to know what the hell they're doing.

"Just trying to hit that window there," Julie says, pointing, handing him the tube of lipstick.

"*Whose* window?"

Sophie says, "My sister's. The third one up." She says it softly, because Ty is an unpleasant man, doesn't say much, and he's cheap with the waiters. He didn't like the jazz either. He never said this out loud, but Sophie could see, by the narrowness of his eyes, the contumelious tension of his mouth, drink after drink, what he was thinking. *Nigger music.* She'd heard the phrase somewhere, on the sidewalk maybe, in an ugly tone. You heard a lot of things on a New York sidewalk, whether you knew what they meant or not.

Ty takes the metal tube in his palm, which is gloved in black leather and exceptionally large. He turns the lipstick just so, and closes his hand into a fist. Sophie steps aside. He winds back his right arm. The lipstick shoots into the air like a bullet and shatters a pane of glass in the center of the lower sash of Virginia's window. An instant later, the slivers rain daintily on the pavement below.

"Dear me," Julie says.

Ty lifts his foot to the running board. "You told me to hit the window. I hit the window. Now can we get the hell out of here before my wife calls the hotel to wish me good morning?"

Sophie watches the facade anxiously, winding her mittened hands around each other. Her pocketbook dangles from her elbow. The curtains part, and a gasp floats down to the sidewalk below. "Sophie? Is that you?"

"Yes!" Sophie whispers, as loud as she can. In the frozen morning air, the sound carries easily. "The door's locked!"

"It's six o'clock in the morning!"

"Is it?"

"You broke my window!"

"I didn't break it! Ty did."

"Who's Ty?"

Ty has already disappeared back in the taxi, behind a grand black slam of the door. "You coming?" he growls to Julie, through a cracked-open window.

"All right, all right," Julie grumbles. "Can you take it from here, darling?"

"I guess so. Virginia?"

Her sister sighs with such monumental emphasis, the sound transforms into a groan by the time it reaches

Sophie's ears. "Coming," she says, and her head melts away, and the curtains fall back together just as the taxi roars from the curb.

"Just who was that awful man who broke my window?" asks Virginia, setting a glass of warm milk on the marble-topped kitchen table at which Sophie is seated. Or rather sprawled. It's a sprawling kind of moment, when you're home at dawn after a disgraceful night on the town, and your brain is achingly acute but the bones of your arms and legs have turned into sand.

The room is wintry—the maid has only just risen to build the fire—and while Sophie's taken off the new mink collar her father gave her for Christmas, she still wears her long black coat, unbuttoned. Her gloves lie in a heap on the table, next to her crimson pocketbook, also new, which appears to have had something blue spilled across its middle. Sophie can't imagine what. The resulting purple stain meanders along the silk, looking a little like Italy and its associated islands—that spot to one side might be Capri, or was it Corfu?—and Sophie supposes the pocketbook is probably ruined. Did that matter anymore? It used to matter terribly. Just like broken windows used to matter.

"I don't know. He's some baseball player Julie knows, visiting the city for the New Year." Sophie sips the milk and closes her eyes, and all at once she's not drinking milk in a newly built kitchen while a stranger bustles about the gleaming Wedgewood range, but reading at the homely wooden table of the makeshift kitchen upstairs—now a proper dining room—drinking milk while the distant hollow sound of the phonograph drifts in from the parlor, playing some tune from *HMS Petticoat*. Father's favorite.

"Well, he wasn't very nice."

Sophie opens her eyes. Virginia settles heavily in the chair next to hers and lifts another glass of milk. She wears an emerald silk kimono over her nightgown, and the lines of her face suggest a night that wasn't especially rich in slumber.

"No, he isn't," Sophie says. "Julie says he's mean as a snake."

"Then why does she step out with him?"

Sophie fingers her glass. Drinks a little. Sobriety is returning—it wasn't that far away to begin with, Sophie's not really fond of cocktails—and the milk forms a nice thick comforting film over the walls of her abused stomach. "I guess she likes it. The danger, I mean."

"She should watch herself."

"Oh, he's leaving town on Friday. Back home to Georgia and his wife and kids."

"Well, I can't say I'm not happy to hear that, Baby dear." Virginia pats her hand and looks up at the clock. The maid, closing the oven door, sweeps a curious glance across the two of them. Sophie can see the girl from the corner of her eye. She can't quite get used to this new intrusion in their lives, the way Virginia and their father can: the remorseless omnipresence of servants, every waking moment, every sleeping one, too. Gives her the creeps.

"You'd better get upstairs," Virginia adds. "You'll want a few hours of rest before that fellow arrives."

"What fellow?"

"Don't you remember? Your cavalier is coming today."

Sophie claps a hand over her mouth. "That's today?"

"You're such a scatterbrain, Baby. Haven't you been looking forward to this for days?"

"I have. I just forgot that today was Wednesday."

"It naturally follows after Tuesday."

"I know, but Tuesday hasn't ended yet."

Virginia laughs and finishes her milk. "For *you*, maybe. And now I've got to go see about that window your baseball player broke. If Father finds out—"

"Oh, you won't tell him, will you?"

"Of course not." Virginia holds up her thumb, and Sophie presses it with her own, the old signal. The thumb pad is cushiony, warm, like the old parlor sofa. Virginia's face behind it has grown a little wistful. "I don't mind. You *should* have a little fun while you can, Baby. Before you get married to Mr. Ochsner."

Sophie drops a remorseful gaze at the table. She *has* had fun. These past few weeks, the fun's trickled right in, excursion by excursion, each one artfully disguised under one excuse or another, a subversive collusion of Virginia and Sophie and Julie against the regime of the Fortescue household. Julie Schuyler, blond and brilliant: *Let's go out and be naughty tonight, somewhere where nobody knows who we are, I know just the place.* And she had. And it was *nice—really nice*—not to sit at home reading for once, listening to the phonograph. Nice and somewhat exotic to drink horrid cocktails that made your head fuzzy, and listen to oddly paced music that made it fuzzier, and then try to dance and end up laughing safe in Julie's long blond arms. Even Julie's baseball player couldn't spoil things, though he *would* keep looking at Sophie as if she were a dish of roasted chestnuts he'd like to crack open, one by one.

All at once Sophie's head is drenched in fatigue. She drops her thumb away to cover a yawn, and when her mouth is back under control, she says to her sister, "My pocketbook is probably ruined, don't you think?"

"You can get another."

"But it's such a waste. Shouldn't it matter?"

Virginia shrugs. "Everything's changed, Baby dear. All our worries are over."

But Virginia's voice is out of tune, a hair flat. On her face there is such an *absence* of joy, such a pancake dullness in her eyes, that Sophie raises her head and shakes off the sleepiness. "Is everything all right, Virgo?"

"Yes."

"Have you heard anything?"

The right-hand side of Virginia's mouth forms a smile. "No. Same as yesterday."

"Well." Sophie picks up her pocketbook and runs her hand along the length of purple Italy. A few feet away, Virginia's hand lies atop the table, caressing her glass of milk, and Sophie (not for the first time) steals a glance at the wedding band that crimps the skin of her sister's telltale fourth finger, just to reassure herself that it still exists. That some physical evidence survives—other than the small child sleeping upstairs, and the letters that appear on the hall table, from time to time—of this phantom brother-in-law from the battlefields of France. Sophie ventures: "I'm sure he'll write soon. As soon as he can."

"Yes, I'm sure."

"He must be miles away from any settlement. Florida's such a big state."

"Well, that's the idea, isn't it? Big and lots of land. Lots of opportunity. Now go to bed, Baby dear. You have a big day tomorrow."

"Today."

Virginia laughs. "Yes, today. I can't wait to see what all the fuss is about. I'm sure it's going to be great fun."

The strap of the pocketbook is a long filigree triple chain, which can either be tucked inside or slung over Sophie's elbow or wrist. A very pretty chain, finely wrought, nothing like the workmanlike chains she encounters in Father's workshop. She fingers it now, slides the delicate metal along the tips of her fingers, making them tingle, and thinks, *I wonder whether you could design a machine to make these, delicate work, but I'll bet you could do it with the right die, with a really precise gear to do the links.*

"I do *like* Mr. Ochsner, though," she says. "He's awfully kind, and he has such manners. He's like the men you read about in books. And his family! The *Ochsners*, Virgo. Like a piece of history."

"He's an aging roué, Baby dear, and needs our money."

"Well, of course. But at least he's grateful. He doesn't act as if he'd be doing *me* the favor, even though he has every right to be a snob, the family he's from. He's related to Paul Revere, you know. *And* Aaron Burr."

Without warning, Virginia leans forward and puts her two hands on either side of Sophie's face. "Look at you. Your lipstick's all smudged. Did that Julie put blacking on your lashes?"

"Yes."

"Well, you'd better wash it off before Father sees you. And use soap. A *lot* of soap."

"All right."

"Now listen to me. I know you want to please Father, and I know he makes it seem like you've got no other choice but to say yes, but that's no reason to marry this Mr. Ochsner if you don't want to. If you don't love him, I mean, or you don't think he loves you the way he should."

"Of course not."

Virginia's eyes have shed that awful film. They're brown and gleaming, just like they used to be, and her hands are delicious on Sophie's cold cheeks. "Not that he *shouldn't* be in love with you, Baby dear. You're such a lovable thing. But he's a New York bachelor. They're a different species. All they care about is the dough, and a good laugh. And I don't want anyone breaking my Baby's heart. I don't care what Father says. I took too much care in raising you."

So Sophie's eyes turn blurry, because she knows what Virginia means, why Virginia's eyes are equally overflowing with caution and brown worry, and darn it all if they're not crying together, crying in each other's arms, crying as if Manhattan Island has just broken off from the rest of America to go drifting alone into the ocean, while the maid rolls her Irish eyes and heads into the breakfast room to light another fire.

Sophie could have slept around the clock, but Virginia wakes her at eleven, holding a glass of water in one hand and a pair of aspirin in the other. "Betty's bringing up a tray of coffee," she says, not very sympathetic.

Sophie, turning her head in the direction of Virginia's voice, reflects that she may have been a little more—how did Julie put it?—a little more blotto last night than previously estimated. Or, alternatively, a nearby quarry has mistakenly delivered a load of rubble into her skull while she slept, by way of an ear.

She takes the aspirin and the water and swallows obediently. "Whatever happened to hair of the dog?"

"Not for you, young lady. Just be glad you weren't arrested last night. The paper's full of some raid the police ran on a place in the Village."

"We were in Harlem. I think."

"Still." Virginia moves to the window and opens the curtain a few inches, causing the sunshine to outline her willowy shape, now clothed in a perfectly ethereal frock of blue silk that recalls the Madonna.

Sophie howls and buries her face in the pillow.

"You'd better get up," Virginia advises. "Your cavalier is due here at noon, and cavaliers are always prompt, I'm told."

So Sophie crawls into an upright position, pushing aside her hair, just as a perfunctory knock hits the door and the maid slides in, bearing a tray that's twice as heavy as she is. Evelyn follows her, squealing *Aunt Sophie! Aunt Sophie!* in two-year-old pidgin. Virginia goes on pulling aside the curtains, sending further shafts of merciless sunshine into the room, and Sophie decides that the teetotalers had it right after all, and she will never touch the demon liquor again.

"My goodness," Virginia says cheerfully. "You look terrible. We'd better get to work."

Lucky for Sophie, Virginia loves a good project, and at two minutes to twelve they descend the stairs, Madonna and virgin sister and beatific child, to join Father in the parlor, all newly redecorated in blue and cream. Sophie's head is still full of rocks, but the sharp edges are blunted by aspirin, and the rattle's not so bad, really, if she doesn't shake her head. She's wearing a dress of delicate fog gray that skims the curves of her calves, and as she pauses in the doorway, she imagines, for just the briefest flicker of an instant, that Father takes her hands and tells her she looks like an angel. Father does that sometimes. To Father, Sophie's always been an angel, as if her mother left behind a little piece of her eternal soul to illuminate them daily, and Sophie just *basks* in this adoration, just *lives* for it.

But only in her imagination.

In reality, Father folds his newspaper, stands up, and inspects her, head to toe. He asks her if she slept well, and she says *Like a baby,* and when that makes her blush because of Virginia, she adds *Right through breakfast!* just as cheerfully as she can, without spilling the rocks in her head.

He peers into her face. His ears are large and extend like a pair of wings from his old-fashioned whiskers, so that Sophie sometimes imagines he can actually hear her thoughts. (Or, in this case, the rattle of the guilty rocks.)

"Is something wrong, Father?" she asks, as innocent as can be.

"Oh, nothing." He shakes his gray head. "For a moment there, I thought you were wearing lip rouge, that's all."

Virginia laughs behind her. "The very idea! Baby wearing lipstick."

"Not our Baby," Father agrees.

Evelyn tugs at her dress. "Aunt Sophie! Aunt Sophie! Peetah's!"

Virginia swoops down and detaches her daughter. "Not today, pumpkin. Aunt Sophie's got a visitor. Mama will take you to Peter's after lunch and buy you a whole bag of lemon drops, all to yourself."

"Lemmy drop!" Evelyn wriggles free and runs for the door.

"Not *yet*, Evelyn!"

Sophie turns to the window. If she cranes her head just so, she can glimpse the stream of people and vehicles gushing forth from the rusty spigot of Third Avenue. "This is so thrilling," she says, in a voice too high by at least an octave. "Shouldn't he be here by now?"

Virginia joins her, carrying Evelyn on her hip. "You'd have thought so. I guess modern cavaliers have all this traffic in their way."

"You mean he's not riding up on a horse?"

"The card didn't say anything about horses."

No, it didn't. But it was a pretty card all the same: ecru, formal, written in a mysteriously lovely script that might have come from a printer, so even and copperplate were its curves and scrolls.

*Mr. Edmund Jay Ochsner presents both his
compliments and his Cavalier*

———————

*Wednesday, the eleventh of January, nineteen
hundred and twenty-two at twelve o'clock*

———————

*if Miss Sophia Fortescue and her Family will be
at home to receive them*

And that was all. So brief and delicious, so dripping with invisible intrigue in the spaces between the elegant black letters. A cavalier! What could that possibly mean? Sophie looked up the word in the dictionary last week, to be sure there wasn't some clue hidden in its French etymology. She discussed the whole affair with Julie Schuyler last night, sometime between a green cocktail and a blue one—oh, perhaps *that* was the source of Italy's appearance on her pocketbook?— and Julie's thin eyebrows rose buoyantly. *Jay Ochsner's sending you a cavalier? Oh, my stars. What fun that will be.* And she tipped her cigarette into the ashtray and zipped her lips, even though Sophie begged for more. No, she wasn't going to spoil Sophie's surprise, she said, not for all the bourbon in all the bathtubs in Kentucky.

And now the cavalier is late, which isn't fair. Caught in traffic like an ordinary mortal. Not that Sophie blames him; at the end of the street, there's the rusty flow of Third Avenue, and beyond that the titantic crammed-up grid of Manhattan Island: delivery wagons and motor omnibuses and taxis and limousines with chauffeurs and endless ordinary automobiles—just like theirs—and it might take an hour to go five blocks in that tangle. Would a cavalier take the subway, if the traffic were *too* awful? It seems unlikely, but then the habits of upper-class New Yorkers are still a mystery to Sophie. It's a world all its own, a rhythm she hasn't quite picked up, no matter how closely she listens, no matter how she thrills to its throb in her veins.

"He isn't that late," says Virginia. "Only a few minutes."

Sophie places her hand on the window frame, which is newly repainted in thick cream, terribly flawless. Father told Virginia to redecorate, after Mr. Ochsner came to call that first time, and Sophie still marvels at the transformation. Creamy trim and blue silk draperies and gilt-framed mirrors above the mantels, so that you caught endless repetitions of yourself as you turned around, each one bemused and lost inside a jigsaw of tasteful new splendor. How could this perfection belong to them? *Sophie's* creamy window frame. *Sophie's* clear and fragile glass, looking down on the cars crawling past, any one of which might contain a cavalier bearing the compliments of the dashing, golden-haired Mr. Ochsner, whose family owned such a glorious, ancient library, who had knights at his beck and call to deliver greetings to young ladies.

What a magical place, Manhattan! What a thrill, what a wallop to live inside it. And sometimes you were bemused and lost, and sometimes you were full of glitter, sometimes your insides sizzled and bubbled and sang with the simple joy of a traffic jam outside your window, one that might or might not contain a genuine, twenty-four-carat knight. A *parfait* creature from another age, galloping free from all that modern steel.

Virginia continues in her housewifely vein. "I've had a buffet luncheon laid out in the dining room, in case he's the hungry kind of cavalier."

"But the card didn't say anything about lunch," Sophie says.

"I thought lunch might be implied in the part about twelve o'clock."

"But eating seems so ordinary and human. Don't you think he'll be offended if we ask him to lunch?"

Virginia pulls away from the window and sets Evelyn on her feet, to go running into the dining room and inspect the rumored buffet. "Baby dear, he's a man. He'll want lunch. *If* he ever gets here."

"Oh, he'll get here," says Sophie, full of confidence, but as the minutes ebb past and Father rises from the settee to walk restlessly up and down the blue-and-cream Persian rug, no knight—hungry or not—emerges from the mass of traffic on the street below. Sophie listens to the distant belch of the horns, the shouts and the roars of engines, the mighty metallic hullaballoo of the Second Avenue El, and above all to the relentless *tick-tick-tick* from the ormolu clock above the mantel—a sound she somehow extracts from all that passionate din, even though she would rather not—but at no time does a squeal of brakes end at the Fortescue doorstep, or a cheerful Manhattan drawl drift up from the entrance.

Father snaps shut the case of his pocket watch. "This had better not be some kind of joke."

"Oh, I'm sure it isn't," says Virginia. "He's just stuck in all that traffic."

Tick-tick-tick. Then a pair of chimes, as the clock delicately suggests twelve thirty.

"I'm famished," says Mr. Fortescue. "What's for lunch?"

Sophie turns. Father's planted his feet in the center of the priceless rug, and his thumbs are hooked in the pockets of his waistcoat. He's built on slender lines, not at all the kind of corpulent figure you expect to find among the wealthy of his sex: more well-dressed egg than man. Maybe because Mr. Fortescue's never been the eggy sort of person, and even the waistcoat and the gold watch are aberrations, interlopers on a body that would rather be wearing a plain broadcloth suit and sitting on a workbench, tinkering with gears and levers. Sophie shares his height—what there is of it—and his narrow shoulders and his incongruously voracious appetite; Virginia (or so Sophie's told) favors their mother, who was tall and extremely slender. Sophie can only wonder how they must have looked together.

"Cold roast meat," says Virginia, "and salads."

"It's wintertime. Luncheon should be hot."

"I didn't know when we'd be serving." Virginia glances at the clock, and then at Sophie. She lifts a pleading eyebrow, as if Sophie can somehow conjure Mr. Ochsner's cavalier by snapping her fingers, or tapping her heels together.

Mr. Fortescue throws up his hands. "What a joke. I should have figured. I should have known it would all go up in smoke, a fellow like that—"

"It's not Mr. Ochsner's fault, exactly. It's the cavalier who—" begins Sophie.

"And that's another thing. What man sends another man to do his courting for him?"

"Maybe it's a custom, among people of Mr. Ochsner's class," says Virginia. "An old custom. I think it's charming and civilized."

"Well, I don't like it. It seems to me, if a man really wanted to make an offer, he'd do it himself instead of sending in some—some—" He flails for a word.

"Oh, I'm sure Mr. Ochsner didn't mean it like that, Father," Sophie says. "I think Virginia's right. It's just an amusing family tradition."

"He comes from an *extremely* old and venerable family, Father," says Virginia.

Mr. Fortescue retrieves his watch from his pocket and flips open the case. "Seems the joke's on us, if you ask me."

"Oh, Father." Sophie looks helplessly at her sister, who shrugs and glances at the door.

"Should have known," said Mr. Fortescue. "These high society nitwits. Should have known it was too good to be true. Let this be a lesson." He shoves his watch back in the pocket of his gray-striped waistcoat. His cheeks are pale; his nose looks as if someone dipped the tip in a raspberry sauce. "I'm hungry. I'm going in to lunch. You're welcome to join me."

He turns to the pocket doors that lead to the dining room, and Sophie flies after him.

"Father, please. Virgo! Have Betty bring him something to eat."

"Good idea," says Virginia.

"I don't want to be brought something to eat. I want to sit down like a civilized man at his civilized table and enjoy my lunch." Mr. Fortescue pushes open one door and then the other, exposing the neatly laid luncheon table and the series of covered dishes on the sideboard beyond.

Sophie takes hold of his arm.

"Please, Father. Weren't you the one to encourage Mr. Ochsner in the first place? Just a few more minutes."

"I've waited long enough already. It's a joke, don't you understand? He's playing one of his jokes on us, playing us for fools. That's what they do, these nobs. They look down on us from Olympus and *laugh*. Now listen to me." He turns at last and places his hand on hers, on her hand that circles his forearm. "You don't let down your guard again, do you hear me? Either of us. I never should have been taken in by that fellow, showing up on our—out of the blue, wanting to—I never should have thought—I never should have said yes."

"It wasn't out of the blue. Julie Schuyler introduced us."

"Well, and who's Julie Schuyler? Dizzy society girl, what's the word? A flapper. Don't trust them, Sophie."

"Julie's perfectly nice. She's from one of the best families in New York."

"And how does my Sophie go around meeting society girls?"

"In the millinery department, Father. I was buying a hat, remember? You told us we could go out shopping, so we went to Bergdorf Goodman on Fifth Avenue, and—"

"Well, don't shop there again, do you hear me? Fifth Avenue. Don't you go shopping with this Schuyler girl again. I never should have—don't know what I was—we'll just go back to the way it was, do you hear me? They're just ciphers, all of them, just a bunch of idiots swanning around in silk jackets because their dads and granddads made some money. Well, I tell you, I think it's time we moved out of New York and found you a nice young man from—from—" He flails with his New Yorker's ignorance of outside geography. Flings his shopworn hands in the air. "I don't know, New Jersey or someplace."

"Father—" whispers Virginia.

"You, too, Virgo. We'll see if that husband of yours is—well, if he's not—well, we'll just keep you to ourselves where you belong. Family, girls. Family's what matters. Family above all." He takes Sophie's hand inside the crook of his elbow and turns them both to face the doorway, where a man stands quietly before the table, wearing an immaculate officer's dress uniform, flanked by the beaming Betty in her crisp white pinafore apron.

The man tucks his hat under his arm, just above his sword, and says, "I couldn't agree more, Mr. Fortescue."

Sophie, during her many afternoon excursions to the New York Public Library on Forty-Second Street, once came upon a volume of portraits from the last century, which occupied her for hours. They were mostly images of society women: women who lived in New York and Boston, or Paris or London, possessing titles and double-barreled names and severely corseted waists, wearing dresses and jewelry that seemed to have grown naturally from their skin. Among these creatures posed the busts of distinguished men, much less interesting, monochrome, grimacing behind the thickets of frizzled hair along their jowls, each one looking more or less like the other.

And then Sophie had turned a page, and there stood an athletic young man in a red hunting jacket next to a burnished chestnut horse. His hat hung from one hand, together with his riding crop, while the other hand contained the horse's reins, just beneath the chin, and (in brilliant contrast to his grizzled male relatives among the earlier pages) he was smiling. Smiling and smooth-skinned and radiant, his red-gold hair matching that of his horse, and Sophie gazed at him in rapture, blinking now and again when her eyeballs became too dazzled, and she wondered what *pill* he had swallowed, what *sun* had shone down on his birth, that he could gather so much electricity beneath his skin. According to the caption, he had died at twenty-seven of enteric fever, and when Sophie returned the next week to see his portrait again, the book was gone. Somebody had checked it out.

Now, then. This young man standing before the luncheon buffet doesn't look like the man in Sophie's portrait, not at all. For one thing, his jacket's olive green instead of red, and his hair's dark instead of red-gold. The fellow in the portrait was more beautiful, too, but then it wasn't his beauty that had caught Sophie's attention, was it? It was the *radiance*, the clean-edged ferocious good humor, the way his smile had *filled* the page to the very edges.

"Good morning," says Mr. Ochsner's cavalier, and he puts one foot forward and sort of bows—bows!—as if anyone does that kind of thing anymore! His face is grave, except for his mouth, which twitches upward at each corner as if the four of them are all party to the same charming joke.

"My name is Captain Octavian Rofrano of the United States Army Air Service, and I've come on behalf of Mr. Edmund Jay Ochsner. Have I the honor of addressing Miss Sophie Fortescue?"

His gaze falls upon Sophie's face, and she's struck with an almost irresistible desire to laugh, to fall down dead of laughter, because what sheltered nineteen-year-old girl can accept that beam of concentrated, smiling attention without falling down dead of something or other?

"Yes," she whispers.

Captain Rofrano's right hand, it turns out, is not securing the headstall of a chestnut Thoroughbred, but a square box of navy-blue leather, stamped in gold. He opens the clasp with an agile white-gloved thumb, and up pops the lid to reveal a perfect miniature rose in bloom, made entirely of tiny diamonds, far too exquisite and complicated and improbable for a mere engagement ring. An engagement ring.

"I offer to you, Miss Fortescue, the betrothal present of the Ochsner family, which has been handed down each generation to the bride of the eldest son, as a symbol of everlasting attachment. Will you accept it?"

Sophie's mouth turns round. She looks from the ring, resting patiently on a bed of old blue velvet, to the solemn face of Captain Rofrano, whose eyes alone are now smiling. But she's only nineteen, and she's seen so little of the world, and eyes are enough for her. Especially a pair of eyes like those.

She pulls her hand from her father's arm, bends her small form into a courtly curtsy, and says yes.

And really, if you yourself were settled right inside Sophie's young skin, wouldn't you do the same?

Chapter 3

Ever since Eve started it all by offering Adam the apple, woman's punishment has been to supply a man with food, and then suffer the consequences when it disagrees with him.

—HELEN ROWLAND

THERESA

Somewhere in Manhattan, the next day

If you're thinking I hauled the Boy straight from that Fourth of July swimming pool and into bed, why, shame on you. Like I intimated earlier, he has principles.

For some reason, as I pickle in a taxi on my way to Greenwich Village for my scheduled Thursday afternoon, regular as rain, going nowhere fast, I ponder those principles. I have a few of them myself: not the same ones, maybe, as you find on Main Street, and certainly not the same ones I commanded twenty-five years ago, or twenty, or even five. But I admire principles, whatever they happen to be, and wherever I happen to find them. I think it takes guts to have principles in this modern age, and even more guts to admit to them.

I remember—and this is a treasured memory, you understand, so indulge me a moment—I remember how I made my way over to him that night, around the open lip of the pool, while he watched my every unsteady step: that took guts, too, I think, on both our parts. Or perhaps it was all the cocktails. My head was buzzing, and so was my skin. I said hello and told him my name, and he nodded.

"I know who you are, Mrs. Marshall."

"Do you? How uncanny. Because I don't remember being introduced."

Instead of replying, he took a drink from the glass in his hand, which might have been water but smelled like gin and tonic. I extracted the cigarette from between his fingers and lifted it to my lips.

"And what do I call you?" I asked.

"Whatever you like, Mrs. Marshall."

"What do *they* call you?" I motioned to the crowd around us.

So he told me his name, and we got to talking. Small talk, you know what I mean. The strangely mild weather: mild, that is, for a New York July. The Babe. How we knew the hosts. What he did for a living, where he lived. It turned out he had returned from France a couple of months ago and taken a job as a junior bond salesman at Sterling Bates, on the corner of Wall and Broad. I asked him to tell me about bonds.

"Government or corporate?" he said.

"Never mind. Tell me about France."

He finished his glass of whatever-it-was and took back the cigarette, of which there wasn't much. "You shouldn't smoke, Mrs. Marshall."

"Why not?"

"My uncle was a doctor. He said they were coffin nails."

"*My* doctor says they're good for my nerves."

"To each his own doctor, I guess."

"Then why do you smoke them?"

He gave me a bored old look that said the answer was too obvious for words, and I remember thinking, at this point, that maybe I was wrong. Maybe there was no frisson, at least on his part; maybe he wasn't interested in flirting at all, now that he'd seen me up close. The water in the swimming pool, picking up the reflection of the torches, still made those funny patterns on his cheeks and forehead, and I couldn't tell the color of his irises. But I could see that he was even younger than I'd thought. The skin around his mouth was taut and thick, and the lips were still full, like a child's. He was twenty at most, I thought. Younger than Tommy. Young and clean and unspoiled.

I stepped in, next to his elbow, and spoke in a soft voice, because I was so frightened. "What were you doing in France?"

"Flying airplanes. Shooting down other ones, when I could."

"But the war ended a year and a half ago."

"I hung around Paris for a bit afterward."

"Ooh la la."

"It wasn't like that," he said.

He was so close I could feel the draft of his eyelashes when he blinked, which wasn't often. The smell of his skin made me think of dandelions. Or newly cut grass. One of those outdoor things. (I later learned that the scent belonged to his shaving soap, a brand he found at an otherwise ordinary drugstore on the corner of Duane and Reade.) He was green and robust and very warm, and his eyes were still regarding me with that peculiar torchlit concentration, and when I put my hand on his arm, the muscle was ropy and vigorous beneath my fingers, and I wanted him so badly—skin, muscle, warmth, everything—my mouth watered. My stomach rumbled.

"Really?" I said. "Maybe you could tell me about it. They tell me I'm a very good listener."

He didn't reply, at least out loud. He just went on looking at me, while the leopard spots jiggled around his face.

I shrugged. "Or you could fetch me a gin and a cigarette, and we could sit here drinking and smoking, and nobody needs to say a thing."

And then he said—God, I'll never forget this—he puts this enormous hand on my shoulder, covers my whole bare shameless shoulder and then some, his big thumb lining up along my collarbone and almost into the tender little hollow of my throat, and he says to me, in this baritone voice that couldn't possibly belong to a twenty-year-old: "Mrs. Marshall, I don't think it's right to go drinking with another man's wife, especially if he's not around to sock me in the face for trying."

I couldn't say anything at first. I don't think I could breathe, I was so angry and ashamed. The Boy has that effect; he can make you feel ashamed of yourself, just by looking at you: not mad, not angry, just melancholy. The way Jesus probably looked at his disciples at the Last Supper. I gathered myself and snapped, "You're such a boy."

He lifted his hand away. "I guess I am, Mrs. Marshall."

And he sort of bowed, and turned away, and as he walked back into the house, I remember how the anger left me in a whoosh, and all I wanted to do was sit and cry. Cry like a baby who's lost her mother.

And maybe that's why I'm pondering all this ancient history, as the taxi inches down Fifth Avenue toward Washington Square, and the dirty white lights wink at me from outside the window. I'm bereft. That feeling he left me with, on that suffocating Fourth of July night, returns to me whenever the Boy is absent from my side, and most especially when we've parted on uncertain terms. I roll down the window, allowing a blast of frigid air into the interior of the taxi, and stick my head bravely out into the Manhattan night to see what's up. What's keeping me from the Boy's apartment on Christopher Street. And it's just traffic. Bawling horns and flashing lights, just people trying to get to another place. Just New Yorkers in a hurry, going nowhere.

When I reach the apartment, the Boy is not around. No matter. I've got a key. He gave me a key right away, the first night I spent here. He had it made specially for me, a locksmith around the corner on Bleecker. "Don't lose it, now," he said, placing the thing in my palm, and I said, dry-mouthed, that I wouldn't. I didn't say that nobody had ever given me a latchkey before.

You didn't trade keys with your lovers; you met when he was home, or you met somewhere else. Keys imply ownership, and lovers are *free free free*, aren't they?

I've brought a picnic. I don't cook—I can boil the Boy a breakfast egg, but even that always turns out too runny or else too hard, though he never complains—so I just haul along provisions cooked by somebody else. And I set a lovely table. The Boy has his mother's old china, a nearly complete set of white-and-ochre Spode, not that we need bouillon dishes, let alone twelve place settings of them. I took out the dinner and dessert plates and the soup bowls and packed the rest back in the crates in the basement. We have some silver I brought down from Fifth Avenue (God knows it's not missed) and the Boy always brings me flowers, extravagant ones, which I put in the vase in the middle of the square wooden table in the miniature hall, wedged between the miniature kitchen and the miniature parlor. It's gorgeously intimate, like a pair of newlyweds just starting out in life.

By the time I whirl inside the front door, the clock has already rung in six o'clock. The Boy will be home from work any minute. I spread out the tablecloth and uncork the wine, and then I open up the cupboard and find the precious Spode plates and the glasses, and the silverware from the drawer, and the napkins, and last of all the empty vase in the center, ready to be filled with hothouse flowers from the shop outside the Christopher Street subway station. Somewhere in the middle of all this, I discover that my hands are a little shaky, so after every dish and glass and spoon is settled in its precise millimeter-fine location, I mix myself a Tom Collins and settle down on the beaten-up sofa with a cigarette to wait for the Boy.

At the time he drove me back to the city on Tuesday morning, he hadn't liked my little idea about the ring, and he let me know it. He was supposed to be working at noon on a Wednesday, didn't I know that? Especially so soon after New Year's Day, when things were getting back to business, when everybody was investing his Christmas bonus, if a fellow was lucky enough to get one. And he hadn't worn his dress uniform in three years, and he didn't appreciate getting buttoned up to perform like some kind of dancing monkey for the pleasure of the leisured classes.

"I'm a member of the leisured classes," I pointed out, "and you don't mind performing for *my* pleasure."

"I do mind, actually, but I do it anyway. I'm your trained monkey."

"You're my beloved."

He said nothing to that. What was the point? It was an argument, after all, with which we were already minutely familiar.

I went on. "Darling, I *need* you to do this. You know my brother isn't the best judge of character, the little dear, and I'd like to see this isn't another of his harebrained schemes. For all we know, they've taken him in."

"Taken him *in*? What for? He hasn't got a pair of dimes to rub together. More likely, it's the other way around, and they're the poor suckers thinking he's got something to offer them."

"He's got plenty to offer them. Better things than money. Position, history—"

"An overdraft."

"But it's a terribly prestigious overdraft."

Well, he smiled at that, just a little bit, and I should have left it there. I really should. But I didn't like that bit about the dancing monkey, you see, and I wanted to set the record straight, so I piped right back up.

"If you mind it so awfully much, why do you keep seeing me?"

He sighed. "You know the answer to that."

"I don't know the answer to anything with you. You're a perfect mystery to me. I suppose it's part of your charm."

"Because I can't stop. I can't stop seeing you."

"Why not?"

"Theresa. Isn't it enough that I'm hooked? Isn't it enough that you've got me revolving around you like a moon? What else do you want to drag out of me?"

"I don't want to drag anything out of you. I just want to understand you."

He brought his fist down on the steering wheel, and we didn't say anything else, not until he pulled up on the corner of Madison Avenue and Sixty-First Street, where he usually let me off, and I said, "But you *will* do it, won't you?"

He got out and went around to open the door for me, and just before I turned away to walk up Madison, he called out *All right, I'll do it!*

So I sent the jeweler down in a taxi that afternoon to the Sterling Bates building on Wall Street (the Boy went on to work that day, he's terribly industrious) and sat in my splendid little office overlooking Central Park, answering letters, wishing I had remembered to kiss him good-bye.

I always kiss him good-bye, just in case it's the last time.

The clock sounds six thirty, and my glass is empty. I fill it again and light another cigarette, and at last a noise appears on the stairs outside the door, a noise not belonging to the madcap city beyond, and I stub out the newly lit cigarette and open the window a crack. I rise from the sofa and straighten my dress and put on a smile.

The door opens, and in walks the Boy, wearing his gray overcoat and his felt fedora hat. He sees the table first, the candles already lit, and his face turns to mine, registering surprise.

"What are you doing here?" he asks.

"If you have to ask."

"You didn't say you were coming."

"It's Thursday, isn't it? But if I'm not welcome, perhaps you might be so kind as to hail me a taxi."

His shoulders bend forward. He sets his briefcase on the floor and removes his hat. His straight, thick hair gleams obediently in the light. "Of course you're welcome, Theresa. You're always welcome. I just thought—well, you walked away without a word. You didn't stop by at all last week. I thought you were mad."

There's a tremendous hollowing in my middle, a void that fills with sweet relief. I make my way around the sofa table, take his hat, and hang it on the stand. "I'm never, ever mad at you, Boyo," I say, and I kiss his hand and his neck and jaw and lips, I remove his tie and his jacket and everything else, and a long time later we are eating our picnic and drinking our wine, and I'm wearing nothing but the Boy's dressing gown and getting beautifully zozzled, and I remember something important.

"So how did it go?"

"How did what go?"

"Yesterday. The ring. Tell me about the patent king and his gilded daughter. Are they grotesquely rich and vulgar?"

The Boy finishes his ham and drinks a little wine. He's wearing his trousers and his white shirt, unbuttoned, and he smokes a cigarette while he eats, an unfathomably degenerate habit for which I have admonished him frequently. After he drinks, he lifts the glass and stares through the wine toward the opposite wall. "No, they weren't vulgar. Not at all."

"But Ox said he's making a million and a half a year."

"If he is, he's not showing it off. They've got a neat little middle-class house off Second Avenue in the Thirties. The furniture looks new, I guess, but it's not what you'd call swanky."

He sets down the wineglass, but he doesn't look at me. His attention is still fixed on the opposite wall, where a fire burns in a small grate, and the modest mantel contains a clock and a framed photograph of his mother.

"Well, how strange," I say.

"Not everybody wants to live on Fifth Avenue, Theresa."

"Then why did he bother to make so much money?"

"Because he likes to invent things, I guess. That's what I thought, anyway, after meeting them."

His voice is absent, his gaze distant. You know the look. His seven-mile stare, I call it, when the Boy's soul levitates right out of my presence to inhabit another world: one to which he rarely invites me along.

"Was she pretty?" I ask.

"Who?"

"The girl. Ox's girl. What's-her-name."

"Sophie. I guess so."

"Lucky Ox. But then everybody's pretty at nineteen, I suppose. It's only later that the underlying architecture starts to matter."

He drinks again and rises from the table. "Her architecture seemed all right to me."

I watch him make his way around the furniture to the hot little fireplace, and for some reason I think of the portrait that hangs in the apartment uptown, which the Boy, of course, has never once entered. (My principles, not his.) I fiddle with the stem of my wineglass. "You should have seen *me* at nineteen."

"I wasn't even born, Theresa."

"Oh, that's right. I'd forgotten I was so very old."

"You're not old. For heaven's sake." He flicks his cigarette into the fireplace. "She's just young. She's very young."

I hardly need ask whom he means, do I? I finish the last drop of wine and say, as dry as can be, "She's your age."

"She's younger than me. She's a baby. She's never left New York, except last year when her father took them to Europe, and even then they only stayed in fancy hotels in the nice parts of town."

I sit back in my chair and tuck my feet onto the seat before me. The Boy has lit another cigarette and smokes it continuously as he stares at the fire, which he laid while I was arranging the food, our accustomed habit, a nice neat companionable division of labor. The flames lick greedily upward at his abdomen.

I reach for the cigarette case. "It sounds as if you had a nice chat together."

"They invited me to lunch afterward."

"I suppose the infant Miss Sophie regaled you with tales of her doll collection and her latest hat?"

"No." At last, the Boy turns to face me. "We talked about art, mostly. She'd just been to the latest Ravenel exhibition, that new gallery above Grand Central."

"Really? Ravenel? I wouldn't have thought that was in her line. A pretty young thing like her."

"It was his post-Cuba work, mostly." He finishes the wine and strolls back to the table to pour himself another glass. The bottle runs out before he's done.

"There's another in the basket," I say. "I didn't know you liked Ravenel."

"I didn't know you wanted to talk about *art*."

The air's gone flat, the room's stuffy and full of smoke. The merry postcoital buzz along my limbs has turned cold and turgid. I want to say something kind about this child, this Sophie: something generous. I really do. But it's as if I've boarded a ship of some kind, have taken command of an ocean liner of immense gross tonnage, and though I can clearly see that our course is leading to a disastrous collision, I can't quite seem to put the engines in reverse. There's no possible way to change direction.

"Of course I don't want to talk about art," I say. "I employ a curator for that."

The Boy flinches. He's turned away from me, rummaging through the basket for the second bottle of wine, and he straightens now and turns, bottle dangling from one hand and cigarette from the other. His face is terrible. "What are you saying, Theresa?" he says quietly.

"Oh, let's not fight."

"Because I did what you asked. I went and took time off from work to deliver your crazy ring—"

"It wasn't my ring."

"But you asked me to do it, and I did. I delivered the ring, I had lunch. It was a nice lunch. They're a good family, a sweet good-looking pair of girls. I left after an hour and went back to work and sold a few ten-year government bonds to a lawyer in Scarsdale. What else do you want to know, Theresa?"

"Nothing," I whisper.

"Nothing." He sets the bottle on the table, but he doesn't open it. "It's always nothing with you, isn't it? Just sex and nothing else. You have a curator to talk art with, a dressmaker for your dresses, a husband to pay for the whole racket. And what am I?"

You're everything.

I snatch my cigarette from the ashtray. "Oh, Boyo, you've gone and turned all serious on me. I was just teasing. You can flirt with all the pretty girls you like. I don't give a damn. What we have is something else, and it suits us perfectly, doesn't it? So don't go ruining things with all your maudlin talk about dressmakers and husbands."

The Boy stands there watching the fluttering of my hand as it maneuvers the cigarette, and he might be a granite statue, he might be the Old Man of the Mountain, if the Old Man had a full head of hair and a firm young face stained with agitation on the extreme outer edges of his cheekbones. He returned from France bearing a number of injuries—if you peer between the unbuttoned edges of his shirt, for example, you can see a shiny patch of skin across his chest where the flames from an engine fire caused his jacket to ignite, and a pinkish-white triangle where a broken rib punctured his skin—but not one bullet or strut or strafe touched his face. I suppose you could call that a miracle. Or luck. The Boy has luck, for all his multitude of scars. He's still alive, after all.

"Sit down, won't you?" I say. "Open the wine like a good boy."

He eases downward and grasps the bottle. A juicy red Burgundy, a 1912 Gevrey-Chambertin from the limitless Marshall cellars. (Now don't cluck your tongue at me; it's not illegal to drink the stuff, you know, just to sell it.) The Boy sets the bottle on the edge of the chair, between his legs, and reaches for the corkscrew.

"I don't know what you've got against her," he says, driving slowly into the cork.

"I haven't got anything against her."

"You have." The cork slides out. He sets down the corkscrew and lights another cigarette, which he sticks between his lips while he pours my glass and then his. "You know, I see pretty girls all the time. I saw them when I was a kid in Connecticut, I saw them in France. I see them every day on the streets of New York. Dime a dozen." He hands me the wine. "You're the one who's married. You're the one with a husband."

"Oh, you're not jealous of *him . . .*"

"I am. I sure am. I think to myself, Why does she stay married to him? And then I think, Well, what have I got to offer her? Just me. No money, no name, no apartment on Fifth Avenue."

"No, Boyo. You're much more than that."

"Really? Because you just told me I wasn't. So which is it?"

"The second," I whisper.

He shakes his head. "Do you know what I thought, that first time I saw you at the van der Wahls' place? Fourth of July? I thought you were the most beautiful woman I'd ever seen. Everybody talked about you as if you were some kind of goddess. And then you came up to me."

"And you sent me away."

"Because I knew what would happen if I didn't."

"This?"

"This." He puts down the wine and reaches forward to lift me onto his lap so I'm straddling him at the waist.

He buries his face between my breasts. "You know, the honest truth, I might have killed myself that summer, just back from France, if it weren't for you."

The Boy's hair is soft in my hands, and his breath is hot. His fingers wander along my hips. He smells of soap and sweat and New York winter air, of youth and vigor. I cradle the indestructible roundness of his skull in my palms and imagine him in the dining room of a modest New York brownstone, sitting next to a fair-haired young lady, talking about art. Her bosom is firm and buoyant, and her cheeks are as pink as his. On the backs of her smooth, white hands, the veins are still invisible. And yet the Boy doesn't care. He doesn't notice.

"I saved you, darling Boyo," I said. "Don't forget that."

"As if I could."

When I first came out, I couldn't stand all the boys my own age. I thought they were silly and scrawny and impossibly callow, that they only wanted to talk about football and baseball, that they couldn't dance and couldn't dress and couldn't pay you a proper compliment. Sylvo was thirty-six years old when we met, almost twenty years older than I was, and when he walked into my parents' opera box that evening, I thought he was a god. He looked immaculate and fully grown, like a stag of mighty antlers, and he sat down next to me and discussed the first act of *Lucia* as if he actually cared about what I thought, as if he actually knew about music. He smelled of richly made shaving soap and cigars. By the end of the evening, I was in love with him.

Does that surprise you? Yes, I was in love with Sylvo, and I expect he was in love with me, in the way that a thirty-six-year-old man loves a beautiful seventeen-year-old girl: covetously, self-indulgently. On the night of our wedding, he set about his matrimonial duty in the manner of a tutor instructing a favored pupil, and when he was finished he put on a dressing gown and smoked a cigar. We were quite happy, I think. We suited each other perfectly; we were each exactly what the other one required. When Tommy was born, ten months later, no man could possibly have been more delighted than Sylvo. Another cigar. (And I suppose he smoked yet another, soon afterward, when his mistress gave birth to their daughter.)

The point is, in my early days, I looked at younger men with nothing but scorn, valuing neither their smooth skin nor their coltish vigor nor their single-minded simplicity. I preferred sophistication in those days, because I didn't understand what sophistication really was, and how it was earned. I preferred wisdom and experience and polish, because I didn't appreciate the sentiment behind a young man's awkward eagerness to please. When I first went to bed with the Boy, he wanted not to instruct, but to be instructed. His flesh was firm under my hands. His skin sprang back from my fingertips. His strength was neverending. Afterward, we shared a cigarette, and then we repeated the exercise, again and again, until we were both half dead, until the sheets were an awful mess. At sunrise, he got up and made me breakfast.

And I decided, right then, that there was something to be said for a young lover, after all.

But we don't have all night this January evening, and anyway the Boy isn't in the mood for limitless exercise. At eleven o'clock we dress each other sleepily and head downstairs and out onto the street, to the frosty corner of Seventh Avenue. The Boy searches the pavement for an empty taxi, to no avail.

"I forgot to ask," I say, as we stand silently on the curb, awaiting the fruits of the next wave of traffic. "Did she say yes?"

"Sophie? Yes, she did. Right away."

"Well, well. So my brother's engaged. Imagine that."

"You don't sound all that happy."

"Darling, she's an unknown. I've never even met her. It's all just—well, it's a bit strange, that's all. How did he meet her? Are they really so rich?"

"Why should that matter, if they're in love?" He peers down at me. "You're shivering."

"It's cold."

He takes me by the hand and pulls me back down Christopher Street.

"Where are we going?"

"Back to my car. I'll drive you home."

"Don't be silly. It'll be past midnight by the time you get back. When are you going to sleep?"

"Theresa," he says, and this time he's grinning, and his grins are so rare that I want to bottle them in vinegar and keep them forever. "When have you ever cared about letting me get some sleep?"

So we climb into the Boy's awful jalopy and he persuades it to start—it's an old Model T, cantankerous in the cold, and I have to sit there in the driver's seat, operating the choke and the ignition, while my hands freeze in their leather gloves and the Boy's arm rotates vigorously before the grille—and then we're off, coughing and sputtering up Seventh Avenue, and the first thing we see is an empty taxi.

"It figures," the Boy says, and he puts the car into high gear and slings his arm around my shoulders.

You'd think that midnight Manhattan would prove easier to navigate than evening Manhattan, but in fact it's just the same, minus the delivery vans. We lurch our way uptown while my hand rests on the Boy's sturdy thigh, and I think how simple it would be to keep going straight up Manhattan, across the Harlem River to the Bronx, and then upstate. Keep going until we found a farm somewhere, nestled in the snow, and no one would ever hear from us again. We would age slowly together, not giving a damn about anything except the crops and the horses and each other, ordering our clothes from the Sears Roebuck catalog and growing our own apples and potatoes. I would toss out all the mirrors, except the one the Boy needs for shaving. Maybe even that.

The Boy pulls the car to the curb, and I look up and realize we've reached the corner of Fifth Avenue and Sixty-Fourth Street, two blocks from the apartment I share with Mr. Marshall.

The Boy stares through the windshield at the restless shadows of Central Park. "You know what? Let's keep going."

"Keep going?"

"You don't need all this, do you? We could head out west and start a new life, and no one would know or care who we are."

The engine coughs again and dies, and the Boy says something under his breath.

"Let me buy you a new car," I say. "Please. A Christmas present."

"You already gave me a Christmas present."

"A New Year present, then."

"I don't want presents." He gets out of the car to crank the engine again. I watch him carefully for the signal. Turn the switch for the spark. My pulse thumps against my ears. *Keep going, keep going, keep going,* I think, in rhythm with the turn of the pistons, and my imagination, for some reason, returns to Sophie Fortescue in her house on Thirty-Second Street, about to sacrifice her eternal future to the dear and witless Edmund Jay Ochsner.

Better the poor thing had run away with the grocer's boy instead.

A sputter and a roar, and then the steady reassuring rattle of a Ford minding its duty. The Boy comes around to the passenger door and opens it. He places his foot on the running board and his hand on the top of the window.

"Well? How about it?"

"How about what?"

"Run away with me."

I love his sharp and frosty nose, his keen eyes beneath the brim of his woolen cap. We've parked in the deep shadow between two lampposts, so I have to imagine the rest. I lean forward and kiss him on his cold mouth.

"I need you to do me a favor, Boyo."

"What's that?"

"I need you to look into this family. The—what was the name?"

He sighs. "Fortescue."

"Fortescue. Something's fishy. Why would a man that rich live in a rinky-dink brownstone so far south and east? It doesn't make sense."

"You know, it's just possible he doesn't care about money the way you do."

"I don't believe it."

He doesn't answer.

I put my gloved hand on his cheek. "Darling, it's my brother we're talking about. I just want to be sure. What if this man's a bootlegger, or something equally awful?"

"Theresa . . ."

"Just ask a few questions. I'm sure he keeps all those piles of money in one of those banks down there. You can ask a question or two for me, can't you?"

Another thing about the Boy: he maintains a terribly slow respiration. Sometimes, when I'm lying next to him, and my hand rests upon the scars of his chest,

I feel as if I'm waiting forever for the next heartbeat, the next intake of air, and panic intrudes. What if he's dying? What if, like an automobile engine—or an airplane, for that matter—his heart and lungs slip into a rhythm so torpid, they begin to stall? And then my Boy will fall from the sky, and be gone from me forever.

At present, I can actually see that alarming breath of his, each puff making its tardy way into the convergent glow of the equidistant lamps, and I count them—*one, two, three, four*—while he stands there blocking the passenger door with his wide shoulders, one foot raised on the running board, his gloved hand gripping the edge of the window, not a muscle flickering in his ropy young body.

"Just a couple of meager questions," I say. "Please? For me. You must admit, it's all rather unusual. No one gets rich in Manhattan without trumpeting that important fact to the entire city."

The Boy moves at last, taking my right hand in his left hand and drawing me out of the car. "All right. But only to prove you wrong."

"I'm never wrong, Boyo. Remember that."

He leans forward to kiss me good night, but we're right smack in the middle of an Upper East Side sidewalk, in the guilty half-lit space between two streetlamps, and even though I'm wearing my hat low upon my forehead and my scarf all the way up to my chin, I know at least three families whose windows overlook this particular patch of Manhattan. I move aside just in time.

"Until Saturday," I say. "I'll come down after the Schuylers' party."

"What if I'm out?"

"You won't be out, darling. You'll be waiting for me like a good boy."

He leans back against the car and folds his arms across his chest.

"Well?" I say.

The Boy reaches inside his pocket and pulls out his cigarette case, the beautiful gold one I gave him for Christmas, engraved on the inside panel: With dearest love to my Boyo, M.T.M.

(My first name is Marie, after my grandmother.)

He doesn't bother reading the inscription again, not at this late hour, though I've caught him at it, from time to time, when he thinks I've fallen asleep. Instead, he puts a cigarette between his lips and strikes the match on the side of the case.

"Yes," he says. "I guess I'll be waiting for you."

Chapter 4

Never trust a husband too far, nor a bachelor too near.

—HELEN ROWLAND

SOPHIE

Thirty-Second Street, Saturday noon

The sound of the doorbell reaches Sophie's ears while she sits cross-legged on the floor of her bedroom, unscrewing the front plate of an old De Forest Audion receiving cabinet.

She's been wanting to get her hands on one for years, not because she's passionately interested in radio transmission, but because she wants to know how the thing works. Well, not quite. She already *knows* how it works, of course: the basic principles by which the radio signal is detected by a wire wrapped around the housing of the glass Audion tube, and the disturbance in its electrical current creates noise in the attached headphones. But she wants to *see* how it works, to take apart the circuits and examine the tubes, and you can only do that if it's sitting right in front of you.

Of course, a device like this would have cost a hundred and fifty dollars when it was first built eight years ago, and Sophie's never had that kind of money at her personal command, not even in her prosperous here-and-now. But a month ago, she spotted a small classified advertisement in the latest issue of *Electrical Experimenter* magazine, offering a used Type R J 6 De Forest radio receiving cabinet for only twenty-five dollars, and while twenty-five dollars is still a great deal of money, she was able to scrape it together from the odd ends of Father's recent largesse. It arrived this morning by special delivery—Father, thank goodness, was in his workshop—and Sophie's been toying with it ever since. Examining each dial, running her fingers delicately along the round glass Audion tube. Like a surgeon, preparing to make an incision in a beloved patient.

In the old days, her room was littered with the carcasses of various machines—a Marconi transmitter, an electric iron, a pop-up toaster, too many Western Electric telephones to count—that kept her brain and her hands occupied during the long hours of the afternoon, when school was finished and Father was in his workshop and Virginia was in France. And then Virginia came home, and Sophie graduated from high school, and in some subtle and invisible way, like the transmission of radio waves across the atmosphere, Sophie came to realize that it was time to put away childish things. And she had. One by one, the devices made their way to the kitchen or the trash heap, depending on their states of usefulness (or, in the case of the electric dynamo, under Sophie's bed, because you never knew when you might need a dynamo!).

But this! A real De Forest receiving cabinet! Too tantalizing to resist, and wasn't it wonderful, really, to immerse yourself once more in the innards of a nice solid useful machine, operating on scientific principles, impervious to emotion and whimsy, doing exactly what you told it to do? A perfect puzzle, for which a perfect solution existed, and a new puzzle at that: a territory she's never explored until now, a miniature world just zinging with the thrill of discovery.

But the ring of the doorbell interrupts all this thrilling symmetry. Sophie raises her head, screwdriver poised in the air, and listens in bemusement to the noises below. Virginia's voice. A male voice.

And the smell, now that she's paying attention, of well-cooked food.

She glances at the clock. Fifteen minutes past twelve!

Sophie scrambles to her feet, tosses the screwdriver on the bed, glances in the mirror on the chest of drawers. Horrors! Her hair all undone, her pinafore still attached. She whips off the pinafore and pins back her hair and flies down the stairs to the dining room, calling out desperate excuses, but her late arrival doesn't seem to bother the two people just settling to the table. One is her sister, and the other, rising politely to his feet, is her cavalier.

"Oh!" She stops and grips the back of the nearest chair. Her brain, still occupied with triodes, makes a sort of confused electrical twitch inside her skull.

"Good afternoon, Miss Fortescue. I hope you'll forgive me, intruding on your Saturday lunch like this."

"Of course not!"

"Mr. Rofrano stopped by to speak with Father," says Virginia, from the opposite side of the table.

Sophie gathers herself and smiles at Mr. Rofrano. "I guess you didn't know that Father's always in his workshop on Saturday mornings."

"So I asked him to lunch," Virginia says.

Mr. Rofrano pulls out a chair for Sophie. "And I can't tell you how grateful I am. A bachelor's Saturday lunch isn't usually so civilized."

"Ham sandwiches?"

"If I'm lucky."

"When we were poor," Sophie says, flicking her napkin to her lap, triodes fizzling and receding into the distance, "Virginia used to make soup from the bones of the Sunday roast."

"Only when we were lucky enough to have Sunday roast at all."

"And then when Virginia was in France with the Red Cross—"

"You went to France?" Mr. Rofrano turns to her sister.

"She met her husband there," Sophie says. "A medical officer. Very dashing."

"Really? Which army?"

Virginia says calmly, "The British one. He was a surgeon in the Medical Corps."

"Good man. I hope to have the chance to meet him."

For a terrible instant, Sophie can't think of a word to say, and even Virginia's immaculate composure seems to have failed her. Mr. Rofrano, noticing the silence, looks up from his soup with a stricken slant to his eyebrows.

"Oh, he's out of town at the moment," Sophie bursts out, a little too shrill, "but I'm sure you'll have the chance before long."

"At the wedding, I hope?"

"The wedding?"

"Your wedding to Mr. Ochsner."

Sophie reaches for the water glass. "Oh! Of course. I'm afraid I haven't gotten used to the idea yet."

"Give her a week," says Virginia, "and I doubt she'll be talking about anything else."

Sophie hopes this is true. She woke up Thursday morning having entirely forgotten that she was engaged to be married at all, until the maid came up and said that Mr. Ochsner was waiting below, and even *then* she wondered, for *several* minutes, why on earth the man would call at such an ungodly hour. She washed and dressed, and she was just pinning her hair when she remembered that little word *Yes*, uttered under the sublime influence of the cavalier's blue eyes, and she realized that Mr. Ochsner was, in fact, the man whose hand she had accepted. Mr. Ochsner was her fiancé.

Not Mr. Rofrano.

"But darling, it's perfect," Julie Schuyler said the next day, as she and Sophie made their way along the bridle path in Central Park, a habit recently introduced to Sophie's Friday mornings. "He's just the kind of husband a girl wants. Young enough to walk unaided, old enough to let you do as you please. You'll have a visiting card to strike everyone dead, and your money will make everything jolly."

"And Father loves the idea."

"Of course he does. Most daddies would do murder to see their little girls so well-placed. The important thing is, do you like him?"

"I adore him."

And it's true! It isn't just that Father pushed the idea so forcefully. She *does* adore Mr. Ochsner—*call me Jay*, he said on Thursday morning, and she tried the syllable out in her head, *Jay Jay Jay*—yes, she does adore Jay. How can she not adore him? He's handsome and dashing and funny. He's jolly, to use Julie's word, and more importantly, he's kind. A bit ribald, maybe, but she likes that about him. She likes his irreverence, which is both youthful and sophisticated at once. She likes the flattering intensity of his interest in her. She's under no illusions about his intelligence, but you can't have everything, can you? And she will be free. Even Father said so: *You can do what you like, Sophie, married to a man like Ochsner. That name is like gold.* A glorious future stands right before her. Soon, as Mrs. Edmund Jay Ochsner, she can go out and meet people. Anyone she likes! She can make friends, like Julie Schuyler, and quench her thirst for things like riding in Central Park on a Friday morning, hearing Julie's stories, stopping to talk with Julie's friends, who are so brash and witty and free and *modern*. They've rarely had guests in her father's house.

Except this one. Mr. Rofrano. Twice in one week! Sophie's mouth heats up with all the things she wants to say, the questions she wants to ask him. He sits next to her, while Virginia sits across, and he eats his soup the way he did on Wednesday, like a man who knows his manners. Over that first lunch, he told her he was raised in Connecticut, near the shore, until he went away to prep when he was fourteen. His father was a stockbroker. He had flown airplanes in France for the new United States Army Air Service, once America entered the war. That was about all she knew, for he liked to turn the conversation away from himself, and they soon discovered a shared passion for the new art going up around all the galleries in town. (*Father hates it, naturally,* she said, sending a sidelong glance in her father's direction, and *Daddies usually do,* he answered, just like Julie had.)

And now he's back. He's right here, sitting by her side, full of mystery and undiscovered detail. "What did you want to ask Father?" she says, almost too thrilled to eat.

"I wanted to talk to him about airplanes, actually. I've been fiddling with a new engine design, and I thought he'd be able to help me. We discussed it a little last week."

A tingle sweeps down Sophie's spine, as if someone's just attached a cathode to her neck. "Ooh! What sort of design?"

"Do you know something about engines?"

"A bit."

Virginia laughs. "Don't be modest, dear. Sophie's a chip off the old block, you know, Mr. Rofrano. She's got a wonderful knack for mechanics. I think she'd spend all day in the workshop with her father, if he let her."

"Would she?"

"I just like tinkering with things, that's all." Sophie turns her gaze to her right hand, gripping the spoon a little too hard.

"I see. And where is this workshop?" asks Mr. Rofrano. He's finished his soup already, and he sets the spoon neatly along the edge of his plate.

"When we were little, he used to work in the little shed in the garden. But once his patents starting making money, he found a shop a few blocks east, a real place, and got a real assistant to help him, instead of just me. I'm sure he'd be happy to discuss this engine of yours . . ." Sophie intercepts a warning look from Virginia and drags to a stop. "That is, if you ask nicely."

"Tell us more about what you do, Mr. Rofrano," says Virginia, and the cavalier obliges, while the soup is taken away by the maid and replaced with cold sliced chicken and mayonnaise. He speaks of interest rates and credit risk, and how business is really picking up again at last: almost as if they were two sensible people instead of a pair of young ladies. Sophie asks him about Mr. Morgan, and whether he really did save Wall Street during the Panic, and how you got to be such a man that others would follow you during a storm like that.

"Reputation," says Mr. Rofrano, without hesitation. "You can like or dislike Mr. Morgan, but when he says a thing, he does it."

There's no sign of Father, even when the cake is brought out for dessert, and as soon as Mr. Rofrano sweeps the final crumb into his mouth, he checks his watch and says he really must go.

"Let me walk you to Father's workshop," Sophie says. "It's only a few blocks away, and I know he'd be delighted to see you."

He laughs. "I'm not so sure."

"Sophie," says Virginia, in her warning voice, but Sophie pretends not to hear and jumps up to fetch her coat, even though they now have a maid to perform such errands.

"It's no trouble," she says, "and I like walking."

"Then I'd be delighted."

They strike out, side by side, at a pace decidedly more measured than Sophie's usual quick stride, neither one pushing the other for greater speed. As if they're mutually reluctant to reach their destination too quickly. Sophie's mouth is dry. She licks her lips and says, "How long have you known Jay?"

"Jay?"

"My fiancé." The word tastes new and fragrant on her tongue.

"Oh. I don't really know him at all, actually. I'm a friend of his sister."

"My goodness! I thought you were pals."

"Pals?" He laughs. "No, we run in different circles, Jay and I."

"Except for his sister."

"Yes. Except her."

Their shoes make a neat, irregular rhythm on the pavement: Sophie's light and clicking heels, Mr. Rofrano's reassuring bass soles. The wind burns her cheeks and smells of snow. "What circles *do* you run in, then?"

"None, really. I work too hard, I guess." He slides his hands into his pockets. "I play hockey, some evenings."

"Hockey? Really?"

"I used to play at school, before I left for France. Hockey and flying." He laughs. "I guess they're not so different, in some ways. Anyway, when I first got back from France, I didn't want to see another airplane as long as I lived, so when autumn came I took the hockey back up."

"When do you play?"

"A couple of nights a week, during the winter. Tuesdays and Fridays."

"How exciting! I don't even know how to skate."

The corner of Second Avenue approaches relentlessly, loud and black under the looming El. A northbound train rumbles up, a block away, and Mr. Rofrano raises his voice. "It's a little tricky starting out, but you get the feel for it. I've been skating since I was a little kid."

"That's the best time to start, isn't it? I've been learning to ride horses with a friend of mine lately, and it's taken me weeks to get the hang of it."

"Only *weeks*?"

"*Only* weeks?" Sophie has to shout above the clatter of the El.

He takes her by the elbow as they start perilously across the avenue. There isn't much traffic, but none of the few vehicles seems inclined to pause. "It can take a lot longer. But you seem like an adventurous girl."

"I don't know about *adventurous*. But I do like to try new things, when I can."

"Yes, I'll bet you do."

They race past an omnibus just in time and duck under the thick steel girders supporting the tracks. "Why do you say that?" Sophie asks.

"What, that you like to try new things? I don't know. The things you've told me. Tinkering around with machines."

"Oh, I don't do that so much any more."

"Why not?"

And just what does she say to that? The truth?

She shrugs. "Too busy, I guess. "

"Anyway, you didn't hesitate when I handed you that ring and asked if you'd like to get married. That's adventurous."

Sophie stops and wheels around to face him, right there under the thunderous El. He's standing before a girder, and his face looks down at hers from the exact center of a pair of parallel lines of rivets. "That's because you made it sound like such an adventure," she says.

"Well, marriage *is* an adventure, I think. Or should be."

"That's what I've always thought. I hope so, anyway. More exciting than this." She points upward to the railroad tracks.

Mr. Rofrano smiles, a lovely warm smile that broadens his face. "What, more exciting than an elevated train?"

"More exciting than being on a rackety old track, going to the same place every day, passing the same stations, never really talking to anybody. Never really *going* anywhere. Locked between your same two rails."

The day is overcast, and anyway it's a New York day, yellow-gray and poisonous with the smoke of a million coal fires, a thousand smokestacks retching prosperity into the air. But a dollop of light still finds Mr. Rofrano's face, through the complicated skeleton of the elevated railway, and as his smile fades, millimeter by millimeter, like a plant left to die by neglect, Sophie notices the true shape of his jaw, the angularity of his chin, and wonders whether he's considered handsome by his friends, or if it's just her.

"And now you want to get married," he says, and Sophie notices another thing: the lightness of his eyes, which examine her in a very grave way that makes her feel just the smallest bit defensive.

"Well, is there anything grander than that? Vowing to love someone for the rest of your life? When you've found the right person, I mean."

Mr. Rofrano rests his shoulders against the steel pillar behind him. "That's the thing, isn't it? Finding the right person."

For some reason, God knows how, Sophie finds the nerve to lean forward and cup her mittened hand around his elbow, and it's larger than she expects, solid and woolly, filling her entire palm. "Oh, you'll find someone, Mr. Rofrano. I'm sure of it. Your perfect girl is just waiting for you, right around the corner. You've just got to *find* each other."

If he's taken aback by her nerve, he doesn't show it. All the curiosity, all the movement in his face seems to have died away with that smile, and he might almost be a waxwork, fixed in concentration at a point just past her right ear. He stands so still, she's almost afraid to breathe. Only the pinkness of his cheekbones suggests life.

A snowflake whirrs past her nose, and another. She lets her hand drop away from his elbow, just as the steel begins to vibrate under the stress of an approaching train. But she doesn't look away. Oh, no. She keeps her sights stuck bang on the fascinating color of his irises, until he can't help himself. He meets her gaze.

"Have you always been so brave?" Mr. Rofrano asks.

"Not always. Just the past couple of months, really."

His lips part, and Sophie thinks he's going to ask her what brought about this recent surge of courage. Or who. And she hopes he will, because she's dying to tell him the whole story, dying to tell him all she's seen and learned, and why. The new world opening before her.

But no. He's just sighing, or maybe it's a groan, swallowed by the noise of the train. He takes her gently by the arm and navigates them both through the steel and the snowflakes to the open air, where his hand falls away.

The whole story is this: They met at the millinery department in Bergdorf Goodman two months ago, and *that* was when everything changed: Sophie's days before Julie, and her days After Julie.

Virginia was there, too, though not altogether willing. She'd wanted to visit one of the more modest millinery shops nearby, but Sophie had never been inside Bergdorf's and begged her sister to go, with a ferocity that made much more sense in the aftermath. So they had walked together from Thirty-Second Street, weaving crosstown and uptown and into the burr of traffic and shoppers that was Fifth Avenue, and Virginia had gripped her pocketbook and looked up the grand six stories that comprised the department store and—well, she hadn't *quite* crossed herself, but she looked as if she wanted to. And Virginia had driven ambulances in France!

"Oh, come along," Sophie said, taking her by the arm and dragging her through the revolving doors, and it was like entering another universe, wasn't it, a universe that contained every possible luxury and nothing but luxury, and smelled opulently of perfume and shoe leather and money.

Money. They had loads of money now: exactly how much, Father wouldn't say. Virginia had a better idea, but she wasn't talking either. All Sophie knew was that her sister's pocketbook contained five hundred dollars, a sum almost beyond the reach of her imagination a single year ago, and that these five hundred dazzling dollars represented no more than a crumb or two of the daily bread that was now theirs, thanks to the ingenious simplicity of Father's pneumatic oxifying drill. Sophie didn't know how they could possibly spend five hundred dollars on something so ordinary as clothes and hats, but as she unwound her scarf—the hall positively shimmered with reckless heat—she thought it might be great fun to try.

In order to reach the millinery department, they had to wind their way through a vast emporium of pocketbooks and gloves and perfume and shoes, through a gentleman's haberdashery and a collection of lush fur coats, until they realized they had missed their destination altogether and doubled back to the elevator, where a uniformed attendant opened and closed the grille and announced the floors in the same stately tone as the elevator attendant at the Paris Ritz had done, last summer. (Except in French.) In fact, Sophie had felt more at home then than she did now, because she spoke French fluently but *this* language—the language spoken by the two ladies murmuring behind her in the car—seemed beyond her grasp, its points of reference too far uptown, inhabiting a separate physical dimension altogether.

They arrived on the third floor, and the attendant called out *Millinery! Ladies ready-to-wear!* in his voice of ceremonial boredom. Virginia and Sophie stepped obediently out, and so did the two women behind them, who were joined also by a quiet girl of perhaps eleven or twelve whom Sophie hadn't noticed until now.

"Go off and find your hat, then," said one of the ladies, in a voice that made Sophie think of a mouthful of marbles.

"Lily?" said the other one. "Come with me and look at lovely hats?"

"Do you mind, Mother?" asked the girl, far too politely for someone her age, and Sophie didn't hear Mother's response because Virginia was already pushing forward toward the millinery in her resourceful way, and Sophie had no choice but to lope on after her.

But never mind, because a few moments later the second woman joined them among the racks of hats— the young girl had evidently gone with her mother instead—and Sophie, settling a wide-brimmed hat over the crown of her head, heard her voice just to the left.

"Not that one, please. Unless you want to look like your mother."

Sophie removed the hat and spun around, and there she was! Julie. Hair of blond, eyes of blue, mouth of mischief (and decidedly of lip rouge as well). She was smiling, taking the edge off her words, and she couldn't have been older than Sophie, though her sophistication radiated outward in luxurious waves.

She lifted another hat from the stand and handed it to Sophie. "Try this one instead. It's close-fitting, frames your pretty face. You've got too pretty a face to hide behind an enormous old brim like that."

Sophie placed the hat on her head and turned to the mirror, and goodness me if the young woman wasn't dead right. The hat surrounded Sophie's face like a picture frame, so that her previously shadowed eyes now looked large and gamine. The mossy color made her hazel eyes greener and her lashes blacker, and suddenly she could see her eyebrows! And they were beautiful! "It's marvelous," she said, turning one way and then another.

"You're the one who's marvelous; the hat just lets everybody see it, which is really the point, don't you think?" The other woman put out a leather-gloved hand. "I'm Julie Schuyler, and you can thank me later."

Sophie took that hand. "Sophie Fortescue."

An instant later, Virginia swooped in, but it was already too late. The spark was struck, and when they had purchased their hats Julie forced everybody downstairs to find a pair of matching gloves in mossy leather, and then they had sat down in the café for tea. At which point, mid-sentence, Julie straightened in her chair and covered her mouth. "Gadzooks! I've forgotten my sister," she exclaimed, but before she rushed back off to the third floor she had slipped her visiting card into Sophie's hand and said to come by for lunch tomorrow, because she was having a little party and needed a new face.

At the party, Julie introduced her to Jay Ochsner, who came calling on Thirty-Second Street the next day. Her father, bemused and suspicious, had taken Mr. Ochsner aside, and to Sophie's surprise they had emerged from this meeting of one mind. *I would like you to encourage this man's suit, Sophie,* were Father's exact instructions, later that evening, and Sophie had. She would do anything to please her father. She had encouraged Mr. Ochsner, and discovered how much fun it was, having a handsome suitor all to yourself, eager to please and flatter you, allowed to escort you to places you'd never been allowed to go, all under the approving eye of a father whose approval came so rarely.

And so it went, for two whole months: shopping and tea and occasional clandestine adventures with Julie, courtship and tea and occasional clandestine kisses from the well-bred Mr. Ochsner. A new world. Maybe even a new Sophie.

So that's the whole story. That's how, in a nutshell, a few hours after bidding Mr. Rofrano good-bye beneath the Second Avenue El, on a bitter Saturday evening in the middle of January, the formerly seraphic Sophie Fortescue possesses an elegant and slightly daring wardrobe to match her elegant and slightly daring fiancé, and no one seems happier than her own father.

"It's how your mother would have wanted it," he says, the absolute and final word on the matter, as Jay settles her coat over her shoulders while a taxi putters outside, waiting to whisk them uptown to a party at the home of Julie's Schuyler cousins: Sophie's first party as an engaged woman.

Of course, Sophie will have to take her father's word for that, because she never knew her mother. Mrs. Fortescue died when she was just a baby.

About those kisses.

There were only four of them, really. The first one arrived in the library of the Ochsner house on

Thirty-Fourth Street, a room of such stupefying riches that Sophie wandered the walls in a kind of trance, running her fingers over the leather bindings, gasping softly to herself. Later, she learned that the rug beneath her feet was a rare Kilim, bought by Jay's grandparents in Istanbul on their wedding tour, and that the pair of Delft urns on the prodigious mantel had been given to his great-grandfather by the Prince of Orange himself, for some obscure reason lost to family legend.

At the time, however, only the room itself enchanted her: the shelves that reached from the floor to the delicately gilded ceiling, the books that filled those shelves. As a child, she had had few options for outside recreation, so with Virginia as her guide, she had explored vast and intricate worlds from the worn cushions of the parlor sofa, only to return those worlds to the nearby public library a week later. Books, after all, were expensive, and it was better to eat than read. So the little shelf in Sophie's bedroom contained a selection of volumes amassed lovingly over successive birthdays and Christmases, and the idea of an entire gilded library, old and venerable, covered with the fingerprints of one's ancestors, never needing to be returned to its rightful owner—why, it stole her will!

So she moved around the room in a slow clockwise rotation, trailed by a smiling Mr. Ochsner—he wasn't

Jay yet, not quite—emitting little gasps from time to time, until she reached the end of one shelf and turned.

"Are all these really *yours?*"

He wore an expression she hadn't seen before, at least on him: a look of heartfelt wonder. The room was large, taking up an entire half of the grand first floor, and the winter light flattened against the side of his face. "Aren't you a doll," he said, laying one hand against the side of her face, and he had leaned forward and kissed her, Sophie Fortescue, her first kiss ever. His lips were soft and confident and left her deliciously breathless, and even though she knew he'd probably never lifted a single one of those books from its shelf, she didn't mind the kiss at all. She thought it was strange and wonderful. In fact, she thought she might like another, and he obliged her a few days later when he came for lunch and presented her with a first edition of *Daniel Deronda*, one she'd especially admired, as a Christmas present.

The third kiss was more daring, arriving on Thursday morning while they sat together on the parlor sofa, admiring the rose-shaped engagement ring on her finger, unexpectedly and temporarily alone, and he had actually pressed her into the cushions then, kissing her lips and chin and neck, springing away just in time when the floorboards creaked outside the door.

And the fourth kiss is happening right now! Right here, in the back seat of the taxi, tasting like gin, more sloppy than she remembers, and not nearly so exciting. Jay smells of peppermint hair oil tonight, and the scent of peppermint always makes her feel sick and slightly terrified. His left hand has just entered her hair, and his right hand unbuttons her coat. She shoves his fingers away and jumps back toward the window. "What are you doing?" she demands, even though it seems perfectly obvious what he's doing. (She hears those words in Julie's voice—*perfectly obvious!* Perfectly obvious what a gentleman's after, now that they're engaged. Julie told her about that, during their ride this morning, and of course Sophie hadn't quite believed her. *We have all got the sex-instinct in varying degrees,* Julie said, ever so matter-of-fact, *and you shouldn't try to suppress it, that's the first requirement of a healthy mind.*)

Jay's face flashes in and out of view as the streetlights slide by. "Darling, we're *engaged,*" he says, just like Julie said he would, and Sophie can't help but laugh, if only to cover the vertiginous state of her stomach.

"What's the joke?" Jay asks, a little injured.

"Nothing. Just behave yourself. We're engaged, but we aren't married."

He reaches for her again. "And what do you know about *that,* Sophie dear?"

"Just enough to know that you should stay on your side of the taxi for now." She picks up his searching hand and winds it securely into her own, in order to slow her jiggling pulse. "There, that's better."

"Now, Sophie. Don't you trust me? I'm a gentleman. I just want to give you a little taste of married life, that's all, so you know what's coming. Nothing to be afraid of." The taxi stops right under a streetlight, exposing a terribly wicked smile on the face of Sophie's intended. His pupils are a little unsteady. The waft of peppermint strikes her again, making her stomach turn. She tries to breathe through her mouth instead of her nose. Anything to quell this unseemly surge of uneasiness in her viscera.

"A taste of gin, more like it."

"Aw, don't run cold on me, Sophie."

"I'm not cold. But a little birdie told me to beware of impromptu petting parties in the back seats of taxis, even when the gentleman in question is the man you're going to marry."

"And what little birdie is that?"

"A very wise birdie." She puts his left hand back in his lap and keeps the right one where she can see it. Julie didn't actually say *Beware*, exactly. She just said that while inhibitions were dangerous to your mental health, a girl still had to choose the right time and place, or she might end up in a pickle.

A pickle. Of course! That's why Sophie's so uneasy just now, in the proximity of the man she's supposed to adore.

The taxi begins moving again. The traffic is noisy and urgent, and Sophie likes the way they're cocooned in sound, crawling atop mad Manhattan Island in company with such a crowd. Thank goodness for Julie, explaining the fundamentals of bachelor management over tea and horses, or who knows what might have happened just now? A pickle, that's what.

Petting. She's heard the word—who hasn't?—but the reality isn't quite what she thought. The kissing itself isn't quite what she thought, either, now that the novelty has worn off, the slightly nauseous thrill of someone else's mouth on yours, and anyway Jay's face looks so unaccountably tired and blotchy and sort of heavy. Was it always so tired and blotchy? Or is it just the light from the streetlamps, not nearly so flattering as the light in the Ochsner library?

Or is it the sick-making hair oil?

Or Julie's worldly advice?

Or is she simply inhibited? Cold, like Jay said. What's the word? *Suppressed.* Her libido all shriveled up and brooding, a danger to her mental health. But how can that be? It wasn't shriveled up before, was it? It wasn't shriveled up when he first kissed her. Just now. Tonight. Suddenly, in the back seat of this taxi, kissing her fiancé seems all wrong, when it should be more right than ever before.

Jay flops back in his seat and begins to sulk—again, just as Julie warned!—and Sophie looks out the window and counts the blocks until they arrive at their destination, a beautiful new apartment building on Park Avenue, and Jay revives just enough to pay the driver with a crumpled dollar bill.

"You haven't told me their names," she says, as he pulls her like a parcel from the taxi to the sidewalk. The cold air blows past her nose. Washes away the stale, peppermint interior of the taxi. She inhales deeply.

"Whose names?" (Jay's still sulking.)

"Our hosts."

"Oh." He looks up at the building, as if the sight of the facade will somehow jog his memory. "Schuyler. Philip Schuyler. Julie's second cousin. He got married last year to his secretary."

"What's her name?"

They're sweeping past the doorman now, and Sophie's hand is wound through the crook of Jay's elbow, and her sensational new engagement ring—an old ring, actually, but new to her—slides loosely around her fourth finger, under the glove. Two months ago, she was almost a schoolgirl; now, it seems, she's fully grown, sweeping into a Park Avenue apartment building on the arm of Mr. Edmund Jay Ochsner, who will soon be her husband. And isn't that why she encouraged Jay to begin with? Because it was time to grow up. To grow up and escape.

"Lucy." He snaps his fingers. "That's it. Her name is Lucy. Lucy Young Schuyler."

But the names of their hosts don't seem to matter, at least at first. Nobody receives them at the door, except a sort of expressionless housekeeper who accepts their coats and turns away down a service hallway. (Maybe manners aren't important among the rich, Sophie thinks.) The light indoors is more golden and less harsh than the streetlights on Park Avenue, and Jay looks transformed: his shirtfront is as stiff as a board and as white as the moon, and his hair is brushed back in a shining metal helmet, streaked by tarnish.

Sophie, her pulse settled, her viscera back in order, a little mortified now at the unexpected failure of her sex-instinct during the taxi ride, tells him how splendid he looks—she leaves out the tarnish, of course—and at last the sulky expression starts to perk back up.

"Splendid, am I? That's good news, at my advanced age. You're looking pretty smashing yourself, now that you mention it." He lifts her hand and kisses the satin that covers her palm.

That's better, isn't it? At least they seem like a newly engaged couple now, winding their affectionate way through the crush of bodies, hand in hand. An instinct rises between Sophie's ribs—maybe not the sex-instinct, but something just as primitive—at the smell of cigarettes and perfume, the musk of human skin. Something she wants but cannot quite identify. A waiter passes by, bearing glasses of foaming champagne. She follows him longingly as he goes. They had champagne the other day, a vintage bottle that Jay brought over from the Ochsner cellar to celebrate the engagement, and Sophie thought it was the nicest thing she had ever tasted. Maybe that's what she wants? Not sex, but champagne.

She turns her head to Jay, who's craning his neck this way and that. "Can you find us some champagne?" she shouts in his ear.

"What's that?"

"Champagne!"

"Sure! But first I want to—oh, there she is!"

"Who?"

Never mind. Off they go, winding back through the crowd, past a fireplace and a buffet table and maybe a thousand cigarettes. Sophie's finding it hard to breathe, but she follows him gamely, hoping there will be champagne at the end of the journey. Champagne! Champagne will make it all better.

There isn't champagne, however. Jay falls to an abrupt halt in front of a milky half-dressed back, on which a beaded jet necklace dangles like an aboriginal tattoo above a swoop of black satin.

He reaches out with his left hand and taps the matching shoulder.

The woman—naturally, the owner of this mesmerizing rear spectacle belongs to the female persuasion— the woman turns her head and registers elegant surprise in one eyebrow.

"Ox?" she inquires, in a voice like the drizzling of cream over dessert. "Whatever are *you* doing in a respectable drawing room on a Saturday night?"

Jay releases Sophie's hand and places his fingertips in the small of her back. "Sisser," he says, like the cat that swallowed the goose that laid the golden egg, "I have the honor of presenting to you your future sister-in-law, Miss Sophia Fortescue."

Chapter 5

Telling lies is a fault in a boy, an art in a lover,
an accomplishment in a bachelor, and second-nature
in a married man.

—HELEN ROWLAND

THERESA

Manhattan, later that night

You know, if it weren't for Man o' War, the Boy and I might never have found each other again. Imagine that: a racehorse decides your fate.

I think it must have been about a week after our unsuccessful encounter at the van der Wahls' swimming pool, the one that nearly reduced me to tears. Naturally I put the whole episode behind me and plunged into a relentless week of—well, of whatever it is I did, before the Boy and I became lovers. I visited friends, I read books, I swam in the ocean, I went to every damned cocktail party between West Hampton and Montauk Point. I believe I competed in a horse show—if memory serves—on my favorite mare, Tiptoe. We won second place over the jumps. The ribbon's hanging in the stable somewhere.

Anyway, we got to talking afterward, me and the horsier set, and the subject of Man o' War came up. Had anyone seen him race yet? It turned out nobody had. We consulted the evening edition and discovered, lo and behold, that the champion was due to start in the Dwyer Stakes at Aqueduct the next day. Or rather—since dawn was nearly breaking—today.

So we went home to our respective houses and slept and changed clothes, and then we drove west in Ned van der Wahl's Buick all the way to Queens, arriving just in time for the third race on the day's card. The Dwyer was the fourth.

The place was jam-packed, as you might imagine. I later heard that forty thousand souls occupied the stands that day. The clubhouse was already full, so we proceeded through the sweaty and unfamiliar grandstand instead, past the long lines of common folk at the betting windows until we hit the fresher air—I speak in relative terms—on the other side. The entrants for the third race were just then emerging from the paddock to parade onto the track, and the bugle called crisply, making my blood stir. As the last notes floated over the heat, someone said, "Hello, isn't it that kid staying with the van der Wahls?"

And it was.

The Boy stood not twenty yards away, leaning his elbows on the rail by the finish pole, visible in flashes as the crowd shifted between us. He wore a light, wrinkled suit and a boater of pale straw low on his forehead against the burning July sun. A folded Racing Form dangled from his left hand, and a cigarette from the right, and he had fixed a ferocious concentration on the animals now jogging down the track.

We called him over, and he straightened and stared at us in perfect astonishment. Even twenty yards away, I noticed the paleness of his eyes against his tanned face. He tucked the Racing Form under his arm and forced his way to where we stood, adjoining the winner's circle, and my blood, already awakened by the call of the bugle, just about boiled in my veins.

He kept away from me at first. He told me later that he was afraid to come close, because he thought the others would notice something. Because I was, after all, Mrs. Sylvester Marshall of Fifth Avenue and Southampton, and he was nothing but a Boy just back from France.

But Nature will have her way, I'm afraid, and by the time the horses had assembled behind the long elastic webbing that marked the starting line, we stood some-how next to each other by the rail, a few yards short of the finish pole, while our friends talked and laughed nearby, not the least bit interested in the race about to begin. Ned van der Wahl's patrician voice floated out confidently among the broad Brooklyn vowels turning the air blue around us. The Boy had put out his ciga-rette, and the Racing Form now occupied both hands, though he was really looking at the horses. His cheeks were pink. I thought of his abrupt departure when I saw him last, and I wondered if perhaps I'd misread the reason.

"Do you have a favorite in this race, Mr. Rofrano?" I asked.

"I put ten dollars down on Number Four to win."

"It sounds as if you're a regular."

He fiddled with the Racing Form. "My dad used to take me to the track on weekends, when I was a kid. I saw Colin win the Belmont in the middle of a rain-storm. That hooked me."

Here on the rail, you could actually hear the faint shouts of the jockeys and the starters, as the horses milled around behind the webbing. It looked like Bedlam. I didn't know how they were going to make a race of it. A minute passed, and another, and the Boy and I didn't say anything, just stood there side by side along the rail, pretending absorption in the spectacle up the track while the sun beat down on the brims of our hats and the crowd hooted and spat. And then, for a strange and pregnant instant, all went still.

The barrier went up.

We kept quiet as the contest took shape. It was a mile, a stakes race for two-year-olds, and it didn't take long, a minute and a half, but it seemed longer. It seemed epic, horses taking the lead and falling back, someone else surging up. As the pack shifted its way down the backstretch, I felt the gradual increase in the Boy's state of tension, nerve by nerve. They rounded the final turn. The rumble of hooves drew nearer and larger, and as the flashes of colored silk clarified in the haze, my own fingers tightened unconsciously into fists, and the Boy's body, arranged by my side, coiled into a live wire. The gamblers roared behind us. The horses thundered by in a fleshy cloud.

I turned to the Boy, a little breathless. "Did he win?"

"Yes, Mrs. Marshall." He smiled. His cheeks were still pink, but this blush had a different fundamental quality to the one before it. "Yes, he did. Shall we go collect my winnings?"

Apparently there's a euphoria associated with winning a bet on a horse race, a kind of invincible glee. I think that's why the Boy made me this reckless offer, at this particular minute, when he had tried so hard and so sternly to stay away before. He wasn't stern now, nor even diffident; he couldn't be stern or diffident when he had just won a ten-dollar bet on a horse at eleven-to-one odds, and I got all caught up in the smoke of his elation and smiled back.

"That sounds divine," I said.

We slipped invisibly past our friends and pried our way through the grumbling grandstand crowd to the betting windows, where the Boy collected his hundred and ten dollars and secured them with a plain silver clip in the inside pocket of his jacket. He looked at his watch. "They should be getting ready in the paddock now, Mrs. Marshall. Do you want to take a look at him?"

"At whom?"

"Why, Man o' War."

I had forgotten all about the big red racehorse. Can you believe it? I followed the Boy through the grandstand gates to the paddock, which was thick and crowded and buzzing. I held my hat and craned my neck, trying to see above all the heads before me, but it was no use, and I shouted in the Boy's nearby ear that we should go back to the track and wait for the great horse there.

"Now, Mrs. Marshall, that's no way to get things done," he said. "Come with me."

He dragged my arm around his elbow and proceeded to slice his way through that crowd, person by person, earning us any number of angry looks and spiteful ejaculations, but I didn't care. The Boy's arm was young and strong beneath my hand, like a green oak, and euphoria still drenched us. By the time he landed against the paddock rail, dragging me with him—or rather against him, because there really wasn't room—we were both laughing. And I don't think I'd laughed (a *real* laugh, I mean, not those brittle false laughs drawn out of you by cocktails and by the merciless demands of the social contract) in two whole years.

The Boy extracted his arm from between our compressed bodies and pointed his right index finger at the open stalls before us. "Look, there he is."

There he is. I don't know if there's been a more magnificent horse, before or since. If there has, I haven't seen him. That beautiful ruddy animal could make you forget anything, could make you forget the war and the communists and the Boy wedged against you. On this hot July day of his fourth year, nineteen hundred and twenty by the Christian calendar, he was a giant. He held his head at an improbably high angle, king over us all, and his chestnut coat was built of fire. He didn't want to be saddled, but saddled he must be, and they got the leather on him, I don't know how. He settled down a bit then, just kicking out a hoof now and again, to remind everyone not to get too friendly. It didn't even occur to me to look at the other horse.

"Isn't he a beauty?" said the Boy, very soft, next to my ear.

He stood right up against my back, pressed there by the crowd around us, so that we couldn't help the indecent proximity, could we? I felt all shameful and electric, like a radio crackling with static. My buttocks fit neatly into his thighs. I could smell his perspiration.

"He's magnificent," I agreed.

The jockeys went up; the horses headed out to the track. There were just two of them, because Man o' War, four races into his three-year-old season, had already scared away everybody else and won each contest under what the Racing Form called a "stout pull," or "eased up," or some other form of sportsmanlike restraint. (How they managed to restrain the colt at all, I couldn't imagine; as he charged furiously into the tunnel, he reminded me of a locomotive.) Today, his lone challenger—so the Boy informed me, as he released me from my intimate prison—was a talented chestnut colt named John P. Grier.

"The poor sacrificial lamb," I said, as we pushed our way back under the grandstand toward the track.

"Well, he's got a fighting chance. He's only carrying a hundred and eight pounds, and Red's carrying a hundred and twenty-six."

"And that makes such a terrible difference?"

"As a rule of thumb, Mrs. Marshall, the track handicappers generally figure a pound of extra weight equals about a length lost in speed, so I guess you could say that Red's giving Grier a head start of eighteen lengths. He's a Whitney colt," the Boy added, as if that made a difference.

"Oh, does Harry own him?"

"Bred him, too. By Whisk Broom, out of a Disguise mare. Care to place a bet?"

I let him put down ten dollars on Man o' War for me, and he put down the rest of his winnings on John P. Grier, just to give the little colt a break. By the time we fought our way back out to the track, the horses had reached the starting line on the other side of the infield. Or so we presumed; we couldn't see a thing, and we hadn't a hope of reaching our earlier position on the rail, let alone finding our friends. The crowd was so densely packed, you couldn't move an inch, except the Boy somehow did: shoving one person aside and then another, selfishly winning us closer to the action.

A roar swept the throng: they're off.

"But I can't see!" I shouted, and the Boy actually elbowed a man off on a nearby bench.

"Say!" the man said angrily, lifting a fist.

"Make way for the lady," said the Boy. The man took one look at the two of us—vigorous Boy, lady of a certain age—and turned away, smashing his hat down on his head until his crown nearly burst through the straw.

The Boy put his hands around my waist and hoisted me up.

Well, I can tell you, that unexpected and gallant action nearly took my breath. I gripped the Boy's steadying fingers with one hand and shaded my eyes with the other—the sun was full on my face—and strained to see across the infield to the galloping horses beyond.

"What's the story?" the Boy shouted.

"I can't tell! I don't see the other horse. It's just Red, I think—no, wait!" I rose on my toes, swaying wildly, clutching the Boy's fingers. "It's the two of them! They're running together! They're coming into the turn, they're side by side! My God!"

The roar around me was like a wall, like I could have flung out my arms and supported myself by sound alone. Strange that so many lone voices could amalgamate into a uniform frantic din. I realized that my own shout was among them, that I'd given up on sentences and begun screaming a primitive *Go! Go!* into the barrage, and I didn't even know which colt I was urging on. Both of them, maybe: the great red horse and Harry Whitney's scrappy challenger, barreling around the turn toward the long, smoky homestretch, flinging themselves recklessly forward and forward, as closely matched as if they were pulling a single carriage.

They say it was one of the greatest races ever, that Dwyer Stakes run in the first year of the new decade after the war. I haven't been to many horse races, so I can't really say one way or another. All I remember is that I came back to life in those last thirty seconds or so: that my cold little heart burst free from its ribs and climbed all the way up my throat to the roof of my mouth, as John P. Grier hung gamely on, taking perhaps two strides for every one of Red's, and they bobbed closer and closer and no one was winning, neither colt had beaten the other, and they couldn't possibly keep this up. They would kill themselves. They would kill me.

On and on, back and forth, my heart throttling my breath, and just as they flashed past the eighth pole (or so I understood later, for I didn't notice that pole at the time) Grier stuck his head out in front.

You wouldn't have thought it possible for that crowd to yell any louder, but it did. We screamed and screamed. The little colt's nose poked out bravely from behind Man o' War's big red body, just about the only thing you could see of him—just that game, game head, taking the lead from the immortal champion.

In the next instant, Red's rider reached back with his whip and struck Man o' War's side.

He hadn't been touched with a whip all season, I believe: not since a single dramatic race the year before, the only race he'd ever lost, and that one because he was boxed in throughout. He'd never been challenged; he'd won all his races handily, rated by his jockey so he wouldn't win by too many lengths and humiliate the Whitneys and Belmonts and Astors who sent their horses against him. No one had ever looked Man o' War in the eye, and now Grier looked him in the eye, Grier pushed his head out in front, and Red's jockey went to the whip.

A single blow, and Man o' War shot forward. In a few strides, he was half a length in front; the jockey hit him again, and Grier was beat. I don't think I'd ever screamed like that. I jumped up and down on the bench, yanking on the Boy's firm hand. Six seconds later, Man o' War streaked past the finish pole, a length and a half in front of gallant John P. Grier, setting a whole new

American record for the mile and an eighth, and they say Grier was never the same. His heart broke right down the middle that afternoon, and while he was still a good colt, maybe even the second-best of his generation, he was never again a great one.

Man o' War went on to smash several more records that year, and won every race.

Afterward, we couldn't find the others, and the Boy offered to drive me back to Southampton in his second-hand Model T, though he expected it might be dark by the time we reached our destination, Mrs. Marshall.

I said yes.

As somebody mentioned earlier, the Boy was staying with the van der Wahls that summer, the summer he got back from France, right before he took the job selling bonds at Sterling Bates. Ned van der Wahl had once worked with the Boy's father at Morgan bank, I believe, and though the Boy wasn't quite of the same social caliber as the van der Wahls—too new, too dark—old Ned was always a gentleman, always the kind of man who'd offer to put up an old colleague's war hero son in his guesthouse for the summer, without regard for the vowel at the end of his surname.

So the Boy has a few connections in our little world, here and there, and I'm always a little anxious that we might bump into each other at some gathering or another, the way we did at the van der Wahls' swimming pool, the way we bumped excruciatingly throughout the rest of that summer of 1920 out on Long Island, pretending we were just the Boy and Mrs. Marshall, exchanging pleasantries regarding the weather and the quality of the company. Anxious and perhaps more, because it *is* a bit of a thrill, those accidental bumpings: an absolute nerve-zapping thrill, to see the Boy's sleek head appear without warning in somebody's drawing room, and his white collar against his golden skin. To talk about stock prices when we really want to talk about sex. Sometimes I think he does it on purpose, just to warm up my blood, to wind up the anticipation for what comes after the party, when we've left the rest of the world behind us.

But he doesn't appear this evening at the Schuylers' Park Avenue apartment, even though I've dropped the details of the affair in his ear more than once. Instead, as I stir my way through the living room to bid farewell to my hostess—I'm a woman of the quaint old manners, you understand, and hostesses must be attended to, even if they were formerly secretaries—I find I am entirely alone, though surrounded by faces I've known my entire life, in drawing rooms and ballrooms and clubs and ocean liners, and the fact of my isolation presses against my temples and my chest in such a way that I'm finding it difficult to breathe. Or maybe it's the smell of cigars drifting from the library.

I discover my host first. "Philip, love," I say, "I'm looking for your charming wife."

"She's putting the baby back to bed. Apparently all our noise woke the poor little tyke, and she wandered into the dining room just as my aunt Prunella toppled into the punch bowl. Can I be of assistance, perhaps?"

I like Philip Schuyler. I like him a great deal, in fact, for I suspect he's a man of fundamental decency, for all that he's nearly as fond of the sauce as he is of his pretty new wife. He has polished blond hair and a face poised handsomely on the verge of ruin, and should one arrive on his doorstep in one's time of trouble, he would undoubtedly deliver up gin and sympathy by the bucketful. He crushes out his cigarette in a nearby ashtray and offers me a look of expectant impatience: a host with *countless* demands on his attention, but he still makes time for you.

To which I shrug. "Just wanted to pay my respects before I left."

"I'm happy to convey them to her." He lifts his glass, but it turns up empty, and his expression of abject, blue-eyed disappointment would soften the hardest heart.

"Do that, love. Tell her I had a smashing time and all that. The food was divine, the company sensational."

He rubs one temple with his thumb. "Did young what's-his-name find you?"

"My brother, you mean? Yes, he did."

"Not your brother. The other fellow. Ned's protégé, the pilot."

One of my shoulders has escaped my coat. I turn my attention to the errant mink sleeve and say, "Why, no. Was Mr. Rofrano here?"

Philip snaps his fingers. "Rofrano! That's it. Yes, he was. And not in a social frame of mind, I'm sorry to say. Peppered me with all kinds of indecent business questions, and then charged off in your direction. You've got to teach him some manners, Theresa, or he'll never fit in."

"I don't need him to fit in." Rather coldly. And then: "What sort of questions?"

"Oh, I don't remember. Something to do with an old client of mine, which of course I couldn't discuss. Confidentiality." He taps his temple, this time with a well-tended index finger. "Very bad form, as the English say."

"How strange."

Philip shakes his head and stares down into his empty glass, and for an instant I imagine he's actually pondering something. "Funny, though. I hadn't thought about that old case in years."

"What old case?"

He looks back up, and a bit of shrewd lawyerly suspicion shapes the squint of his eyes. He picks up my hand and kisses the gloved knuckles, like a man who does that kind of thing often. "Now, why don't you just ask him yourself? Two good friends like the pair of you."

I extract my hand and gather up my pocketbook. "Trust me, love. Friendship has nothing to do with it."

I have begun the evening alone, and alone I remain as I travel down the elevator directed by one red-coated attendant and allow another red-coated attendant to hail me a taxi from the frozen street outside. The coldest day of the year, the cabbie informs me, setting off down Park Avenue toward the beckoning lights, and I tell him I'm not surprised to hear that.

I've never felt colder.

"There you are," I tell the Boy, when at last I slide atop a neighboring stool at the Christopher Club, the place next door to his apartment. Our usual haunt. I set my pocketbook on the bar and signal the proprietor, all of which serves to disguise my relief at the sight of the Boy's heavy black hair, gleaming under the lights.

"Here I am."

"I thought we agreed to meet at your place."

"I got a little restless. I figured you'd know where I was."

I accept the martini between my fingers and nod my gratitude to Christopher. The musicians are taking a break, it seems, and the Boy's dear voice is rather eerily audible, in the absence of trumpet and saxophone. "You might have left a note, just to be sure."

"I guess I might."

The martini is pure corrosive and peels my throat. One of these days I'm going to die of gin like this. I set down the glass and cover the Boy's hand with mine. "Let's not fight, hmm? It's much nicer for both of us when we don't fight. Give me a kiss."

He turns his head and kisses me, but his lips are hard and his heart's not in it. I ask him what's the matter. Have I done something awful?

"No." He fingers his glass. There's an ashtray at his elbow, filled with the sordid remains of perhaps five or six cigarettes. Another one decorates his hand, half-finished. He lifts it to his lips.

"Has someone else done something awful?"

"Maybe."

"Come on, now. Talk to me, Boyo, or nobody gets to have any fun tonight."

The Boy drinks the rest of his whatever-it-is—whisky, I guess—and signals for another. "It's nothing, okay? How was your evening?"

"My evening was delightful. You'll never guess who turned up. Ox's little bonbon, just as sweet as could be."

"*Sophie* was there?"

"Is that her name? I'd forgotten. Anyway, she was just darling. She was wearing the prettiest little dress, all in pink. It brought out her round sweet cheeks. Like a doll, really. I can see why Ox is so smitten, aside from the money, of course. I think they're perfect for each other."

"He's far too old for her."

"I don't think he minds."

"I meant her. *She* should mind. A used-up old bachelor like him."

"Boyo, darling, are you casting aspersions on my brother?"

"He's got the brains of an orang-utang and the morals of an alley cat, and you know it."

The gin doesn't burn so much now. Indeed, it's rather refreshing. I drain the chalice and ask the Boy if he's got another cigarette. "I never heard you object to poor Ox before," I say, as he lights me up.

"He's never tried to marry an innocent young girl before."

"Not *tried* to marry." I blow out the smoke in long gusts. "*Is* marrying. She's agreed to marry him, very much of her own accord. That was your doing, remember? She looked awfully jolly at the party, by the way. Smiling the whole while, just as pleased as could be. She's wearing her manacle. I made her take off her glove to show me. Made such a fuss over her. It's a shame you weren't there."

"Yeah, a real shame."

"Of course, I still have my reservations about that curious father of hers, and how he got his money, and how much he's really got. But if you haven't found out anything awful . . . Have you, Boyo?"

"Have I what?"

"Found out anything awful about the Fortescues."

Christopher—not his real name, by the by, but then I expect you already guessed that—Christopher slides by and presents the Boy with another drink. The Boy takes the glass between his fingers and sort of rotates it on the surface of the bar, clockwise, making wet little interconnected circles in the wood. (The Boy usually drinks his whisky neat, but tonight there's ice for some reason, ice on the coldest day of the year.) The hum of voices around us is more subdued than usual, the mood less reckless and more maudlin, as if everybody's stayed home because of the frozen streets, the smell of impending snow in the air. The instruments sit abandoned on their chairs in the corner of the room, and I'm beginning to wonder if their owners are planning to return.

"Boyo?"

"Yes?"

"The Fortescues."

He picks up the whisky at last and takes a drink, maybe half a glass in one gulp. The ice clinks and falls. "Still asking around."

"Well, let me know what you find out, won't you? Before too much longer. Not that I'm not coming around to wonder whether it matters. These are modern times, aren't they? Love conquers all. Who really cares if the old man's hiding a skeleton or two? My God, haven't we all got *skeletons*!"

The Boy winces slightly, and I'm not sure whether it's my words, or the brittle quality of the laugh that goes with them.

I continue. "It's a lovely ring, isn't it? The Ochsner family ring, I mean. Did you know that my—"

"You know what, Theresa?"

"What's that, darling?"

"I think I'm going to call it a night." He slings back his whisky and rises from the stool.

I stub out the cigarette in the ashtray, attend to my drink, and follow him up. "I was just going to suggest the same thing."

"I mean *alone*, Theresa. I'm sorry. It's been a long week."

A few notes wobble softly from the trumpet behind me. The musicians have returned after all, it seems.

I say lightly, "The coldest night of the year, and you want to sleep alone?"

"I'm sorry. Maybe I've got a flu coming on, or something. I'm tired as sin."

"Ah, but not so tired that you couldn't make an appearance at a certain party uptown, isn't that right?"

The Boy's eyes widen a little. His mouth tenses at the corners, and admits defeat. "I looked around for you. You must have been hiding."

"Who, me? I was in plain sight, I thought. Unless I just fade into the background for you now."

"You know that's not true."

The saxophone's joined the trumpet, and a bass player thrums a question. I lift my hands into the Boy's hair and pull him down for a kiss—kissing's so much easier than talking—and for a second or two he obeys me, opening his mouth, allowing me a taste of himself. Relief! Triumph! I still have my Boy; he's still *mine*, God knows why, warm and green and relentless, the source of all life. His lips are charged with whisky, and it tastes better than gin. Better than anything. I test his tongue, and he pulls away.

"Not here, Theresa."

"Then let's go."

"I said not tonight. I'm not up to it."

I step backward. The band has begun to play in earnest, filling the air with noise, noise. My throat hurts. *Not up to it.*

"All right. Find me my coat and a taxi."

"I'll drive you back."

"That's not necessary. After all, you're a tired Boyo tonight. Tired as—what was it? Tired as sin."

He brings the coat, and a moment later we stand silently on Seventh Avenue, examining the approaching cars while the wind whistles along the brims of our hats. One of the vehicles swerves toward us. The Boy opens the door for me.

"Good night, then," I say.

He bends down to kiss me. "Good night."

"And Boyo?" I reach up and touch his icy cheek with my thumb. "You're going to have to learn how to lie a little better, or you'll never get on in this world."

I climb swiftly into the taxi and slam the door all by myself, so he won't have a chance to answer me. Not that he seems to have anything plausible at the ready, though, judging by the stricken young expression on his face as it slides past my frosted window.

I hope I haven't given the impression that I don't get on with my husband. Quite the contrary! We've been good friends for over two decades, ever since I walked into his dressing room, asked his valet to leave, and demanded to know whether the author of a certain spiteful anonymous note (*spiteful* and *anonymous* do tend to go together, I've always found) had her facts absolutely straight.

He remained calm. He asked to see the note, and I obliged him. He said that it was true, that he had, in fact, conceived a child with another woman shortly after conceiving Tommy with me; moreover, he still kept this woman and her baby under—as we quaintly called it in those days—his *protection*. He didn't say whether he was actually still fucking her, but then it hardly needed saying, did it? A lovely word, *protection*. Means ownership. And if you own something, by rights, you are allowed to fuck it.

I then asked, rather tremulously, whether he was in love with this woman. For some time, he considered his answer. He poured me a glass of sherry and made me sit on the little settee he kept there. He was very kind. He sat next to me and took my hand and explained that he did love this woman, but not in the same way he cared for me; that in fact I was not to feel threatened at all by these little adventures of his. Perhaps, one day, I would like to have adventures of my own, and he was a fair man, a very fair man, and he fully understood that he had no grounds to object to my adventures, provided I conducted them prudently.

I told him I wanted a divorce.

Very well, he said. If I wanted a divorce, he would give me a divorce, but he asked me to consider the consequences. After all, we had a very pleasant life together, didn't we? Nothing had materially changed between us. We got along well. We made each other laugh; we enjoyed many of the same interests; we had the same ideas of how life should be lived. We were of the same kind. We had a son together, a handsome and brilliant boy who was the light of Sylvo's life; he looked very much forward to the forthcoming birth of our second child, and it was his dearest hope that we should have even more together. Our partnership was the central fact around which our pleasant life revolved. Did that mean nothing to me?

He said all this in such a sincere voice, and I found— well, maybe it was the sherry, too—that he did make a great deal of sense. I did care for him. I didn't want to live without him. I didn't want to deprive our children of their father. I simply wanted him all to myself, and wasn't that, in a sense, ungenerous of me? Did I really require his devoted presence every moment of the day? Did this mistress of his make him any less attentive to his family, did it subtract in any way from the thousand personal qualities I knew and liked about him? If he had slept with other women before our marriage—and of course he had—did it matter, logically, that he slept with other women now? Would I not perhaps like to have the promised excitement of my own lover one day, while maintaining the perfect security of a tranquil marriage?

And—let's be honest—were not most of our own friends married under similar understandings? Did I think I was somehow immune to this particular disorder?

At Sylvo's urging, I went away to think about these things. It was nearly summer, and I took Tommy and went out to the house on Long Island, though nobody else had yet arrived in town. We played on the beach and splashed in the cold May currents, until one afternoon, when the sun was hot and a few other families had begun to appear on the shore, Tommy stood up on his fat little legs and began to cry. *Papa*, he said. *I want Papa.*

Now, you must understand what an adorable infant Tommy was, and how I worshipped him. Sylvo and

I both did. In my childish enthusiasm, I'd insisted on nursing the baby myself, and even now—especially now—I spent every spare moment in his company, to the nanny's bemusement. He was so handsome, such a dear little lad. He had the funniest ways, the most heart-melting expressions. He stood there in the sand with his little red pail in one hand, and his little red shovel in the other, and the tears streamed down his little red cheeks. And I thought, I must find a way through this. I must give Tommy what he needs.

I scooped him up and called for the nanny and told her to pack his things, because we were going back to the city. We took the train and arrived by dinnertime. Sylvo was there, preparing to dine alone; he had promised me not to visit this woman while I was considering the matter of our marriage, and he was a man of his word. He stood at once when I entered the room, and I realized then that he had kept his promise. A small thing, maybe, but it decided me.

Very well, I said. I won't ask for a divorce. I won't ask you not to have lovers, so long as you are discreet, and so long as you present no further bastards on my doorstep, and so long—here my voice broke, and the tears gathered in my eyes—so long as we remain *first* in your life.

For a moment, he stood quite still, saying nothing. I remember that, how his lips pressed together, and I remember thinking that I had made a terrible mistake with my demands. That I was only twenty years old, after all, and he was nearly forty. I had no power over him at all. First in his life? What a hoot.

Then he began to move. He pushed back his chair and walked around the end of the table in my direction, and when he reached me—I was trembling now—he took both my hands and thanked me for my generosity. And I don't know how it was, but I took my seat at the table as if nothing had happened. I ate my dinner and conversed with my husband. Our lives simply resumed, carrying this new understanding between us. Oliver came along, and then a stillborn girl, and then darling Billy, and I received no more anonymous notes in the morning post. No whispers from well-meaning friends. Sylvo could not have been more courteously discreet.

Indeed, it wasn't until I was nursing Billy that I noticed Sylvo paying particular attention to a pretty young widow of our acquaintance, and by then—rather to my surprise—instead of tasting jealousy, I knew a kind of dry compassion. After all, I now possessed such a supreme confidence in our importance in Sylvo's life—in my own beauty and power, aged twenty-six—that his sexual interest in a pretty widow didn't bother me at all. Let him enjoy himself while I devote myself to my baby son, I thought, and I'm positive that he did exactly that, although he kept his promise and enjoyed himself *just* as a gentleman should.

So it went for many years, and though our marriage ebbed and flowed in a natural human rhythm—we had, to be perfectly honest, more ebbed than flowed in the past few years—we continued to honor the agreement we had made that evening, and our home was always a refuge of professional friendship into which, by unspoken consent, no transient loves could penetrate.

Tonight, as the taxi at last approaches the familiar stretch of Fifth Avenue, and our apartment building that grows like a limestone monument from the pavement, I find myself inhaling a deep measure of ice-cold relief. These are natural human rhythms, I think, like the ebbing and flowing of a marriage, like the joys and heartbreaks of life itself. So the Boy was cross tonight. So his attention's been temporarily diverted to an unspoiled girl of nineteen; so he hasn't been *quite* honest with me about something. He's young and virile—*exceptionally* virile—and he certainly can't go to bed with this innocent and affianced Sophie. Within days, he'll crave me as before. Maybe more, because he will have gone without sex all that time, and his hopeless desire for the bright little Sophie will sublimate into desire for me. (I am up-to-date on all the latest psychology, even if I don't go in for it myself.)

In the meantime, I have this apartment, and this comfortable life, and this husband and these sons, and while the apartment's probably empty at the moment— husband in Sutton Place, sons grown and gone—it's still mine. It's *my* emptiness. And old Sylvo will be back by morning, and the boys will visit eventually, and the Boy will return to me. Thanks to the Boy, nothing's so bleak and lonely as it seemed a few years ago, when Billy left to prep and the place was empty—thoroughly, echoingly empty—for the first time since we moved in.

I greet the doorman and the elevator attendant as cheerfully as I possibly can, and peace settles over me as we trundle upward to the fourteenth floor, which belongs entirely to us: twelve rooms and a substantial terrace overlooking the park, the most beautiful metropolitan sunsets in the world. I fish for the key in my pocketbook. The car arrives with a clank; the attendant opens the door and the grille and wishes me good night, even though it's actually morning.

I say *Good night, Val.*

Inside, the apartment is quiet, the housekeeper and maid in bed, but to my surprise a light shines under the door in the library, as I pass by on my way to the bedroom. I push it open, thinking wildly that maybe one of my boys has come home at last, my God, maybe it's even Tommy.

But it isn't Tommy, or his brothers. It's Sylvo, who rises from his desk and kisses me tenderly, and then sits me down on the leather Chesterfield sofa, hands me a glass of cream sherry, and tells me he wants a divorce.

Chapter 6

*In love, somehow, a man's heart is either exceeding
the speed limit, or getting parked in the wrong place.*

—HELEN ROWLAND

SOPHIE

A little earlier that evening

Sophie seems to have misplaced her fiancé. Well, it
wasn't her fault! One minute he was standing by
her side, introducing her to some willowy pillar of society, and the next minute he's gone, vanished, leaving Sophie to gamely invent small talk with a woman
whose mouth looks as if it's been washed in hot water
and shrunk to half its original size.

Five minutes later, Jay has not reappeared, and Sophie's run out of observations on the weather—*Brrr!*—
and the lady's relationship to the host—*cousins*, always
cousins—and that book everyone's been talking

about—*indecent*. At some point, Sophie realizes she doesn't even know her companion's name. She faintly remembers hearing Jay's voice as he introduced them, but—oh, so horribly raw and tenderfoot!—she was fixing her attention too raptly on the face now before her, which bears such mesmerizing traces of former beauty that Sophie can't quite figure out where it's all gone wrong. Her skin is still smooth, after all, except for a few crinkles around the eyes. Her hair hasn't gone gray. Maybe it's that constipated mouth, from which the shrunken little words squeeze reluctantly, one by one; or else the fact that she isn't wearing any cosmetics at all, not even a bit of lip rouge to pinken her conversation. Her colorless face just disapproves of them all. Even Sophie. Especially Sophie.

"Oh, I didn't find it indecent at all," Sophie chirps back. "I thought it was wonderfully daring. After all, it's only what everybody thinks inside, but doesn't say out loud."

"*I* don't think those things," the lady replies, her longest sentence yet.

"Maybe you're only suppressing them." Sophie smiles kindly. "You know, the very *first* requirement of mental health is—"

"Why, Sophie, darling!" A pair of arms encircles Sophie's waist, and a sticky kiss finds her cheek. "I've been looking all over for you, and here you are, all tête à tête with my own sister!"

"Your *sister*?"

"Yes! Isn't it grand? Christina, Sophie's going to marry Jay Ochsner, the lucky thing."

"So I understand," says Christina, and now Sophie remembers where she heard that voice before: in the elevator of Bergdorf Goodman's, full of marbles.

Julie continues. "The thing is, I desperately need to borrow Sophie for just an instant, if you can *possibly* spare her. A friend of mine who won't believe Jay's engaged unless she actually sees the ring. Not that I blame her!"

Christina's mouth adjusts to a tense and insincere smile. "Not at all. A pleasure to make your acquaintance, Miss Fortescue."

"A pleasure, Mrs.—"

"Dane," says Julie's sister, just before she turns away.

"You've got to forgive her, I suppose," Julie says, as she drags Sophie in an experienced serpentine through the closely packed drawing room. "Her husband came back from the war an absolute wreck, and I can't seem to persuade her to find a substitute. I don't think she's had any fun since nineteen seventeen."

"How dreadful for her!"

"Isn't it? *Now* you see what I mean about suppressing the sex-instinct. The damage it does to your psychology!"

Julie's fingers bite into Sophie's hand as they writhe through the crowd, reaching a pocket of air at last. She lifts a glass of champagne from a passing waiter and hands it to Sophie. "Here you are, darling. You look as if you need it. That was really unhandsome of Jay, leaving you with my sister like that, all tender and unarmed. Was she perfectly awful to you?"

Champagne at last. Sophie tilts her chin and takes a *long* sip, and it's just as lovely as she remembers, tickling her throat and her brain both at once. "Not too awful," she says, thinking of Mrs. Dane's tragic husband and her suppressed sex-instinct. Would Sophie turn out like that, some day soon? After all, the sex-instinct doesn't seem to run high in her, either, except perhaps during those first kisses, or when reading indecent novels, which hardly counted. So maybe her unconscious suppression is already so steely that—

"You're too sweet, darling. Say what you think. My sister's a sad old Mrs. Grundy, and you're indebted to me for rescuing you."

"Rescuing me?"

Julie's found her own champagne by now, and she gestures with the glass. She's beautifully dressed in a shimmery low-waisted frock that flatters the modern angularity of her figure, and her lips are a dark and dangerous scarlet. The exact symmetry of her blond curls leaves Sophie feeling faintly frizzy. "With my mythical friend, remember? The one who wants to meet your engagement ring."

"Oh! I'd forgotten about her."

"It doesn't help that you're keeping the pretty bauble under wraps like that."

Sophie examines her left glove. "I already had to show it off once this evening, to Jay's sister."

"Oh, to the great Mrs. Marshall! Do tell."

"Tell what?"

"Well, what was she like? I've never met her, though I've seen her from afar. The Queen Vamp."

Sophie peers between the beautiful bodies and says absently, "She's very lovely. Much kinder than your sister. She's going to throw us an engagement party."

"There you are, then. An engagement party on Fifth Avenue! You've arrived, my darling, truly arrived." Julie looks one way and another. "Where's the lucky fellow, by the way?"

"Actually, I haven't the slightest idea. He disappeared about half an hour ago."

"Even better. You're coming along with me."

"Where to?" says Sophie, following Julie's immaculate blond curls once more, thinking they're headed for another room, more private; or else a terrace of some kind, overlooking Park Avenue, where Julie could indulge in a cigarette or a cocktail without any matronly disapproval dampening the experience. Not that much disapproval circulates in the Schuyler drawing room at the moment. Giggles, lipstick, tobacco, juice of juniper. But not disapproval, as if the new modern tempo has even beat its syncopated rhythms into the salons of the Upper East Side, and nobody gives a damn about anything any more.

Julie turns her head just enough to display the neat ripple of her hair, winging past the upper curve of her ear before it meets the knot at her nape. "Downtown, of course. I've fallen in love again, sweet Sophie, and I'm in desperate need of a chaperone."

The thing about Julie, she doesn't give a damn. Sophie, who grew up inside the claustrophobia of the house on Thirty-Second Street, hardly dreaming of escape, can't quite comprehend the audacity with which Julie departs from Park Avenue, hails herself a taxi, and drags Sophie inside: never asking for permission, never bidding farewell to her hostess, never informing Sophie's luckless fiancé where they've gone.

"He deserves it, for abandoning you to my sister," Julie says, when Sophie raises this point of etiquette, above the sputtering engine of the taxi.

"That's true."

"Anyway, you're not joined at the hip, just because you're engaged. That's the old way of doing things. It's a new world out there, kiddo, waiting to be explored." She taps the window of the taxi with her short, lacquered fingernail.

"But why?" asks Sophie. "Wasn't the old world good enough?"

"God, no. Look at our parents. Look at the war they foisted on us, all that nonsense about honor and duty and sacrifice. What did that ever get anybody? Dead, that's all. Dead with nothing to show for it. Or else like my brother-in-law, coughing up each poor lung, bit by bit, trying to get the poison out. We're free now, Sophie, *free.* We've got the vote, we've got cars and jobs and freedom."

"But you don't have a job."

"Well, I *could* have one. I *should.*" Julie reaches into her pocketbook and produces a cigarette case. "I've been thinking about it, actually. It's all the rage, don't you know, having jobs. Cousin Philip's a lawyer. I'm thinking of asking him to take me on."

"But you haven't studied the law, have you?"

"Oh, I imagine he'd find me something." She lights the cigarette and hands it to Sophie, who shakes her head. "The only trouble is you've got to be awake so awfully early in the morning. But that's not a problem for *you*, is it?"

"Me? But I'm getting married."

"All the more reason. It never does any good to sit around the house, waiting for your man to arrive. *That's* the old rules."

Julie crosses her legs, displaying an extraordinary amount of stocking. Sophie thought that hemlines were supposed to be going down again, after the shocking excess of the past couple of years, but Julie's calves don't seem to care what the fashion editors say. Her stockings aren't white or decorous black, but the color of skin.

"I can't imagine what I could do," Sophie says. "I didn't learn anything especially useful at school, just English and French and mathematics and all that, and Father wouldn't hear of sending me to college."

"No, I imagine not. But you have lots of interests, haven't you? What do you especially like?"

"Well, I—nothing, really. Nothing I could make a living at. Books and art, mostly."

"But there's something else, isn't there? You hesitated."

"It's nothing."

Julie takes her hand. "Darling, you've got to learn to let these things out in the open. You're going to fester from within, and then where will you be? An old festering housewife, like my sister."

"I like machines."

"What's that? Don't mumble it, like a ninny. Say it out loud! I . . . LIKE . . ."

"MACHINES!"

"*Machines?*" Julie's so surprised, she drops Sophie's hand into her lap, kerplonk. She points out the window, where a nearby taxi putters alongside. "Do you mean . . . well, engines?"

"Not just engines, I guess. Everything. I like . . . well, I've always liked to figure out how things work. Since I was a child."

"Like a . . . a *mechanic?*" As she might say *prostitute.*

"Like my father." Sophie makes a watery laugh and returns her fingers to her own lap. "I used to help Father in his workshop, when I was younger. He showed me how to fix the car and that kind of thing. He said I had a knack for it."

"A *knack* for it? How very . . . well. Why not? Apples not falling far and that kind of thing. Only . . . *really?* More than, say . . . oh, magazines?"

"I wanted to be just like him when I was little. I didn't have a mother, you know."

"Oh, your *mother*! In that case, it makes tremendous sense, now that I think about it. A withdrawal of maternal attention can have the most awful effect on your subconscious. You attached yourself to your father instead, and—well, goodness me, it's a wonder you weren't dressing yourself up in short pants." She opens up her pocketbook and rummages inside. "I suppose that's awfully useful, though. A little *oily*, maybe, but useful. Do you go about the house, fixing things?"

"No. Father does all that, and anyway, he doesn't let me help him anymore. A thing of the past."

Julie produces a cigarette and lights herself up. "Because it's not ladylike, I suppose?"

"Something like that."

"Well."

"Yes. *Well.*" Sophie laughs again. "Not really a suitable job, is it? Can you just see Jay's face? *I'm off to the garage, darling.*"

"Well, it wouldn't have to be a garage, would it? Dirty things, garages. What about a nice clean . . . you know, a place where you could still"—Julie twists her fingers about, fitting some imaginary bolt—"but without the . . . well, without spoiling your hands."

Sophie turns to the window. The lining of her chest is raw, as if she's swallowed a sword or a blunt razor. "Never mind. It's just an old hobby, that's all. I've grown up now."

"Yes, you have, thank God. Still, it's a talent, isn't it? I'll ask around and see what I can find for you. Maybe a place with an architect, or—well, those men who design things."

"An engineer."

"That's it."

"But I really—"

"No objections. It would do you all kinds of good." Julie waves away the smoke with her elegant, ungloved hand. "You can start when you're back from your honeymoon."

"Honeymoon?"

"Yes, honeymoon. Everybody takes them now. You should go away for two or three weeks at least, get it all out of your system."

"Get what out of my system?"

"Darling," Julie says pityingly. "Sex."

Sex. A year ago, Sophie hadn't even thought about sex, and now it's all around her, right out in the open. It's all anyone can talk about. The films are full of it, and so are the books and theaters. It's as if a dazzling new color has suddenly been added to the rainbow, and you didn't realize what you were missing before, except that sometimes it's a little *too* dazzling, isn't it? You sort of wish that the landscape would calm down a bit, from time to time. To give your eyes a little rest. To think about something else. But nobody else seems to feel the way Sophie does. Nobody else seems to want to rest their eyes a single minute. Nobody wants to think about anything else.

They arrive at their destination, a plain brick-fronted house in an unfamiliar neighborhood. Julie trips right up to the door and rings the doorbell, and a few seconds later a small window slides open and Julie leans forward and says something across the dark rectangle. Sophie shrinks inside her coat. The air is terribly cold, colder even than it was when they left Park Avenue, and tiny snowflakes are swirling like dust beneath the streetlamp on the corner. The door opens, and Julie drags her inside.

By now, Sophie's familiar with the procedure. At first, there's just an ordinary hallway, bare and damp, like any boardinghouse or tenement on just about any street in Manhattan. Somebody shows them down a narrow flight of stairs, smelling like urine, and opens an unpromising door at the bottom. And bang, poof! Out comes a burst of jazz and laughter, and cigarettes and fun. Julie swoops inside, and Sophie follows her, straight to a small round table in the corner where a man sits waiting for them, arms crossed, nursing a low-ball and a smoke and a few empty glasses.

"Peter, duck! I knew I could count on you." Julie drops a kiss on the man's cheek and turns to drag Sophie into range. "Darling, this is Sophie Fortescue, Jay Ochsner's brand-new fiancée. Sophie, this is Peter van der Wahl, a friend of the family."

Peter van der Wahl sets down drink and cigarette and rises to greet her. He's a man of modest proportions: hair brown, eyes blue, face pleasantly well-bred. He doesn't seem a bit sauced, despite the empty glasses standing before him. He smiles politely and tells her how pleased he is to meet her. Sophie likes him at once, but she can't quite encompass the idea that Julie Schuyler's fallen in love with *this* fellow. Just like that.

"I'm always happy to meet another friend of Julie's," she says warily, and Peter pulls out a chair for her and makes a signal in the direction of the bar, which takes up most of the rest of the room.

"Oh, I've known Peter all my life," says Julie. "It's one of my earliest memories, isn't it? When one of the Bouvier boys kicked over my sandcastle—well, it wasn't much of a sandcastle, I was only two or three—and Peter came in and punched him in the nose. How old were you, darling? Six?"

"Five."

"An older man." Julie winks. "We've been friends ever since. He does my bidding and doesn't complain, and I reward him whenever I can."

Sophie looked back and forth between the two of them.

"Give a girl some of that ciggy, Peter," says Julie, and she helps herself. "Hasn't he arrived yet?"

"Not yet. He had something to do first, he said."

The world begins to right itself. "Hasn't *who* arrived yet?" Sophie asks.

"Why, the fellow I've fallen in love with." Julie hands back the cigarette. "My goodness, you don't think I meant *Peter*, do you?"

"I didn't—"

"My God, that would be like kissing one of my brothers."

A waitress arrives, bearing a tray of loaded highball glasses, which she sets on the table, one by venomous one. From the expression on Peter's quiet face, Sophie guesses that Julie's sentiments aren't returned in quite the same fraternal flavor. Poor man. Wouldn't it be just awful, to be hopelessly in love with Julie Schuyler?

Julie selects one of the glasses and examines it—not that carefully—against what light she can find. "No, it just so happens that Peter's acquainted with the object of my affections, and he's kindly offered to make the introduction for us."

"You haven't met him yet?"

"No. I've only seen him from afar. He walked into the party tonight and *murdered* me from across the room."

"Murdered you?"

Julie places a hand on her heart. "Murdered me."

Peter turns his eyes upward to inspect the ceiling. "This happens twice a week, you understand."

"Oh, but this time it's *real*, Peter. I haven't stopped thinking about him."

"Really? That's—oh, three whole hours?"

"Applesauce. Haven't you heard of love at first sight?"

"You haven't even met."

"For God's sake, don't be such a wet blanket, Peter. You're making me anxious." She finishes her drink, snatches the cigarette from Peter's fingers, and stubs it out in the ashtray. "Dance with me. It'll settle my nerves."

"You haven't got any nerves," he says, but he stands up anyway and allows her to drag him off to the few square yards of linoleum flooring in front of the musicians, which is packed with frenetic dancers: feet flying, hands splayed. Sophie looks after them for a stunned few seconds, until Julie's blond head is swallowed whole, leaving only a single erect black feather to shimmy above them like a periscope.

Sophie returns her attention to the table before her, and the several glasses standing atop it, reminding her of downtown itself: all those buildings perched on such a tiny speck of land. The great weight of the Woolworth tower, reigning like a colossus. She picks one up and sniffs the rim. A medicinal smell assails her nostrils, like a hospital disinfectant.

And that's the drink that Julie's already finished.

She tries another one—an untouched glass—and extracts a little sip, just to prove she's not afraid of it. Her tongue sizzles. Stiffens in shock. Goes a little numb. And then she looks up, because a shadow has just darkened the table, and it can't possibly be Julie and Peter, can it? The music's not over.

The funny thing is, she's had a premonition all along. She's had the feeling that something's coming, something unexpected and secretly delightful, or else she wouldn't have abandoned her fiancé at the Schuylers' party uptown. She wouldn't have climbed into a taxi with Julie Schuyler and left for parts unknown if she hadn't felt this waggling in her stomach, this tingling in her fingers beneath the satin and the rose-shaped engagement ring. Something's arriving at her door, something marvelous, and she remembers—just as she turns from her highball glass, choking a little—where she's felt this familiar anticipation before.

So it's not a surprise, is it, when she lifts her gaze to find Mr. Rofrano's shadowed face staring down at her.

"Hello, there," she gasps, just before the coughing fit strikes.

By the time Julie and Peter return, damp and scintillating, the coughing has died away, though the blushing has not. She knows her cheeks are pink—she suffers the telltale scorch of her own blood, right there under the skin—and probably her nose and neck, as well. Such a terrible blusher. Mr. Rofrano has drawn up a chair and offered her his handkerchief, which she's just handed shyly back to him, and now he leans forward to ask her a question.

As his black head bends to hers, Sophie turns to hear him better, and who should swing her head and meet Sophie's gaze at that exact instant? Julie, that's who. (Uncanny, isn't it? How animals know when someone's watching.) Julie stops dead, and her eyes move back and forth, cavalier and Sophie, and from the expression on her face, she's just been murdered for the second time this evening.

Mr. Rofrano rises politely from his chair. "Peter," he says, nodding at Julie's partner.

"Rofrano. Glad to see you." Gladness is not the tenor of Peter's voice, however. "This is Julie Schuyler. You know Philip, of course? She's his cousin."

Julie draws near and holds out her hand. "My goodness, Sophie. Do you two know each other?"

"I met Miss Fortescue last week, when I had the honor of presenting her with a—a token from an admirer."

"*You're* Sophie's cavalier?"

"Isn't it amazing? Such a small world," Sophie trills.

"Yes, it is." Julie leans over and snatches a drink. "I don't think there's more than two dozen people in it, sometimes."

"Four hundred, isn't that right? The capacity of Mrs. Astor's ballroom," says Mr. Rofrano.

"Oh, that's just a story. Anyway, her house is long gone, and the ballroom with it." She slings back the entire drink, all at once, and blinks her eyes furiously to keep it down.

Peter places one hand at the small of her back. "Careful, now."

"Don't be silly. I think I'd like to dance some more, darling, if you don't mind?" She turns her head briefly to Mr. Rofrano. "A pleasure to meet you. Take good care of my little Sophie while I'm gone, won't you?"

Later, as Mr. Rofrano sees her home in a taxi, Sophie can't quite decide what Julie meant by that. Did she suspect some sort of attraction between the two of them, Sophie and Mr. Rofrano? Or had some other piece of knowledge fallen into place, from that jigsaw of ephemera that constituted the habits and customs of the New York upper class?

Sophie hadn't danced with him, after all. She'd steered her eyes scrupulously away from Octavian's face, because she was engaged to another man, and Julie was smitten. They had chatted stiffly, conscious of this awkward thing between them, this fiction of impartiality. But you couldn't fool Julie, could you? And Julie had obviously not been fooled.

Sophie stares at the gloved hands in her lap and says, "I hope I haven't put you too far out of your way."

"Of course not. Anyway, I'm not about to send a girl home by herself in the middle of the night."

"That's very kind of you."

"Kindness has nothing to do with it," he says, almost under his breath, and then: "If you don't mind my asking, shouldn't your fiancé be around to do this kind of thing?"

"We left him uptown at a party."

"Oh, of course. The Schuylers."

"How did you know that?"

He hesitates. "Well, I was there, too, for a bit."

"Oh. You should have said hello."

"I didn't see you, or I might have."

Sophie frowns, because there's some fatal hole of logic there, but she's too sleepy and too tipsy to locate it. The sleepiness has come over her like a blanket, since stepping into the taxi with Mr. Rofrano, and all she wants on this earth is to boldly lay her head on his woolen shoulder and plunge into an abyss of sleep from which she wouldn't climb out for days. Already her eyelids are sagging. "Oh, of course you were there. How silly of me. That's where Julie spotted you."

"Did she?"

"Yes. You murdered her from across the room—"

"I certainly didn't mean to."

"—so she was forced to ask Peter to introduce you." Sophie pauses. "How do you know Peter?"

"I stayed at his family's place in Long Island a couple of summers ago. I was just back from France. Not too sure what I wanted to do with myself. Whether I wanted to do anything at all."

"And did you find out? What you wanted to do, I mean?"

"I guess I did. I thought I did, anyway."

The streets are passing quickly, too quickly. In a few minutes they will arrive on Thirty-Second Street, and Sophie will bid Mr. Rofrano good-bye and resume her life as the fiancée of Jay Ochsner. Planning a wedding and a honeymoon and a home together. "Selling bonds, you mean?"

"It's a living, I guess."

She doesn't reply. Maybe if they don't speak, the time will pass more slowly, and she can simply relish Mr. Rofrano's presence beside her, aspect by aspect. Very solid and warm, smelling like cigarettes and the sweaty, alcoholic dankness of the establishment from which they've recently emerged. (*You'll see my Sophie home, won't you, Mr. Rofrano?* Julie said, sporting as only Julie could be, falling sideways into Peter, and Mr. Rofrano said of course he would.) His upper leg lies about a foot and a half from her upper leg, but she can feel him anyway, can perceive his presence on her skin as if they're actually touching. Or maybe it's just the cocktails? She only drank one, but the effect is far in excess of any old glass of champagne, blurring lines and skin and clothes and borders until she can't quite locate the territory where Sophie ends, or where Mr. Rofrano begins.

Mr. Rofrano doesn't speak either, and in some strange way—much like the imagined touching of their bodies, when there is none—the silence itself seems to speak for them, querying and replying back and forth. Until Sophie asks, a little too forcefully: "But what do you *really* want to do, then?"

"Now that's a funny question," he says slowly.

"What's so funny about it?"

"For one thing, no one's ever asked me before."

"Nobody? Not your parents or anybody?"

"My parents are dead."

"Oh!" Sophie squeezes her hands together. "I'm so terribly sorry. How stupid of me."

"That's all right. You had no way of knowing."

"But you never talked about them, so I should have realized . . ."

"It doesn't matter. It happened a while ago."

"My mother died when I was a baby, and I haven't stopped missing her."

"Did she? Well, I'm sorry for that." He sets his hands on his knees, fingers spread. His thumbs rub against the sides of his trousers. "Do you mind if I ask how she died?"

"I—I don't know exactly. A sudden sickness of some kind. I don't think they knew what it was, really. What about your parents?"

There is a brief hesitation before he answers. "My father shot himself over some sort of bad investment when I was fourteen—"

"Oh, Mr. Rofrano!"

"And my mother died of the 'flu when I was in France."

"How terrible for you. I'm so sorry."

"It was a blow, I guess." His fingers flex on his knees. "I got the news in December of 1918. My aunt sent the telegram. The war was over, but I hadn't gotten my demobilization papers yet. They held the funeral without me."

"Oh, Mr. Rofrano."

"Anyway, I guess that's why I stayed around Paris for a while, afterward."

"Because you had no one to go back to," Sophie whispers. She reaches bravely across the eighteen inches and lays her hand—the left hand, the one hiding an engagement ring under the glove—on his, and begins a sentence that she regrets an instant later. "How I wish . . ."

"Wish what?"

"Nothing." Twenty-Fourth Street. Only a minute or two left. Eight blocks of frozen pavement. Sophie withdraws her hand and says, hurriedly now, "You didn't answer my question. What you *really* want to do."

"I don't know."

"But you must know, deep down. You must know what's missing."

He lifts his hands from his knees and folds his arms against his chest. "I used to love flying, until the war."

"But you don't anymore?"

"I didn't, for a long time. I didn't want to see an airplane ever again."

"But you can't do that. You can't turn your back on the thing you love most."

"I didn't say I loved it the most."

"Still, it was a passion of yours, wasn't it? There was a reason you loved it, there was a reason you loved flying that had nothing to do with shooting down other airplanes and killing people. So that reason must still exist inside you, waiting for the—the—the tide to go back out."

"I don't know," he says. "I don't know."

They lapse again into silence, and Sophie thinks that maybe she shouldn't have spoken so eagerly and so passionately. A fault of hers: her reckless enthusiasm for romantic causes, so out of temper with the times. Nobody believes in romantic causes any more, especially not people who fought in the war, like Mr. Rofrano. In fact, it's telling and even absolutely symbolic of the modern cynicism that he has gone from jousting in the sky, like a medieval knight, to selling government bonds from the security of his telephone in his tiny office (or so Sophie imagines it) on the corner of Wall and Broad.

The taxi lurches into Thirty-Second Street, and Sophie, jolted to the present, opens up her pocketbook to hunt for the fare.

"Don't be silly," says Mr. Rofrano. He reaches over and closes the pocketbook, and for just an instant their fingers tangle up, before Mr. Rofrano withdraws to open the door.

He walks her up the steps. Sophie thanks him and asks if he has the time. He looks at his wristwatch and says it's nearly two o'clock, and is anyone up to let her in? She tells him she has a latchkey and produces it from her pocketbook as proof.

Mr. Rofrano waits to make sure that the key works, that the lock isn't frozen and the door opens under her hand. "Thank you," she says again, turning to face him. "I suppose it's good night, then."

He takes her hand. "Good night."

They stand there a moment, holding hands, peering at each other. The wind whistles against her left ear, and then dies away.

"Look," he says softly, "what about going somewhere tomorrow?"

"I—I'm going to church with my family in the morning. Eight o'clock."

"After that? Say, nine-thirty? I can meet you on the corner of Third Avenue, in my car."

"I—" She glances up behind her, at the windows of the house. "I don't see why not, as long as I'm back for dinner. Where are we going?"

He releases her hand and makes a little sigh, as if he's been holding his breath all this time. "It's a surprise," he says, and turns to leap down the stairs to the sidewalk, and the taxi waiting by the curb.

The New York Herald-Times, May 30, 1922

TIT AND TATTLE, BY PATTY CAKE

They like to start these things off with a bang, these Connecticut prosecuting attorneys, and regular readers of this column know that you can't get much more bang for your dollar than Miss Julie Schuyler. Or simply JULIE, as we like to call her, in big bold typeface, with or without an exclamation point.

Now, we all know what she was doing there in the witness stand, and we all know the likely nature of her testimony. So let's fix our attention on more important things: namely, how she looked. Why, ravishing, of course! She's gone and bobbed her pretty blond hair—a bit of a cliché, at this point, but the style really does suit her, unlike many of the girls who try out a little barber-shop rebellion. I've heard from some quarters that Julie is a reluctant witness for the prosecution, but she didn't look reluctant to me. Far from it. She answered the gentleman's questions with nothing short of aplomb, and let me tell you, aplomb isn't an easy thing to achieve when the mercury rises above eighty-eight degrees by ten o'clock in the morning. Even the judge was charmed, and in a race of digits between the mercury and the judge's age, why, I wouldn't want to lay down a bet.

In between witty asides and some very elegant eyebrow-raising, Miss Schuyler managed to convey that she had become friends with the accused's daughter in the hat department at the Bergdorf Goodman emporium on Fifth Avenue in October of 1921, and despite numerous luncheons, teas, shopping excursions, and goodness knows what else in the company of Miss Fortescue, she never met the Patent King himself. Why? Because he didn't want to be met, apparently. In fact, Miss Schuyler believes herself to be the first friend of Miss Fortescue's acquaintance, for Miss Fortescue was kept under strict lock and key for the first nineteen years of her life, in the manner of Rapunzel, and the far greater part of the Fortescue-Schuyler antics were undertaken without the knowledge or permission of the accused. *Why?* inquired the prosecution, and Miss Schuyler shrugged her elegant shoulders and said she couldn't imagine. *Try,* said the prosecution, in so many words, and naturally the defense sprang to its feet and objected—*Conjecture, Your Honor!*—and His Honor stirred himself to agree. So. Off with Miss Julie Schuyler, to the great regret of the court.

Next to be called was that far less bewitching, but more informative figure: the infamous Downstairs Tenant, Mrs. Kelly, she of the soda bread. You will not be surprised to learn that she Never Trusted That Man (here she narrowed her eyes and cast a steely one at the accused, who made no response) and feared very much for the safety of Those Sweet Girls (here a gaze of maternal softness at the Patent Princesses, also unacknowledged) under his care. In order to confirm her suspicions about his character, she crept one evening to his place of work, a small garage nearby where the great inventor did his incomprehensible things with his inconceivable gadgets, and she searched through his private papers. Instead of ordering her arrested on the spot for criminal trespass, the prosecution was moved to ask her what she discovered. Nothing of note, she replied, shaking her head, but she was interrupted in her midnight work by none other than the accused himself, who threatened her with a sharp instrument and swore he'd make her rue the day if she ever returned. Naturally, she ran home, packed her things, and gave notice by way of a basket of soda bread. (At this point in her testimony, she indicated a basket she had left behind her on the bench, with which she invited the court to refresh itself.)

I shall spare you, dear readers, the remaining details of Mrs. Kelly's hour in the witness box, and the recess which followed, because I should be very un-happy if you stopped reading at that point and missed what I have to say about the final witness of the day, Mr. Philip Schuyler, who (you may speculate, and you would be correct) is related in some way to Miss Julie Schuyler. They are cousins, and both handsome in that rakish blond Schuyler manner, but Mr. Schuyler is a lawyer of some repute, and his testimony was perhaps the most anxiously awaited of the day, not least because it was the last.

By the time Mr. Schuyler took the stand, the temperature had reached its considerable zenith, and we—audience and jury—were not especially moved to tolerate a lengthy recital of unimportant details. The prosecution, perhaps sensing this collective mood, cut straight to the chase. In what capacity was Mr. Schuyler acquainted with the accused? He had done some legal work for Mr. Fortescue, some years before, when the first of his patents came to be registered. In particular, Mr. Fortescue was concerned about the legality of his patents, since he did not possess a legal birth certificate, nor proof of identification. They had been lost in a fire. Mr. Schuyler had then assisted Mr. Fortescue in reconstructing his lost identity, and helped him form a corporation by which his patents could be registered and licensed, without Mr. Fortescue's personal privacy being disturbed.

Had Mr. Schuyler, at any time, felt that there was anything more suspicious behind Mr. Fortescue's lack of identifying paperwork?

Mr. Schuyler paused before he answered. No, he told the court firmly. He had not.

At this point, Mr. Schuyler's testimony came to an end, and upon cross-examination he revealed nothing new.

So it is left to Mr. Octavian Rofrano, ladies and gentlemen, to provide some fireworks for our entertainment tomorrow. As one of the prosecution's key witnesses, he is expected to electrify us, much in the manner that he seems to have electrified the lovely and discerning Mrs. Marshall.

That is, if tonight's expected thunderstorms don't anticipate him in the task.

Chapter 7

The woman who appeals to a man's vanity may stimulate him, the woman who appeals to his heart may attract him, but it is the woman who appeals to his imagination who gets him.

—HELEN ROWLAND

SOPHIE

Sunday morning, bright and early

Too bright, really. Last night's paltry fall of snow has given way to a sky made of blue ice, and a brilliant sun fixed at its eastern end.

But Sophie is looking west, not east: down Thirty-Second Street toward Third Avenue at thirty-two minutes past nine o'clock in the morning, the sun at her back. Her leather half-boots clatter along the sidewalk, echoing the clatter of her heart, which seems to be in the grip of some sort of irrational worry. Some kind of panic. Two minutes late! What if he's one of those punctual military men who can't abide tardy women? What if he's like her father, whose silence has just blighted the entire Sunday morning routine of breakfast and church, because Sophie arrived in the dining room—bleary but clean-scrubbed—at four minutes past seven o'clock instead of six-fifty-nine?

But then she sees her cavalier, standing between a lamppost and an old Model T, dressed for the countryside in a brown Norfolk suit and a wool cap pulled down over his forehead. He lifts his arm and waves, and Sophie thinks, *Whatever you do, don't run to him.*

She runs anyway.

"I'm sorry for being late!" she gasps, holding down her hat with one hand, so she won't try to touch him. "Father always insists on sitting down together after church, and I had to make a ridiculous excuse to get away, since it's Sunday and the shops are closed. I hope you haven't been waiting long."

"Not too long." He opens the door for her—the car is pointing north—and goes around front to crank the engine. "Mind switching the ignition for me? Where the key's sticking out, by the wheel."

Sophie knows how to start an old Model T. After all, her father only got rid of theirs a couple of years ago, trading it in to buy a secondhand Oldsmobile, which he parks in a garage across the street from his work-shop—it used to be a livery stable—and pays the boys there a dollar a week to keep it shined up and away from the other cars. But that old Ford was Sophie's respon-sibility. Father had shown her how to clean the paint-work, how to change the oil and the tires, how to keep the engine running, how to drive it. (In comparison to the boys at the garage, she received only a dime a week for these services.) In consequence, Sophie's something of an expert when it comes to the pre-war Model T. She reaches over and pulls out the choke, and turns the ignition switch as Mr. Rofrano's shoulder pumps up and down, priming the engine. At his signal, she turns the key in the starter to magneto. Another quick move-ment of Mr. Rofrano's shoulder. The engine coughs twice, hovers precariously, and then catches.

Mr. Rofrano lifts his head and sticks up his thumb in victory, and beneath the shadow of his cap brim his smile is wide and happy. Sophie's absurdly proud of herself. She slides back over to the passenger seat and returns his smile when the door opens and he swings into place beside her, bringing with him the smell of fresh soap and cold air. His left hand eases the spark retard lever, until the pistons purr happily.

"Off we go," he says.

"But where?"

"Connecticut."

"Oh." Sophie's elation ebbs just a bit. Connecticut—well, there's nothing *wrong* with Connecticut, she's heard it's a perfectly *pleasant* place, but it's not exactly known for adventure, is it? (She almost adds the word *romance*, until she remembers, just in time, that she is someone else's fiancée.)

On the other hand, unless she was perhaps expecting Mr. Rofrano to whisk them off to an ocean liner waiting on the west side piers, there isn't much choice for a Sunday morning outing within easy driving distance of the center of Manhattan. Long Island, maybe? New Jersey?

"What's in Connecticut?" she asks.

"You'll see."

Even on a Sunday morning, the traffic has already cleared away the snow that fell in the night, and anyway, it wasn't much of a snow. It's too cold to snow properly, Sophie says.

"Well, I'm glad it didn't, or it would have spoiled our plans. Are you sleepy?"

"No."

"I thought you might be sleepy, going to bed so late. You can lie down, if you like. It's going to be a couple of hours at least."

Sophie doesn't think she's ever going to want to sleep again, not the way her nerves are dancing now. But maybe Mr. Rofrano's right, maybe she should rest for an hour or so, so she'll be fresh for whatever it is they're going to do, up in Connecticut in the middle of the bitter January cold.

"All right," she says, and she curls as tight as a kitten on the seat, just touching Mr. Rofrano's woolen leg with the top of her head, and she must have gone straight to sleep, because the next thing she knows, the car is bouncing to a stop and the engine cuts off into silence.

As far as Sophie knows, she's never been to Connecticut. She's been to Europe, but not Connecticut—isn't that strange? Her life, until last summer, was circumscribed by a certain number of blocks around the narrow brownstone house on Thirty-Second Street, a realm that contained a butcher and several grocers, a bakery and a dress shop, a church and a magnificent public library: who could want for more, really? Until graduating two years ago, she attended a nearby girls' academy, but her father never encouraged any friendships with her classmates, and expected her to return home directly after classes were finished, clutching Virginia's firm hand.

Virginia had a little more freedom. Virginia joined the Red Cross at their church, and when a call went out for volunteers in France, Virginia had asked their father if she could go. To Sophie's surprise, he had said yes, after a period of silent consideration. And Virginia had gone. For eighteen months, she had lived in France, and she came back pregnant, wearing a slim gold ring on her finger, and her husband was going to join them just as soon as he could settle his affairs. Then Evelyn had been born, and the husband hadn't arrived. Only letters, and then even those had ceased, about a year ago. He was in Florida, Virginia said. In Florida with his brother, recovering the family fortune by the age-old method: land speculation. There's a rush on, after all, and as soon as he can make things suitable for a wife and a child, he'll send for them.

Well, Sophie hasn't been to Florida, either, and she isn't sure she wants to. But she *did* want to go to Europe, as Virginia had, and when Evelyn turned a nice safe two years of age, Sophie asked if they might go, and (again, to her surprise) her father said *Yes*. So off they went, in a pair of first-class cabins on the magnificent brand-new RMS *Majestic*, keeping to themselves, and they were gone two months and saw everything that wasn't wrecked by the war. They went to Paris and Rome and Florence; they went to London, though for some reason they didn't look in on Virginia's husband's family. And they came home and resumed their lives, but Sophie hasn't quite felt the same since. She feels as if Europe has changed her a little, has made her impatient with her familiar twenty blocks on the eastern side of the island of Manhattan, and that was her state of mind when she met Julie Schuyler. That she hadn't seen enough, not nearly enough. That there's a beautiful, glimmering world from which she's been shielded until now, and she wants to see it. She wants to see what glories it contains.

She wants to see Connecticut. Only thirty miles away from the middle of Manhattan Island, and she's never been there, not once that she can remember.

"There it is," says Mr. Rofrano, setting the brake.

Sophie springs up and peers through the windshield at a winter field, on the other side of a weathered gray-brown fence. The grass is the same color as the wood: dull and shorn, dusted by a thin film of snow that settled more thickly in the hollows. "Is this Connecticut?" she asks.

"Yes."

"It looks bleaker than I thought."

"Well, it's winter, isn't it? Put on your hat and mittens."

He opens the door and climbs out, and Sophie finds her hat and mittens and wraps her muffler snugly about her neck. Mr. Rofrano opens the passenger door and helps her out, and the blast of air that accompanies him is so bitterly frigid that she gasps.

"All right?" says Mr. Rofrano, and his breath makes clouds in the air.

"It's awfully cold!"

"Do you want to stay in the car?"

She takes her hand from his and shoves it inside the pocket of her coat. "Well, of course not."

"I didn't think you would."

As compliments go, it's rather spare—hardly even recognizable, to the naked eye, as a compliment at all—but Mr. Rofrano smiles as he gives it to her, and his eyes are so warm with approval that the atmosphere itself seems to thaw by several degrees, and the wind blows more gently on her cheeks.

Sophie turns. "Where are we, exactly?"

"We're in Avon. See this field in front of us?"

"That's a field?" she says disdainfully.

"In the summer, it is. It's the infield of a racetrack. We're parked on the track itself, if you haven't noticed."

Sophie looks around them in surprise, and discovers that he's right. The dirt under her boots stretches in a track on either side, before curving around the fence and disappearing. Behind her there's a small wooden grandstand, mournfully empty.

"But why are we here? There can't be any races."

Mr. Rofrano nods at the field before them. "That's where I saw my first airplane. They held a big air show here, back in 1911, when I was a kid, just before I left for school. Poppa took me. It was September, a gorgeous clear blue-skied day. You could see for miles. They took off from the infield right here"—he nods again—"and went up in the air and did all these acrobatics. Looping the loop, that kind of thing. I just stood there by the fence with my mouth open."

"My goodness." Sophie tries to picture this barren landscape covered with green grass and clean white airplanes, with spectators in sunlit dresses. Those beautiful big hats everybody used to wear, before the war shrunk everything down, hats and dresses and lives.

"Poppa asked if I'd like to go up in one, and I said, *Boy, would I.*" He laughs. "So Poppa went up to the man who was promoting the thing and asked how much it cost to take a ride. I don't know how much, but Poppa was pretty flush back then. Came out all right after the panic, somehow. Anyway, up I went. It was only about ten minutes, but it changed my life. I thought I'd never been so happy. I looked down at the earth beneath us, and it looked so small and pretty, the people on it so inconsequential. And yet somehow, you know—this is the paradox, I guess—it was all the more dear and precious for being so tiny. You couldn't see the flaws. You felt protective of it all."

"Like a child with a dollhouse."

"I don't know. Something like that. Anyway, I fell in love, not just with the beauty of it but the freedom, too. The speed and the wind and the elemental thrill. The summer before college, I got a job as a mechanic at an air field, and I learned from the inside out. By then it was nineteen seventeen, we were in the war at last, and I couldn't wait to get out there. I was in college for about a month before I turned eighteen. I quit the next day."

"And you enlisted in the Air Service."

"Yes." He draws in a long breath, and as it comes out, bit by bit, he reaches inside his pocket and brings forth a shiny cigarette case, an expensive one. "Mind if I smoke?"

"No, of course not."

He lights the cigarette and smokes quietly for a moment. Sophie's toes are frozen inside her boots. She stamps her feet a couple of times, trying to get his attention, to wake him out of his trance. When that doesn't work, she takes his arm. "Show me the place," she says.

"What place?"

"The place where you stood, watching the airplanes."

He nods. "Right over there."

"Come on, then." She tugs his arm and drags him to the fence—drags, because his steps are reluctant—and when they arrive she removes her hand from the crook of his elbow and leans against the topmost board. "Lean with me, like this," she says, and he obeys her. "Now close your eyes and pretend."

"Pretend?"

"All right. *Imagine.* Is that a better word? Imagine you're ten or eleven again, and you're watching an airplane go up into the sky for the first time. Imagine you're climbing inside for the first time—"

"This is ridiculous."

"Because it's so cold out?"

"Not because it's cold out. Because I'm not eleven years old any more. Because it's not September, it's January. Because . . ." He allows the word to hover there, in its own little cloud of vapor, containing any number of obstacles. Any number of heartbreaks that Sophie, living quietly and predictably inside her twenty square blocks of Manhattan Island, knows nothing of.

"Then why did you bring me here?" she asks.

"I don't know. Why did you come?"

"Because you asked me to. You needed me for something."

The cigarette is nearly finished. Mr. Rofrano drops the end in the dead grass and grinds it thoroughly with the toe of his shoe, and then he turns to face her, propping his lean body on the fence with his right elbow. "Maybe I did. But that doesn't mean you should have agreed."

"Why not?"

"You're engaged to Jay Ochsner, for one thing. For another, you hardly know me. You get into a car with me and let me drive you off alone, without a chaperone or anything like that, for hours into the countryside. I might be anyone."

"The Big Bad Wolf?"

"I'm not joking. Do you make a habit of this kind of thing?"

"I've never done this kind of thing. But you're my cavalier, Mr. Rofrano. You're here to watch over me, isn't that right?"

He looks down at her with shocked eyes and doesn't reply.

Sophie puts her hand on his, there on the fence rail, her thick woolen mitten on his leather glove. "I'm not stupid, Mr. Rofrano. I'm not as sheltered as you think.

I know what a good man is. I know whom I can trust. I wouldn't get into a car with just any old fellow, would I?"

He glances down at her hand on his, and then—a little slowly, as if the act requires courage—returns his gaze to her face. He looks so somber! Sophie wants to wrap her arms around his waist and lay her head on his chest. She wants to pour comfort between his ribs, to anoint his troubled forehead.

"No, you wouldn't," he says.

He's wearing a peculiar expression now, one that Sophie can't fathom. His lovely straight nose is red from the cold. So are his lips. His eyes, out here in the winter sun, have turned the most beautiful shade of arctic blue, like the water beneath an iceberg, and Sophie loves all these colors in him. Isn't it marvelous, Sophie wants to say. Isn't it simply marvelous being here in this January field with you. Isn't it marvelous just to be *alive* with you, breathing in all this bracing air, blinking our eyes, beating our hearts, alive, *alive.*

"You're sensational," he murmurs, so softly that Sophie isn't quite sure she heard him properly.

She leans forward. "What's that?"

"Nothing." He picks up her hand and kisses the back of the mitten, right before he tucks the arm back inside his elbow. "Come along, Miss Fortescue. I think

I have something else to show you, on the way back to New York."

The roads are quiet and empty as they curl their way southwest. The shoreline makes a sharp right turn at the New York border, Mr. Rofrano explains, and if you stand on a Connecticut beach and gaze out to sea—Long Island Sound, that is—you'll be facing due south. Not until Massachusetts does it all straighten out again, everything in its rightful place, the foam-topped Atlantic Ocean stretching eastward to the brink of Europe.

"To France," Sophie says. "Do you think someone will ever fly across in an airplane?"

"I expect so, eventually. If we want it badly enough."

"Did you ever want to try?"

"I don't know. I guess I never really thought about it."

"Not even when you were young?"

He laughs. "I'm not *that* old, am I?"

"I mean before the war."

Mr. Rofrano quits laughing and rubs his leathery thumb against his forehead. The air inside the Ford is close and smoky, filled with human scent. "Maybe I did. I guess we were all full of dreams, then. But it was all a tin-pot fantasy. The airplanes we had then, they were just wood and glue and canvas. Then the war came in and the airplanes got better. They got a lot better, real fast—that's war for you, I guess. But we lost the nerve. We stopped dreaming. All we dreamt about was fighting. Fighting and surviving the fight. Flying across the ocean, well, there wasn't much object in that." He pauses. "And then all the good pilots got killed."

"Not all of them. *You* weren't killed."

"I got lucky."

"And you were good, too."

He shrugs.

"I'll bet you were really good, weren't you? I'll bet you were the best pilot in your squadron."

Mr. Rofrano finishes the cigarette he's smoking and tips the stub into the draft. They're approaching a village of some kind, a few tired clapboard houses huddled against the edge of the turnpike. "Yes," he says, slowing the car, bouncing over the frozen ruts, and then, "Could you open up the basket in the back? I could use a ham sandwich."

By the time they return to the Boston Post Road, the afternoon is turning middle-aged and the ham sandwiches are all gone. Mr. Rofrano stops at a service station for gas. He checks the oil and the tire pressure. They had a flat a while back, and Sophie helped him patch it up. "You know something about cars, do you?" he said, and Sophie smiled and said *A little.*

But she took in his admiring smile and thought, Mr. Rofrano is the kind of man who likes girls who know something about cars. That's something, isn't it?

"Where are we now?" she asks, peering out the window. The persistent sunshine has warmed the air a few degrees, and the low fieldstone wall rimming the roadside has lost its bluish cast. (*Real* cold—not thirty degrees or twenty degrees but even lower, that genuine frigidity that visits New York only a few times each winter—has a special color all its own.)

"Just outside of Stamford."

"And where are we going? If I'm allowed to ask."

"Sure you can ask. Doesn't mean I'm going to answer you."

She pulls her head back in and looks at him. Possibly there's a smile curling up the corner of his mouth, but it's hard to tell. She reaches out to take his chin and get a better look. "Oh, you're joking, aren't you?"

"Maybe."

"You've got a bit of ham, you know. Right there under your lip." She brushes it away. "Am I allowed to guess?"

He turns back to the road. "Go ahead."

"Is it in Connecticut?"

"Yes. Barely."

"Greenwich?" she guesses. (Greenwich lies close to Stamford, doesn't it?)

"Yes. A part of Greenwich."

"Near the water, or away?"

"Near the water. It's where I grew up. Since I was eight years old, anyway."

"Your childhood house! Does your family still own it?"

"No." He pauses. "My aunt had it sold when Mama died. Some family from New York bought it. They use it as a summer place."

"So nobody's living there now?"

"I guess not."

The road's paved all through Stamford and into Greenwich, and the Ford runs reliably up and down the hills, past the farms and houses and the clusters of storefronts. Here and there, in the hollows and in the lees of the buildings, piles of crusty gray snow still linger from some earlier storm. Sometimes Long Island Sound flashes into view, in between the brown slopes and the barren trees, and Sophie says something about how you can see things better in winter, without all the leaves.

"That's my favorite part," says Mr. Rofrano. "That's what we get in return for the cold. You can see all the hidden things."

"Yes!" Sophie says eagerly, because when she tried to explain this to Julie Schuyler one afternoon, walking through the park, Julie only laughed and told her she was a funny thing. Julie said that she hated winter, that she was going to marry an extremely rich man just for the purpose of having a house to move to during the winter, somewhere south where it never got cold.

"In France . . ." Mr. Rofrano begins promisingly.

"Yes? In France?"

He leans one elbow on the edge of the doorframe. "I missed the autumns here. The good old New England autumn. You don't get all the colors there. The maples and the birch and the elm. But especially the maples. I missed the maples."

"Maybe that's why you came home," Sophie says. "For the maple trees."

"Maybe so." But his tone is too thin, too agreeable, and Sophie knows he's not telling her the truth. Not all of it, at any rate.

"Well, whatever the reason, I'm glad you did. I'm very grateful you came back home."

He doesn't reply. He doesn't say a word, in fact, until they turn off the post road and onto an unpaved street, lined with elm trees at perfect intervals, leading south toward the water. They pass under the railroad tracks—the New Haven line, Mr. Rofrano tells her, when she asks—and then up a winding hill that flattens out into a straight and empty street. Each enormous house is set at the center of an immaculate dun lawn, and the boxwoods have been tucked under burlap for a long winter's sleep.

"Welcome to Greenwich," Mr. Rofrano says, and there is just enough irony in his voice to make Sophie wonder.

A few minutes later, Mr. Rofrano parks the Ford under the far-reaching skeleton of an oak tree and points to a large white clapboard house. "That's it," he says.

"Your old house?"

"They've painted the trim green," he says. "It used to be black."

"It's very pretty. Who had the turret bedroom?"

He drums his thumbs against the steering wheel. "I did."

Sophie opens the door.

"Where are you going?"

"To walk around, of course. Nobody's here."

Sophie marches forward across the lawn, without looking back, and a moment later the car door slams shut behind her. She smiles and tucks in her muffler. A set of wicker furniture remains on the porch, although the cushions have been removed. She settles herself in a chair and nods at Mr. Rofrano as he climbs the porch steps and comes to a stop before her, hands on hips. "Join me? I'm afraid there's no lemonade."

"There's a better view out back, you know. Clear across the sound to Long Island."

"Oh, why didn't you say so?"

She springs back to her feet and follows Mr. Rofrano around the side of the house—the porch is wide and continuous, containing all the artifacts of summer living, down to a swing that creaks in some faint current of air—until they turn the corner and find the capacious terrace. More wicker. Mr. Rofrano pulls out a chair with flourish. Sophie nods her thanks and sinks into her seat. Before her, the lawn swoops straight down to the water, and the wind hits her hard enough to hurt.

"It's a bit nippy," she admits.

Mr. Rofrano sits down beside her. "Well, that's what makes it such a great summer place. The breeze off the water. Right down there, now, that's the boathouse. Poppa taught me to sail in that harbor." He pauses. "Well, that's not true, exactly. He had a fellow come out from the club, a sailing instructor. He taught us together."

"But that must have been wonderful! Learning how to sail with your father."

"You think so? The club instructor didn't think much of it, that's for sure, a gentleman who couldn't sail. But we weren't like the other families around here, the society families. My grandfather was born in Italy. He came here with his family in the seventies, when he was about thirteen or fourteen. They started a shop, made some money, and then Nonno met my grandmother on the El one morning. Fell in love. She was Irish."

"Oh, my. I'll bet your great-grandparents didn't like that."

He chuckles. "The families weren't too happy about it, but it seems Poppa was on the way already, so they got married and made the best of it."

"I can just picture the wedding. All those disapproving parents scowling at each other, and your grandparents dancing together in the middle." Sophie laughs. "Did they live happily ever after?"

"More or less. That's how I remember them, anyway. Smiling at each other. Arguing and then making up. Nonno took over the grocery, and then Poppa landed a job as a runner at Sterling Bates, right out of school, and worked his way up to stockbroker by the time he was twenty-two."

"Ambitious?"

"I'll say. My mother, she was one of the partners' daughters. That's how we ended up in Greenwich, you know. Poppa didn't want her to have to leave her own kind, if you know what I mean. So we moved out here, and he did his best to fit in. The sailing, I mean, and tennis and all the rest of it. They sent me to prep in Massachusetts."

"How did you like that?"

"It was all right. My mother's family kept up the school fees after Poppa died. They set up a trust for us both." He takes out a cigarette. "It wasn't the same, though. Summers weren't the same without him. Quiet and awful. The summer before college, it was just like . . ." He fumbles with his lighter, which turns shy before the wind, and at last he turns his back to the sea to shelter the flame.

She waits until he lights the cigarette, until the smoke streams confidently from the tip and the smell of tobacco reaches the roof of her mouth. He is so lean, she thinks. Lean and bony. Obstinate jaw and cheekbones covered by fresh new skin, made ruddy by the cold. Her fingers are numb inside her mittens, and the wind bites her nose. "Could you see the sea from your turret window?" she asks.

Mr. Rofrano's hand halts at his lips, and for an instant Sophie catches a stricken expression on his face. He lowers the cigarette, without inhaling, and says, "Why do you ask?"

"Oh, it's just a dream of mine. When I was a little girl, I used to wish I had a turret window, overlooking the sea. Wouldn't it be wonderful? You could sit and read there, and when you looked up, the sea would be right there. You could daydream for hours."

Mr. Rofrano leans forward, resting his forearms on his knees, and knits his hands together. The cigarette sticks out between his knuckles, flaring orange in a sudden gust. Sophie follows his gaze, out past the shoreline, and for the first time she notices an island, about a half-mile out to sea, and a stone lighthouse squatting at one end, its tower sticking up like an overgrown chimney from the plain square house of the lightkeeper. She opens her mouth to ask Mr. Rofrano about the island and the lighthouse—did he ever land there in his sailboat, has he ever been inside?—but he speaks first.

"Yes. Yes, I could see the sea from my room."

Sophie stands up. "Can we go inside?"

"Go inside?"

"Why not? Nobody's there. And you lived there once; it belongs to you."

"I don't think the police would see it that way."

Sophie lifts her hand to her brow and makes a show of looking around them. "I don't see any police, do you?"

Her hat catches the distant afternoon sun, and as she looks down at Mr. Rofrano, she feels as if she's bathing in it. Bathing in warmth, surrounded by a halo of sunshine. Look up, she thinks. Look up at me. Look at Sophie in the center of her irresistible sunshine halo.

But he doesn't.

He sighs, drops his cigarette on a flagstone, and rises to his feet. "Crazy dame."

There used to be a wobbly window, he tells her. A sash, warped by the sun, that didn't fit perfectly in its frame, so the latch wouldn't slide into place.

"Where was it?"

He sighs again and looks up at the blue sky. "The breakfast room. But I'm sure they've had it fixed by now."

They haven't. With a bit of muscular persuasion, the sash jerks right up. It's a nice big window, spacious and summery, and Sophie, lifted to the opening between Mr. Rofrano's two large hands, wriggles easily inside and tumbles to the floor.

"I'm all right!" she says brightly, and picks herself up. She unlocks the French door to the right and lets Mr. Rofrano inside. "It's cold, though."

"Of course. They would have turned off the boiler when they packed up in September." He looks around, sliding his gaze up and down the walls, frowning. "This is a rotten idea."

"It's a *wonderful* idea." Sophie takes in a deep breath, filling her chest with the smell of wood and dust and camphor. "Show me your room. I want to sit exactly where you used to sit, looking out to sea. This *is* why you brought me here, isn't it?"

Mr. Rofrano's gaze falls on her, and in the dim and unlit room, designed to catch the morning light, Sophie loses the color of his eyes. She finds herself longing for this missing detail, the way you long for the saltshaker when it's disappeared from the table.

"I guess it is, after all," he says quietly, and he takes her by the mitten and leads her out into a hallway and up the wide staircase. The house is whisper-still around them, except for the creak of the floorboards beneath their feet, and decorated sparsely with white paint and watercolor seascapes.

"Does it look the same?" Sophie asks.

"Not at all. My mother loved her flocked wallpaper and her oriental rugs. It's like a different house."

"What a shame."

"Actually, it looks better now. Lighter."

If the house looks lighter now, Sophie thinks, how dark was it before? But she follows Mr. Rofrano obediently down the creaking hallway to the very end, past closed white doors and yet more watercolors, until he comes to a stop and rests his hand on a brass doorknob.

"Go on," she says.

He straightens his shoulders and opens the door, and Sophie pushes past him and gasps. "How *beautiful*! Oh, Mr. Rofrano! How *lucky* you were!"

She rushes to the round turret at the far corner, rimmed by a creamy window seat topped with blue cushions, and presses her nose to the window glass. The view reaches right across the lawn and the shoreline, encompassing Long Island Sound and the island with the lighthouse, until it lands on the faint winter-brown strip of Long Island and the blue sky above. A few white waves curl on the top of the water, appearing and disappearing in the cadence of the wind and current. Sophie lifts one leg and sinks her knee into the cushion.

"How did you ever leave this?" she says. "It must have been awful."

There is a clink of metal and the elegant scratch of a matchstick, quite distinct in the undisturbed air of the turret room, as Mr. Rofrano lights another cigarette. He must be running out by now, surely? He crosses the room in slow footsteps that make the floor groan behind her, and comes to a stop just to her left, not quite touching her shoulder. If she concentrates, she can detect his breath on the lobe of her ear, on the edge of her jaw.

"There was a story about this house, you know," he says softly.

"Really? What kind of story?"

"Not a nice one, I'm afraid."

"A ghost story?"

"Something like that."

"How awful."

"It was. It was pretty awful," he says. "It was a murder."

"My goodness! Not while you were there, I hope?"

"No, no. It was the owner before us. The family who sold us the house, although they'd moved out a while before. It sat there for a couple of years. No one would buy it, until Poppa came along. By then the price was so low, he couldn't resist the bargain. And he wasn't a local, he wasn't one of them, so no one told him until later."

"Of course they wouldn't, the rotten snobs." She turns around and sits on the window seat. "What happened?"

Mr. Rofrano joins her, a decorous foot or two away on the dusty blue cushion. "They never knew, exactly. I finally heard the story from the neighbor boy. A servant found the mother dead one afternoon. She was on the floor, covered with blood. Her throat was slit."

"How horrible! Was anyone else in the house?"

Mr. Rofrano lifts the cigarette to his lips. "Yes. Her daughter."

"Oh, no!"

"She was two or three years old, I think. She was actually inside the room, with the body. According to the servant, the girl thought her mother was sleeping. She was trying to wake her up."

"Oh, no. Oh, no. The poor thing."

"Yes. The other daughter was older. She was still at school."

"And her husband? He was at work?"

"That's what he claimed at the time, though as he worked alone, in a garage, for hours on end, no one could actually vouch for him." Mr. Rofrano says all this deliberately, in a dispassionate voice, as if reciting evidence in a courtroom.

Sophie waits for him to continue the story—Did the husband do it? Was there an arrest, a sensational trial?—but he only goes on smoking quietly, staring at a collection of framed photographs hanging from the opposite wall, which is painted in buttercup yellow and trimmed with cream. She nudges him with her elbow. "Well?"

"Well, what?"

"What happened next?"

Mr. Rofrano rises from the window seat and walks to the washstand. He tips a long crumb of ash into the soap dish. "They disappeared."

"*What?*"

"The entire family. They just disappeared. Left the house and the furniture inside it, about a week after the funeral, and nobody heard from them since." He turns around and leans against the washstand, crossing one leg over the other, studying Sophie carefully.

"But that's crazy! Why would he disappear, if he didn't do it?"

"A good question. I always wondered."

Sophie looks around wildly. "My goodness! It wasn't *this* room, was it?"

"No, no. It happened in the kitchen. The neighbor boy told me this was the little girl's room. She'd just been moved out of the nursery, you see, because the mother was seven months gone with another baby when she died."

Sophie covers her face with her hands. "Oh, no."

The floorboards groan again, and Sophie feels the cushion stretch to accommodate Mr. Rofrano's bony frame, back in place beside her.

"The neighbor kid told me it was a baby boy," he says, "but I don't know if that's true. Sometimes kids make things up."

"But the rest of it is true?"

He nods. "I looked it all up in the newspapers. It was big news around here. But then it settled down eventually, when they couldn't find the family."

"I hope they're all right," Sophie whispers. "Those poor sisters."

"I always hoped so." He leans his head back against the window and examines the ceiling. His hands curl around the edge of the window seat, one on each side of his legs, as if he's holding on for balance. When he speaks, his voice is hardly more than a whisper: just clouds of frosty breath dissolving into the dry winter air. "I used to lie in my bed here and think about that little girl, you know? The one who found her mother's body. The one who slept in this room. Sometimes I almost thought I could feel her with me, like she was still playing there, with her toys. Waiting for her mother to wake up again."

Sophie touches his hand. "Oh, Mr. Rofrano."

"Kind of silly, I guess. But I didn't have any brothers or sisters. There was only me. So maybe I just . . ."

"Just what?"

"Nothing. Anyway, I never forgot that girl. I just kept thinking about her and thinking about her. They had her picture in the newspaper, and I clipped it out and kept it in my wallet. Kept it in my pocket, when I was flying." The cigarette is gone from his fingers—maybe he left it in the washstand—and he stares down at Sophie's hand that covers his own. "Something about her eyes. Like she was looking right into me, from her picture. Right into my heart. I know that sounds stupid."

"Did you ever try to find her?"

"I thought about it, when I got back from France. I meant to, actually. And then I got busy with other things, and I guess I just put it all behind me. In the past, you know, with Poppa and Mama and everyone else." He stands up and pulls her with him. "Come along. I'd better get you back to New York, before your father figures out you're not gadding around with Julie Schuyler."

Sophie keeps his hand and folds her other mitten over the top, like a sandwich. "Do you know what I think?"

"I wouldn't dare to guess, Miss Fortescue."

"I think you should find this girl."

He stares down at her and breathes without sound. "Why do you say that?" he says at last.

"Because I think she's the *one*, the one you're meant for. I think it's fate. I think you've been missing her all your life."

"I've never even met her."

"Yes, you have. In your dreams, you have. You lived in the same room, you breathed the same air. You're *connected*." She pauses. "But you already know that, don't you? You've carried her in your pocket all these years. I'll bet you've looked for her in every single face, every single woman you've ever met. Haven't you?"

"God in heaven," he whispers.

She squeezes his fingers between her palms. The mittens are thick, but she can feel the ridges of his knuckles, the heavy lines of his bones, and the weight of them fills her with certainty. "Go find her, Mr. Rofrano. Go find her and make her happy. You belong to her."

Again the soundless breathing, the mature consideration. The house creaks faintly, the wind hoots around a corner. Mr. Rofrano lifts his other hand and touches the corner of Sophie's mouth with his thumb, a swift swipe, like she's left a crumb behind or something.

Or *something*.

"Oh, I *do*, do I?" he murmurs. "To *her*?"

"Yes."

"Well, maybe she doesn't want me. Maybe she doesn't need a fellow like me, all broken up and scarred. What if she's already got someone to make her happy?"

"Then you should cut him out, of course. She'd be much happier with you, in my humble feminine opinion. Scars and all. She'd be the luckiest girl in the world."

"I see." He presses her fingers. "But what about *you*, Miss Fortescue? Aren't *you* the luckiest girl in the world?"

"Who, me?"

"Yes. Don't you belong to Jay Ochsner?"

The question interrupts all that lovely certainty warming her belly. The mystic alchemy of this seaside turret bedroom, by which she, Sophie Fortescue, seems somehow transformed from her leaden East Thirty-Second Street self into the girl in Mr. Rofrano's picture, the girl he loves, the *one*. Jay Ochsner? She hasn't thought about Jay in hours, and his intrusion into this intimate winter idyll strikes her as—well, intrusion. Where he doesn't belong.

"I guess so," she replies.

"You guess so?"

"Yes! I mean, of course I do. We're engaged to be married, after all." *Married:* what a clang that word makes, in the frigid air of Mr. Rofrano's childhood bedroom. Another intrusion.

"That's what I thought. Since I was the one who popped the question, after all. And I can still hear the sound of your voice saying *Yes*. You were pretty certain about that."

"Yes, I was."

Mr. Rofrano plucks away Sophie's mittened fingers, opening the sandwich, so that the two of them, Sophie and Mr. Rofrano, are left standing there in the middle of the room, linked at both hands, staring absurdly at each other. Like a couple at the altar, she thinks. His lips are pink, parted just a crack, as if he's about to say something. Ask a question. Say *I do.*

Wouldn't that be crazy?

"I guess we'd better get back to New York," Sophie whispers.

"I guess we'd better," Mr. Rofrano agrees.

But he doesn't let go.

Chapter 8

*And verily, a woman need know but one man well,
in order to understand all men; whereas a man may
know all women and not understand one of them.*

—HELEN ROWLAND

THERESA

Monday morning, about ten o'clock or so

U ntil this morning, I have never visited the Boy's
place of employment, but everybody knows
where to find the Sterling Bates & Company building:
right there at the intersection of Wall and Broad, coyly
cornering the Stock Exchange.

I was the one who got him the job in the first place,
after all. Well, that's not quite true. I *urged* him to find
himself a means of gainful employment, to keep himself
busy during the day once the first autumn zephyr blew
us all back into the city, like so many fallen leaves. *Idle*

hands do the devil's work, I reminded him, sometime in the tranquil center of August, and then I took said hands into my own and settled them right where they could do the devil's work to my utmost satisfaction. It was the middle of the day, and we had been lovers for about a month by then, but I was already planning for the future. Already laying out a means by which the Boy could settle into a little nest at just the right distance from the Upper East Side—not too far for convenience, not too close for discretion—and I could pay him a visit or two, from time to time.

I knew, of course, that he wouldn't allow me to keep him. He wasn't that sort of Boy, then or now. Besides, he has a tendency to brood if left to his own devices, and I did have other claims on my time, loath as I was to face them in the middle of that summer of nineteen twenty. So. A job he must have, and a job he easily found, once I planted a little whisper in Ned van der Wahl's ear. *That houseguest of yours, that nice boy just back from France, the son of your old friend, don't you think he'd make a fine new stockbroker at your firm? He seems to be perking up a bit. A career in finance might be just the thing for him.* And what do you know? Ned had the same good idea as I did. He was just waiting for the end of summer to suggest it. The boy needed time to rest up a bit, after all he'd been through, and now that I mentioned it, he *was* perking up. He was perking up nicely. So off to Sterling Bates he went, except in bonds instead of stocks, because they happened to have an opening on the government desk at that exact moment. Kismet, or something.

You saved my life that summer, the Boy likes to tell me, and I modestly think he's right. I have only to remember the sight of his face, that evening when he dropped me off at Windermere after Man o' War's race, to know how far he's come since then. The triumphant elation of the racetrack had worn off by then, and we had driven most of the way in silence—two long hours of silence, just picture it—punctuated only rarely by observations on the weather, on the entertainment afforded by Ned van der Wahl to his guests, on the splendid race we'd just witnessed. That was how I liked it. I don't go in for soul-searching, for this modern passion for psycho-analysis. Examining every last detail of your childhood, every last itch in your subconscious. Generally speaking, the less I know about the contents of a person's soul, the better I like him.

Anyway. We pulled up in the exact apex of the tidy crescent drive at Windermere—we kept the gravel raked daily, as a matter of moral order, and still do—and I asked the Boy if he'd like to come in for a nightcap. Although there wasn't much company, I was afraid. My husband was in the city that week.

A nice gilt-edged invitation, wasn't it, and I fully expected him to accept.

He peered up the steps and back down to my face. His eyes were sick and dull. "No, thank you," he said, and he got out of the car and opened the door for me, like a gentleman. He shook my hand good-bye and puttered off down the drive, and that was the last I saw of him for a week, poor thing. One hand on the wheel, clenched hard, and the other elbow propped on the doorframe. Stupid Boy, I thought, a little slighted and angry, but I couldn't get that picture out of my head. The unhappy angle of his face.

Six nights later, having drunk a couple of martinis with a couple of friends at the Maidstone Club, having tried and failed to catch the Boy around town all week, I decided enough was enough. I stood up in the middle of someone's sentence, tossed down the third martini, stubbed out my cigarette, and drove on over to Ned van der Wahl's guesthouse to trap the Boy in his own lair.

But that's another story, and anyway, the reason I'm thinking about all this, the reason I'm dredging up all this history, is because that ancient scenario bears a remarkable resemblance to my present situation. Unable to find the Boy around town yesterday, I'm driving downtown this Monday morning to ambush him at his office, and my fingers are trembling, my lips are clenched just as hard as they were back then.

"Mr. Octavian Rofrano," I tell the secretary out front, just as crisp as can be. (I might have telephoned him from the box on the street below, of course, but it seems to me that a woman standing in the reception area inside your place of employment is much harder to ignore than a woman standing in a telephone box on the street outside your place of employment.)

"Do you have an appointment?" she inquires, as pert as can be. She's wearing the latest suit and a bobbed haircut, and she thinks she's awfully smart. Smarter than a Fifth Avenue matron of a certain age, at any rate, however attractive the matron's figure and however expensive her dress.

I administer my most dragonly stare, the one that used to set my boys all a-quiver when they were guilty little sprouts. "Just tell him Mrs. Marshall is here to see him."

"Yes, ma'am." (Meekly.)

A moment later, the Boy strides free from the interior doorway and wheels to a stop in the middle of that plush marble reception area. His eyes are wide and alarmed, and his shoulders are just the way I like them, inside that suit of dignified gray charcoal for which I measured him myself. "Mrs. Marshall!" he exclaims. "Is something the matter?"

I rise from my chair and straighten my gloves on my wrists. "Indeed there is, Mr. Rofrano. Shall we find somewhere for you to buy me a cup of coffee?"

The Boy takes me to a coffee shop a few blocks away, making rather endearingly furtive glances all about us. He orders coffee and cinnamon buns and lights me a cigarette, and I notice that his hands are almost as nervous as mine.

"Couldn't this wait until tomorrow?" he asks. "I was going to talk to you about something, when you came over."

"Not really."

He lights his own cigarette, but he doesn't do anything with it, just holds it between his fingers and stares at the burning end. "You do know that everyone's going to hear about this, you coming to see me at work."

"Oh, never mind that. Everybody already knows about us."

He looks up. "What do you mean?"

"I mean secrets don't last long in this town. Didn't you know that?"

"Nobody ever said anything to me."

"Darling, nobody ever would. Anyway, it doesn't matter any more." The waitress arrives bearing coffee and buns, and I utilize this natural pause in the conversation to gather my thoughts and—I suppose—my courage. After all, it's a bold thing I'm doing, isn't it? And not the kind of bold thing I usually do.

"Why not?" says the Boy, as the waitress steps away.

I add cream. "Why not what?"

"Why doesn't it matter?" He grips the coffee cup and leans forward. His face is all pink, his bones practically jumping forth from behind his smooth young skin. I adore his skin. I adore him. His eyebrows knit anxiously together as he continues: "Are you ending this?"

"*Ending* this?" I stir in the sugar and lift the cup with both hands, so it doesn't shake in my fingers. The coffee is just right, sweet and creamy. "No, Boyo. The opposite. I've changed my mind entirely." Set down the cup, fix him in the eye. "I've decided to accept your offer of marriage, after all."

From the shock in his face, I can tell this is the last thing he expects from me. I believe his eyes actually change color—or is it continents?—from Mediterranean to Antarctic. The pink drains away from his skin.

"I don't understand," he says, in a voice like the spray of fine gravel at the apex of a crescent-shaped driveway.

"I've changed my mind, that's all. I've thought about it long and hard, and I realized you're right. All this sneaking about, it's bad for the soul. Manhattan's bad for the soul. We should go away together and start over, and—well, maybe we can have a baby after all, it's not al*together* impossible, and—well." I blink once or twice—it seems my eyes are stinging, maybe someone's cutting up an onion in the back—and lift the coffee again. "Anyway. What do you think?"

The shock is still present, or rather the color's still absent. The Boy fidgets with his cigarette, sips his coffee, and says, without looking at me, "What about your husband? The boys?"

"Oh, they'll get used to the idea. The boys have their own lives now, after all, and Sylvo . . ." I rattle to a halt, because I can't lie. I can't lie to my Boyo. "Sylvo wants a divorce."

"A *what*?"

"A divorce, of course. We can't get married without one, can we?" I laugh; or rather, I intend to laugh. The resulting sound comes out more like a particularly repellent giggle, the kind that no red-blooded man would want to shackle himself against for eternity. "Sylvo's finally decided to move with the times and marry his mistress. Isn't it precious? So we're free, darling Boyo. There's nothing in our way. I'm sure he'll settle plenty of money on me to keep things quiet, enough to buy us a fine new start somewhere. What do you think about California?"

He's never thought about California, I can tell. California is the furthest thing from his dear little mind. He reaches out and touches my hand. "When did this happen?"

"When did what happen?" My voice is still far too high.

"When did Sylvo tell you he wanted a divorce?"

"Oh, that? I believe it was Saturday night. Yes. Saturday night, after I got home." *Tap, tap* in the ashtray. "He was awfully nice about it. I didn't know you could say a thing like that so nicely."

"Oh, Theresa."

"My goodness, you don't think I'm *upset* about it, do you? It's *sensational* news. We're free! It's what we've always wanted, isn't it? A gift on a silver platter, engraved *Mr. and Mrs. Octavian Rofrano, Junior,* just exactly the way you signed all those naughty hotel registers. We'll be respectable at last."

"Theresa," he whispers.

"Nothing too fancy, of course. I think a City Hall wedding would be adequate, don't you think? A small party afterward, just a few friends. Jay will have married his little woman by then. They can serve as witnesses, I suppose. What's the matter, Boyo? You're not saying much."

"I'm sorry. Just a little shocked, I guess. A week ago you turned me down flat. I thought it was hopeless."

"Well, things have changed since then, haven't they? All the obstacles are gone, and do you know something? I'm glad. I'm glad Sylvo was brave enough to part with the old ways. It's a whole new world, and divorce isn't such a scandal anymore. If two people aren't suited to each other, haven't been suited in some time, why, they should shake hands as friends and find someone else." I brush his knuckle with my thumb. "And we've certainly established how well we're suited, haven't we?"

He looks up from his coffee. "There's more to marriage than *that*, Theresa."

"Of course there is. But sex is fundamental, that's what all the scientists say. Sylvo and I haven't gone to bed in years, and how can you call that a marriage? Say!" I put down my cigarette and snap my fingers. "We can have a double wedding, can't we? If the divorce comes through quickly enough, I mean."

"A double wedding?"

"You and me, and Jay and little Sophie."

The Boy releases my hand and sticks all ten fingers in his hair.

"What's the matter?" I ask. "Is something wrong?"

"No. Nothing. I mean—I'm sorry, I just—I'm taking it all in, that's all."

"Is this about Jay? Have you found out something awful about that girl?"

"Damn it, Theresa," he mutters.

"Because it doesn't matter. I don't give a damn anymore. Her father can be a convicted felon, for all I care. They love each other, and that's all that matters."

He pulls his hands out of his hair and stares at me. "Do they? Love each other?"

There is something about the way he asks this question. Something about the slant of his eyebrows, or maybe the color of his eyes, which seem to be moving north again, to warmer climes.

I crush out my cigarette in a kind of rolling motion, clockwise, taking my time. "Why, Boyo," I say. "Why do you care?"

The tiniest pause. "I don't."

It appears my fingers are cold. They *seem* cold, anyway, as I take careful hold of the coffee cup. I don't lacquer my nails. That would be vulgar. But I do trim them nicely, a little longer than I used to, and they're really quite elegant, poised against all that cheap white ceramic. It's just the rest of the hand that troubles me. The veins that pop out in awful sea-green profusion whenever I lower my claws below the level of my heart. The lines around my knuckles. The excess of color in my capillaries. Most of the time, you can hide all this mess under your gloves, but when you're smoking and drinking coffee in a joint like this, the gloves come off. You sit naked before your companion. Your age is written on your hands, plain to read, and there's nothing you can do about that, is there?

"Tell me something, Boyo," I say, staring at my telltale veins. "What did you want to tell me tomorrow?"

"What's that?"

"You had something to tell me. And then I jumped on in with my own news, awfully rude of me. But now it's your turn."

His lips part, but nothing comes out.

"Did it have anything to do with your whereabouts yesterday? I tried to telephone you, again and again, but there was no answer."

"I was out. Out for a drive."

"Yes, so I guessed. I actually went down to your apartment and asked at the garage. They said you'd left early."

"I drove to Connecticut. Back to my old haunts."

"By yourself?"

Another pause, even tinier than the one before. But at least he has the guts to look me in the eye. "No. I took Sophie Fortescue with me."

"*Did* you? Another man's fiancée?"

"You asked me to find out more about her."

The coffee is tepid now, but I drink it anyway. "And did you?"

"I don't know. I think so, yes."

"Anything scandalous? Anything I should know about?"

"No," he says, a little too fiercely, and my heart, my God, I think it actually stops for an instant or two. Freezes right up in my chest. Chokes and sputters like an engine that won't start properly. The coffee rises in my throat, and I swallow it back.

"Good," I say, just as fiercely. I lift a cinnamon bun from the plate between us and bite down hard. The waitress stops by with the coffee pot. Refills us both. I stir in the cream and the sugar. The Boy takes his black. He lights another cigarette and opens his mouth to say something. I jump in first.

"It's a funny thing, Boyo. I was just thinking—as I drove down here in the taxi to tell you the good news—I was staring out the window and remembering that first time I showed up at your place in East Hampton. Ned van der Wahl's guesthouse. Do you remember?"

"Of course I do, Theresa."

His voice is soft with compassion, and I hate the sound of it. I hate the sound of his compassion. I hate that habitual stillness of his, the way his fingers, after a brief and singular nervous interlude at the beginning of our little chat, have once more acquired an extreme economy of motion.

I say sharply, "You were drunk, as I recall."

"I'd been drinking. I drank a lot that summer."

"Well, of course you did. We were both drinking a little too much than was good for us, weren't we? I was half-drunk myself, I think, or I might never have had the nerve to turn up at your virtuous door at a quarter to midnight in the middle of summer." I turn my head to the window and the curious absence of traffic on the sidewalk outside. Maybe it's the cold. A lone man walks by, huddled inside his overcoat, his scarf wound up to his nose: just a faded black bundle topped by a worn felt hat. Across the street, a luncheonette waits for the noontime crowd. HOT SOUP 5¢. There are a lot of restaurants in New York these days. They're popping up all over. Everyone's eating out; no one wants to stay at home and cook dinner anymore.

"You didn't look that nervous," the Boy says quietly.

"Well, I was. I was scared as hell. I was forty-two years old and I'd never done that before. You were my first, Boyo. My first affair in all those years. Did I ever tell you that?"

"No."

"I'm almost ashamed to admit it, really. But there you are. And there I was. And there you *were*, all young and strong and perfect, and I'd never wanted anything so much as I wanted you. Just to *see* you, that night, just to see the color of your eyes and the—the—well, you've got this *skin*, Boyo, this utterly delicious skin. It's so firm and fresh, even after a drink or two." A couple of girls walk by. They're wearing smart clothes, cheap but up-to-date—you've seen them around, haven't you, those new coats with the dropped waists, the straight mannish silhouettes?—and their heads are bent together, all sharp and smiling beneath a pair of identical small hats. Twenty-two, twenty-three. About the Boy's age, I suppose. Secretaries? Typing pool? There's a shimmer of business around them, an industrious energy. They're going to conquer the world, one typewriter key at a time. I say, in a whisper now, "I just wanted to see you again, that night. That's all. That would have been enough. I never thought you would actually fall for an old bird like me."

"You weren't old, Theresa."

"But I wasn't in the first bloom of youth, was I?" I turn back to him and smile. "Although I do think I've aged rather gracefully. I've kept myself up."

"You're a beautiful woman, and you know it. Don't pretend you don't."

"I'll never forget the sight of your face, when you opened that door. You were wearing blue-striped pajamas and a blue dressing gown. Dark blue, with little brown paisley swirls. And a cigarette in your hand, just like that one." I gesture, a flutter of my fingertips. "You didn't look a bit surprised to see me."

"Well, I was."

"Do you remember what I was wearing?"

He rubs his thumb along the edge of the saucer. "You were wearing a red dress and a diamond necklace. And your shoes were dangling from your left hand."

"It was a hot night, after all."

I allow that to sink in for a moment. I can see he's remembering; his gaze has dropped straight into his coffee cup, and his lips are parted a little. Regards the Boy, you have to pay attention to the small clues, the minute movements that allow you some glimpse into the workings of that immaculate mind of his. His breath seems to be a little shallow. That's good. Let him remember. God knows I can't forget. Even now, my heart starts to find that same thudding tempo, and my nerves tingle anxiously on my arms and between my legs, all because of a single indelible memory: The Boy, like a lean, hard rope all wound up inside that dark blue dressing gown, and the tender hollow of his throat just visible at the parting of his pajamas, which he's neglected to button all the way up.

"Good evening, Mr. Rofrano," I said.

And he looked me up and he looked me down, and he looked me right back up again, landing softly inside my forehead. "Good evening, Mrs. Marshall. It's a little late, isn't it?"

His voice was just a little slurry, just enough that I knew he'd been drinking. I placed my palm against the doorjamb and asked if I could have that nightcap now. *What nightcap?* he wanted to know, and I said the nightcap I'd offered him a week ago, after he brought me home from the racetrack. I was still thirsty, I told him.

So he thought about this. Motionless. Fixed as a pillar of salt. I don't think he even blinked. He just stood there, considering me, considering the offer before him. The seconds passed, the mockingbirds sang in the tree by the door. And I could tell when he gave in. His lips parted a little—the way they're doing now—and the skin beneath his eyes sort of relaxed (if that's the word) in such a way that only then, at that instant, did I realize he'd been tense to begin with. That my appearance at his door had constituted an unexpected test of his resolve, and that his resolve had just been defeated by my red dress and my bare feet, and by the abyss of loneliness that split him open from stern to bowsprit, and maybe by the half-empty bottle of skee just visible on the table behind him.

He stepped back from the doorway and said, "Help yourself, Mrs. Marshall."

So I did.

The Boy finds me a taxi on Broadway and promises to leave work early. Good, I tell him. I'll bring dinner. We can celebrate.

He doesn't look much like celebrating. His face is still and heavy as he opens the taxi door for me and waits while I settle myself inside. I lift my gaze to thank him and the shock of his expression travels all the way through my belly to the soles of my feet.

"What's the matter, Boyo? You look as if I've passed you a sentence of death. It's only marriage, after all."

He's got one hand braced on the door of the taxi, one hand braced on the back of the seat, behind my neck. The taxi sputters and rattles impatiently around us. The Boy angles his head to my ear and says, "Was that the truth, back there?"

"I always tell you the truth, Boyo."

"I mean that you'd never had an affair, before that night. That I was the first . . ."

He leaves a word dangling, and I supply it for him.

"Lover. Yes, Boyo." I find his hand, the one on the back of the seat, and kiss the backs of his leather knuckles. "You were my first lover, and my last."

His breath is white and steady. He bends down to kiss me good-bye, and his lips are warm. "I'll see you tonight, then."

"Don't be late."

The Boy nods and takes his hand back. He slams the door shut and turns away, and the driver says, "Where to, ma'am?"

For some reason, the word *ma'am* makes me wince. I lean back against the seat and stare at the Boy's diminishing body as it strides up Broadway toward Wall Street, all business, one more charcoal overcoat, one more snug fedora hat bobbing among the others, down the cold gray January canyons of downtown Manhattan.

I give the driver my brother's address on Park Avenue.

You know, we're really quite close, Ox and I, despite our obvious differences. Our mother retired to her fainting couch soon after his birth and hasn't really risen from it since, so I had the raising of him. I couldn't do much about his lack of brains, but I made sure he minded his manners and learned to ride a horse properly, and I kept him from eloping with the showgirl who kindly relieved him of his virginity and his allowance when he was seventeen, the summer before he left for Princeton. (No easy feat on my part, I assure you; Ox can be remarkably stubborn, where women are concerned.)

And it was Ox who delivered me the news of Tommy's death, two days after the Armistice. I was staying with an old Westover friend in Boston at the time, and the War Department telegram had naturally gone to Fifth Avenue. Sylvo was too broken-up to tell me himself, I suppose, so my brother jumped aboard the next train and reached me that evening, just as we were about to leave for dinner. (To celebrate the war's end, ironically enough, and our own immense relief at having been left personally unscathed by its horrors.) There I stood in the foyer, laughing, all dressed up in blue silk and gloved to the elbow, when the heavy brass knocker fell on the door—*clunk!*—my God, I can still hear the exact metallic clang it made, key of G minor— and we fell silent, the three of us, my friend and her husband and me. Terrible silence. The butler opened the door, and I knew what had happened, the instant I saw Ox's face. Maybe even before.

I screamed, *Tommy!*

And Ox. Dear Ox. He leapt forward, just in time, and held me up against his chest. He said that it was 'flu, that Tommy had fallen ill during a weekend's leave in Paris; that he had died at the American hospital in Neuilly on the same day as the Armistice itself. Just awful. Just an awful damned unlucky break. I don't remember much of the next day or two, but I remember Ox was there the whole time, and Sylvo wasn't. Sylvo stayed home in New York and made all the arrangements, bringing back the body and where to bury him and so on. Important details, of course, and I was grateful not to have to take charge of them myself. But it was Ox who kept me alive, in those first forty-eight hours of the rest of my life.

And I think to myself, as the taxi lurches slowly uptown, how uncanny it was that he should have been so compassionate. I mean, *Ox!* He hasn't got a child of his own, after all—at least one we're aware of—so he couldn't have known that particular passion that takes up residence in your heart, when you first have a baby. Of course, he knew and loved Tommy. Who couldn't love Tommy, that lovely gilded child, that laughing and brilliant boy? My golden one, my darling twinkle-eyed son, who looked so inexpressibly fortissimo in his second lieutenant's uniform on the morning he left for France. But Ox's love was an uncle's love for his nephew, a different thing entirely. Tommy did not inhabit his soul. Tommy did not run inside Ox's blood and lay himself down along the bones and muscles of Ox's chest, so that the loss of him sometimes impeded Ox's ability to breathe.

But somehow Ox had understood. God knows why.

None of this goes any way to explain why Ox should be at home in his Park Avenue bachelor digs at Monday lunchtime, nor why I should expect to find him there. Call it instinct. Call it feminine intuition. Call it a sister's intimate knowledge of her brother's slovenly ways.

"Shouldn't you be at work, brother darling?" I inquired, as I plucked off my gloves and tossed them on a Louis Quatorze commode, the gilding of which had seen better centuries.

"Ridiculous question."

"Someone has to ask it. I presume the partners at Willig and White are more indulgent than I am, or you wouldn't have a job at all."

"*Job* is such a crass word, Sisser." Ox lifts his feet from the sofa cushion, in order to make room for me. He's holding a quilted bag to his head with one hand, and a tall glass of hair of the dog in the other.

"Most of life's inescapable necessities are crass," I observe, dropping a kiss on my brother's forehead. "That doesn't make them any less necessary. Are you really expecting me to sit on this?"

"It's a perfectly respectable sofa."

"It's a disgrace. You need a wife, Ox. The sooner, the better."

"That *is* the plan, after all."

"Really? How soon?"

He removes the bag from his head and takes a sip from his glass. "As soon as possible, so far as I know. She's supposed to give me the happy date upon consultation with Papa."

I manage, after some effort, to discover a chair that isn't already inhabited by crumbs and spills of one kind and another. "Hasn't she consulted with Papa already? Or is she too busy with other affairs?"

"She hasn't got any other affairs, Sisser. It's all part of her charm."

I settle myself in the chair and offer my brother a guileless smile. "Are you *quite* certain of that?"

"Of course I am. I hope you're not suggesting otherwise?"

"Not at all. As long as you're confident of her, why should I be otherwise? I'm sure her outing yesterday was entirely innocent."

He chokes on his drink. "What's that?"

"Her outing. Yesterday. Surely she's told you all about it?"

"I—that is—yesterday, did you say?"

"Yesterday. Sunday. The day after Saturday night, when the two of you attended that party together? Philip Schuyler and his little secretary wife? I presume you saw her home yourself, of course."

Ox's face turns a rather sickly shade, not that it bore all that healthy a tint before. "Not exactly."

"No? But of course you entrusted the care of your precious darling to someone—well, trustworthy?"

"I—I can't honestly remember. But she did get home all right. I'm quite sure of that. I sent around flowers the next morning, and—and—" His face screws up into an object resembling nothing so much as a crumpled tissue.

"And she replied? She came around to your place in gloves and Sunday bonnet, and administered her healing hand to your troubled brow?"

"Now, see here, Sisser," he says, gathering up strength again, "if you've got something to say, say it."

"Oh, you know how it is, Ox. A woman in my position hears so many things."

"Nothing against Sophie! I'd smash the face of any fella who said a word against her. She's as innocent as an angel."

"No doubt at all." I lengthen my gaze to consider the tarnished silver cigarette box on the lamp table, next to Ox's pink ear. "Still, she's a human being, isn't she? A young lady."

"Well, yes. Of course she is."

"And like all young ladies, she appreciates a little attention from the man who's supposed to admire her. The man she's going to marry. She likes to be wooed, and adored, and made much of."

Ox considers this, frowning. He rubs his forehead with his thumb, as if to ignite the gray matter inside.

"Ox," I say tenderly, "you can't just ignore her, just because she's agreed to marry you. Until the vows are exchanged—and *soon*, God willing—she's still free to back out of the deal. You've got to remind her, and remind her, and *remind* her, what a wonderful man she's getting." I reach over and pat his knee. "You've got to *woo* her, darling, or someone else will."

"Say. What are you getting at? Are you suggesting she was stepping out with some other fella yesterday?"

"I'm not suggesting anything. She's a sweet girl. I'm sure she wouldn't do anything to betray you. But she's so young, Ox. So young and inexperienced. These pretty girls, their heads are turned so easily, and men can be such awful *cads* these days." I examine my fingernails. "Really, if I were you, I'd scrub myself up and head down to Thirty-Second Street, flowers and chocolates in hand, and I wouldn't leave her side for an *instant* until she gives you a wedding date. An *early* date. A handsome devil like you, I'm sure you'll secure her enthusiastic cooperation in no time."

"Well, naturally." He straightens himself against the sofa and contemplates—guessing from the look on his face, anyway—the possible daring boundaries of Sophie's enthusiasm. Perhaps, at this point, I ought to mention that my brother remains in a state of what we once politely called *dishabille*. His pajamas are rumpled, his green silk dressing gown is untied and open across his chest, and his lovely golden-brown hair runs greasily amok across his skull. I should charitably describe his face as bloated. To scrub himself up, as I suggested, might take him the greater part of the day's remains. Not that he seems to have plans for any better occupation. (His actual occupation included.)

I remove the glass from his hand. "I'm quite serious, Ox. You're about to become a married man, if you're lucky enough to persuade her to the altar itself. It's time to start acting like one."

"Well, *I* haven't seen all that many married men dance constant attendance on their wives."

I tip back the glass and drain what remains. "I expect most marriages would be a good deal happier if they did."

Maybe I said it too bitterly. Maybe there was something in my expression. Or maybe it's just Ox: as thick as two planks in ordinary life, but nonetheless attuned by some primeval blood instinct to the rippling of my unhappiness in the ether. He lifts his eyebrows and leans forward, and a lock of his untidy hair drops across his forehead. He pushes it back and says, "Something going on with you, Sisser?"

"If you must know, I'm getting a divorce."

The words pop out before I can consider their wisdom; or maybe I've been wanting to say this all along, since that moment early Sunday morning when Sylvo closed the front door behind him, in a singularly echoing thump, and left me in a stunned and lonely heap on the library sofa, clutching a glass of cream sherry. To throw myself on my brother's chest and surround myself in his wordless understanding. I finger the empty tumbler and fix him with a bright and expectant smile. *Getting a divorce.* How modern it sounds.

Ox sneezes messily and pulls out his handkerchief. "Gadzooks, Sisser! Say it ain't so."

"It's so." I shrug helplessly. "I'd had enough, I guess. All the other women and the—well, the lack of understanding. We haven't been man and wife in years, really. Not since Tommy died."

"Yes, but—*divorce.*"

"Everybody's getting divorces these days, Ox. Nobody cares about the old rules anymore."

"Still." He blows his nose, shakes his head. "I thought some things were sacred. I thought the two of you would soldier on and grow old together."

"Ox, we hardly even *talk* to each other any more. We're like strangers occupying the same apartment, and not all that often at that."

"I suppose it doesn't help that you're in love with that kid of yours."

I drop the glass on the rug. *"What?"*

"That Rofrano kid. Come on, Sisser. You think I didn't know?"

"I don't know *what* you're talking about."

My brother sighs and rises creakily to his feet: stuffing the silk handkerchief back in his silk pocket, swooping up the fallen glass as he goes. "Well, I'm sorry you're throwing in the towel, that's all. It's a damned shame, the way you two can toss away a quarter of a century of marriage like that."

"My God. Listen to you, the moralist."

"Like you said, I'm getting married myself. I've got to be a moralist, haven't I? I've got to believe in what I'm doing, or what's the point?"

He turns and walks to the kitchen with the empty glass. I hear a ceramic clink, the squeak of the faucet, the rush of running water, and I call to him: "I'll just let myself out, then."

"Do that," he calls back.

I should march straight out the door, after that remark. I should march straight out and find a taxi. But where would I go? Sylvo's back at our apartment, packing up. He's already rented a bachelor apartment of his own, in accordance with the terms of the legal separation that necessarily precedes a legal divorce. Everything's in motion, like a train chugging inexorably out of the station, and I'd really rather not head to the platform at the moment and watch it leave. Watch Sylvo leave.

I follow my brother into the kitchen and place my hand on his shoulder.

"Ox," I say softly.

He doesn't turn. "Sisser."

"I meant what I said. Clean yourself up and go pay attention to your fiancée. And do me a favor, brother dear?"

"What's that, Sisser?"

"Don't ever stop."

Chapter 9

A bachelor never quite gets over the idea
that he is a thing of beauty and a boy forever.

—HELEN ROWLAND

SOPHIE

Earlier that day

The flowers stand in the middle of the breakfast table, in a tall and unfamiliar crystal vase. Sophie counts at least a dozen red roses, six fragrant stargazer lilies, and four hydrangeas of the most delicately perfect blue. She adds cream to her coffee and says, "My goodness. Who sent the flowers? They must have cost a fortune at this time of year."

"Your fiancé sent them," Virginia says. "They arrived at lunchtime yesterday."

"*Jay* sent them? Did he stop by?"

"No. Just the flowers."

Virginia's attention is directed not at Sophie or the flowers, but at her daughter, who's attempting to clean up a spill of egg yolk with a slice of buttered toast. Father's already at his workshop; he left even before Sophie came down this morning, chased by a resolute slam of the front door that seemed—at least to Sophie's guilty ears—to promise a reckoning later. Due to a pair of flat tires, she hadn't arrived home until well past dinner, by which time Father had already retired. Only a note remained of him, pushed under her door that morning, the contents of which made her stomach drop.

I presume you will have ready a reasonable explanation for your absence last night by lunchtime today.

"Did Father see them?"

"Of course he did."

"Did he say anything?"

Virginia straightens at last and turns to Sophie. Her expression is both harried and compassionate, and rather startlingly pale. Or is it the morning sunshine, slanting at last through the window to whiten her face? She says, tilting her head, "Did you think he would?"

Sophie glances at Evelyn's dark head, bent listlessly over her breakfast. She lowers her voice almost to a whisper. "Was he awfully upset last night?"

"You know he never gets upset, Baby. But he was very, very worried. You should have tried to find a telephone."

"We did! The man in the service station let us use his. But the operator couldn't seem to connect the call. I think she was drunk."

"Where was this service station?"

Sophie hesitates. "Connecticut."

"Connecticut!" The teaspoon drops from Virginia's hand and hits the edge of the table, before landing with a soft thump on the rug. Virginia makes no move to recover it. "What on earth were you doing in Connecticut?"

What, indeed?

Sophie lifts her coffee and drinks long, and when she can't put an answer off any longer, when she can't think of a suitable half-truth that isn't an outright lie, she sets down the cup in the saucer and says, "He was showing me the house where he grew up."

"Sophie!"

"What?"

Virginia looks at Evelyn, whose small, flushed face is buried in a cup of weak tea fortified with milk: her favorite drink. She bends down and picks up the spoon, laying it carefully above her plate. "We'll speak about this later," she says, in a voice Sophie recognizes from her own childhood, when Virgo was more a mother to her than a sister.

In other words, Sophie's in trouble. But it was worth it, this trouble, wasn't it? And when she explains everything to Virginia—the frozen airfield, the beautiful turreted house in Greenwich, Octavian himself—then her sister will understand. Virginia believes in the same things Sophie does. Virginia will advise her. Virginia will help her do what needs to be done.

But until then. That awful note under her door. Father's never been the warmest of parents, but the brief and arctic quality of his message—even the letters looked stiff and frigid, etched onto the page with an ice pick—destroyed all the feather-edged euphoria that had dusted her off to sleep last night, all the anticipation that nudged her awake this morning. And oh! The memory of that moment when Octavian had almost kissed her, there in the turret bedroom while the winter sunset was just beginning to soften the horizon, and then decided against kissing at the last instant, in such a tender, longing way that was almost as good as being kissed in fact. (Certainly lovelier than being kissed by a corked Jay Ochsner in the back seat of a taxicab, reeking of peppermint hair oil.)

He had gazed at her for maybe a half a minute longer, and it was the quietest and most eternal thirty seconds of Sophie's life. His eyes were flattened of all color and still beautiful. He hadn't even blinked, he was so still, and yet she could hear every thought in his head. *Not now. We'll make things right first.* We'll do this right, because this thing that lies between us is too perfect, too transparent to darken with the slightest tint of sin.

"You're smiling," he said at last, though not smiling himself.

"Of course I am," she replied, and he released one of her hands and led her out of the room by the other, down the stairs and out the front door, which they had to leave unlocked. Oh, well. They hadn't said a word. He tucked her into the Ford and they started the engine together in a wordless synchronicity of action, and about fifty yards back down the unpaved road the first tire went flat.

At the time, it hadn't occurred to Sophie that this might be an omen. After all, tires went flat regularly.

But then another tire had blown out, badly enough that they had to limp into a service station, and by the time it was fixed the sun had gone down, and they had found a nearby chophouse for dinner. He had called her Miss Fortescue and she had said he could use her first name now, if he liked, and he had smiled—at last!—and told her that in that case, she would have to call him Octavian. Only fair.

"It's an awfully grand name," she said. "Don't you have a nickname?"

He hesitated. "No."

"Then Octavian it is. Sophie and Octavian."

Thinking about it now, she realizes that was a bold thing to say, but it didn't seem bold at the time, over pork chops and fried potatoes on the post road, while the sunset died and the stars popped out in the navy sky. Bold enough that they were sitting there at all, the two of them; bold enough that it was well past nine o'clock by the time they rolled down Third Avenue and around the corner of Thirty-Second Street. He gave her a piece of paper with a number written on it. His telephone exchange—SPRing—followed by 4892. "If you need anything," he said, and those were the last words she heard from him. Not *I'll swing by tomorrow at lunchtime*, or *Let's meet again soon*. Not even *Goodbye, Sophie* or *Gosh, I had a swell time today* on the steps, while she slipped inside the front door. No more words at all. As if he'd lost the ability to speak. She looked back over her shoulder, but he'd already turned and hurried down the sidewalk to the Ford, which was parked by the empty curb, a few houses down.

But words aren't necessary, are they? Sophie knows what he couldn't say. And against the awful might of Father's note, Sophie has that scrap of paper with the telephone number tucked inside her pocket right now, resting against her leg, like a talisman. It's going to give her the courage to tell her father she can't marry Jay Ochsner, after all. It's going to give her the courage to explain this change of heart to Jay himself.

And when she's done all these things, well, that paper's going to give her the courage to pick up the telephone, ask the operator to connect her, and tell Octavian that yes, in fact, she thinks she does need something.

She needs him.

Father doesn't arrive home for lunch, which isn't unusual on its own. Sometimes, when he's especially absorbed in one of his new gadgets, he won't come home all day and all night, and it's Sophie's job to bring him a hot meal in a covered dish and a bottle of milk—he doesn't drink any kind of liquor—and to make sure the cot in the workshop has clean blankets.

So Sophie sits down to lunch in the kitchen by herself. Evelyn's earlier fretfulness has turned into a fever, and Virginia now hovers anxiously over her daughter's bed in the nursery upstairs. The house has taken on that edgy, nerveless atmosphere of the brink of collapse. Sophie eats her soup and places her left hand on top of her pocket, while the cook bustles around the range. Maybe she should telephone Octavian now. (But isn't he at work?) Maybe she should put on her coat and hat and gloves and take the train downtown, to find the office where he works and tell him she absolutely must speak to him, she couldn't bear waiting around any longer for things to happen to her. Waiting to ask permission, when she knows what Father's answer will be: *No.* Sophie should stick to her word. Octavian Rofrano is just a boy, a boy with a slight job and no family and nothing but future before him. Jay Ochsner can take care of her. Jay Ochsner can protect her, the way Father has protected her so carefully all these years.

The soup is half-finished, but Sophie isn't hungry. She stands up and sets her napkin next to her bowl. "Thank you, Dot," she says to the cook, and she turns and walks up the stairs toward the hall, and later on, she's never certain whether she meant to visit her father's workshop first and inform him of her decision, or whether she intended to go straight to Octavian.

Because the instant she reaches the landing, the brass knocker comes crashing down on its plate, and— in the grip of some sort of fantastical hope, maybe— she bounds to the door and throws it open.

And what do you know? Jay Ochsner himself stands there under the steely clouds, cheeks pink from a recent shave, bearing a box of chocolates in one hand and a bunch of crimson roses in the other.

"Darling." He steps forward and kisses her on the lips. He tastes like oranges and cocktails. "I've missed you like crazy."

The funny thing is, she can't quite put her finger on *why*. Why a man who seemed so dashing and amusing and well-ironed and attractive a few days ago, so incontrovertibly *right* a fellow for a girl to marry, now seems so unquestionably wrong. It's not as if he's changed. Not a bit! He remains exactly the same, in every indivisible detail, as the man who first kissed her in the library of the Ochsner town house on Thirty-Fourth Street. His smile is still toothsome, his manners carelessly well-bred. Is she really so fickle as that?

They sit on the sofa. Betty brings tea and cake, the cake Sophie didn't eat for dessert. The flowers are dispatched downstairs to be placed in a vase. Virginia staggers through the doorway, smoothing her dress, face all haggard. "Mr. Ochsner! What a lovely surprise."

He stands at once and takes Virginia's hands. (He's a terrific gentleman, Sophie reminds herself, trying to be fair.) He looks into Virginia's eyes and says, "Why, is something wrong, Mrs. Fitzwilliam?"

"My daughter's a bit ill this morning, that's all," she says. "A touch of fever."

"My sympathies. Terrible ordeal. My sister used to go distracted whenever her boys were poorly, though I assure you it always came out right in the end." He pauses and catches his breath, as if remembering something.

"Well, thank you. That's reassuring," says Virgo. "I'm a trained nurse, which ought to make me steadier, but it seems I'm just as hopeless as any mother."

He smiles and gestures to an armchair. "Come sit down and have some tea. I was just talking to Sophie about setting a date. Maybe you can help us."

"I don't know about that. Isn't this between the two of you?"

Jay waits until Virginia's settled herself in an armchair before resuming his own seat at Sophie's side. "She can't seem to decide."

Virginia pours herself a cup of tea and offers Sophie an inquisitive eyebrow.

"I'd like to talk to Father first," Sophie says.

Virginia sets aside the strainer. "Well, it isn't as though we have a great many conflicting engagements. Doesn't Father want the wedding as soon as possible?"

"My thoughts exactly!" exclaims Jay. He seizes Sophie's hand and kisses the knuckles. "The sooner the better. I know you young ladies like to savor a long courtship, but I've waited long enough to be a married man. I'd like to be off on our honeymoon before springtime, wouldn't you?"

"I—I really hadn't thought about that."

Another kiss. "Where would you like to go, darling? Somewhere warm, I think, don't you? What about South America?"

South America. In fact, Sophie would love to visit South America; just not with Jay Ochsner. She tugs her hand away and reaches for a piece of cake, though she still isn't hungry. She might never be hungry again, at this rate. Her face is hot, her stomach tight. South America with Jay Ochsner. In a flash, she sees the luxuriously overheated stateroom of an ocean liner, skimming past an Amazonian jungle, while Jay reclines in a deck chair wearing a silk dressing gown, like an aging Rudolf Valentino.

"No," she says, "I'd rather not, really."

"No? What about Africa, then? We could go on safari. Always wanted to go on safari." He makes a motion, as if firing a rifle into the clock above the mantel.

"Mr. Ochsner," Virginia says gently, "let's consider the wedding first."

"Oh! Right. Getting ahead of myself, aren't I? There must always be a wedding before a honeymoon, mustn't there?"

Virginia stirs in a spoonful of honey. "Naturally."

The first bite of cake makes Sophie feel sick. She sets it aside on a tiny new plate and picks up her tea. "Either way, I don't think we should consider any of this without consulting Father first. I suppose he'll be paying for everything, after all."

That stings. As well it should.

Jay coughs into his hand and presses his fingers together, on top of his knee. "*Well.*"

"*Sophie,*" says Virginia, in a low voice.

Sophie just sips her tea. "So it's Father's decision, don't you think? I'll speak to him about it as soon as he arrives home from his workshop, and we'll let you know what we decide."

"You don't think we should perhaps toss a few dates into the air, just for speculation?"

"No. I think we should wait."

"Wait?" Jay looks at Virginia, and then at the tea. "But I don't want to wait."

"Jay, you sound just like a sulky boy who hasn't got what he wanted for Christmas," Sophie says. "Surely thirty-eight years on this earth must have taught you a *little* more patience than that?"

"Now, how *can* I be patient, my love, when it's your darling self I'm going to marry? I'd have to be made of stone." He picks up her hand again—the one that doesn't contain a teacup—and presses the fingers against his lips. She's going to be left with a tattoo if he keeps this up. "I'd marry you tomorrow if I could. Tonight."

Virginia clicks her cup back into its saucer. "Mr. Ochsner. This is really unsuitable."

"I'm sorry." He grins at her, the kind of effortless, lopsided smile that must have gotten him anything he wanted, at one time. When he was a child. "She's just irresistible, isn't she? And once a confirmed bachelor makes up his mind that he's going to marry, why, he doesn't want to remain single a minute longer than necessary."

Sophie rests her teacup on her leg, right near the pocket where Octavian Rofrano's telephone number waits for her to act upon it. *Now*, she thinks. *Now* is the moment when she should speak.

Open your mouth, Sophie. Say what needs to be said. *Speak*, for God's sake.

Sophie opens her mouth, but a grim, fatherly voice emerges from the doorway before the words stand a chance.

"My thoughts *exactly*, Mr. Ochsner."

She's a coward.

All she had to do, really, was to stand up and say those words. Stand up and say, "I'm very sorry, the two of you; I know you both desire this marriage to take place as soon as possible. But I'm afraid I've made a mistake. I was swept along by the excitement of it all, by my inexperience, by my eagerness to do what everyone wants of me, and now that I've had a chance to reflect on what it all means—why, I just can't. Not with Mr. Ochsner, anyway. And that's it."

A good speech, isn't it? Full of resolve, a dignified reflection. Impossible to argue. A girl who knows her own mind and isn't going to let you persuade her otherwise. She rehearsed the words to herself as she sat there on the sofa next to Mr. Ochsner, while Virgo poured Father a cup of tea, and Father and Mr. Ochsner discussed their mutual satisfaction with the match. (Why don't they marry each other, then?) Several times, she cleared her throat and set down her teacup. Several times, when someone posed her a question, she prepared to reply in the manner of the paragraph above.

And could not.

The look on her father's face just strangled the words in her throat. The pig iron in his eyes pressed and pressed against her resolute vowels and courageous consonants, until they crumbled against the wall of her esophagus, ashes to ashes, drenched in tea.

Now Jay is rising to his feet, beaming from every surface. Even his hands are beaming. They are going to be married on the fourteenth of February! Just a small ceremony, followed by dinner on Thirty-Second Street, only family and the odd close friend. And then off for the honeymoon! Father thinks South America is a splendid idea. Stay as long as you like. He'll look out for a house for the newlyweds, have it all ready and fixed up by the time you return.

"Father," Sophie says, "may I speak to you for a moment?"

"Sophie. We don't want to be rude."

"Oh, I'm in no hurry," says Jay, checking his watch to be sure. "Though I guess it wouldn't do any harm to stop by the office and see if I'm supposed to be in court."

"Dear me! You'd better be off, then."

"Ha! Only joking, dear heart. I practice corporate law, don't you know. Never spent a day in court in my life."

"Sophie," says Father, "why don't you see Mr. Ochsner out?"

The hallway is chillier than the parlor. Sophie hands Jay his coat and his round hat from the stand against the wall. He puts them on and winds his scarf about his throat. Sophie stands carefully back, but that doesn't stop him from reaching out to take her by the shoulders. "They aren't coming out yet, are they?" he asks.

"Not yet."

"Good." He bends down and kisses her, so forcefully that Sophie staggers back against the opposite wall and gasps into his tea-scented mouth.

"Mr. Ochsner!"

He goes on kissing her. He hasn't put on his gloves yet—they're resting on the small console next to the umbrella stand—and his hands slip downward from her shoulders to the edge of her blouse. She works her fingertips into the space between his rib cage and her chest and pushes him away.

"Someone's coming!"

"I don't hear anyone." As if he's listening, or even cares. His eyelids have slipped downward, maybe he's about to fall asleep, except that the rest of his face is flushed, and his mouth is toothily half-open, and his chest pumps like a small machine beneath the lapels of his black overcoat, and Sophie is astonished that she once actually *wanted* him to kiss her. That she actually once thought she wanted to marry him.

She presses her palms against the wall. "Listen to me. I don't want to get married."

"What's that?"

"I can't marry you!"

The eyelids lift; the teeth disappear. "Can't marry me? What does that mean?"

"I just can't, that's all." She tries to remember all her careful, reasoned words, but they've stuck somewhere on the wall of her skull, impossible to retrieve. "I've thought it over, and I can't."

"Nonsense." He reaches for her again. "It's just nerves, that's all."

"It's not nerves."

"Every bride gets nerves."

Sophie pushes against his ribs again, but this time his embrace is interminable. Like resisting the walls of a canyon. He holds her close and croons in her ear.

"We don't have to get married on Valentine's Day, you know. That was just an idea. We can wait a little longer, until you're used to the idea."

"I won't get used to the idea, I assure you." But her protest is muffled against the wool of his overcoat.

Jay sets her away, keeping hold of her shoulders with his wiry hands. "Then let's elope. What do you say? We could sit here turning it over in our heads until the roses start blooming, but sometimes the best thing to do is to jump right in. Like learning to swim!"

"Learning to swim?"

"Exactly! We'll run off to Niagara or someplace this weekend, and I'll show you how terrific married life can be. I'll spoil you rotten, Sophie."

"I think that's a terrible idea."

"It's a wonderful idea! You don't know what you're missing, that's all."

"I have an idea, and that's all I need."

"Now, darling." He sweeps her back into his arms. "I know there's a passionate girl inside there, just waiting to come out, and I intend to see that she breaks free. If we elope—"

A mighty shove, and she's free. "You're not listening, Jay. We're not eloping. We're not getting married. I—"

Jay puts a single finger to her lips. "Shh. Don't say any more. I understand. My sister warned me about all this. She was married young, too, to a fellow a few years older. And you know what? It all turned out just fine. There are advantages, you know, when youth marries experience. Just you put yourself at ease, darling, and let me take care of everything. Why, I'll make you so happy, you won't see straight."

He slings his hat back on his head—like a born gentleman, he's taken it off to kiss her—and winks that sleepy blue eye at her, an eye that's winked a million times to a million girls, and adds just the right amount of somnolence to make it work. She can't deny he's a charming man, if you liked that kind of charm. She can't deny his classy fingertips, his creamy self-satisfaction, his ability to show her the world and all that's in it. Maybe a week ago, he *was* just the right man for her. Just the right ticket out of this black-and-white tiled hallway on Thirty-Second Street and into the wide blue-skied world. Even Father approved.

But that was last week. That was before Connecticut.

"But I'm not—" she begins, but Jay Ochsner is already opening the door, waving his hand in the air, departing in a breeze of cold, dirty air.

The breath goes out of her. Her brave shoulders deflate, and then she straightens and kicks the door, leaving a small dent in the glossy new paint.

"Sophie, my dear," comes a fatherly voice behind her, quite calm, "did I hear you properly?"

Sophie spins.

Father stands before her, arms akimbo atop his spindly hips. The pig iron is back in his eyes, double strength. His hair, a little greasy from his labors, falls in thick pieces onto his forehead. Actually, he's still a handsome man, if he were cleaned up properly from the hours spent dogging over his latest design. If he were a gentleman like Jay Ochsner, who seemed to stop off at work only when the whim struck. But Father, for all his shiny new wealth, is a working man. He doesn't give a damn about the money and the leisure that ought to come with it; he's only happy when he's absorbed in some project: so absorbed that he can't think about anything else, until his whole world has sunk into a few precise millimeters of metal that might or might not change the course of civilization.

Father's not a gentleman, and it shows. His skin is tough, his clothes are unkempt. In the symmetry of his features, there's an accidental air, utterly untended and mostly unnoticed. He needs a wife, the way a lawn needs a gardener. Funny, Sophie's only just thought of it now.

A wife, Father. That's what you need. Two grown-up daughters just aren't enough anymore.

She says clearly, "I said, I don't want to marry Mr. Ochsner after all."

"That's what I thought."

"So it's off. The wedding. You can explain the whole thing to Mr. Ochsner. He doesn't seem to be taking my word for it."

"No, of course not." Far too calm. He pushes his hair back from his forehead and tugs at his right ear-lobe. An old tic. Means he's thinking about something. Pondering. "And what, may I ask, do you propose to do instead? Find someone else to marry?"

For some reason, this question ignites a certain spark of defiance inside Sophie's belly. She tips her chin upward. "I don't see that I need to marry anyone at all. I'm thinking of getting a job, in fact."

"A job! Well, now."

"Everyone's getting jobs these days. Girls, I mean. You can't just sit around anymore, waiting to get married. I might take a stenography course, or maybe work at a magazine. Or an engineer's office. You must remember how clever I am with mechanics. It wasn't *that* long ago."

"Oh, I see. Seems my daughter's been out acquiring a few modern ideas."

The air in the hallway is quite cold. Sophie feels the hairs prickling her arms, the hardness of the tiles beneath her shoes. Father's not bothered by cold, of course. He's spent so much time in his drafty old workshop, he's impervious. As if he's got some kind of internal combustion in operation, right inside his rib cage, chugging out faithful quantities of British thermal units to keep him toasty beneath that tough old skin.

"Yes, I have. I have lots of modern ideas," she says bravely. "It's a new age, isn't it? We've done away with the old world."

"Have you, now? I don't know about that. Looks pretty solid around here to me."

"Well, the war, for one thing. The old ideas brought us nothing but misery and death, and it's time we threw off the shackles of the past and—"

"Do you know what I think, Sophie?"

"Yes, Father?"

"I think you don't know a damned thing, that's what. Getting a job? I guess that's not really a choice for most girls, is it? Never has been. There's just a few of you lucky enough to have someone to provide for the family, without your having to get your own hands dirty. And now jobs are the fashion. The new craze. It's going to emancipate you, is that the idea?"

"I just think it would be much more interesting and useful than running around doing nothing."

Father rubs and tugs at his earlobe. Rolls and worries it. "Well, I think you have no idea what it means to work for a living. I think you imagine it's a fine and pretty thing, the world out there, and it's not."

"I don't think it's fine and pretty at all. I think it's *interesting.*"

"Interesting! You don't know what interesting is, Sophie, or you'd be glad not to have it. I thought . . ." The hand drops away from his ear and falls to his side. "I thought, when you finished school, I thought maybe it was time to give you a bit more freedom, to let you make a few young friends and see a little more of life. Both of you. And look what it's done."

As if on cue, a thin cry drifts down the stairs, shushed quickly.

Father waves his hand at the hallway behind him. "You see? Virginia's got a baby on her hands and some kind of new-fangled phantom of a husband who doesn't see fit to visit. *You* think you should be out in the world, getting your hands dirty, instead of starting a nice clean virtuous new life with an upstanding member of society. You have no idea, the two of you, no *idea* what it takes to make a real life, out of raw clay, out of your own two hands." He holds up his palms, his knobby fingers. "You see this? All I want is for my two girls to start their own families, to have a brand-new life. To go pure and unstained from this house into a better one. I thought, if they can just have new names. A new start."

"Oh, Father—"

"But it seems I've made a mistake. You don't have a clue, Sophie, not a *clue* what waits out there for the unwary woman. You think you're so modern. You think I'm just a conservative old fool, sticking to the old ways. But I'm right. You'll see that I'm right."

Sophie's beginning to shiver. It must be the cold. She folds her arms and meets her father's gaze: an act that requires all the bravery she can muster out of the contents of her pocket. The slip of paper etched with a promising number. "What does that mean?"

"No more going out with that Schuyler girl, for one thing. No more sneaking out—don't think I don't know about that—and no more question of hiring yourself out for money. We've got plenty of money; I've seen to that."

"You can't keep me trapped in here!"

"Can't I? I can, Sophie, but I won't. You're a good girl. I know you won't disobey me. Will you, Sophie?"

His voice, as he says this, is so dreadful it might as well be a threat. Sophie knows that voice well; it's been her companion all her life. Since her earliest memory, her father's voice has tugged on her conscience, dragged on her shame and her desire to please him. To elicit some small smile or word of praise. The choice is always clear: she can be a good girl, or she can disobey him. And she has always chosen the former, hasn't she? She's always been a good girl.

Sophie wavers, physically *wavers*, there on her feet in the chilly hall. Her father's face swims before her eyes, and she sees, for a brief instant, the view from a turret window toward the sea, except that it's summer instead of winter, and there is a clean white sailboat beating hard for the lighthouse, against the wind, tack on tack, and she cannot tear her gaze away.

Then it's gone.

Sophie turns to the hall stand and lifts her coat from its peg.

"No," she says, and she walks right out the door, without her hat.

Chapter 10

Every man wants a woman to appeal to his better side,
his nobler instincts, and his higher nature—and another
woman to help him forget them.

—HELEN ROWLAND

THERESA

About the same time

Billy's waiting for me at the apartment. My youngest. I'm afraid I spoiled him, once upon a time,
but then you're apt to do that with your baby. You want
to hold onto his precious youth with both hands, because it's your youth too, isn't it? If *he's* still a baby, you
can't be all that old yourself.

He's not a baby now, however. He jumps from one
of the armchairs in the drawing room, and his polished blond head nearly scrapes against the ceiling.

He snatches a cigarette from his mouth and says, "Ma! There you are!"

I accept his kiss and ask him what kind of nerve he's got, smoking his filthy cigarettes in my drawing room. He puts out the gasper. I tell him that's better, and then I ask why he's here at all. Isn't Princeton keeping track of its freshmen anymore?

(And don't call me *Ma*, for God's sake. This is Manhattan Island, not the middle of the Oklahoma Territory.)

"Mama, Oklahoma's been a state for a while now," he protests, and then, agreeably childlike, he seems to remember why he's here in the first place. "Look, what's going on? I got a hysterical telegram from Ollie this morning, something about the two of you getting a divorce."

I remove my gloves and hat and toss them on the nearest table. "I am most certainly *not* divorcing your brother. Would you mind pouring me a drink, darling?"

He skids to the cabinet. "You know what I mean!"

"If you're speaking about your father and me, then yes. It's true. I suppose Papa must have written to Ollie already—"

Billy whirls around, empty glass in hand. His face is tragic. "Mama!"

"Would you mind with that drink, darling? Parched."

"You can't let him do it." Rattle of glassware, clink of bottle stopper. "You just can't!"

"How do you know it wasn't *me* who asked your father for a divorce?"

"Because you'd never do that. You've always stuck together, even when . . ." His hands pause in their work.

"Even when he had other women?"

"You weren't supposed to know about that."

"Darling," I say gently, "the drink."

He brings me my sherry, and a sleek martini for himself. He sits next to me on the sofa, looking adorably helpless. His lower lip is pink and trembling as it accepts the absurd rim of the glass.

"Now listen," I say. "It's not so bad. Lots of people get divorces these days. Look at the Astors, my goodness."

Billy nods miserably.

"Papa and I will always remain the best of friends, and—well." I'm trying to think of some other hopeful aspect of the situation, and I find I can't. *I'm sure you'll adore your new stepmother* hardly seems tactful, at the moment. And I can't possibly mention the Boy, not yet. The Boy's only five years older than Billy. The Boy's younger than Billy's brothers, both of them. (Though, to be fair, Ollie's only got him beat by a few months.

Another fact I'd do well not to point out, at a tender moment like this.)

"Is Dad going to marry his mistress?" asks Billy.

The sherry sputters. "You're not supposed to know about that."

"I'm not a kid, Ma. For Chrissakes."

"William Marshall. I don't care what sort of language they allow you at college these days, but in this house, we speak like civilized human beings."

He picks himself up abruptly from the sofa. Billy's always moved around like that, in sudden, sharp movements like the chop of an axe. I don't know where he gets it from. There's nothing sharp about Sylvo, unless you count the pressed edges of his clothing, and his valet's responsible for those.

Billy jolts to a stop before the enormous gilt-framed Church landscape that hangs on the wall opposite the fireplace. Some Adirondack view or another. "It's sort of rich, in a way. You two getting a divorce, at the same time that Uncle Ox decides to get married."

"A reversal of the natural order, you mean?"

"Something like that. I guess you could call it irony."

"Modern life is packed with irony, I'm told."

He lifts his hand and fingers the bumps and swirls on the gilded frame. "Nothing's the same. Not since Tommy died."

"No."

"Things used to be happy around here. We used to have people over. You and Dad and all those dinner parties. Remember those parties you used to throw?"

"Such fun."

"Everybody used to come. Isn't this a grand place for a party? All these rooms, all this space. All this pretty art. Now it's all going to waste. Everything's going to waste, the whole world." Billy whirls and points a pair of accusing eyebrows in my direction. "You're letting it rot, because you can't get over Tommy being gone."

"That's not true."

"When was the last time you threw a party around here?"

"We've had people over, all the time."

"But a *party*, Ma."

I set down the empty glass and unfold from the sofa, as I used to do, except it doesn't offer quite the same effect, now that he's so much taller than I am. "That's got nothing to do with your brother."

Billy meets my eye for a second or two, and then he hangs his head down toward his drink. Swish, swish. "I'm sorry, Ma. I didn't mean it that way. I just miss the old days, that's all. Just wish we could go back to how things were, before the rotten war came along and ruined everything. Go back to when we were happy."

"Darling, parties don't make people happy."

"Well, they're a start, aren't they? At least a party gives you the chance to pretend you're happy."

He swallows down the last of his martini in the flick of an elbow, and I observe him minutely as he strides back to the cabinet and pours himself another. He's very good at it. Coats the ice with vermouth, strains it back out, adds the gin. Probably had lots of practice, and yet he's only just nineteen. About the same age as Ox's girl. Wasn't Prohibition supposed to put a stop to all this expert drinking? I distinctly remember one of those dour firebrands promising something like that: a return to a godly, sober family life, everyone gathered by the matrimonial fireside, sipping their . . . well, whatever it was you sipped, when you couldn't have a real drink. Milk? Lemonade?

Now look at us, a couple of years later. We're a nation of incipient alcoholics, even the youth. Even especially the youth. I suppose that's irony, too.

"Maybe you're right, darling," I say.

"About what?"

"Maybe this apartment could stand a good party."

The telephone jingles just as I'm headed for the door, valise in hand. I attempt to sneak out anyway, but the housekeeper pounds after me. It's your brother, Mrs. Marshall! He says it's important!

"She wants to break off the engagement, Sis," Ox tells me, tone of disbelief.

I close my eyes. Refuse to panic.

"Oh, Ox. What did you say to her?"

"Nothing! I did exactly as you said. I brought flowers and chocolate. I talked about a honeymoon in South America, sunshine, the works. I asked her to set a date. And do you know what she did? She practically threw me out the door."

"Maybe she doesn't like South America."

"I can't believe you're joking at a time like this."

"Ox, there's nothing to worry about. She's just young, that's all. Maybe she's had a chat with her mother about the duties of marriage, and it's given her a case of nerves."

"Her mother's dead, Sisser."

"An aunt, then. I wouldn't worry about it."

A whooshy sigh at the other end. "You're certain?"

"Absolutely. It's a terribly nerve-wracking idea, for a sheltered girl like that."

"You don't think she's frigid, do you?"

"Frigid? What on earth does that mean?"

"I mean maybe she doesn't like sex."

"Ox, my goodness, she's a virgin of nineteen years. How does *she* know if she likes sex or not? For heaven's sake. That's *your* job. *Make* her like it. You've got a couple of decades worth of know-how, I should think. Use them to your advantage." I tap one fingernail against the base of the telephone. It's the ancient Western Electric candlestick we keep in the hallway; not nearly so nice as the Grabaphone in Sylvo's study, and certainly not as private. There is a niche in the wall, specially designed for telephone use, but you've got to stand against the wall and make it snappy, because there's nowhere to sit. My diamond bracelet slides down my wrist to clink against the nickel plating, and I add (inspired): "A bit of jewelry wouldn't hurt, either. Jewelry works wonders on the female nerves."

"I can't afford jewelry."

"Ask Mother for some of hers. She never wears it, anyway. Tell her it's for the party I'm going to throw you."

"What party?"

"Didn't I promise you two angels an engagement party? It's going to be the show of the season. One week from today. No! Two weeks. Everyone's going to be there, and I'd just like to see your little bird slip her traces after that. Now I really must be off, darling. Keep your chin up. Loss of confidence is fatal in these matters. Take her out on the town, show her a ripping time or two. Jazz conquers virtue, I've heard."

There's another despondent sigh. "I don't know, Sis. I was thinking maybe I should give her some room to breathe. Think it over, realize she can't do without me."

"No!" The word bursts straight into the mouthpiece, causing a static fizz to fill the wires, causing operators up and down Manhattan Island to jump right out of their seats. "Absolutely not, Ox. Don't even think of it. You've got to keep her right under your wing, do you hear me? Don't let her spend a single evening alone."

"Sis, she'll be sick of me!"

"Now, what kind of talk is that? You're getting married. You'll have plenty of time to ignore each other after the ceremony, trust me."

"But—"

"I'm not going to hear another word of this, Ox. Now's not the time to give up. You just march right back there and take the girl in your arms and kiss her senseless."

"But I—"

"Good-bye, Ox."

I drop the earpiece in the cradle and press my back against the wall. But just for a second or two. I wasn't raised to slouch.

The first time I visited the Boy in his brand-new Village apartment, I was horrified. He picked it out himself, of course; he wouldn't hear of me tramping around the Village on his behalf, and the result, I suppose, was exactly what you'd expect.

I didn't say anything. As far as the Boy knew, I was charmed by the bohemian furniture and the fin de siècle draperies, the what-once-was burgundy velvet and the more-hole-than Oriental rugs. Anyway, the furnishings weren't the object of the exercise, were they? And who needs plates when you're too busy to eat.

But I took note, nonetheless—a comprehensive mental inventory, you might say—and over the course of the next year and a half I've smuggled in various household comforts, one by one, like a modern-day Ram Dass, pretending not to do a thing while the Boy pretends not to notice. Satisfactory on all sides, wouldn't you think?

Why, even now, packed inside my valise, I've got a stack of fresh linens and some fine French soap, which I intend to distribute discreetly before the Boy arrives home from work, so we can maintain our pleasant little pantomime. But the Boy, it seems, has beaten me to it. The door is already unlocked, and when I push it open and peek around the corner, he's standing in his shirtsleeves by the window, looking over the jagged Himalayan range of rooftops as if contemplating a possible crossing.

I set down the valise next to my shoes. "Hello there, Boyo. You're home early."

"As ordered." He turns away and leans over the lamp table to stub out a cigarette. "How are you, Theresa?"

I remove my hat and gloves and toss them on a credenza that used to decorate the back hallway at Windermere. "Billy's heard the news. He stopped by to console me."

"So it's decided, then?"

"Of course it's decided. Sylvo isn't the kind of man who second-guesses himself." I unbutton my coat and slide it down my arms, and it's uncharacteristic of the Boy that he doesn't cross the room to assist me in this maneuver. There's a hat stand near the door, and I place the coat on one of the hooks and turn to my lover, straightening my dress, patting my cheeks, like a nervous young bride.

The Boy, naturally, hasn't moved a muscle. One hand sits on his hips, knuckles first, and the other, I now perceive, holds a drink of some kind. Nearly finished. The light is already dying behind him, and a terrible shadow crosses his face, as if he's transformed into stone. Maybe he has. Maybe it's just a granite Boy who confronts me now, a carved statue without blood or bone or beating heart. Maybe I'm too late for him.

I nod to the glass. "I don't suppose you've got another one of those?"

"Of course." He speaks! He moves! He makes his way to the kitchen, leaving me to contemplate the vast difference between his style of movement and Billy's, and how strange it was that two young men born less than five years apart could evolve along such divergent paths. The apartment is chilly, and I realize that the Boy hasn't lit a fire. The radiator bangs fruitlessly near the window. I cross my arms and tell myself it's because of the cold.

Such is the miniature nature of the kitchen, I catch glimpses of the Boy as he goes about his work, moving precisely between icebox and cabinet. When he returns, I extract one hand to accept the drink, and I clink it against the Boy's own glass, which is newly filled. "To fresh beginnings," I say, and to everyone's shock, my own most of all, a pair of tears springs in tandem from my eyes.

"Oh, Theresa," the Boy says, and he sets down the drink and gathers my poor sobbing self into his arms, against his chest, which is so much larger and warmer and substantial than my own, a thick rock shelter of a chest. "Oh, Theresa," he says again, caressing my back while the tears continue to fall, inexplicable and unchecked and entirely—I swear it—unstudied. "You'll be all right. We'll be all right."

You may or may not have believed me this morning, when I told the Boy he was my first love affair. Regards the truth, I'll let you decide for yourself. But I will say this, beyond all doubt: I was the *Boy's* first lover.

He didn't actually say so, of course, and I didn't ask. (One doesn't ask a man a question like that, if he doesn't volunteer the information beforehand.) But I couldn't help noticing the hesitant way in which he unfastened my dress for the first time. The wondering way in which he beheld each new fragment of exposed skin, as if he were translating an ancient and unknown poem into his native language, with the aid of a secret dictionary. Why, he hardly even knew how to kiss, at first. I had to nudge his lips open and demonstrate the tender inner workings of the caress, though—to be fair—he caught on like lightning, once he got the general idea.

I unwrapped him carefully, like the gift he was, and he shuddered when my fingertips encountered his skin, as if he thought I might hurt him. I don't think either of us said a word. The bedroom was hot and quite small—I can't quite remember how we got there—and I sat down on the bed and kissed his stomach, and that was when his muscles convulsed. That was when he came, helpless, into my possession. The moon was full and blew straight through the window onto his skin, and I thought I had never seen anything so new and perfect, so utterly clean, as the naked Boy before me. I kissed his ribs and the scars on his chest, I rose on my knees and kissed his ropy shoulders and warm neck, while my hands slid downward to encompass the curve of his buttocks.

He's mine, I thought.

I told him to open his eyes, and he did. The pupils were dilated, the encircling irises gray in the moonlight. I took his hands and showed him where to touch me, and how to touch me, but when his poor starved fingertips shook against the tips of my breasts, I could see he wasn't going to last another minute. So I drew him down on the bed and opened my merciful legs, and here's the funny thing about Nature: the Boy knew what to do with me after that. He found the rhythm in an instant, he drove and drove in the manner of a tender machine, watching my face the whole time, expression of wonder and torture, and my God, I can still feel the way my flesh hurtled at last. I can still perceive the dampness of his skin. I can still hear my cry, and his.

Afterward, in the silver quiet, I knew regret, the way you feel when you walk across a field of snow and ravage its immaculate surface, and yet your regret cannot quite swallow your primitive pleasure in the act of desecration. I suppose it helped that the pleasure was mutual. When at last he lifted his head, I was relieved to see that he was smiling. *Thank you,* he said, and I replied—what else?—*Any time.*

Any time turned out to be fifteen minutes later, and then twice more before the early midsummer dawn. By then he was practically an expert. Immensely pleased with himself, like the Boy he was. Immensely pleased, too, with the snowy multitude of footprints now corrupting his formerly pristine skin, and when I woke, rather groggily, I discovered that the smell of bacon and coffee had roused me. A new day had crept over the horizon, and the Boy was making me breakfast.

But midsummer is long past, and now it's the middle of winter. The cold drives us under the covers, and the Boy's shirt still dangles from his shoulders as he hovers above me, eyes closed, in the familiar old rhythm. The silence afterward isn't because there's too much to say, but because there's too little.

Still, I nestle myself into the warmth of his side. The heaviness of his arm comforts me. There's no smell on earth I love more than the scent of his skin, and the tobacco that burns at his fingertips into the solemn air of the bedroom, and I cannot lose all this. I cannot lose the Boy, because then there will be nothing left of me.

I suppose we fall asleep. I'm considering how hungry I am, and how I can't possibly move, can't willingly extract myself from the Boy's embrace in order to rummage dinner from the shelves of the kitchen. A terrible conundrum. Then I'm opening my eyes, and the air is much darker than it should be, and that sound in the other room turns out to be a ringing telephone.

I ought to nudge the Boy awake, but he's sleeping so peacefully I haven't the heart to disturb him. (Or so I tell myself, anyway.) I lift his arm away and rise from the bed, taking the dressing gown from the chair as I go, and the telephone is still jangling by the time I reach the living room.

"Hello," I say, just that single word, and the first thing I notice is the sound of jazz in the background, a tune with which I'm familiar. The band at the Christopher Club plays it all the time. The trumpet player—a man I much admire—favors that very riff, up and down a minor scale, ending in a mournful question.

Somewhere inside the music lies a sweet young voice that hesitates before it replies. "Hello? Hello? I'm sorry, I think I have the wrong connection. I was trying to reach SPRing 5682."

I wrap the cord around my hand and stare out the window at the purple twilight, the small and desolate lights flickering from the surrounding buildings. "No, you have the right number."

She hesitates again. "Is this Mr. Rofrano's residence?"

"Yes, it is. But I'm afraid he's fast asleep at the moment, the little dear. Would you like me to wake him for you?"

"No, thank you."

"Shall I give him a message?"

"No! No, thank you. Good—good evening."

The line goes dead, and I replace the handset in the cradle. The lamp is still burning on the nearby table, and beneath the lamp sits my drink, golden, untouched, the ice chips melted away. The bedroom door stands ajar, about a foot of black space.

I cross the room and close the door.

When I return to the telephone, I lift the handset and wait for the operator, ever so patiently.

"Exchange and number, please."

"ATWater 2203."

My brother answers right away, for which mercy I thank God. I speak softly. "Ox, darling. I don't suppose you've got your armor all shined up, have you?"

"My armor?"

"Because there's a damsel in great distress down here at the Christopher Club, probably crying into her juice this very instant, and I think you'd better ride on in to rescue her at the earliest possible opportunity."

"A damsel? Do you mean *Sophie*? At the *Christopher* Club?"

"It's my best guess, I'm afraid."

"But how—"

"*How* isn't the point at the moment, darling. The poor little thing. What's important is that someone rescues her, the sooner the better."

"All right, all right."

"That's my good brother. Make sure she's all right, won't you? And get her home intact, for heaven's sake."

There's no reply, just the satisfying click of the line going dead, and I replace the receiver and reach for the drink. I've finished half of it before I become aware of the faint breath of wind at my neck.

I turn, and the white-shouldered ghost of the Boy stands before me in the bedroom doorway. The muscles of his face are clenched in shock, and I don't suppose I shall ever forget the agonized shape of his eyes.

"You're awake," I say softly.

Chapter 11

A man's heart may have a secret sanctuary
where only one woman may enter, but it is full
of little anterooms which are seldom vacant.

—HELEN ROWLAND

SOPHIE

At the Christopher Club, the next instant

The bartender has a sympathetic face. When at last Sophie lifts her gaze from the telephone, she finds it regarding her, only a few feet away: slim brown eyes and crescent mouth. "Drink, miss?" he says, and then: "On the house."

Sophie considers the offer. "What do you suggest?"

"A nice girl like you? I can make something up."

The nod she sends him is probably numb. Certainly the rest of her is numb, a nice thick absence of feeling that coats her skin from scalp to pinkie toe. The film seems especially thick over her ears, but that might be because of the racket from the jazz band in the corner, or the buzz from the telephone receiver. Sophie had taken in the words on the other end, but the woman's voice still seems to be vibrating the bones of her inner ear, instead of penetrating to the gray matter beyond.

He's fast asleep.

Well, but didn't the lady in the Sterling Bates foyer say something similar? *He's gone home for the day, I'm afraid,* in an awfully professional voice, deflating Sophie's buoyant pink-cheeked hopes just like that. So now Octavian was asleep. Probably he'd had a hard day at work, or maybe—oh, dreadful thought!—maybe he was *sick*! All that cold air yesterday. Sophie made him sit outside, while the winter wind blew straight on from Long Island Sound, turning an incipient cold into full-blown influenza, and likely pneumonia as well. Poor Octavian!

But the numbness in Sophie's cheek and jaw suggests otherwise. Though her mental faculties seem to have taken on the sluggish syncopation of the music playing behind her, they still retain the sense to wonder why, if Octavian had the 'flu, his female companion should seem so unconcerned for his health—*the little dear,* she said—and, above all, why she should have the unquestioned right to wake him from his slumbers.

Sophie knows the answer to that question, of course. She isn't stupid, nor half so naïve as she has the right to be. But the gray matter is nonetheless reluctant to accept this obvious explanation. The gray matter would rather remain numb, thank you very much. Numb and unreachable. She accepts the drink from the bartender and arranges her lips around the rim. Not so bad, if you remembered not to breathe.

She smiles her thanks, and the bartender's mouth makes a hesitant movement, as if he's thinking of asking a question. But the music is loud and shrill, and a gaggle of clamorous patrons has just burst through the door, and he shrugs and walks away instead, wiping his hands on his dishcloth.

The bartender. The bar. So forbidden and masculine, an unimaginable place for a nice girl to find herself—*alone!*—until now. Until suddenly girls and boys are going to saloons together, and they aren't called saloons any more. A whole new vocabulary is springing up overnight, it seems, like mushrooms or crocuses, all clustered around the underground slaking of illegal thirst, and it seems the more illegal the thirst is, the more ordinary and acceptable it's become to slake it in mixed company, among strangers. And the vocabulary has something to do with that, doesn't it? Hooch, speakeasy, blotto. Silly words, trivializing the laws they're breaking. Trivializing everything in the world. Sophie lays her palm on the dented brown surface before her. The wood is slightly tacky, as if someone's spilled a drink or two. Something as sugary as the concoction in Sophie's other hand.

Down the length of the bar, the newcomers are giggling and screeching. Three men and two women. The women are dressed in black satin trimmed with feathers and glittering beads, and sequined bands run across their foreheads like midnight canals. Their lipstick is so red, it's almost black, and Sophie finds herself mesmerized by the graphic movement of their mouths. Realizes, as she does so, that she doesn't belong here. She's not one of them. She's not a member of the tribe. Maybe she can repeat a remembered password and gain entry, maybe they won't throw her out because they remember her from Saturday, maybe a girl has just as much right to a glass of bootleg liquor as a boy, if she wants one.

But maybe she doesn't want one.

Maybe Father's right. Maybe all this freedom doesn't make you any happier, after all. Maybe, if you take a chance, if you break out of prison and ride an ocean liner all the way across the Atlantic to a war-battered continent, all you get is a husband lost in Florida and a baby with a fever. Maybe, if you take a chance, if you break out of prison to track down the man you might be falling in love with and throw your vulnerable new heart into his hands, all you get is a worldly female voice on the other end of the telephone line, telling you you're too late.

Sophie rises from the stool. The drink is only half-finished, but she doesn't want any more. If she had a dollar bill, she would place it on the sticky wood next to the glass, but she doesn't have a dollar bill. She doesn't have a dime; that's why she came here, because she left her father's house this afternoon without even the money for a public telephone call in her coat pocket.

Virginia and Father must be frantic by now. Darkness has fallen over Manhattan, and Sophie's thirty blocks from home, and she will have to walk. Home seems awfully nice, just now. Home doesn't seem like a prison at all, next to this sweaty, cacophonous medicine cave down a narrow staircase in Greenwich Village.

The bartender appears, like magic. "You leaving?"

"Yes, I'm afraid so."

"You can't go out by yourself. Lemme call you a taxi."

A taxi sounds heavenly. Except she's broke.

"No, thank you. I can manage."

"On the house?" He smiles at her hopefully, the nicest bartender in the world. Weren't these speakeasy men supposed to have Thompson machine guns hiding under the counter? This one looks as young as she is, as fundamentally decent as a newspaper boy, except he's selling the demon liquor instead of news.

Sophie hovers. Opens her mouth. Says—

"*Sophie*! Darling. There you are."

Mrs. Marshall is terribly reassuring. "I've telephoned my brother," she says, slipping off one leather glove and then the other. "He'll be *right* down to fetch you."

"I really don't need—"

"Darling, he *wants* to." Mrs. Marshall touches the back of her hand. "He's thoroughly in love with you, you know."

"Is he?"

"Of course he is. Why, look at you! How can he help it? Octavian." She turns to the man sitting quietly to her left. "Wouldn't you fall just *headfirst* into love with our Sophie, if you weren't already going to marry me?"

How friendly she is. Of course she's laying her claim—Sophie can't fault her for that—but she doesn't seem to bear Sophie the slightest bit of resentment for having telephoned this handsome young fiancé as if she has a right to. (Another emblem of the modern new world, that you could have a husband and a fiancé at the same time, and admit that paradox publicly.) How much does Mrs. Marshall know about yesterday's drive to Connecticut? Does she know about yesterday at all? In her cheerful voice and unworried forehead, there's no sign.

As for Octavian? Who knows. Who cares. Sophie won't look at him. She hears him reply, polite and faintly agonized, but she tips up her drink to block him out. Something's building in her head, ringing in her ears, and she's afraid that if she sees Octavian's face, the thing will ignite. Maybe even explode, messily and prematurely. "There was no need for both of you to come," she says. "Especially since Mr. Rofrano was *asleep.*"

"Oh, the telephone woke him up, I'm afraid. And of course he wouldn't *hear* of leaving either of us without some sort of protection, at this hour. What on earth were you thinking, my dear, coming to the Christopher Club all by yourself?"

"I didn't have any money for a telephone," Sophie mumbles.

"Dear me. Are you in trouble of some kind?"

"No." Sophie looks up and smiles. "Not anymore. Just a little quarrel with my father, and I've realized he was right, after all."

"Good girl. Fathers usually are, you know."

What was that about the cold? Sophie is as hot as blazes now. Perspiration trickles down her back, between her breasts. Her cheeks are glowing. The backs of her legs are damp in their stockings, molding her to the round wooden seat beneath her. She can't look at Octavian, but she doesn't need to: he just sits there drinking and smoking and not saying anything. Waiting for her to acknowledge him. Waiting, no doubt, to telegraph some kind of mute apology from those fabulous chameleon eyes of his.

Waiting for her to say something. Waiting for her to toss her drink in his face and scream, *How could you? She's as old as your mother! How could you go to bed with her, after what happened between us yesterday? How could you love her? Her, Mrs. Marshall, of all people?*

Well, she won't. Sophie can be a grown-up, too. Sophie can play grown-up games, if she puts her mind to it.

"By the way, my dear," Mrs. Marshall continues, "I was absolutely serious about that engagement party. Next Saturday, I think. Or perhaps the following week, just to give ourselves enough time? We want to be sure everyone can come. Things are a bit messy because of my divorce, but we'll put our best face to the world, won't we? That's the only thing to do, when the world thinks it's caught you flat on your bottom."

Sophie says, "That sounds delightful, Mrs. Marshall."

"I'll make you the toast of the town, Sophie dear. Manhattan could really use a bright new face to rage over, and yours is both terribly bright and terribly new. I expect you'll be on a first-name basis with the society page and someone will name a dessert in your honor. Or a cocktail."

Octavian makes a noise in his throat, almost inaudible, and finishes his drink.

"And you *must* call me Theresa," Mrs. Marshall continues. "We're going to be sisters, after all. The best of friends."

A welcome draft hits Sophie's cheek, and she turns hopefully to the door.

"Jay!" she exclaims, and she springs from her seat and throws her arms around his astonished neck and kisses him, right there in front of everybody, in front of Octavian and Mrs. Marshall and the bartender and the whole world, until the women in their black feathers and sequined headbands start laughing and applauding, and the band, just returning to the instruments after a break, breaks out into a jazzy trumpet rendition of Mendelssohn.

"Don't forget!" calls Mrs. Marshall, as a beaming Jay leads her out the door to his waiting car. "The first Saturday of February! The party of the year. I promise."

Chapter 12

The hardest task in a girl's life is to prove to a man that his intentions are serious.

—HELEN ROWLAND

THERESA

Returning home, a moment later

I don't know why you're so disgruntled," I say to the Boy. My arm is tucked securely inside the corner of his elbow, but I can tell he doesn't want it there. I can feel his skin recoiling from mine.

"She's just a girl, Theresa. You're toying with her, like a cat."

"I'm not toying with her. I wish her nothing but joy. I'll do anything to make certain she's happy with Jay."

He doesn't reply. We emerge from the building and into the open air. It's past eight o'clock, and the streets are settling into quiet, the Manhattan sort of quiet, in which taxis rattle past and people hurry down the side-walk, but at a lessened pace, a reduced volume. You can breathe a little, even if the air is dank and sour and oily, and smells of rotting garbage.

I stop in my tracks and pull the Boy around to face me. "Listen to me," I whisper. "Look at me. Do you think I'd wish a marriage like mine on any girl? Do you think I'd wish that kind of heartbreak on her? Grief and divorce and everything in pieces?"

He looks sorrowfully into my face. "No."

"Of course not." I place my hands on his cheeks and savor his warmth through the leather. A nearby streetlamp gives off a gaseous yellow glow. "She needs out of that house. She needs a husband to give her a loving freedom, and a friend to guide her through the thickets. I'll be that friend, Boyo, I swear it. I'll keep my brother on the straight and narrow, I'll make sure he's a good husband. Whatever she needs, I'll give it to her."

That's all. That's all I can say to him, because I've run out of oxygen. I've burned it all up in honesty, and the back of my throat is scorched. I suppose you don't believe me. But I assure you, I'm no villain. I'm well aware that I've taken something our sweet Sophie wants, because I happen to need it more, and because a girl like that can't possibly appreciate a Boy like him.

302 • BEATRIZ WILLIAMS

But I want to repay her. Maybe there's nothing I can give her to make up for the loss of the Boy, no possible gift in my possession, but I'll try. I'll give her what I can.

And maybe the Boy, looking down on me like that, in such a terrifying way, doesn't understand all this. Maybe he does. Either way, he's not telling.

But he does bend down and place a chaste kiss on my lips, and we continue next door and up the stairs to his apartment, where he lets me in with his key.

Chapter 13

*Before marriage, a man declares that he would
lay down his life to serve you; after marriage, he
won't even lay down his newspaper to talk to you.*

—HELEN ROWLAND

SOPHIE

**Returning home, a quarter of an hour after
that**

J ay keeps his hand on the small of her back, all the
way up the front steps. *Just let me do the talking,* he
said, on the way over, and she lets him do the talking.

"Here she is, safe and sound!" he announces cheerfully, and Sophie is smothered by a sudden descent of
arms and kisses. "We had a grand time."

"All that time, she was with you?" Father says.

"Yep." Jay nods with vigor, and then his face turns
beautifully puzzled. "Wait a minute. You didn't *know*
she was with me?"

"She didn't leave a word behind."

Jay turns a reproachful gaze on Sophie. "Darling. Your poor father." Back to Father. "She came running after me, when I left. We went out to tea and had a long talk. I guess we lost track of time."

What a brilliant liar, Sophie thinks. His face so open and guileless, the untruths slipping so glibly from his mouth. The funny thing is, she rather admires him for it. Maybe this talent of his doesn't bode well for married life, but there's something so alluring about a man who can pull the wool over Father's eyes—*Father's* eyes!—without even troubling to blush.

In the middle of Sophie's present misery, it's the only small joy.

"Well," Father says, "all's well that ends well, I guess."

"Indeed it is, sir. But there's more good news. I'm delighted to say that Sophie's agreed to a Valentine's Day wedding, and what's more, my sister's going to make it all official with a grand party at her apartment, the first Saturday of February. Isn't that right, Sophie darling?"

"Yes, it is," Sophie says.

And Father's slapping Jay's back, and Jay's tolerating it manfully, and the air buzzes with masculine congratulation and relief. Sophie takes a kiss on each cheek, and she even slips her arm around Jay's, just to be a good sport.

Only Virginia remains quiet, near the stairs, and her face is heavy with some expression that might, or might not, be the anxious exhaustion of a mother tending a sick child.

Don't worry, Sophie wants to tell her. I know what I'm doing. Just you wait and watch me.

But Virginia doesn't wait. She turns and treads back up the stairs, back up to Evelyn's little room on the top floor, and Sophie turns back to her fiancé and keeps her secrets to herself.

The New York Herald-Times, May 31, 1922

TIT AND TATTLE, BY PATTY CAKE

As promised, the scrumptious Mr. Octavian Rofrano climbed into the witness box of the Trial of the Century this morning, electric and refreshing as one of those thunderstorms that tumbled over the horizon late yesterday afternoon, breaking the heat at last.

Much to everyone's disappointment, he showed no sign of the wounds he sustained early last February, when the whole affair came to the attention of the public and the police department. His refusal to press any charges against the accused, you remember, has remained one of the most celebrated (and speculated-upon) facts of the whole case. Nonetheless, here he is, called as a witness by the prosecution, so I suppose he had a greater scheme in mind.

Mr. Rofrano is one of those rare specimens, a very young man—he was one of our greatest aces in the late war, counting eleven enemy planes to his credit—who has the self-possession of the middle-aged. I would not actually call him handsome. His face is a little too lean and hungry for my drawing-room taste. But his eyes are an arresting shade of aquamarine blue, his hair is dark and glossy, his complexion is somewhat swarthy, and he exudes a great deal of energy without moving an inch. There you have it.

He answered the attorney's questions with ready honesty, if not exactly an excess of words. As a friend of the lucky Mrs. Marshall, he told us, he was asked by that lady to do a little quiet investigation into the nether branches of the Fortescue tree, because not every girl, however dazzlingly wealthy, makes a suitable bride for a family so old and august as the Ochsners, who have led New York society since the Revolution. (This last observation is mine, by the way: Mr. Rofrano answers all questions with utmost economy and no opinions whatsoever; the prosecuting attorney, like a surgical dentist, is made to work hard for every fact he draws out.) He undertook his appointed task in the usual underhanded manner, by insinuating himself into the friendship of the Fortescues, until he was able to discover that they were not, in fact, Fortescues at all. That Mr. John Ephraim Fortescue was really none other than Mr. Montague Charles Faninal, who had disappeared from public notice sixteen years earlier following the murder of his wife in the family home in Greenwich, Connecticut.

Upon further questioning, Mr. Rofrano admitted that his interest in the case was more than casual, for he himself had been raised to manhood within that same unfortunate building. He would not otherwise have made the connection, it seems, because when asked how his suspicions were first raised—considering, that is, how well the accused had covered all traces of his previous existence—Mr. Rofrano replied simply, "His ears."

(Having been presented with an unobstructed prospect of said organs—perhaps *wings* will provide the reader with a more accurate description—for the past three days, I can confirm that no amount of careful disguise, by beard or by hat, could obscure this singular and unfortunate feature of the accused's person. If, as Mr. Rofrano admits, he has studied this case from childhood—photographs, newspaper articles, and the like—I don't wonder that he should look upon those ears with the same familiarity as a long-lost relative.)

In any case, once the first alarm was rung, Mr. Rofrano's quick intellect began to gather other telling details: the names and ages of the daughters, the long absence of a mother, the curious reclusiveness of the family despite its riches. The singular profession of the accused, and his habit of disappearing for fathomless hours into his workshop. Further inquiries—such as that made of

Mr. Philip Schuyler—soon hardened his suspicions into certainty.

The prosecution then attempted a line of questioning to do with Mr. Rofrano's childhood memories of the case, to which the defense objected—*Hearsay!*—on the grounds that he had obtained his information from a neighbor, unreliable because of their mutual youth and the dozen or so years that had passed in the meantime. The defense then took over cross-examination of the witness, to which Mr. Rofrano responded—to the extent one can determine Mr. Rofrano's emotional state at all— with some relief.

Why, the defense wanted to know, having formed this startling suspicion, did Mr. Rofrano not immediately report his discovery to the police? Mr. Rofrano replied that he had no proof at all, that the crime had occurred nearly two decades earlier, and that he had no wish to inflict such an ordeal upon the family of the accused, who were only young girls at the time of the awful event, and who would be greatly disturbed to learn all the grisly details of their poor mother's demise. As the younger Miss Fortescue was engaged to be married, and the elder was already bound in matrimony, they would soon be removed from their father's immediate physical influence in any case. On the other hand, Mr. Rofrano worried the threat of prosecution could inspire the heretofore complacent Mr. Fortescue—if, indeed, he *were* the killer—to commit some desperate act that might place the young ladies in danger.

Weighing all these considerations, and with due respect for the presumption of innocence, Mr. Rofrano said he decided that the safety and happiness of Miss Fortescue and her sister must, in this case, be placed above the demands of criminal justice.

Mr. Rofrano uttered this speech—longer by many degrees than any previous statement—without a single glance toward the two ladies in question, nor the accused himself. As to whether his words elicited any emotion from the former Misses Fortescue, I had no way to determine, other than the fact that both remained quietly in their seats, and disdained any audible reaction.

The defense, perhaps not surprisingly, did not dwell upon the dramatic events of the fourth of February, and Mr. Rofrano was dismissed with the admonition to hold himself ready for recall, should either side require further testimony from him.

Adjournment was then called until the next morning. As the temperature in the courtroom had, by this time, descended to a more habitable height, there was some disappointment that we would not have the opportunity to hear from Mrs. Lumley, the Scarsdale housewife who once served as a humble char in the Faninal household in Greenwich, now raised to respectability by a munificent husband, and on whose testimony the prosecution's case is expected to hinge.

I suppose that in criminal justice, as in all else, such good things must come in their own time.

Chapter 14

You will never win if you never begin.

—HELEN ROWLAND

SOPHIE

February the fourth, just past seven o'clock in the evening

Father's waiting in the parlor when Sophie sails down the stairs in her party clothes. She was hoping to avoid him, but you can't avoid Father when he wants to be found. He folds the newspaper and climbs to his feet, and to her surprise he's wearing evening dress, black and white and crisp all over.

"Why, you're not *coming*?" she gasps.

"Why not? It's my daughter's engagement party, isn't it?" He meets her dismay with an unexpected smile, and Sophie, bewildered, detects wave after tiny wave of satisfaction shimmering from his skin, like he's applied some strange new variety of shaving soap with a tonic effect. A different man from the one who stomped home from the workshop last night, muttering dusty nothings into the wallpaper.

"Yes, but—"

He laughs. Laughs! Laughs and uses her old nickname. "Never fear, Baby. I'll come along later and linger at the back. You won't even notice I'm there."

Sophie hovers. Wavers. Starts forward a few steps and brushes his satin lapel. Where on earth did he get that jacket? Her fingers are shaking a little; her brain is recalculating. Somewhere in the corner, the gramophone is singing tinnily, some kind of sentimental nonsense. "Don't be silly. I *want* you there. It's just a surprise, that's all. Last I heard, you'd decided not to come. It was just me and Virginia."

"Well, it's not my kind of party, you know. It's the kind of thing your mother would have loved." He takes her fingers, another unexpected gesture. "But I just— well, Baby, I'm not a man of many words. I haven't been the most affectionate papa, I guess—"

"Don't be ridiculous. You're the best father in the world. You've given us a wonderful home, and a—a— that time in Europe, and . . ."

How strange, he won't let go of her hand. His eyes are steady, but without all the awful steel. She can't look away. She can't quite remember what she was saying.

Then the gaze drops. Down to their linked hands.

"I just wanted to keep you safe, that's all," he mumbles.

"Well, you've done that, all right," she says brightly, "and now look! Off we go, into the future."

"Yes. A good, solid future. Trust me on this, Baby. Ochsner will make you happy. He might seem a little rackety, but he's a good man. A good man. He'll give you everything I can't, and maybe—well, one day . . ." He looks up and finds her again, and this time it's as if he's pleading, just a little, in the corners of his eyebrows. As if there's something he needs from her.

Wonderful. Just wonderful. *Just* what Sophie needs right now, when she's all resolved, when her plans are laid. She glances over her shoulder, hoping to see Virginia descending at last, and turns back with a faint laugh. "Oh, Father. You're not getting sentimental on me, are you? It's just a party."

And the plea disappears, just like that, leaving his eyebrows back at their ordinary angles. He tugs an earlobe and steps back, dropping her hand. "Just a party. You're right. Go on and enjoy yourself, I guess. Virginia will keep an eye on you for me."

"And you'll be there, too."

"I'll be there, too. Just for the toast, mind you. I can't take any more than that."

Oh, *only* the toast, Sophie thinks. A thin-skinned bubble of laughter rises in her throat. At least he's going to get his money's worth.

Virginia's voice floats down the stairway. "Sophie! The taxi's here!"

Sophie smiles and leans forward to kiss her father's cheek. The skin is drier than she remembers, like he's transforming into paper. An old man with two grown daughters.

She pats the cheek she's just kissed: an act of supreme and modern boldness, but he doesn't seem to mind.

"It's going to be spectacular, I promise."

Sophie has this funny habit, when she's walking down the street or entering a room. She's doing it now, from the back of the taxi, in the middle of Fifth Avenue, on the way uptown to her engagement party.

Sophie was only two years old when her mother died, and she doesn't remember her at all. Virginia says that's a good thing. *You never knew Mother*, she says, *so you never had a chance to miss her.*

Sophie doesn't agree, though she'd never say this to Virginia. Her sister cared for her so devotedly as a child, and she might be hurt. But Sophie grew into girlhood bearing a small yet distressing fissure in the center of her heart, and she was always looking for ways to fill the gap. There was Virgo, of course. There was the house-maid who came to live with them, a maid-of-all-work, really: a young woman from Brooklyn who gave Sophie sweets from the pocket of her pinafore apron, and who had a little girl of her own who was being brought up by relatives upstate. This was a *secret*, Muriel told Sophie, showing her the photograph, and Sophie ate the sweets and kept the secret and listened to her stories in the kitchen during the evening, when Muriel was doing the dishes. Until Muriel was dismissed, quite suddenly and without explanation, and Sophie turned to Mrs. Kelly and her soda bread downstairs.

The funny thing was, Sophie never really believed her mother was dead at all. In her childish way, she felt that Mother had only gone away, for some tragic reason of the variety you read about in sentimental novels, and that she was actually lurking around New York in some kind of disguise, watching over her family and *longing* to rejoin them. Sophie used to look for her, on the way home from school, or walking around the neighborhood. She would look in taxi windows and through library shelves; she would peek into the back rooms of shops and at every face they passed along the sidewalks. Hoping for a flash of recognition. Hoping that, if she—Sophie—were good enough and sweet enough and generally irresistible, her mother might be tempted to return to them.

Until Sophie turned twelve or thirteen, and she put away childish things. She understood her mother really was dead—yes, lifeless, expired, banished from human existence—and she wasn't coming back, no matter how well Sophie behaved. *How did she die?* she finally asked Virginia, and Virgo said that she had become very sick, and one day she was too sick to go on.

That was all Virginia would say. She wouldn't talk about what Mother was like, or where they used to live, or why they came to New York after she died. Only a few small, blurred photographs remained of that previous existence: one on Father's bedside table, and three in the scrapbook Virgo keeps in her chest of drawers. (Mother was one of those people who hated having her photograph taken, apparently.) *You look like her,* that was all Sophie was told, and she used to gaze into the mirror, turning this way and that, wondering which features were borrowed from this mysterious woman who was present at her birth, and which belong only to Sophie.

But childish habits are hard to break, and when the taxi staggers into a knot of traffic on the corner of Forty-Ninth Street, Sophie's gaze falls first on the face of a black-coated woman hurrying south along the sidewalk, brows all worried, clutching a pocketbook in her left hand; then a lady of massive bosom, steaming along like an ocean liner, flanked by two giggling girls; then a woman wearing a small hat, very neat and businesslike, carrying a valise that bounced against her leg.

Virginia nudges her. "What are you thinking about, Baby?"

"I was thinking about Mother."

"Mother! My goodness. Why?"

"I don't know. Because it's my engagement party, I suppose. Every girl wants her mother to attend her moment of triumph."

Virgo takes her hand and squeezes it. "She would be so proud of you, Baby. Look at you. All grown up and beautiful."

"I don't know about beautiful, but I do feel rather grown-up."

"Your *dress* is certainly grown up." Virginia's tone stops just short of admiration.

"Julie helped me pick it out. We had a grand time at B. Altman's, trying everything on. It's a shame you couldn't come."

"You should have had something made for you, an occasion like this."

"There wasn't time. Anyway, who wants to sit around a dressmaker's shop for endless fittings, when you can have anything you like in a department store?"

They still haven't moved. It's Fifth Avenue, always crowded. A beautiful new bronze and granite tower rises from the center of the avenue, topped by a light shining white for *GO*—mocking them, really, because there's nowhere to move. A few dozen horns burp in outrage. Unconcerned, the light switches back to green.

"Let's walk," says Sophie.

"Walk! But your shoes!"

"It's only a dozen blocks or so. I'll bet we get there sooner than the taxi."

"Oh, Baby, no—"

But Sophie doesn't listen. She takes a dollar bill from the sequined bag at her wrist and shoves it over the seat at the driver. "Come on," she says, reaching for the door handle.

Poor Virgo. She's spent the past two weeks nursing a sick child, fever up and down, rashes appearing and disappearing, hardly two hours' consecutive sleep. Little Evelyn's doing better today, but now her mother's a ruin. Her dress is ancient—of course, she hasn't had time to shop—and her serene face is no match for her fatigue. Her old-fashioned hair is done up at the nape of her neck, without a sequin or a joyous feather in sight. But she's here. She's gathered up her strength for an evening out, her first bit of fun in ages—maybe ever—and as they clatter up the sidewalk, maneuvering around gray-hatted businessmen and floral-scented secretaries and the odd late shopper, Sophie feels the smallest bit guilty.

Maybe she should warn Virginia of what's to come.

But no. Virginia—serene, staid Virgo—will be horrified. Virginia will try to talk her out of it. Virginia's expression will stretch into astonished horror—*Oh, Sophie, no!*—and Sophie's such a good girl, how can she resist a heart-tugging appeal like that? No, no, no. Virgo's going to be just as surprised as the rest of them.

It's going to be grand. It's going to be—as Julie Schuyler puts it—*fireworks.*

Chapter 15

When a girl marries, she exchanges the attentions of many men for the inattention of one.

—HELEN ROWLAND

THERESA

A dozen blocks north, two hours later

You can tell right away if a party's going to rise or fall, can't you, and this one's soaring straight up to the heavens. Like a helium balloon on a cold morning.

I'd like to claim all the credit, but that wouldn't be fair. In the first place, the weather's showing a bit of thaw, at least temporarily, and there's nothing like the thawing-out of a cold February to lend everyone that bubbly springtime feeling, like there's hope for the world after all. And there *is* hope, my goodness! Business is picking up again, I've heard, and people are beginning to shed that haze of dread that's hung about ever since the war ended. All those fears—communists, anarchists, influenza—are lifting from our shoulders. Maybe another disaster isn't waiting around the corner, after all. Maybe we can take our shoes off and have a sneaky drink and a good time, and fate won't sock us for it. Or maybe fate will sock us anyway, whether we're having a good time or not, so we might as well have a good time while we can.

Or maybe it's just me. I'm happy, really *happy*, for the first time in ages. Everything's working out. Sylvo's being a gentleman about the divorce—taking all the blame, offering plenty of compensation—and the Boy seems to have forgotten his passing fancy for the Fortescue girl. We're making plans to head out to California, once the papers are signed—the Boy says he's *through* with New York, he wants to make a whole new start, far away from old Manhattan Island—and the only thing left is to break that news to Ollie and Billy. But they won't mind, will they? California's only three days away, ensconced in a comfortable Pullman car, and when you get there, you have sunshine and clean air and a nice wholesome ocean. And oranges! You can pick them right off the trees, I've heard.

So that's settled, and in the meantime there's this party. I decided on a South America theme, just to whet the appetites of the happy couple, and the place really does take your breath. I've spared no expense. There's an Amazonian jungle in the foyer, and the drawing room is Rio de Janeiro. I've dressed the staff in native garb, as depicted in the color plates of *The Illustrated Guide to South America,* and while I'm afraid the cook had some difficulty in finding authentic recipes for the aboriginal cuisine, we do have a sufficiency of imported pineapples.

As for my costume. Well! I think I've quite outdone myself. The Boy's eyes practically swelled with admiration when I emerged from my dressing room, and while I can't exactly move my head with ease, the entire ensemble's really more comfortable than you'd think. For example, when the Boy set down his drink and set about testing my seams, we were able to arrange ourselves on the edge of the dressing table without too much trouble, hoisting skirts and unbuttoning trousers, and the very haste and passion with which the Boy consummated his admiration made the effort all worthwhile. Why, he didn't even stop to put out his cigarette: just *bang, bang, bang,* while the fag dangled from his teeth, and his desperate fingers dug into my hips. It was exactly what I needed, at such a moment, and while my wrists still ache from the effort of bracing myself on that damned table, my hair is nonetheless full of the Boy's hot breath, and my skin is flushed, and every rocky doubt has melted away under the geological pressure of copulation.

He's mine, yes, the Boy is thoroughly *mine* once more.

The Boy has principles, and he's not going to engage in unbridled sexual intercourse with a woman if his intentions aren't fixed upon marriage.

Speaking of marriage! There she is now, the blushing bride. I'll admit she looks ravishing, far more than she ought. Her dress is cherry-red and trimmed in jet, and her hair, without actually being bobbed, is parted on the side and arranged in ripples over her ears, then gathered at her neck in such a way that it *suggests* bobbing. I believe she's actually wearing lipstick. She's standing under a palm tree with Julie Schuyler, sipping champagne— Sylvo's vintage Pol Roger is being sacrificed for the occasion—and when she turns the other way I can't help noticing that her dress plunges into an alluring U at the back, adorned by a web of jet beads dangling right down her spine. I believe I've got a similar necklace myself.

"Holy cow," says Billy, handing me a martini. "Who's that?"

I tip the glass to my lips and drizzle a measure of gin down my throat before I reply. "Your new aunt."

There's a second or two of awe.

"I need another drink," Billy says, and he turns on his heel and heads back to the bar in the Amazon.

Left adrift, I turn to engage a few ladies to my right. Of the Boy, there's no trace. I suspect he's curing in the smoke of the library with the other recluses. It took me ages to persuade him to attend the party at all—he insists that we shouldn't make our association public until after the divorce—and so we've got to continue pretending cordial indifference, to the amusement of our guests. The blushing groom is equally absent—no, there he is, chatting in the corner, looking starched and handsome in the muted lighting, merely mellowed instead of dissipated—and my attention falls on a woman standing by herself, a few feet from Ox's shoulder, looking as if she's been elbowed aside by a more ambitious arm and doesn't particularly care.

I murmur a flattering excuse to my companion and edge my way through the throng—growing nicely, it seems, while a column of new recruits still marches two-by-two past the welcoming jungle—toward this unfamiliar woman, whose face reminds me of someone I've met before.

To be sure, the face is unadorned, and the dress beneath it—dark green, high-waisted, long-skirted—is as old and tired as her hairstyle. I'd call her pretty, except that beauty's the last thing on her mind. Her lips are pale, and her eyes are dull. Her skin is creamy and unlined, suggesting youth, except for the faint furrows that appear between her brows, when you approach close enough to say hello. Not a trace of rouge or powder or blacking, and still she arrests you. It's her eyebrows, I think, thick and straight and slanted a few degrees upward at the ends; or else the shape of her bones, which are graceful and permanent beneath that lackluster skin, rescuing her from plainness. Austere, I think they call it, and nothing like the big-eyed, heart-shaped charm of Miss Sophie Fortescue. Except—

"Why, you're her sister, aren't you?" I burst out, quite unlike me.

"I beg your pardon?"

I extend my hand. "I'm Theresa Marshall. I believe we're shortly going to become related."

"Oh, yes! Of course. Virginia Fitzwilliam." She shakes my hand, and the touch is far more firm and confident than I might have expected. Her palms aren't delicate at all. "I believe we missed you when we arrived."

"I'm afraid I took entirely too long getting dressed. This headpiece!" I touch a papier-mâché pineapple and laugh. My wrists ache triumphantly at the memory. Bang, bang, bang. "I'm enchanted to meet you at last, however. Sophie's such a dear, sweet thing. My brother is beside himself."

"Indeed," she replies carefully. "We're terribly grateful for the welcome. It's the kind of party one only reads about in the newspapers."

"Is it? How kind. But you'll find yourself accustomed to them in no time, I assure you. Ox loves a good party."

"Ox?"

"My brother. I see you haven't got a drink yet, which is absolutely scandalous." I signal to one of the waiters and pluck a glass of champagne from the tray. "Here you are. Go on. It's not going to kill you, whatever those rabble-rousers say."

"I've had champagne before, Mrs. Marshall," says Mrs. Fitzwilliam, rather sternly. "It's just that my daughter's been ill, and I would rather not indulge myself."

"You have a daughter? But you're so *young*!"

She smiles, but it's not the smile of flattery acknowledged. It's a smile that says she knows she's being flattered, and she sees right through you. She extracts a few drops of champagne from her glass and says, "I'm nearly twenty-seven, I'm afraid."

"But where's your husband?" Fingertips to mouth. Quick, shocked gasp. "Not the *war*, I hope."

"My husband's in Florida at the moment, looking after some investments." She admits another sip, more generous this time.

"How very dull. But at least your father's here, I hope? I haven't had the pleasure of meeting him yet. Such an accomplished fellow; I think I'll shiver in my shoes when we're introduced at last."

"He does have that effect." The smile again. "But he's not terribly social, I'm afraid. He's promised to look in for an hour or so, but I expect he'll just stay in the background."

"Well, do bring him over to say hello, at least. It won't do for us to meet for the first time at the ceremony." Mrs. Fitzwilliam looks a little uncertain, and I add: "The *marriage* ceremony, I mean."

"Yes, of course."

We appear to have exhausted Mrs. Fitzwilliam's capacity for conversation, and yet I find I can't quite abandon her to the wolves. I cast about, and my desperate gaze falls at once upon Sophie Fortescue—well, she's hard to miss, isn't she, all jet-beaded and cherry-dazzling—and I remark on how well she seems to be enjoying herself.

At last, a warm channel opens up in Mrs. Fitzwilliam's frozen voice. "Sophie's always had a tremendous capacity for joy. It's what I love most about her. Everyone does."

Those last two words, I think, are unnecessary. Here I stand, still pulsing with confidence, my skin still bearing the imprint of the Boy's reassuring desire for me, and Mrs. Fitzwilliam *must* go and say a thing like that. *Everyone does.* Everyone loves Sophie.

Really, how uninvited.

"No doubt," I say. "She certainly enjoyed herself in Connecticut with Mr. Rofrano, the other weekend. Or so I've heard."

Rather like the Boy, Mrs. Fitzwilliam doesn't react much to the stab of this little arrow. The two of them, they're cut from the same scratch-resistant cloth. But those are the ones who feel it most, aren't they? The ones who don't show the scratches.

"In Connecticut? Oh, yes. I'd forgotten about that."

"He drove her all over. They even visited the town where he grew up. I can't imagine why. He's just sentimental like that, I suppose."

"The town where he grew up," she repeats. "And where *is* that, exactly? I don't recall what Sophie said."

"One of the shore towns. Greenwich, I believe." I tap the corner of my mouth and nod. "Yes. Greenwich."

"Greenwich. I see." She isn't looking at me, but rather at Miss Fortescue herself, who's flown over to the corner of the room where the musicians have just filed in. There's going to be dancing, you see, right after we toast the newly engaged couple and send them off in a happy fox-trot around the drawing room. "I didn't realize that you and Mr. Rofrano were acquainted, Mrs. Marshall."

"Didn't you? But that's how Ox found him to begin with, you know. I suggested Mr. Rofrano as the perfect man for the job."

"Cavalier, you mean?"

"Cavalier and private investigator." I laugh, very light. "One has to make sure one's dear brother has picked himself out a suitable bride. And Octavian's marvelously *thorough,* in everything he does. A perfect fellow for the job."

Mrs. Fitzwilliam's face is quite pale: though, on second thought, it was pale beforehand, and maybe I'm only now noticing how *awfully* pale it is. As if her life's been drained away from her face. She continues to stare across the room and maybe across the Hudson River itself, and her voice is cold, cold. "Then I certainly hope Sophie's met with your approval."

"Naturally she has."

Her face turns at last, but not toward me. She looks past my left ear toward the foliage in the foyer. "And there's my father now. If you'll excuse me, Mrs. Marshall. I need to have a word with him."

I follow her gaze, and to my surprise, the great man looks rather ordinary. He may be earning millions, but they haven't put a single pound of flesh on his gray-trimmed frame, nor an ounce of ease in his bearing. His ears are enormous, the first thing you notice. He peers around him, bewildered, and lights on our direction with relief.

"Splendid!" I say. "I'll come along and you can introduce us."

Now she turns and fixes me, and my goodness, you wouldn't think such a slender, queer, plainish thing could deliver such a ferocious stare. "I'm afraid it's a private matter, Mrs. Marshall. But I'll bring him around later."

And she walks away from me, just like that. As if she isn't scared of me a bit.

As I surmised, the Boy's in the library, smoking in the company of the other tobacco-worshipping gentlemen. He's even speaking to one of them, next to a window that's been cracked open just enough to support life.

"There you are," I say, quite without regard for discretion. I snake my arm through his and smile at his companion, whose name escapes me at the moment, though his face is familiar. I'm told this is a consequence of turning forty. Your brain is so stuffed with useless bits of information that when a new fact trots in, wagging its tail, wanting a treat, something's got to give.

The Boy gives me an odd look. "Mrs. Marshall? Is something the matter?"

"Goodness me, no! Nothing *matters* anymore, hadn't you heard?"

The other gentleman laughs. Canning, that's it. And his sweetly stout little wife, the one with the earlobes that sag beneath the weight of too many diamonds, because Canning's money came in railroads and he got out before the creditors got in. Sylvo told me this, many years ago, chuckling as he said it. Wily fellow, that Canning.

But the Boy doesn't smile, only lifts his eyebrows expectantly. I ask him if he's seen the lucky man lying around somewhere.

"Lucky man?"

"Why, my brother, of course! I seem to have lost track of him. I don't know if you've caught sight of his fiancée, but she's making a real stir out there. I'm wondering if it's time to make the toast before someone gets hurt."

The Boy's eyebrows aren't satisfied with this answer, but he makes the best of it. "Right over there," he says, after only a brief pause, and I follow his nod to a cozy pair of armchairs next to the fire, where my brother sits deep in single-malt conversation with my nearly ex-husband, cigars twirling in the breeze.

I clap my hands, and the room snaps to guilty attention.

"Gentlemen," I announce, "if you'll snuff out your cigars and follow me to the drawing room, it's time for our main attraction."

By the time we reach the drawing room, I've exchanged the Boy's arm for that of the lucky man, who seems to have developed a case of the nerves.

"You're awfully quiet, Ox, for a man who's about to see his dearest dreams come true."

"That's why I'm quiet."

"Ox. *You,* superstitious?"

"There's such a thing as things going too well, Sisser," he whispers back.

"Nonsense. Buck up. Have you seen her dress?"

"Sensational, isn't it?"

"I suppose that's one way to describe it."

We turn the corner from the hallway, and Rio de Janeiro spreads out before us, populated by a throng of overdressed and half-ossified New Yorkers from the very best families. You can pick out Miss Sophie Fortescue right away. She's the one holding a glass of champagne (a different one from the first, I'll bet) and surrounded by all the admiring gentlemen, lapels flapping in eagerness to make a good impression for that moment (soon enough, they'll bet) when the joys of matrimony wear thin.

The orchestra leader is watching me dutifully. I make a signal.

Trumpet flourish.

Only a short one, however. I enjoy a touch of the theater, but everything must be in good taste. Even my palm trees contain just three or four imitation cocoanuts each. I lead my brother along the obedient parting in the crowd, in the manner of a father walking his daughter down the aisle, to the exact circle where the delectable Sophie awaits, holding her champagne against her cherry-red breast, admirably collected, betraying not a single stray nerve.

But there's something wrong, isn't there? I've seen plenty of aspiring brides in my time, believe me, and none of them regards the approach of her beloved with that kind of coy arch to her eyebrows, with that kind of mischievous curl to her bottom lip. As if she's got a secret she's just bursting to tell us all. She lifts one hand to fiddle with the tiny beads at her throat, and I'm only slightly mollified to see that she's still wearing her engagement ring, which splinters the light from three separate electric sconces and sends it dancing in graceful leopard-spot patterns on the walls.

The warning bells clang in my head. I have the strangest idea that I've transformed into Charon, and am leading my poor unwitting brother into the underworld. His palm is awfully damp next to mine. So maybe I'm not crazy. Maybe he's feeling this, too.

A swell of applause lifts us along the final steps. Nothing to do but go on, straight into the teeth of Miss Fortescue's mischievous smile.

"Mesdames et messieurs." I reach her and take the ringed left hand into mine, so that I'm standing at the intersection of Fortescue and Ochsner, holding a hand from each, a human link between fiancée and fleeced. "My dear friends. I am so *delighted* to have you join us this evening, as we celebrate the engagement—at *long* last—of my darling brother Jay, the light of my life, the thorn in my side, and once the most confirmed bachelor of my acquaintance"—my God, the girl is absolutely squirming now, like a fish on a hook—"to my dear and lovely sister-to-be, Miss Sophie Fortescue. Miss Fortescue—*Sophie*—let me be the first to embrace you, before I turn you over to my eager brother—"

"Actually—" says Miss Fortescue, just as I turn to plant a quelling kiss on that dewy young cheek.

"And now, I give you Ox!" I exclaim, slinging my brother into her arms, in an effort to stifle what comes next.

"Actually—" she says again, and I signal desperately to the orchestra leader, who whips the musicians into a noisy fox-trot. Ox wraps his hand around her waist and snatches her fingers, spilling champagne on the floor, as if I gave a damn about floors at the moment.

"ACTUALLY—" she shouts, above the music and the applause and the laughter and Ox's frantic dancing. "EVERYBODY! WAIT!"

She tugs herself free from Ox's embrace and staggers to the orchestra leader, and I'll be damned if she doesn't snatch the baton right from the poor fellow's hand. The musicians—astonished, rudderless—trip all over the notes and land in a discordant heap atop the next measure.

"That's better," says Miss Fortescue, and she doesn't need to shout this time, because the room has fallen into the most delicate, primeval silence. She spins slowly to the bodies arrayed before her, all the rich and the great in this fair city, and not one of us can move a finger. Not even me. Certainly not Ox. We wait—breathlessly, fearfully—for her to speak.

The mischievous smile is all flattened out, replaced by a most solemn, big-eyed charm. She touches her rippling hair with one hand and lifts her half-empty champagne glass with the other.

"I'm afraid there's been a change of plans," she says.

Chapter 16

When you see what some women marry, you realize how they must hate to work for a living.

—HELEN ROWLAND

SOPHIE

At the very same instant

For the first time in over two weeks, Sophie experiences a moment of doubt.

Julie warned her about this, so it's really no surprise—standing there in front of all those legendary people, wearing a daring dress, holding a champagne glass and a ridiculous baton—that the nerves jolt back to life and fizzle under her skin. The beads stick to her rakishly exposed back. Is it her, or has the room grown intolerably humid in the past few minutes? Or perhaps that's all part of Mrs. Marshall's tropical theme.

Just remember what you're trying to achieve, darling, Julie said. *Remember the alternative if you fail.*

The alternative. Sophie glimpses Jay, entombed in shock at the front of the crowd. A terrified lock of hair has broken free from the glossy shield on top of his head, to drag untended across his brow. Poor Jay. Was she really in awe of him once? He looks like a schoolboy in the grip of some terrible aging disease. A cocoanut hovers dangerously above his skull. He will be terribly, terribly disappointed, won't he? But he'll get over it. Some other girl will accompany him to South America, if she can afford it. Some other girl will make the bargain.

As all these women have. They are all ages, spread out before her, all stages of love and matrimony and divorce. All hair colors, all shapes, all degrees of beauty. Some are dressed fashionably, some frumpily. Some entertain glints of intelligence in their eyes, and some are irreversibly dull. But they have all exchanged their independence for security. Not one woman, Sophie's willing to bet, ajoins her husband right now, like a loving married couple. Not a Vanderbilt, not an Astor, not a Morgan nor a Schuyler nor any other of the illustrious names ringing in Sophie's ears, the people with whom she will be expected to associate, as the wife of an old Knickerbocker scion.

Not one of these women has earned a single penny in her life, has she? Her clothes, her apartment, her house in the country, her jewels, her shoes, the bottle of milk in her icebox: all of them have been paid for by the industry of some other person. She is beautifully, uselessly, benevolently beholden. Left to herself, she couldn't possibly sustain this luxury. She couldn't even sustain necessity.

And Sophie's the same. Her father's money, her father's hard-earned patents. He did it all for Virginia and Sophie, he says, so they would be comfortable. And they *are* comfortable! But they're beholden. She and Virgo are in his thrall, just like every woman in this room exists in thrall, whether she realizes it or not. Whether she resents it or not.

As for the men. Equally variable. Some have earned wealth, and some have inherited it. Some—like Jay himself—are required to marry it. But would Sophie want to marry any one of them? Exchange the thrall of her father for the thrall of someone else?

There's been a change of plans.

Sophie is not going to marry Jay Ochsner. She's not going to live under her father's roof, spending her father's money, marrying a man of her father's choosing. No, not any longer. Not another minute!

Sophie's going to take an apartment with Julie Schuyler. She's going to apply for a job in an engineer's office, or a manufacturer of some kind, answering telephones if she has to, studying at night, taking on more and more responsibility, until she's huddling over the sketches and blueprints herself. Until she's designing and building things herself. She'll be in thrall to her boss, maybe, but it's a different kind of thrall. An honest, democratic thrall, with no hypocrisy attached to it.

Everyone's getting a job. Well, so is Sophie.

She lifts her glass a little higher and thanks God there's no sign of Octavian, no reproachful eyes to overturn her resolve. Instead, there's Julie Schuyler, golden and smiling. She stands just to the right of center, waiting for her cue: not far, in fact, from the tropical figure of Mrs. Theresa Marshall, whose elegant face is now splattered with horror.

"Ladies and gentlemen," Sophie begins, and that's all that anyone ever hears of Sophie Fortescue's declaration of independence, because the crack of a gun echoes madly down the corridor and off the walls of Rio de Janeiro, setting the cocoanuts to trembling, and everybody just screams.

The New York Herald-Times, June 2, 1922

TIT AND TATTLE, BY PATTY CAKE

Well! It seems your humble correspondent still possesses the capacity to be surprised, after all. We all filed into the courtroom this morning, expecting to be regaled with blood and gore courtesy of the much-risen-in-the-world Mrs. Lumley, and instead the prosecution—with a decided air of triumph—called the splendidly named Mr. Giuseppe Magnifico to the attention of the court.

Who is Mr. Magnifico, you ask? Why, none other than the gardener, about whom much has been rumored but never proved, for the simple fact that he could not be found. Well, he's been found, dear readers, and I must urge you to dismiss any small children and otherwise delicate minds from the room, for the substance of his testimony proved more shocking and morally degenerate than we newspapermen could have dared to hope.

He is a colorful character, Mr. Magnifico, and fully worthy of his name. He plays to type with extraordinary precision, down to his baroque black mustache and his extremely slick hair. He seemed, of all things, to desire the admiration of the court stenographer, a most stern and high-necked lady of perhaps thirty-five or forty, and bent himself to this task with utmost charm, though the lady (to her credit) gave him no encouragement whatever.

Possibly she was too busy transcribing Mr. Magnifico's sentences, for there were many of them, often long and tangled, and always entertaining. I am afraid I shall have to summarize, or I shall never meet the six o'clock deadline mandated by my long-suffering editor.

Mr. Magnifico, I am sorry to report, was indeed engaged in a friendship of an immoral and adulterous nature with the victim, Mrs. Virginia Claire Faninal. I must admit that I cannot blame her entirely, when I compare the earthy—if rather viscous—charm of Mr. Magnifico with the charm entirely absent in the accused, he of the Wright Brothers ears. It was Mr. Magnifico's belief (confirmed, so he claims, by Mrs. Faninal herself) that the child she was shortly to deliver redounded not to the credit of Mr. Faninal, but to that of his humble gardener, who, by virtue of his profession, apparently knew a thing or two about planting seeds.

Now, these revelations are not altogether surprising in themselves. You will remember that we, the curious public, suspected as much, following those hints that made their way into the fact-hungry press when some

enterprising reporter first obtained notes from the inter-
views given to the Greenwich police department by the
now-Mrs. Lumley, in the days after the murder itself.
(Let it be a warning to all persons contemplating the sin
of adultery, that the kitchen maid will inevitably know
your secret.) But Mr. Magnifico has now confirmed
before the court what was previously mere speculation, on the part of Mrs. Lumley and the investigators
themselves, and what is more, Mr. Magnifico explained,
shaking his head, he did not believe that he was the only
person enjoying the favor of Mrs. Faninal's fair company.

At this, the accused himself did not wait for his attorney, but rose to his own feet and objected to Mr. Magnifico's claims as speculation.

No, Mr. Magnifico insisted. He himself had witnessed
Mrs. Faninal so engaged while Mr. Faninal was away
from the house, though, out of respect, he would refuse
to name publicly the occasion or the man. But he would
say this: that he believed Mrs. Faninal was neither morally corrupt nor weak-willed, and that her actions were
the result of some sickness of her mind. He had, in fact,
ended the liaison for that reason, and he was afraid for
Mrs. Faninal's health when he did, so dramatic was her
reaction to this dismissal.

Mr. Magnifico said much more, of course, but those
were the points most relevant to this case, and as I still

have the contributions of Mr. and Mrs. Lumley to relate, I am afraid I must refer you to the rest of this newspaper for a more comprehensive account of Mr. Magnifico and his testimony.

After such exhausting entertainment, I suppose we were grateful for the evidence of the next witness, Mr. Lumley, the husband of the one-time kitchen maid, whose ascent into respectable matrimony and mother-hood should be applauded as the very apex of the American Dream.

A small, plain man, Mr. Lumley seemed to have been called by the prosecution to vouch for the respectability of his wife, an office he performed admirably, if rather snorishly. Under questioning, he asserted that which we already knew: that he met her some two weeks after the murder, when she dined alone at the Bluebeard Restaurant in Scarsdale, an establishment owned by him at the time. As he had not followed the case in the newspapers—he is not, it seems, a man interested in sensational news, preferring instead to fix his attention on the business pages, poor fellow—he did not recognize her face. He was, however, struck by the air of fetching distress that surrounded her (her pretty face, one presumes, had nothing to do with it) and upon learning of her role in the affair, was moved to do the chivalrous thing and marry her. (His face, as he regarded his wife, contained a commendable trace of tenderness, which did him much credit in the eyes of the courtroom.) Had she ever spoken of the events of that day? the prosecution delicately inquired, and he said that of course she had, at the outset of their friendship, but she had scarcely ever referred to it since. She had wanted to put such a distressing affair behind her, and he had quite understood her reluctance. A terrible affair, he said, shaking his head, and I believe I caught an extremely quick glance directed at the accused: one sharp with rebuke.

He seemed to be speaking the truth, too, for Mrs. Lumley, who made her entrance after the noontime recess, appeared reluctant in the extreme to discuss her recollections of that fateful day. She glanced often in the direction of the accused, though under her brow and in such a manner that communicated her unwillingness actually to meet his eye. Nonetheless, she answered the questions put to her without additional prompting, and so we learned how, on the morning in question, after cleaning the upstairs rooms, she came down to discover the body of Mrs. Faninal lying on the kitchen floor, and the pathetic figure of the youngest Miss Faninal, smeared with blood, kneeling next to her mother, urging her to wake.

Mrs. Lumley maintained her composure throughout this description, though her face was pale, and I believe her fingers shook. Her husband, now sitting in one of the rear benches, fixed a sympathetic eye on her throughout. She confirmed her suspicion that Mrs. Faninal had indeed seduced the gardener, Mr. Magnifico, into an adulterous association, but she would not speculate on the parentage of the unborn child. She insisted, however, that Mrs. Faninal was an excellent mother in all respects, almost too doting, especially on the younger child. At this point, she seemed to seek out the faces of the accused's daughters in the crowd, and her expression of agony is impossible to describe, leading one to comprehend some inkling of the dreadful scene in the Faninal kitchen that morning.

The prosecution then gently steered her toward the facts of the discovery: the kitchen door left ajar, the kettle left whistling on the stove. Mr. Faninal had left for his workshop early that morning, as was his habit, and to her knowledge he had not returned, though as she was upstairs, in the rooms facing away from the street and the front drive, it was, she agreed, possible that she hadn't noticed.

The defense then climbed to its feet. In her opinion, asked the accused's attorney, was Mr. Faninal aware of his wife's adultery? Did he ever display any hint of jealousy?

Mrs. Lumley's plump face softened into compassion. She had no way of knowing, for Mr. Faninal was in all ways solicitous of his wife and her welfare, and his obvious grief upon learning of the tragedy had struck Mrs. Lumley's heart with deep force.

You may well be astonished by this revelation, for the court certainly was. Until now, we had heard nothing—and seen nothing—to dispute the notion that Mr. Faninal was a cold, determined, charmless man, and a father who kept his daughters under the most rigorous control. But Mrs. Lumley, as she spoke, regarded the accused with true feeling, though Mr. Faninal sat with bowed head and did not make any sign that he comprehended her.

We were thus left, on this extraordinary day, with the most extraordinary surprise of all: the possibility that Mr. Faninal might not prove the cold-hearted murderer we imagined.

Or perhaps he will. In a week or two, I suppose, we'll have the final verdict.

Chapter 17

*Between lovers, a little confession is
a dangerous thing.*

—HELEN ROWLAND

SOPHIE

East Thirty-Second Street, the thirteenth of June

For some reason, Sophie's surprised to find that the latchkey fits the lock, and the door to her childhood home glides open beneath her hand. Not even a creak. "Hello?" she calls, but there's no answer from Dot or Betty. They're probably out. Why would they hang about the house all day, with no family to take care of?

The hallway is strange in its familiarity. The black-and-white floor presents the same checkerboard she used to count when she was small, the same chipped and missing tiles, the same dark lines at the corners that no amount of scrubbing will lift. To her left, the old hat rack stands empty, except for a lingering umbrella beneath. The mirror hangs beside it, forming the same small oval, disfigured by the same pattern of tarnish to its silvering, and its dustless surface suggests that someone, at least, is doing her job faithfully.

Sophie removes her hat and gloves and puts them in their accustomed places: hat on the hook, gloves on the table. She isn't wearing a jacket—the heat returned like a bludgeon the other day—so the key goes back in her pocketbook, which she also leaves on the table. She takes in a deep breath—*home!*—and it smells different somehow, too much wood and not enough smoke, too bright with lemon polish to be its ordinary self.

But none of us is her ordinary self, anymore, she thinks. We will never be ourselves again.

In a way, she's glad to find the house empty. She came here to be alone, after all, even though today is the kind of day you're supposed to share with your sister, with your dearest friend. You are supposed to commiserate, to mutually console, to hold each other's weeping hearts, to pour each other syrupy glasses of cordial and discuss—if you can bear it—What Is To Be Done.

Instead, Sophie has come here. Alone. And though Virgo didn't say so—of course she wouldn't—Sophie suspects that her sister is just as relieved not to have to support any company tonight. We are both hollow, she thinks, examining her wide and uninhabited eyes in the mirror. We are drained of words. We are drained of cordial. We are sans everything.

The eyes stare back, not blinking, until Sophie turns away.

The air is cooler than she expects, defying the immense and slow-moving heat outside. Dot and Betty must be keeping the curtains drawn, the lamps off, the oven unlit, the doors shut. At the end of the hall, the stairs tilt invitingly upward, padded by the stylish blue runner Virginia ordered last year, but Sophie cannot face her bedroom yet. Cannot face the tidy abandonment inside. Too many relics of the Sophie left behind. The half-assembled De Forest radio receiver, shoved under the bed. The inner workings of a clock decorating the surface of the bureau. The few well-thumbed issues of *Popular Mechanics* hidden among her books. The rose-shaped engagement ring in its box inside the drawer.

For a moment, Sophie continues to stand in the hallway, facing the stairs, hand resting on her pocketbook. She isn't conscious of the passage of time, only of the cool air on her cheek, and the blessed, invisible quiet. The way the contented motes of dust hang in the atmosphere, undisturbed, because no one is moving, no one is talking, no one even exists except Sophie. If she stands still enough, she can almost believe it. She can believe—like Prospero—that the entire course of the last four months is just a vision of her imagination, an elaborate play enacted by her subconscious. An insubstantial pageant. Our revels now ended.

But the revels weren't ended. Outside these walls, the farce continued, and Sophie must play her part, mustn't she? Like everyone else. She must wake up again.

She gives her pocketbook a last pat and opens one of the double doors into the parlor. The drapes are closed to the afternoon sun, and the room is dark and smells of beeswax. Sophie pauses at the sofa table to pick up a photograph of Virginia in her Red Cross uniform, taken just before she left for France, and a throat clears in the corner of the room.

Sophie gasps and spins. The photograph slips from her fingers and lands softly on the rug.

"Miss Fortescue," says Octavian.

He's standing before Father's favorite armchair, as if he's just risen from its comfort. For a shocked instant, Sophie imagines he really *is* her father, that today's events really *were* all a great mistake, an illusion, and Father's been released from prison and is somehow already home, wearing a pale suit and a striped necktie.

But the mirage ends in the next tick of the mantel clock, because the figure is too tall and youthful, and the voice—well, she knows that voice, even if the face is covered by shadow. She bends down and lifts Virginia's photograph and brushes the glass with her hand, not because it's damaged but because she doesn't want to look up.

"The maid let me in," continues Octavian, when she doesn't reply. "I hope I'm not intruding."

Sophie looks up and lets out an astonished breath that might once, in an earlier Sophie, have been a laugh. "Isn't that exactly what you're doing?"

"I'm sorry." He reaches for his hat, resting beneath the lamp. "I'll go, of course, if you want me to. But your sister told me you were coming home this afternoon, and I thought—well, I haven't had a chance to speak to you since January."

"I didn't think we had anything to say to each other."

The brim of the hat beats softly against his chest. "Sophie—Miss Fortescue—"

"Faninal," she says coldly.

"You have every right, I guess, to be angry with me. But I want you to know that all this—the way things turned out, what happened today in that courtroom— it's the last thing I wanted. I would have taken it all to my grave, if I could have."

Sophie fixes her gaze on the rhythm of that hat brim over his heart, the nervous flex of his finger joints. Her eyes are growing accustomed to the dusky light, so that the details become visible, one by one: his suit is gray, the stripes on his necktie are blue, the pressed creases of his trousers are softened by the heat. She thinks his fingers are more tanned than before, but they're otherwise familiar in each tiny hair and crescent nail; more familiar than the room around them, more familiar than the house itself. Except that they're moving, beating that uneasy hat, a most peculiar feature.

"I know that," she whispers.

The hat stops moving. "I was hoping you would." A deep pause. "I knew you would."

"Of course I knew. But I can't forgive you for it."

"No. I suppose that's fair."

He gives the hat a spin, puts it on his head, takes it off again. A bizarre flurry of moment. By contrast, Sophie feels as if she's turned to stone. If she wanted to move, if she wanted to step toward him or away, if she wanted to turn and open the curtains and flood the room with hot summer light, she couldn't. Even her eyes are disinclined to blink.

He bursts out, "What happened today in court—"

"No! I don't want to talk about it."

"I just want to say how shocked I was. I thought things were going the other way. We were all convinced about the gardener. Your father's lawyers did a brilliant job of—"

"Please, Octavian." Sophie lifts a tired hand, palm outward. "I can't even think about it."

"Sophie—"

"Please, Octavian. Mr. Rofrano."

Octavian runs his fingers over his head, as if he's surprised not to find his hat resting there. His polished black shoes stand a little apart, preparing to carry him to the door if she tells him to leave, knowing he's got no reason to stand there. No right to stand there. And she *should* tell him to leave. She *will* tell him to leave. In just a few more seconds, when she can summon the will.

"What will you do now?" he asks.

"I don't know. My father's just been convicted of murdering my mother, Mr. Rofrano, by an impartial jury of his peers. He's not planning to appeal. I suppose they're going to sentence him to death shortly. We are to hold ourselves at the court's pleasure. No doubt the lawyers will telephone me when I'm needed."

"But you can't be staying here alone!"

"Why not? The servants are here." She moves at last, sinking into the sofa, and it feels unexpectedly luxurious, to sit on a sofa instead of a hard bench. She takes a deep breath, and the air tastes of dust. The sofa cushions, apparently, haven't been so well tended as the plane surfaces. "Anyway, I'm tired of people. I don't want to talk to another human being, as long as I live."

"I'm sorry." He puts the hat on his head, this time with decision, and steps away from the armchair. "I shouldn't have come. I'll leave you in peace."

"No!"

He pauses.

"I'm sorry. I mean, you can leave if you wish. If you need to leave now."

"Do you want me to stay?"

Now that she's used to it, the room doesn't seem cool anymore. An intolerable warmth squeezes her temples. Her fingertips, pressed together in a web over her knees, stick damply in place. She imagines a glass of lemonade, tall and choked with ice, sweating into her hand. She imagines the springtime she's missed, the tulips she never noticed, the blue sky outside that beckons everyone but her.

"I—I don't know." Sophie looks, at last, into Octavian's face. He's tanned, and more tired and lean than before, but his eyes are large and soft with compassion. *Real* compassion, not the synthetic kind that squishes the faces of all those people in the courtroom, as they steal glimpses of her, snatches of her, the tragic Daughter of the Accused. A compassion that's really curiosity, morbidity, the way you manufacture sorrow for someone struck by a streetcar, or someone two houses away who has just received one of those awful War Department telegrams. A compassion that makes her sick to her stomach.

But Octavian's compassion isn't sick-making. His compassion knows her, understands what she's suffering, comprehends the dangerous state of her nerves. Octavian's compassion makes her veins rustle, makes her heartbeat double. Restless. Reckless. She wants to ask, *Where is Mrs. Marshall?* But instead she shrugs. "If you *want* to stay . . ."

"No. I don't want to stay *here*."

"Then you should go."

He holds out his hand. "But you shouldn't stay here either. Come with me."

Sophie begins to laugh, high and hysterical. "Come with *you?*"

"Why not?"

"After what happened last time?"

"Nothing happened last time, did it? Nothing would have changed, if we had or hadn't gone."

"But it was wrong of us. I had Jay, and you had— you had someone, too. I fooled myself into thinking we were just taking an innocent ride together, but it wasn't innocent. *I* was innocent, that's all."

But Octavian is shaking his head. "You're still innocent, Sophie. You don't know what corruption is, and that's why there was nothing wrong with what we did. There still isn't."

Something about the firmness of his voice. She wavers.

He curls his fingers invitingly. "Come on, now. You could use a little fresh air."

"There isn't any fresh air, not between here and the equator."

But she rises anyway and, after an instant's hesitation, places her naked hand against Octavian's naked hand, and it seems, despite the firmness of his voice, he's just as damp as she is. Just as afraid.

Once they're under way, rumbling eastward along Thirty-Second Street in the familiar Ford, Sophie inquires, as a matter of duty, after the whereabouts of Mrs. Marshall.

"Theresa's back at the apartment, I believe."

"Yours, or hers?"

Octavian slows the car to negotiate the crossing of Second Avenue. "Hers."

"Does she know where you are?"

"Yes. I told her I was going to look in on you. Make sure you were doing all right, after what happened today."

"What did she say?" Sophie asks relentlessly.

"If you're asking whether she *cares* we're together, I suppose she does. But she understands. She agreed I should go."

"I see. We have her permission."

"It's not like that."

"Yes, it is."

Octavian falls silent. He doesn't want to fight with her, she thinks, but maybe he understands why she *does* want to fight. Why she's spoiling for a bit of spat. Sophie turns her head and watches the houses slide by, the little striped awnings above the shops, the pavement blistering under the sun. The leaves on the trees are still pale and new, drooping in exhaustion. Summer has begun too early. The draft blows hot against Sophie's face, filled with exhaust and rot. She holds her hat brim to keep the shade steady over her face.

"Where are we going?"

"Long Island. A little place I've been visiting lately. I hope you'll approve." He speaks loudly, belting his words over the draft and the engine's roar, and Sophie thinks how stupid this is, stupid and reckless, driving to Long Island with another woman's fiancé. Look what happened the last time.

But that was another Sophie, another girl, innocent and undamaged. This Sophie has so much less to lose.

Over the Brooklyn Bridge. Through the ragtag streets of Brooklyn, then the orderly rows and yards of Queens, then open space, the air a little fresher, the smell a little greener. Sophie has lost interest in any possible destination. Whatever it is, she never wants to get there. Just ride and ride, the wind blowing in your face, the silence long and comfortable between you and your driver.

Maybe he's taking her to the beach. Maybe he's taking her to a seaside hotel. Maybe they're going to have a love affair, discreet and smoky, ending badly, like a modern novel. Sophie doesn't care. When your father has stood up in a court of law that very morning, all smart and polished, eyes heavy and unslept in, and received a verdict of *guilty* on a charge of murder in the first degree; when the crime is of a most bloody and nerveless nature; when the victim in the case is none other than your own mother . . . well, why on earth would you ever care about anything, ever again? The shock. Yesterday the final statements were made, the defense had outlined once more its minute and carefully wrought rebuttal to the prosecution. The jury was supposed to head into the deliberation room piled high and thick with reasonable doubt, and the newspapers were supposed to report the wan yet optimistic expressions on the faces of the accused and his family. Acquittal: you could almost smell it in the air.

Now this. Driving away, away, not caring where you were going as long as your destination was another world from a sweaty marble courtroom, from the rows and rows of people who wanted to know how you *felt.*

"Stop the car," she says.

"What's that?"

"STOP THE CAR!"

He throws back the throttle and hits the brake pedal, and the Ford shimmies to a halt by the side of the road. Sophie yanks the door handle and springs from her seat, away from the smell of the engine, the hot leather, taking large gulps of air into her chest, and when she opens her eyes she discovers she's standing on the edge of a pasture, inches from a fence of old split rails. The grass is luxuriously green, nourished by a series of recent downpours. About fifty yards away, a pair of horses grazes in a kind of fevered delirium, tearing mouthfuls of tender blades from the earth. One is a bay, the other a luminous chestnut. Their tails whisk away the flies in a strange and unexpected rhythm that reminds Sophie of the beat of a jazz band, long ago.

She places her hands on the topmost rail and the panic recedes, bit by bit, into the long, flicking tails and the idle rattle of the engine behind her.

Octavian comes to a stop at her left shoulder. The corner of his jacket brushes her sleeve. "Look at the fat, shiny things."

"They're in heaven. All this lovely grass."

He puts his hands in his trouser pockets and sets one foot on the bottom rail. "It used to amaze me, you know. Up there in the air, you could see the armies, the wrecked towns and the trenches, the craters and the mud between them. And then, a few miles away, pastures like this. Cows grazing. Not many horses; the armies took every poor brute they could get their hands on. But cows and stable yards full of geese and pigs, and crops growing in the fields. Just as peaceful as could be, and yet you could hear the shells screaming, the boom of the guns."

"It must have been extraordinary, to fly up above the battlefield like that."

"Yes. When you're in a trench, there's no reason to it. Passages every which way, mud and rats and general disorder. But from the air, you see the pattern. You see what a marvel it all is. Especially the German lines. *Damned* marvelous, you know? Just a remarkable display of human genius, when put to the test, when your life's at stake. And it all looked so peaceful, up there. Like a game, like a kind of bizarre picnic. You couldn't imagine there were men being killed down there."

"Until the enemy planes found you, I suppose."

"Yes, then it was all madness."

Behind them, the engine misses a stroke, catches, and then stalls out. One of the horses—the chestnut—lifts his head, as if noticing their intrusion for the first time. He remains quite still, except for the occasional whisk of his tail, and examines the two of them in drunken, brown-eyed tranquillity, before returning his attention to the richness of the meadow.

"And then afterward," Octavian continues, "you would land at your airfield, several miles behind the lines, surrounded by all the farms you'd been looking at from above, and you couldn't believe you were still alive. There was just this unreality to it. They would take your plane back to the hangar, the mechanics would, and fix up anything that had gotten hit or broken, and I would go back to my commanding officer and make my report. Tell him if I'd seen anything unusual, who'd been killed, whether I'd killed anyone. Still unreal. And then, when I was dismissed, when most of the squadron went to the mess and drank, I would go out walking. They have these long, straight white roads in France, shaded by trees. I would look at the animals, at the women and children doing the chores, and I felt like an alien being. Like I didn't belong in the world anymore, in the world of fields and cows and women and children. But I liked to watch them, anyway. It made me feel that something was still normal, that things still grew and thrived, even if I wasn't one of them anymore."

"Yes," Sophie says, a little like a sob, and his arm falls around her arm, and she turns her face into the hollow of his shoulder, and she doesn't cry. Her eyes remain perfectly dry, against the flat, slightly damp weave of Octavian's jacket, the solid muscle of his understanding. Like a pair of horses standing together, head to rump, flicking their tails in mutual relief of what plagues them.

By now, Sophie suspects she knows where Octavian is taking them, and she's right. He parks the Ford in a lot of packed clay, along a neat row of other parked cars, and sets the brake.

"The squadron came here for final training, a million years ago," he says. "I nearly crashed over that bluff, once. Now it's a civilian airfield. They're building a golf course out of part of it, right over there, near the motor parkway."

"Can we go inside?"

"That's the general idea."

He turns off the engine and gets out of the car. Sophie, rather than waiting, opens the door herself and shakes out her rumpled clothes. She's still wearing her court suit, a neat skirt of navy blue and a high-necked ivory blouse, though she's taken off the matching low-waisted navy jacket and discarded it on the back seat. Her hair is pinned low, just above her nape, and her shoes are square and low-heeled. Her hat, fashionably small, is really insufficient against the sun, and she holds her hand to her brow to obstruct the glare as she gazes across the field.

"Why, it's enormous!"

"It was even bigger before, trust me. Swarming with planes and men. Come along. It's getting late."

He takes her hand and leads her along the rutted pathway to the hangars, which rise up from the field in a series of white barrel roofs. Easily distinguished from the air, Sophie thinks. The low, busy drone of an airplane engine begins to build in her ears, and she looks up just in time to see a pair of pale wings pass overhead, wobbling back and forth, making for the wide plain of shorn grass to her right. She stops to watch. She's never actually seen an airplane land before, and her body reacts as if the whole world's at stake. Her pulse accelerates, her hand tightens around Octavian's fingers. The machine looks so fragile, like a moth. She imagines that a single improper gust could send it tumbling through the air. Her breath stops. It's going too fast, too fast, it will never make the runway, it will crash into the grass.

And then it touches the earth. Bounces, touches again, rolls speedily away until the sound of the engine fades, and another one takes its place. Sophie turns, amazed, to Octavian. "I thought he was going to crash! How do you do it?"

"Oh, there's nothing to it, as long as your plane is sound and the weather's not too bad. Although you couldn't pay me to fly an old tub like that Vickers Vimy." He tugs on her hand. "Come along. I'm going to show you a real airplane."

Roosevelt Field. Named after President Roosevelt's son Quentin, who was killed in combat over France, one beautiful summer day. "Did you know him?" asks Sophie.

"Yes."

He doesn't elaborate. He's walking briskly, a half step ahead, still holding her hand. Ahead of them, at the end of the narrow roadway, the row of identical plain white hangars catches the angle of the afternoon sun, much larger than they appeared from a distance.

Each one is painted with the name of some optimistic aviation company. Octavian heads past a line of shining biplanes, propeller noses tilted eagerly to the sky, straight for the third hangar from the left. The doors are wide open, the atmosphere lazy and scented with machine oil: the smell of Sophie's childhood, the smell of discovery. A man sits in a chair, just inside a triangle of shade from the roof, reading a newspaper. NO SMOKING, reads a large sign above his flat cap. He looks up, and his face, deeply tanned, stretches into a toothy young smile.

"Why, Mr. Rofrano! What brings you here today?"

"Afternoon, Taylor. Miss Fortescue here is curious about airplanes." Octavian releases her hand and motions to the small of her back, not quite touching her dress.

"Then she's come to the right place with the right fella. Want me to show her around for you?"

"Thanks a million." (Heavy on the irony.) "But I think I've got this covered. Is the new Curtiss inside?"

"No, she's right out there." Taylor nods to the row of biplanes. "Take her for a spin?"

"Maybe later. Sophie?"

She follows him into the shadows. The floor is beaten earth, the windows dusty and not very light. The place seems to have been baking in the sun all day, and without the breeze to cool her skin, Sophie feels as if she's stepped into an oven. Except this oven contains airplanes instead of bread—two of them, in fact, each being operated on by a couple of sweaty, grease-smudged surgeons in dungarees and nothing else.

Sophie stops and covers her mouth. "Oh, my."

"What's that? Oh." Octavian laughs. "I guess things can get a little masculine around here. I hope you're not offended?"

"Of course not."

But she says the words a little too loudly, and the men all turn in a kind of astonished unison, hands still stuck on the wings and the engine parts. Someone whistles, so soft it's almost respectful, and another one mutters something Sophie can't hear.

"Say that again," Octavian calls out amiably, not breaking stride, "and I'll knock your lights out."

There's a chorus of laughter, which Sophie recognizes wistfully as the sound of a happy crew, a group of men working well together, engaged like the gears of an engine. The sound of purpose. Octavian has it, too, whistling a little as he leads her to a door at the back, a small hot office with a north-facing window that Octavian forces open. "That's better," he says, taking off his hat and tossing it on the corner of a wide, plain desk, stacked with papers. The room smells of pencil shavings.

"But the airplanes are outside," Sophie says.

He looks up from the desk. "What's that?"

"You were going to show me a real airplane, weren't you?"

"Yes." He holds up a stack of papers, bound together. "Right here."

"There?"

"The airplane I'm designing. Enclosed cabin, six-seater. Aluminum skin. Two wing-mount engines. She's a beauty, isn't she?"

Sophie's blood starts in her veins. She moves to stand next to him, before the desk. She stares down at the image on the page, the elegant bird crisscrossed with razor lines and small, sharp notations in capital letters. She flips a page: the front perspective. "You designed this?"

"Yes. I'm on leave from the bank at the moment—too notorious, my supervisor said, in so many words—so I've been coming out here instead."

She looks up into a face she doesn't recognize, an Octavian transformed from famished into fed. His eyes are warm and happy. "You were put on leave because of me?"

"Not because of *you*. Because of the whole thing."

"Because of me."

He turns back to the drawing. "Anyway, I had to do something. I couldn't just hang around the city, bored and useless. And I kept thinking about what you told me, driving back from the Christopher Club, that first night."

Sophie blinks her eyes, because the memory returns, without warning, and in such acute, daylight clarity that it pains her. "Really? What did I say?" As if she doesn't remember.

Octavian's hand passes across the topmost sheet, smoothing down the curled edges. Unlike her, he's not wearing gloves, and his skin is leathered, his knuckles large, as if he's been using his fingers relentlessly; not in writing and drafting, but in labor. "You said that I couldn't turn my back on the thing I loved most," he says.

"Oh, that's right." She lets out a small, soft laugh. "How young and silly of me."

"You said—I can hear your voice exactly—you said that there was a reason I loved flying so much, and that reason still existed, waiting for the tide to go back out."

"Well. You have an excellent memory."

He picks up a pencil and makes a minute adjustment to one of the struts. "I think I remember just about everything you ever said to me."

She could say, *How flattering,* or something equally light and flirtatious and dismissive. *Charming as ever, I see.* Except that he isn't trying to flatter her, and he's never really been charming, has he? Not nearly as charming as Jay was.

She places her fingers on his fist and draws the pencil away. "Do you know what I'd like?"

"No."

"I'd like to fly."

Sophie doesn't stop to think about it, not until she's actually buckled into the passenger seat, staring at the thin, golden strip of skin between Octavian's leather cap and the collar of his jacket, and it's too late.

The airplane rolls with frightening buoyancy toward the end of the grassy field, not far from where the Ford is parked. She leans forward and tries to yell in his ear. *Stop! I've changed my mind! It's all a great mistake!* But her throat is stiff, the words won't rise. The canvas straps hold her in place. She reaches out to touch his shoulder, and then to shake it. He turns and lifts his hand, thumbs up. He's smiling beneath his goggles— she can't see his eyes at all—and the engine whines like a large, impertinent insect in her ear.

Oh, heavens.

How stupid. How awfully, fatally stupid. Octavian can't even imagine that she wants to turn back; she was so enthusiastic, so insistent, practically dragging him to the row of biplanes. She took his hand and levered herself cheerfully into her seat. In her newfound recklessness, she thought she didn't give a damn. She thought she didn't care what became of her. It turns out, she cares after all. She wants to live! But Octavian seems to be mistaking the panic in her face for exhilaration. He pats her hand that grips his shoulder and turns back to the controls, and she wonders how he can even see the field ahead, when they're pointed upward like this, like a pair of fools, watching the blur of the propeller against the blue sky, watching a cloud take shape into a cat. Or is it a zebra? The airplane turns sharply, and Sophie's spasmodic gloved hands grip the slippery metal edge of the cockpit, and she shuts her eyes.

But she can't shut out the sense of motion, the building momentum. She can't shut out the draft against her cheeks, or the screaming pitch of the engine, or the way the machine bounces and strains for the sky. She opens her eyes just as the bouncing smoothes away and her stomach falls to the ground, and her chest takes on weight but her head soars giddily upward.

You are flying, she thinks. *You are flying.*

And it's all right. The airplane is strong, the engine doesn't miss a stroke. The wings lift them steadily toward the sun. When she gathers enough courage to turn her head, the entire horizon opens before her, all of Long Island, the hazy patchwork farms, the skinny yellow beach, the stripe of navy sea. The white dots of the sailboats, the gray spots of merchant shipping. The whole world in elaborate, mesmerizing miniature.

The plane banks left, and they're turning toward the ocean, tilting to the earth, still climbing. Another ripple of panic. But this is Octavian, she reminds herself. If you're going to go flying, you might as well have an ace for your pilot, a man who's chased enemy Fokkers and been chased in return, who's flown a machine nimbly through the various fronts of war and weather, who can certainly handle a well-kept civilian airplane on a tranquil summer afternoon.

Trust the machine, she thinks. Machines won't fail you, as long as you treat them right.

The air is cooler up here, and she's glad for the jacket covering her shoulders, which Octavian insisted she wear. She was wrong about everything. She thought the sun would bathe them in warmth; that the sky would be calm and peaceful. But the draft rushes against her ears and the sides of the plane, and the engine roars beyond that. The wings level out. They're headed southeast, judging by the sun. Below them, the fields are getting smaller, compacting into yards and parks. More buildings, more streets. She wants to ask Octavian where they're going, but when she speaks, she can't even hear her own voice. The words disappear in the wind behind them, unheard.

They've stopped climbing. They're soaring above the earth at a nice level pace, and it almost seems normal now. The muscles of Sophie's abdomen unclench slowly. She looks over the edge and wonders how fast they're going. So many questions she should have asked before they left, but she was carried along by her own recklessness, by her own determination to do something dangerous and forbidden. Now the madness has passed. There is no danger. There's just Brooklyn coming into view, Prospect Park, a cluster of tall buildings, the factories and smokestacks near the shore, belching out their noxious clouds. Over there, the Navy Yard, she thinks. A pair of battle cruisers sits against the docks, and they look like toy ships, or the models they had on display at the Cunard offices when the Fortescue family booked passage to Europe last year. A lifetime ago.

Octavian removes his arm from the controls and points to the right. Sophie's gaze lifts obediently, and there it is! Manhattan Island! Long, bristling, industrious Manhattan, packed tight with gray buildings in a rippling pattern, taller at the tip and then flattening out, and then rising again at midtown. A trio of bridges arch delicately across the East River, which is crowded with ships, glittering in the sun. Farther north, the Queensboro Bridge stands a little blurry in the summer haze, no longer mighty but miniature. Up here, you can't see the dirt and smoke and garbage. You can't see a bit of empty ground either, not a blade of grass anywhere. As if the buildings are just floating on the water, and there are so many of them, the whole thing should sink straight to the bottom. But it doesn't. The city gleams and strains toward the sky. It's invincible, eternal.

Sophie realizes they're over open water now, making a slow arc around New York Harbor and the very tip of downtown. Octavian points again, to the left this time, and she tears her gaze away from Manhattan just in time to see the Statue of Liberty rising above the water like a miracle, pale against the dark water. It's too much, Sophie thinks. It's too much beauty at once, wonder after wonder breaking over you, until you can't even breathe. You can't think.

They round the harbor and drone up the Hudson River. Sophie tries to notice the details now: to pick out one particular building and examine its windows and shape, the water tank fixed to its roof, and imagine who lives there or works there. The Sterling Bates building lies in that jumble there somewhere, on the eastern side, and here is Greenwich Village and

Octavian's apartment and that damned speakeasy, with the decent, well-meaning bartender. To the north and east, the house where Sophie grew up, the neighborhood she knows, everything familiar. Everything she thought she knew; the childhood she thought she had. Coming up, the piers studded with ocean liners, the points of departure and return. She closes her eyes. It's too much.

Ahead of her, Octavian silently flies the airplane, looking over the sides now and again, making adjustments. A gust of wind catches them, an instant of dizzying loft, and Octavian rides it out without a flinch. She realizes—consciously, for the first time—that her life, at this instant, is entirely in his control. That she's trusted him once more, and that this leap of trust constitutes the real danger, the real gamble of the day. And maybe that's the reason they're up here in the air to begin with? To fly them both back to January.

Sophie stretches forward and runs her thumb along the back of Octavian's neck, along that tanned stripe below the leather cap. The skin is softer than she expects, warmer, and she thinks how *glad* she is that he's alive, what a miracle life is.

How the world makes so much more sense from above.

Chapter 18

Jealousy is the tie that binds, and binds, and binds.

—HELEN ROWLAND

THERESA

Stamford, Connecticut, an hour or two earlier

If you'd told me, in the summer of 1920, that my love affair with the Boy would lead inevitably here—this door with the peeling paint and the broken knocker, in the shabbiest waterfront corner of Stamford, Connecticut, begging the occupant to open the door—I'd have told you that I wouldn't stand for such a thing.

I, Mrs. Theodore Sylvester Marshall of Fifth Avenue, have never stood before such a shabby door in my life, but I'm doing it now, God knows why. I have a plan, or rather the suspicion of a plan, and if Mr. Giuseppe Magnifico must be reasoned with—begged with, cajoled, seduced even—then Mrs. Marshall must hold her nose and seduce. I suppose it's not the first time I've sold my charms for the greater good.

I've never actually visited the place before, but I know the address. Who do you imagine tracked down the little devil to begin with? I paid a fair fortune to the Pinkerton Agency for this information, and I suppose the Pinkerton Agency—and Il Magnifico himself— did not disappoint. The trouble is, he's gone back to earth, and I'm having the devil of a time digging him out again.

"Now, Mr. Magnifico," I say. "*Giuseppe.*" (More of a purr, that one. So much easier to purr in Italian.)

"Go away, Mrs. Marshall. I have nothing to say!"

"But you must, surely. I promise, I won't go to the police. I just want to know the truth."

"The truth, she is not important! Mr. Faninal, he is guilty. The jury say the truth!"

"Now, Giuseppe. We both know that's not so."

There is a harrumph.

"Giuseppe. You know you can trust me. Haven't I done *exactly* as I promised so far?" I pause to tap my fingernails against the edge of my pocketbook. The heat's not so bad here, really. There's a stiff little breeze coming off the sound, and it moderates the concentrated air of the street, the sticky awfulness that makes summer so unendurable in Manhattan, and nearly as bad in the slums of the lesser cities. By rights, I should be reclining among the dunes at Windermere. I should be enjoying the pleasant life with which God has seen fit to reward me, for my sins.

If it weren't for the Boy.

"Giuseppe," I say, a little more sternly. "I really shall have to call the police, if you don't open the door. I'm in possession of a certain scrap of information that will shine an entirely new light on this case."

"This case, she is closed! Mr. Faninal murdered his wife, that is all."

"Giuseppe. We both know that's *not so.*"

Harrumph.

"Very well." (Theatrical sigh.) "I suppose I've got no choice but to call in that nice Inspector Hopkins. The one who interviewed you before, remember? I'm sure he'll be delighted to know you've been lying to him, and to the court. Under oath, isn't that right?"

There is a quick click of the lock, and the door jerks open so decisively that I tumble, rather than stalk, into the hallway.

Oh, yes. The Boy has a lot to answer for, damn him.

In case you're interested, I was lying about that scrap of information. (I find I've been lying about a lot of things lately, scattering untruths about the place like so many stockings, discarded in the—what do the novels call it?—the heat of passion.) In fact, I haven't got a thing, but I do feel a certain amount of ownership as regards Giuseppe Magnifico, having scraped him off the bottom of the proverbial barrel with my own two hands, and those of the Pinkerton Agency. I feel as if he owes me.

One thousand dollars, to be exact.

"I have say all I can say," he grumbles. He has also evidently been drinking again, and the neatness of his magnifico mustache is quite ruined. He is a gentleman, however, and he shoos an enormous tabby cat out of an armchair for me. I'm too much of a lady to refuse.

"Thank you," I say, settling on the extreme edge. "However, I don't believe you, I'm afraid. I feel very much as if you're still hiding things from me."

"There is nothing important. Anyway, Mr. Faninal is verdict guilty." He spreads out his helpless hands. "What more can we do?"

"But we both know he didn't do it, Giuseppe. Justice itself should prompt you to act."

Justice is evidently not a cause that resonates with Mr. Magnifico. I can't say I blame him. His history with the law is lengthy and complicated, gone over at considerable length by the defense, during the endless hot hours of the trial. The crimes themselves are mostly of the petty kind, barring the odd assault thrown in for self-defense, but believe me, I quite understand that those are just the crimes we know about. He shrugs his shoulders and takes a chair. The tabby promptly occupies his lap. The room smells like the contents of a saucepan, along with a peculiar acrid odor that I presume has something to do with the cats, of which there are several.

"I do what you ask," he says, caressing the pussy in his lap with long and languorous strokes. "I talk to the police, I go to court, I say what I have to say. Is not my fault if Mr. Faninal get the swing. Is *his* fault, for kill his wife."

"He didn't kill his wife," I say.

"How are you so certain of this?"

I lean forward. "Because I am, Mr. Magnifico. In any case, it's no concern of yours. You know the terms of our agreement. Mr. Faninal is to be acquitted, or you don't get the rest of your money."

"So keep your money!"

Probably it was a mistake to give the man five hundred dollars at the outset, although his debts were so pressing—and by pressing, I mean actually *pressing*, by the sort of fellows one doesn't desire inside one's drawing room—that I felt I couldn't refuse. Now, cleared of immediate want, Giuseppe apparently has no need of my money. He's not a greedy man, I'll give him that. (Greedy for money, anyway.)

As to whether Mr. Faninal is or is not a murderer, I haven't the faintest idea, no more than you do. Like Mr. Magnifico, I have little interest in the justice of the matter. Mrs. Faninal seems to have been a rather un-principled sort of creature, exhibiting no art or virtue at all in her indiscriminate, indiscreet adultery. She did not, of course, deserve to die brutally for her sins. But fifteen years of prison—and innocent or not Mr. Fani-nal has served a sort of prison sentence, in my view, for all that the prison was a comfortable one—must surely go some small way in the balance against what the French (perhaps too forgivingly) call a *crime pas-sionnel*. That sort of betrayal, after all, can drive an ordinary man quite out of his ordinary senses.

Regardless, the damned jury has overturned all our plans for Faninal's acquittal, and instead of breathing a sigh of relief and retiring to Southampton for the summer, while the lawyers toil away on my divorce and the Boy, cleared of all chivalrous obligation toward the too-fair Sophie, prepares himself for matrimony, I'm wallowing in cat hair in a stinking house in Connecti-cut, and forgive me if my temper's running short with the unforthcoming Mr. Magnifico.

I open my mouth to tell him so.

But the fellow surprises me.

"You want to know who kill Mrs. Faninal?" he says. "You ask the girls. The girls know."

"The girls? Do you mean the Faninal sisters? Sophie and Virginia?"

He folds his arms and settles back in his armchair, nodding, and his eyes are so keen and dark that I get the suspicion I've been robbed of my five hundred dollars. A tremor rattles my belly, not for the first time in Mr. Magnifico's company, and I settle one hand on my pocketbook, which contains a small but reasonably effective pistol.

We regard each other, eye to eye, while the tabby nudges his hand with her nose.

"Ask the girls," he says again, that's all, and there's nothing I can do but rise from the armchair, to be replaced by a cat.

Regards Mrs. Virginia Fitzwilliam, I have little opinion. I haven't spoken to her since that disastrous party at the beginning of February, and—as I'm sure you know already—she's not the sort of person to reveal herself to any old spectator across a crowded room.

I do know that she's staying at the Pickwick Arms Hotel in Greenwich, about a half hour's drive straight down the Boston Post Road from the courthouse in Stamford. The Patent Princesses quietly took up a suite there at the beginning of the trial, and such is the extreme discretion of the proprietors, there is no press at all outside, even today, a fact for which I'm grateful.

The press. Have I mentioned them? Omnivorous, omnipresent little creatures, flashing their bulbs and shouting their questions. I half expected to find one of them lurking outside Mr. Magnifico's insalubrious abode when I slipped out the door, chased by the feral scent of cat urine, but there was only Ox's battered Packard, thank God, being eyed by a mangy fellow leaning against an electricity pole across the street.

You can imagine the haste with which I started the engine and roared out of that place. Never, I hope, to return.

The Pickwick Arms, on the other hand. Awfully tasteful, and you can't deny I've got a fine appreciation for aesthetics, whatever you think of my morals. It's not one of those glamorous grand hotels, heavens no. Those are strictly for out-of-town adulterers, and the Pickwick is thoroughly respectable. It's designed to look like an English inn of roughly Tudor provenance, reassuring you of its prestige by means of peaked roofs, half-timbered facades, and garden forecourts: a stockbroker's suburban mansion writ large. I expect the rooms are furnished in chintz. I leave Ox's Packard in the circular drive, keys in the ignition, and tug off my gloves upon entering the warm, floral-scented lobby. A bellboy approaches me with comforting obsequiousness. Does Madam have any luggage?

Madam does not, I tell him, but she should very much appreciate his taking a message upstairs to the suite currently occupied by Mrs. Fitzwilliam.

The bellboy's demeanor changes instantly from servility to suspicion, manifested in the adjustment of his cap an inch farther up his forehead, to reveal a pair of slim brown eyes. "I'm afraid that particular guest has asked not to be disturbed."

"My dear boy," I say, "do I *look* like a reporter, or a member of the curious public? Tell Mrs. Fitzwilliam that Mrs. Marshall has a private matter to discuss with her. I assure you she'll agree to receive me."

The bellboy bites his lip. Poor fellow. I expect he's been hoodwinked already; these members of the press can be so damned devious.

I tuck my pocketbook under my arm and tell him he's welcome to discuss the matter with the manager before proceeding. I'll be waiting right here.

A discreet yet spirited discussion ensues behind the front desk while I settle myself on a chintz sofa and observe the tranquil comings and goings of the Pickwick set. Everybody's got a country house in Greenwich these days; it seems to be the done thing, if you like horses and people who like horses. Elsie Rockefeller tells me that the town's filling up with professional men who take the train into New York every day, leaving behind wife, children, and faithful hound in a handsome four-bedroom house with a half-acre yard. I sometimes envy them, these ordinary people of the professional classes. Maybe the husband's not exactly behaving himself in the city, maybe the wife's taking to drink when the kids are in school and there's nothing left to do but join the bridge club and the charity committee and redecorate the dining room. But there's a security to it, isn't there? The boundaries of your life are neatly defined. You are not beset by mad passions for unsuitable objects. You don't find yourself embroiled in murder.

Or maybe you do. Why, I might appear perfectly normal to one of these linen-suited ladies passing across the lounge, just as normal and correct as they appear to me. I don't suppose anyone's fully immune to the temptation of a Boy. These days, nobody can say she will never get divorced, or go mad, or get murdered. Nobody can tell who's who.

"Mrs. Marshall?" It's the manager, calm brown mustache and all.

"Yes?"

"Mrs. Fitzwilliam asks me to escort you to her suite."

Hotels, of late, remind me naturally of the Boy: an irritating effect at the present instant, as I'm trying not to think of him at all. The Boy interrupts my customary mental sharpness, the necessary detachment with which I arrange my worldly dealings. To remember the Boy, just now, is to remember that he's spending *his* afternoon consoling the shocked and grieving Sophie, and to imagine just *how* he might be consoling her at this particular moment. Hardly conducive to mental sharpness, as I'm sure you understand.

So. I shall ignore the frisson of anticipation that activates my lungs as I follow the gray-suited manager down the fourth-floor hallway of the Pickwick Arms, and I won't consult my feelings on the subject of the Boy himself. I've got pressing matters, *practical* matters to conclude. Facts that beg my attention. Objects to pursue.

That I am losing my Boy, inch by precious inch, bears no relation at all to the matter at hand.

Do you know, after observing her for some weeks in the confines of that dreadful courtroom, I have come to feel that Mrs. Fitzwilliam and I might be real friends, if we can get past the fundamental incompatibility of our temperaments. She's packing a trunk as I enter—no maid for her—and a little girl in a rosy pinafore plays with a set of blocks near the open window. Her daughter, I presume. I haven't laid eyes on the rumored child until now. Pretty thing. I take Mrs. Fitzwilliam's outstretched hand and thank her for taking a moment to see me.

"Of course," she says. "May I offer you some tea?"

"Iced, if you don't mind."

She addresses the manager, who still looms protectively near the door. "Mr. Simpkins, could you arrange for iced tea? And lemonade for Evelyn."

"Of course, Mrs. Fitzwilliam."

When the door closes, she moves to the desk and busies herself with the articles there. She's removed her jacket, but her neat patterned blouse and unexceptional navy skirt remain in place, terribly dignified. "I apologize for the heat, Mrs. Marshall. We don't seem to be getting much air today."

"Not at all. The city's worse, believe me."

"Evelyn, darling," she says, addressing the tyke, "would you mind going into the bedroom and fetching your toys? Mama's packing our suitcases now."

Little Evelyn rises to her little feet—evidently Mama is a figure of some authority, a fact I can appreciate for the miracle it is, these days—and trundles off to the door on the opposite wall, leaving the two of us alone in the parlor.

"Did you have something particular to communicate, Mrs. Marshall? Or merely sympathies?" She flutters back and forth between desk and suitcase, and I suspect she's trying to disguise a little untoward trembling. (It's a trick I employ myself, from time to time, when confronted by an immovable Boy.) She continues, arranging papers, not looking at me, "I'm afraid my sister isn't here, at the moment. She wanted a little privacy, after the shock this morning, and went back to our house in the city."

"Yes, I know." I set my gloves and pocketbook on the sofa table. "Is there anything I can do for you? You seem distressed."

"Do I? Actually, I feel quite calm. I suppose it will all sink in shortly, and then I'll be in pieces." She sets the papers in a leather portfolio and the portfolio in the trunk. "Did you say you *knew* that Sophie's in the city?"

"Yes. Mr. Rofrano has gone to meet her there."

That stops her. She turns to me, hand on waist, eyes rather wide-ish. "Mr. Rofrano?"

"Yes. Do you mind if I sit down? The heat." Rather than wait for permission, I allow a chintz armchair to absorb me into its thickets.

"Mr. Rofrano," she says again. "Do you think that's wise?"

"If you're asking whether I trust Mr. Rofrano, I do. He *is* my fiancé, after all, and while you may question his judgment in that regard, I challenge you to question his honor."

She studies me without embarrassment, nods, and turns back to the desk. Someone's been busy there; it's covered with reports and folders and stacks of correspondence held together with plain black string. There is also a slip of paper that looks dangerously like a telegram, not that I'm snooping. I wonder, not for the first time, about Mr. Fitzwilliam. Whether he actually exists. She's wearing a ring, but you can buy a ring anywhere, can't you? Seduced and abandoned, the old story.

"Very well," she says, "but that's not why you're here, is it?"

"No. I have a keen interest, Mrs. Fitzwilliam, a very keen interest in your father's acquittal—"

"Then I'm afraid you must have been terribly disappointed this morning, when he was convicted of the crime."

"I was as shocked as anyone. Or perhaps *bemused* is a better word. Why the jury would convict him, when the courtroom was clearly consumed by a titillating flame of reasonable doubt. I suppose the dear fellows figured someone had to pay, and it might as well be him."

She turns her head. "You don't believe he killed her?"

"You speak so dispassionately, Mrs. Fitzwilliam. These are your parents we're talking about. Do you really believe your father capable of murder?"

"I wouldn't have thought so, no. But I don't necessarily consider myself an infallible judge of human character."

Aha! I think, just as a knock strikes the door, and the refreshments arrive. This minute clue into Mrs. Fitzwilliam's past gives me far more satisfaction than it should, and perhaps a grain of hope that she might, after all, be inclined to confide in me.

I sip my iced tea decorously while the waiter leaves and Mrs. Fitzwilliam settles Evelyn in the bedroom with her lemonade and cookies. A breeze at last makes its way through the open window, scented very faintly by the sea. I rise and carry my drink to the view, and it's not my fault if the desk rests along my path, and the telegram lying atop the desk, and I so happen to notice the words *Cocoa Beach* at the beginning of the typescript before I direct my gaze virtuously out the window.

The Pickwick Arms occupies a commanding position at the top of a hill, and if I strain my eyes through
the haze, I believe I can make out a sliver of Long Island
Sound, and Long Island beyond. I'm consumed with a
passionate longing for Windermere. For the dunes and
the crashing ocean. The boys, sunburned and salty,
digging channels in the sand with their tiny shovels.
The sun crawling over the infinite sky.

The bedroom door closes softly behind me. I say,
without turning, "What was she like? Your mother."

"Why do you ask?"

"Believe it or not, my dear, I *am* here to help you. I
was the one who dug up Mr. Magnifico, did you know
that? I want nothing more than a happy conclusion to
this awful matter."

"But why? Why do you care?"

I turn, holding my wet glass close to my chest, and
smile sincerely. "Why, because of Ox. I'd do anything
to help my brother."

She looks amazed. "But they're not engaged anymore. Sophie hasn't worn the ring since February. I
presume she means to return it, now that the trial's all
over."

"Ah, but you see, my brother is still deeply in love
with her. He wants to marry her, whatever happens.
But he's been awfully worried about how all this is

affecting her. If there's a shred of hope that Mr. Fortescue—"

"Faninal."

"—that your father's innocent, why, Ox wants—*we*
want—to keep on laboring in pursuit of justice. For
your father's sake, and for yours."

"And because you want Sophie beholden to you. You
want her to feel as if she's obliged to marry the man
who rescued her father from the gallows."

"There's no such things as the gallows anymore,
dear. They're quite outdated."

I am sorry to say that Mrs. Fitzwilliam doesn't appreciate my little quip. I heave a suffering sigh in the
face of her disapproving gaze. She hasn't got the pretty
blue eyes of her sister; hers are more pale and washed
of color. Gray, I should call them, though I've never
been satisfied with that description. It's more of a blue
that didn't have quite enough will to bloom.

"My mother's character, Mrs. Marshall," she says,
after delivering me that chiller, "has been thoroughly
dissected in a public courtroom over the past two
weeks. I can't imagine what else you need to know."

"But is it *true*, all of it? Was she really so bad?"

"For what it's worth, I don't think she was bad. I
think she was ill. I *knew* she was ill, even when I was a
child, and I didn't understand."

"Do you mean she went mad?"

She returns to the desk. "No. But she changed, after Sophie was born. I was six years old. She was like Sophie before that, all full of sunshine and love. And the light went out of her. I don't know why. My father didn't know what to do. He started spending more and more time in his workshop. They both had some family money, so he didn't really need to work, but—well, I guess it was just easier for him. He doesn't like to be helpless. He likes to fix things when they're broken, and my mother refused to be fixed, like one of his machines, and he got—*angry*, I guess. You know how people hate things they don't understand."

I don't know what brought on this lengthy confession. I'm not the kind of person in whom most women choose to confide. I imagine they think I'm like Mr. Faninal, that I'll set about trying to fix them, and I believe most women—like poor Mrs. Faninal—don't really want to be fixed. Or (more likely) they understand the impossibility of really fixing a person, the way you fix a car or a rusty hinge. They just want someone to share the burden. Fair enough, I suppose. So I stand there quietly by the window and allow Mrs. Fitzwilliam to share her burden with me—it's not unlike what she said in court, under oath, except that somehow it is—without interruption. I have the idea that she won't tolerate any leading questions, she's far too clever for that, so when she pauses for breath, I simply say, "I guess we're all guilty of that, from time to time."

She's looking down at one of those bundles of correspondence, tied so snugly in waxed black string. She picks up the telegram, folds it in half, and slips it inside. "I don't know about all those other men. I never saw her do anything wrong like that. Or maybe I just don't remember. I was so young."

"It's a shame your sister doesn't remember anything."

"A shame? I've always thought it a blessing."

"Yes, of course. For her peace of mind. I only meant from the practical point of view. Finding out exactly what happened, that morning."

Mrs. Fitzwilliam sets the bundle of papers in the trunk and turns to me fiercely. "Well, you haven't had to live with this all these years, have you? You haven't spent fifteen years trying to bury it all. Everything you knew, everything you were. Every possible suspicion."

She speaks softly, because of the little girl in the room next door, but her intensity—the tautness of her face, the force of her words—pins me to the window, speechless. Another hot breeze strikes the small of my back. I curl my left hand around the wooden frame.

"Yes." Her arms fold across her chest. "Just *imagine* that for a moment, Mrs. Marshall. Just imagine growing up with that suspicion."

"I wish"—my throat is dry, making speech difficult—"I wish I could relieve you of that."

She stalks to the desk. More papers. An ebony pencil case. "You can't. It's already done. He's been found guilty, and he hasn't objected to that verdict, either to Sophie and me or to the public, and now I have only to regret that I didn't take Sophie away with me when I could. That I left her alone with him when I went to France."

"You believe he committed the crime, then?"

"Oh, yes. Father never testified. He never actually claimed he didn't do it, did he? And he doesn't lie," she says, with a bitterness that might mean all kinds of things. She chucks the objects into the trunk. "And here's something else, something I didn't tell them in court, though I probably should have."

Ask the girls, Giuseppe said. *The girls know.*

The hair goes all electric on my arms. A tingle makes its way down the column of my spine, and back up again, and I set my glass on the windowsill—the ice is beginning to clatter about, betraying my nerves— and say, "My goodness. Why ever not?"

"Why *not*? Did you ever have a father, Mrs. Marshall?"

"Not that I can recall. He died of a corrupted liver when I was seven. Lost his fortune in the panic, I'm told, and naturally turned to drink, as a gentleman should."

"Well, I'm sorry about that," she says, a little mollified. "But if he had lived, and he were sitting there in the courtroom, watching you as you testified, and no one asked you that specific question, no one *thought* to ask it. Because of course, nobody imagined . . ."

"Imagined what?"

She perches on the edge of an armchair, next to the trunk. A leather portfolio rests in her hands. She looks into the empty fireplace, or maybe the set of irons next to it; hard to tell, from this angle. Her hair is soft and waving, just covering her ears, and my goodness if she doesn't look appealing. What a cad, this soi-disant husband of hers. I've a mind to track him down myself, real or not, and give him a good shaking.

"That he was in love," she whispers.

I wait for her to go on, but she doesn't oblige me. She's thinking very hard now, biting her lip. Wondering if she can trust me.

I had a daughter once. Don't you remember? I knew she was a girl, growing there in my womb; she just felt different, somehow, from the boys who preceded her.

I went so far as to decorate the nursery in pinks and laces, to make unbearably frilly clothes for her with my own two hands. Sylvo thought I was crazy. Maybe I was. Anyway, they let me look at her, after she was born. She was so clean and white and peaceful, such a lovely pure little thing. You would hardly know she was dead. Her fingernails were like pearls. I touched her fist for a moment, slightly curled upon her pillow, and her hair, which was light brown and still damp from the delivery, and then her miniature round nose. Then they took her away to ready her for burial. Before she was put in her casket, I made them dress her in one of those frightful pink frocks I sewed for her, in the ecstasy of my anticipation. The rest I gave away to the foundling hospital, except for a small knit cap, which I kept in my drawer. From time to time, I took that cap from its hiding place, and I imagined the little girl she would have been. I would think, Let's see, she is two years old now and starting to talk in sentences, she is six years old and reading her picture books, she is seventeen years old and falling in love for the first time, probably with some unsuitable lad. Just like her mother.

And if she has some confession to make, some burden in her heart that needs sharing, I will settle myself next to her and take her cool, soft hand between mine, and say something like:

"In love with whom, dear?"

And, in a dry, heartbroken voice, she will tell me the truth.

Chapter 19

Don't waste time trying to break a man's heart;
be satisfied if you can manage to chip it in a
brand new place.

—HELEN ROWLAND

SOPHIE

Roosevelt Field, Long Island

An hour later, when Octavian has landed the air-plane and brought it neatly back in line with its fel-lows; when he has removed his helmet and goggles and Sophie's helmet and goggles and put them back in the hangar; when he's run his hands a last time over the fu-selage, the way you check a horse's legs for soundness, and exchanged pleasantries with the mechanics; he turns to Sophie and suggests a cup of coffee at the airfield café.

She nods yes. Octavian takes her hand, and she walks beside him on her unsteady legs toward the cluster of buildings on the western side of the field. The grass is warm and well beaten; she can smell its good greenness, the scent of summer. She loves the comfortable silence between them. She loves the weight of his fingers around hers, the way they tether her to the present moment, the present rectangle of sunlit meadow, instead of what lies beyond.

It's too hot to stay inside, so Octavian carries the coffee and sandwiches outside and they make a picnic on the grass, near the parked Ford, watching the airplanes drone past, landing and taking off and circling above in a delicate aeronautical ballet.

Sophie swallows and says, "I wish we didn't have to leave. I wish we could just stay right here."

"I know."

That's all. *I know.* Sophie wants to ask him if he loves Mrs. Marshall, and if he *does* love her, why is he here with Sophie, holding hands with Sophie? And if he *doesn't* love Mrs. Marshall, why the devil is he marrying her?

Instead she says, "Your airplane. Is that what you want to do? Design airplanes?"

"It's the future," he says. "Everybody will be flying soon. Getting inside an airplane will be no more strange than getting into an automobile."

"And you'll be in the middle of it."

"I hope so."

"You will. It's what you were made for. It's why you're alive."

He finishes his sandwich and pulls out his cigarette case. Beneath the peak of his flat cap, his eyes point east, across the runway, where a plane is just now touching its wheels to the grass, up the bluff to the second airfield. "He was a good man, Roosevelt. You'd think he'd be a bore, or a snob, growing up in the White House and all that. *I* thought he would. But he wasn't. He was a smart fellow, a good pilot. The kind of fellow who'd draw off enemy fire to save the rest of the squadron, and not stop to think about it. He lasted about a month, once we started combat patrols. The Boche dropped a message a couple of weeks later, saying he'd been shot down behind their lines, and they'd buried him with full military honors. Better than getting blown out of recognition by a shell, I guess."

"I can't bear to think about it. I can't believe you survived."

He lights the cigarette slowly. "Do you know how long the average pilot stayed alive? About six weeks. Six weeks, Sophie. Every time I went up, I figured I wasn't coming back. That my luck had run out."

"But it didn't."

"It didn't. Then I stopped believing in luck at all. It was just chance."

"Aren't they the same thing?"

"No. Luck's a conscious thing, isn't it? It means someone's on your side. Fate's on your side. Chance is just chance. A random play of numbers. And that's all it is, a one-in-a-thousand chance that I'm sitting here with you, eating a sandwich, smoking a cigarette, instead of buried under a pair of crossed propeller blades on the French frontier."

"Well, I think you're wrong. I think it *is* luck. There's a reason you survived."

"No, there isn't. Why should God choose me, instead of Quentin Roosevelt? He's the better man."

Sophie sets aside the crust of her sandwich and leans back on her elbows, watching Octavian smoke his cigarette, squint-eyed and thoughtful. It must be five or six o'clock, but the sun is still high. It's midsummer, they have hours yet before the day is over. Before the light is gone.

"Because there's something you're meant to do," she says. "Something you're meant to be."

He turns to her, and his face is tender. "What about you, Sophie? What are you meant to be?"

"I don't know. At the moment it's rather bleak, isn't it?" She laughs dryly. "I'm the daughter of the murderer, the pathetic little girl who tried to wake her murdered mother. Forever notorious for an act I don't even remember."

"You really don't remember? Not a thing? You were almost three, weren't you?"

She shakes her head. "Julie says I've repressed the memory. That's what your subconscious does, when you live through something awful. It buries the memory deep down, where you can't find it."

"Well, I wish to God my subconscious would do the same for me." He flicks ash into the nearby turf. "Instead, it's the opposite."

Sophie's hand, lying on the ground, starts to play with the grass. She plucks out one blade, and another. "It's been the strangest thing, sitting there in court every day. Hearing this thing described, this little girl described, and she might as well be a stranger. And she's me. I sat there on that kitchen floor, I saw it all. I saw my father murder my mother." She lowers herself all the way back and stares at the sky. The grass prickles her ears, the back of her neck. "Is that why you took me there? Hoping I'd remember something?"

"My God, no. What makes you say that?"

"I don't know. I've just been wondering."

"Sophie." He moves beside her, and she turns her head, just enough to see him. "No. You were the one who wanted to go inside, remember? I just wanted—well, I'm not sure what I wanted, exactly. I already knew who you were. I didn't have any proof, but I felt it. I knew it. You just—you fit. There was this hole"—he brushes his sternum with his thumb, the thumb holding the cigarette—"and you fit there. And the house was where I first found you. So I just—it was an impulse. A stupid impulse. If I hadn't taken you there, your father wouldn't have suspected—"

"We don't know that for certain."

"Yes, we do. I do. I know what he said to me, that night at Theresa's apartment, while everyone was giving speeches. He thought I was going to expose you all." He lifts the cigarette, what there's left of it. "You know the rest."

"He threatened you, and you fought him off, and he took out his pistol, his stupid pistol he always carried around."

"Don't fret. I don't blame him. I might have done the same, if I had you to protect. You and your sister."

If I had you. But he doesn't have her, does he? He has Mrs. Marshall to protect. Mrs. Marshall to love.

Sophie turns back to the sky. "Tell me. When are you getting married?"

A pair of men walk by, a few yards away, talking in loud nasal voices. Something about a man named

Carter who's a terrible pilot, going to kill himself, and for some reason this is a good joke. Octavian waits until the nasal laughs have faded before he replies, in a flat pitch, "As soon as the divorce comes through. That's the plan, anyway. Then we're heading out to California. A lot of pilots out there these days, plenty of opportunity."

"That's wonderful. I expect to hear great things from you."

Her tone is too bright, and she knows it. How false she sounds, how brittle. Aren't they supposed to be honest together, at this point? What does it take anymore, for two people to say what they really mean?

"Listen," he says. "For what it's worth—"

"Don't."

"You have every right to be angry. You should be angry."

"I was angry. I was so angry, that night I found out. Over the telephone!" A dry little laugh. "Now it doesn't matter."

He doesn't reply, and Sophie closes her eyes. A drowsiness has begun to creep over her, a kind of relief after all the strain and exhaustion of the preceding months. The strain and exhaustion that await her when she returns. She hears the faint drone of an insect, or maybe it's another airplane. There is a rustle, a sigh. A weight coming down, as Octavian settles back in the grass next to her.

"As I said. For what it's worth. I meant to end things with Theresa, after I met you. I hated what we were doing together, but I couldn't stop, because I needed what she had to give me. And then *you* danced in, and I knew—I thought I knew—"

"Please don't."

"She lost a son in the war. Awful thing. And then her husband, that same day we drove to Connecticut together, he told her he wanted a divorce. He wanted to marry his mistress. That very same day I found you, after all those years. So if you want to talk about luck—"

"Then we were never meant to fall in love, I guess."

Above them, or maybe across the field—lying here in the grass, Sophie can't really tell—an engine sputters, coughs, and then catches again. She listens carefully to the reassuring buzz. The sign of life.

"No," he says. "It's too late for that. At least on my side."

"Then God is cruel."

"Or it's just chance again. Dumb, random chance."

Sophie rolls over to face him. His nose points straight to the sky, tipped with sunshine. His arms are folded behind his head, and the cigarette is gone. He loves her. He just said so, didn't he, unless she mis-understood. She says quietly, "No. It's not chance, it's who you are. She needs you, and you're too good to leave her."

"What about you? Do you need me?"

"About as much as you need me, I guess."

He closes his eyes. His chest rises and falls. "I hope not. I hope you don't."

Sophie puts her hand at the meeting of his ribs. Her white cotton glove is smeared with dirt and oil. "If you ask me," she says, "what's worse is not feeling anything at all."

"Well, then. What if I *am* asking you?"

Her hand looks so proper there, encased in cotton, resting on Octavian's shirt. "When I realized there was something between you two, you and Mrs. Marshall, of all women, I was furious. I was madly jealous. And it was *exhilarating*. It was almost as good as falling in love with you. And then Father was arrested, and I stopped feeling either one. I was so numb and shocked I didn't care. You could have married her the next day and had a dozen children, and I wouldn't have cared. The most terrible thing of all, like your heart is stricken inside your body." She curls her finger around a button. "I would rather hate you again than go back to feeling nothing."

He removes one arm from behind his head and traps her hand against his chest. "So you *don't* hate me anymore?"

"No. Well, I never really did, did I? I was just angry. Every time I closed my eyes, those weeks before the party, I thought of the two of you together, like lovers, and I couldn't stand it." She stares at his profile. At his eyelashes, of all things: thick and dark against the bridge of his nose. Lighter at the tips, or is that the sun? She whispers, "I still can't."

There is no answer to that, and Sophie doesn't expect one. The sky is warm on the crown of her head—she's taken off her hat, and so has he—and the drowsiness returns, along with a sense of slow rupture, as if she's cooking from within, and the drowsiness is just a symptom of her malady. His voice stirs her, just as her eyes are closing.

"What if I tell you—Sophie—what if I tell you that we aren't lovers? Theresa and—that I haven't—that we haven't . . . not for some time."

"Some time?"

"Since the night of the party."

She opens her eyes. His cheeks are stained with raspberry beneath his tan. "Is that true?"

"Yes."

"But why?"

His sigh moves her hand. "It wasn't honest. She's married. It never felt honest, even at the beginning, when I thought I was in love with her."

"Then why didn't you ever stop?"

"Because I was afraid I would go back to what I was before. What I was when the war ended. When everyone was dead."

His heart beats under her hand. The rhythm communicates through his shirt and her glove, and echoes back through the pulse in his fingers. It's a slow pulse, so slow it frightens her. She keeps longing for the next beat. The spaces between them are almost unendurable.

"Anyway," he continues, "I *have* stopped. At least until her divorce comes through. Until . . ."

Thump-thump.

Thump-thump.

"Until what?"

His head turns. His eyes are quite blue now, reflecting the sky. A shadow passes over his skin, gone in a flash, in the mad drone of another airplane.

"You tell me," he says.

In the car, he kisses her. One minute he's sitting there, hands on the wheel. He's just cranked the engine; he pulls down the spark retard until the pistons smooth out into a contented rumble. His hand goes down to release the parking brake, and then, just before touching the lever, makes a U-turn instead, crossing over the small divide between his body and hers, taking her softly by the cheek. The kiss is fervent and awkward. She tries to turn sideways and so does he, but his legs are too long and their mouths come apart.

"I'm sorry," he says.

"Don't be." She takes off her gloves and picks up his hand, which has fallen on his thigh, and she places it on the placket of her blouse. He unbuttons the top button, the second, the third, and his fingers ease between the two edges to lie against the damp, delicate crepe de chine camisole that covers her chest. The top of the Ford is open; anyone can see them. She leans recklessly forward and kisses him, and this time it works better, because they're both ready. He kisses her beautifully, quite slow, gentle as the tide; his mouth is warm and tastes of tobacco. Better than Jay, better than anything. His fingers slip inside the camisole to touch her breast, to examine the curve and the weight of her, the texture at the very tip, minute and thorough, until she's staggered by her own audacity, by the way a man's fingers feel upon your naked skin, when you actually want them there. Hot and fizzy. He breaks off first, panting a little, and there is a moment of perfect wonder, staring at each other.

"I don't want to stop," she confesses.

He closes his eyes and pulls his hand free, and she holds the back of his neck and leans into his chest. Well, his pulse is certainly faster *now*, she thinks, listening to the eager contractions of muscle. Thump-*thump*! Thump-*thump*! His breath is humid in her hair. She laughs against his shirt and murmurs, "At least that's over, anyway. At least we can't regret we never even kissed."

He says, "Are your servants living in?"

"I think so. They're supposed to be."

He strokes the back of her hair. She thinks maybe she'll lift her head and kiss him again, just to see what's next; and then, belatedly, she realizes what he meant about the servants and her blood goes whoosh in her veins. Is it really possible? Of course it is. There's nothing to stop them, is there? No parents and chaperones, no unhealthy repression of the sexual instinct. She's almost sick at the prospect, dizzy with either daring or anticipation or fear. What would Father say? Father doesn't matter anymore. Father doesn't exist. This kiss—this act—a declaration of independence.

She lifts her head. "Are you going to kiss me again, or are you going to take me home?"

He reaches back and unwinds her arm, kissing the inside of her wrist as it passes by. "Take you home, I guess," he says, and he releases the floor lever with his left hand and presses the reverse pedal with his right foot.

They head west, toward Queens Village and Jamaica Avenue, and the sun is starting to fall, casting a glare across the windshield. The empty roads fill suddenly with traffic, and Octavian steps gently on the brake and slips the engine back into low gear.

"What's the matter?" Sophie asks.

"I think it's the racetrack," he says. "It's Belmont day."

"Belmont day?"

"The Belmont Stakes. Big race for three-year-olds. The track's right over there. Belmont Park." He lifts a single index finger from the steering wheel to point north.

"I didn't know you followed the races."

"An old hobby." He pauses. "I saw Man o' War win the Dwyer Stakes a couple of years ago, over at Aqueduct. That was some race." Another pause. He rubs the wheel with his thumbs and adds, "That was the last time I went, actually."

"Horses and airplanes." She laughs. "That's you, exactly."

"Is it?"

"The past and the future, running inside you like parallel lines. And you want to straddle them both. You see the beauty in both. Horses *and* airplanes."

The car ahead lurches forward. Octavian moves the throttle, and the Ford follows, into a skein of dust, growling with effort.

"Maybe," he says.

They've stopped at a drive. A long line of cars waits to emerge from the beaten earth of a parking area. Octavian sticks out his head and addresses the driver of an elderly electric Columbia runabout. "Hey, buddy! Who won?"

"Pillory!" the man calls back. "Beat the favorite by three lengths."

Octavian pulls back in and turns to Sophie, smiling perhaps as wide as she's ever seen him, smiling like a hungry crocodile, teeth aligned in perfect order. "Well, that's something, anyway. I just won a hundred and forty bucks."

But something happens, as they cross the Queensboro Bridge and crawl back into Manhattan. The mood shifts and falls, like the sun dropping behind the buildings to the west, and the echoing metropolitan noise petrifies the air between them. Sophie, thinking for maybe the hundredth time about the kiss at the airfield, feels for the first time that they have done something wrong.

"I don't know . . ." she begins as they turn down First Avenue.

"Know what?"

"Whether you should stay the night!"

"Stay the *night*?" He sounds stunned.

"Didn't you mean . . . ?"

"What?"

"When you asked about the servants."

The uptown traffic is sweating and impatient, all eager to get home after a long day's toil. The Ford has rumbled to a stop. In the face of this banal detail—-people navigating the city's dirty, crowded, eternal grid—Sophie is overcome with embarrassment. Octavian's hand on her breast—how shameful! When, just that morning, her father was deemed guilty of her mother's murder.

"Sophie," Octavian says, "I didn't mean . . . What I meant was that you shouldn't be alone. All by yourself in that house. I meant that we would find someone to stay, if the servants weren't there when we got back, because the reporters might find you, or some crazy fellow who's fixed on the trial, or God knows what else."

"Oh," she says miserably. The car moves forward again, another few feet.

"The thing is, Theresa's expecting me for dinner."

"Of course."

"I'm already late."

"Then you should hurry back."

"Sophie, don't be sore. I can't just—I can't be cruel. I owe her everything. There's—well, there's more to her than you think."

"I don't want you to be cruel. Didn't I say that already?"

"I'm sorry. I shouldn't have kissed you like that. I've been regretting it ever—"

"Don't! Don't regret it. It's just a kiss. She has to give us something, doesn't she? She doesn't get to keep all of you." She stares down at her lap, her rumpled navy skirt, her stained white gloves clutched miserably atop. The necessity of Octavian's leg right up against hers, on the narrow seat of a Model T.

He brings his fist down on his leg and swears under his breath.

The lurching seems to be making her a little sick. She turns her head again and looks out the side, where a flower shop is just closing for the evening. A man in a dirty apron rolls in a green-striped awning. Roses are in season, blooming inside every inch of the rectangular plate-glass window, and a sign in the corner reads WEDDINGS GLADLY CATERED FOR. INQUIRE WITHIN.

"Horse and airplane," Sophie murmurs to herself.

"What's that?"

She turns back and reaches for his hand. "I'm not going to make you choose. I'd never do that to you. You were meant to make some other girl happy, some *woman*, and I'll just take off and soar into the sky, and no one will catch me."

He doesn't reply, and the rest of the drive is just like that, New York talking around them, life going on, stopping and starting, noisy and arrhythmic, and Sophie thinks, *So this is good-bye.*

By the time they reach the house on Thirty-Second Street, the sky is purple and the sun has fallen behind the buildings to the west, and Julie Schuyler has taken possession of the topmost step, wearing a beaded dress that catches a glitter or two from the streetlights. A sparkling clip adorns the side of her bobbed hair, sagging a little, as if she's just returned from a night out. Or maybe desecration is the intended effect? She rises to her feet when the Ford pulls up to the curb.

Octavian peers across Sophie, through the passenger window. "Who's that?"

"Julie Schuyler." Sophie tugs ferociously on the door handle. "There might be news."

But Julie just brushes down her dress as Sophie climbs out of the car. Her smile is crimson and insincere. "I thought you shouldn't be alone tonight. I can see you've already had the same bright idea, however."

Behind Sophie, the other door slams shut. Octavian, revealing himself. Julie's gaze lifts, takes in the sight, and returns to Sophie. Her eyebrows, freshly plucked, are high and delicate on her forehead.

"Mr. Rofrano was just taking me home," Sophie says.

"I'm sure he was. And now that I know you're in good hands, I'll be on my way."

Sophie turns her head. Octavian's still standing by the driver's door, watching them. His hands rest lightly on the frame, dressed in leather driving gloves. His flat cap is drawn low over his forehead.

She turns back to Julie. "He wasn't staying, though."

"No?"

"No. Just took me for a drive. I needed a little air."

"Is that so?"

Sophie holds up her hand. "Word of honor."

The crimson lips part a little. Maybe it's a smile, maybe not. You never really know with Julie; you never know exactly where you stand with her. That's part of the thrill, isn't it? Unpicking the threads of her costume.

"Well, then." Julie Schuyler lifts one bare hand and makes a shooing movement toward the Ford, sending a tangle of gold bangles to crash around her elbow. "We'll just send him back to Mama, won't we."

Julie Schuyler always knows where the skeletons lurk in the closet, and she likewise always knows where the bottle of liquor lurks in the cabinet. She produces one now and holds it high, examining the label against the light. "Kentucky bourbon, by God. Where did you get this?"

Sophie shrugs. "I don't know. It's my father's."

"Nothing more suitable to zozzle us tonight, then."

"I don't want to get zozzled."

"Try," says Julie, and voilà, they're sitting on the parlor sofa, trading the bottle between them while the passing headlamps trace, at irregular intervals, along the cracks in the drapes. Julie lights a cigarette and asks what Sophie's planning to do now.

"I was thinking of applying for a job in an engineer's office," Sophie says, swishing the bourbon in the bottle and wishing she liked the taste. She thinks, *Octavian's having dinner with her now, remember?* Octavian's kissing her now, and you *told* him he could, you little fool, you stupid noble little girl. You sent him off to her.

Sophie draws breath, tilts back, and forces the burn down her throat.

"A job? What about your money?"

"I don't know. It's Father's money."

"Well, it's yours now, isn't it? I mean, once he's— *well*."

Once he's dead. Obviously, Father will shortly be sentenced to death, won't he? For the crime of capital murder. And soon after that, they will carry out the sentence. Swift, efficient justice. A life for a life. One man to the gallows, another man to Mrs. Marshall. Sophie all by herself.

She lifts the bottle and swallows again.

"That wasn't very tactful, was it?" Julie says. "My apologies. I know it's dreadful. He's your father, after all."

"Yes." Sophie's eyes are stinging. She blinks and says, "I don't know about the money. I haven't thought about it."

"What a good girl you are. Thank goodness you've got me to think about it for you. All that lovely dough, divided into loaves between the two of you. You could open your own engineering office, if you like." She swallows, much more luxuriously than Sophie, cigarette balanced between her fingers, and hands back the bottle. "You could do whatever you want."

"I don't know how I can touch his money."

"You'll find it in you, I'm sure. We always do."

The third swallow isn't so bad. Sophie feels she's getting the hang of this. She wipes the corner of her mouth with her thumb and asks Julie if she can try her cigarette.

"Have your own," Julie says generously, and she reaches for her pocketbook and rummages inside. Her cigarette case is enameled in a giddy red-and-white design, edged with gold. She produces a long, new cigarette and sticks it between Sophie's lips. "You really need lipstick to do it properly," she advises.

"I left my lipstick behind at the hotel."

"I've got some." Julie paints Sophie's lips, working around the unlit cigarette. Her eyes narrow in concentration, and Sophie notices she's got blacking on her eyelashes, and a very thin line of kohl articulates the shape of her eyelid. When she draws back to judge her handiwork, she looks adventurous and unnaturally wide-awake, as if her blue irises are jumping from her face. "There. Much better," she says, and she sets aside the lipstick and lights Sophie's cigarette with a match struck from the side of her red-and-white enamel case.

Later, when they've foraged for dinner in the icebox and both servants have failed to turn up, Sophie invites Julie to stay for the night. She glances at her slender gold wristwatch, and then at the plain black-and-white clock on the kitchen wall.

"Well. Since you so obviously need me."

"I don't need you."

"Yes, you do. Someone needs to take your mind off the fact that your beau is having dinner with another woman at this very moment, and probably more than dinner."

"He's not my beau."

"But you're in love with him."

"It doesn't make any difference, does it? Nothing makes any difference." Sophie shuts one eye and stares at the inch or two of bourbon remaining in the bottle, which stands in the center of the table, like an honored guest. "We are such stuff as dreams are made on."

"That's Shakespeare."

"Yes."

Julie wags a finger. "You're not allowed to go flinging around Billy-boy at a time like this. Willy-nilly."

"Says who?"

"Says me. You can jus—you can justify anything with a little Shakespeare. Give yourself a nice glossy shield of—cleverness."

"But we *are* clever, darling. We're awfully clever. Look at us!" Sophie opens her arms. "*You're* going to start an engineering firm with me, and *we're* going to share a grand apartment and have lots of lovers and never, *ever* get married."

"Says who?"

"Says me. That's what I'm going to do."

Julie shakes her head. "You can count me out, sister."

"Oh no you don't. You're brave enough to get me into this, but you won't see it through?"

"But it's different with you. It's *your* money. Or *will* be yours, when your father—well."

"You have money, too."

"My parents' money, Sophie. It's a trem—trenem—it's a *great* difference." She frowns, looks around the room, and discovers her cigarette case lying on top of the icebox. Bracing herself carefully on the table, she rises to her feet. "And they won't stand for this."

"For sharing an apartment with me?"

"No. I don't think they'd care as much about that." With some difficulty, she lights the cigarette, and then—apparently exhausted by the effort—collapses back against the icebox, puffing quietly. "It's the rest of it. Making my own money."

Sophie frowns. So hard to concentrate, when the world is so beautifully muddled. "But you were going to get a job anyway, weren't you? With me. We were going to get an apartment together and find work and be indepen—dependent and modern."

"Oh, a *job*! But that's nothing, darling. You can't make a real living on a mere job. *My* kind of living, I mean, the kind that will keep me in the style to which I'm tragically accustomed." She waves her hand, butterfly-like. "As long as I need my allowance, they've got me in the end, right? I can only stray so far, like a little doggie on a leash."

"But you'll be with me."

Julie shakes her head slowly. "I can't take your money, dearest. Not even for the sake of eman— enamci—freedom. The creed, you know."

"What creed?"

"The creed that says we don't sponge off our dearie-wums."

"But I *need* you!" Sophie wails. "I can't run my firm without you! You know so much more about— managing people—and *economics*!" (She says it carefully, so as not to embarrass herself: *e-co-nom-ics.*)

Julie's smooth face takes on a bit of wrinkle at the forehead. "But engineering's so grubby. Can't you run a department store instead?"

"But I don't know anything about that."

Julie reaches down and takes off a shoe, fumbling with the buckle until it slides free from her stocking. She holds it up before her. "You see this?"

"I think so."

"What is it?"

"A shoe?"

"Exactly! It's just a shoe, darling. You don't have to know everything about it. You just have to know if you like it. You have to have the guts to say, *I like this shoe, damn it, and every woman in New York is going to wear it next season.* And you *have* that kind of guts, Sophie. You do." She wobbles. Braces herself against the icebox. A bit of startled ash drops from the end of her cigarette. "I don't, though. I have the guts to bob my hair and smoke in public, but I don't have the guts to scratch for my own worms. That's a special kind of brave, my sweet, and Julie doesn't have it."

Sophie leans her cheek into the palm of her hand and thinks that Julie looks awfully brave enough to her. She stands teetering on the pinnacle of the present sleek moment. Her breasts are flattened by a state-of-the-art brassiere. Her waist doesn't exist. Her skirt hovers dangerously at the middle of her shin. Her lips are round and rosy, her hair short and curled and burnished. In her modern costume, she makes you think of a juvenile, fresh and unspoiled and yet utterly naughty: a girl who will give you all the good times you crave, without all the messy grown-up consequences. Julie blazes a fearless new trail, just by standing there in her glittering, straight-edged best, trailing a cigarette from her hand.

Sophie rises from the table and staggers toward the blurry image of Julie, leaning against her icebox. She takes the shoe and kneels down to replace it on Julie's slender foot, encased in its delicate stocking of daring flesh-colored silk. The beaded dress, which looked gray outside in the streetlights, is actually the color of moss.

"I think you do, though," Sophie says. "I think you *are* brave enough. Just go out there and do it. You don't need all the dresses and the luxury. You just need spirit. You need a soul."

"But I'm afraid I haven't got that little thing." Julie kneels next to her on the kitchen floor. "It's not so bad, though. I'm having the time of my life. It's just absolutely ripping, isn't it? A smashing success. Eventually I'll have to get married, I guess, when my parents lose patience with me, but I think I've got a few years left. A few years and a lot of fun."

Sophie stares at Julie's eyes, which are now ringed in soft charcoal smudges. "I don't understand. You're the bravest girl I know."

"God, no. What a thing to say." Julie giggles quietly and settles her head in Sophie's lap. "Don't you see how conventional I am? I'm never going to bite the hand that feeds me. Maybe a nibble from time to time, just to keep them on their toes. But give up this?" She lifts a section of dress. "No."

"You can if you want to."

"But I won't. That's your kind of courage, not mine."

Sophie runs her finger along the waving golden line of Julie's hair, until it ends in the diamond clip. Actually, it's not diamonds. It's rhinestones or some other costume jewel, very up-to-date, glittering with irony. Julie's eyes are closing. The cigarette sags against the floor.

"And our little life is rounded with a sleep," Sophie whispers.

Julie's faded pink lips create a tiny smile. She lifts her hand—her left hand, not the one with the cigarette—from the hygienic linoleum floor and curls it around Sophie's fingers, atop the rhinestones.

"O brave new world," she whispers back, "that has such people in it."

Telephone.

The word tears across Sophie's mind, leaving a wide and painful gash. Or maybe it's the noise itself, the persistent *brring-brring* that will not be denied. The word keeps tearing, and the noise keeps *brring-ing,* but she can't put the two ideas together.

She lifts her head. "Come in!" she gasps out.

Brring-brring.

Sophie opens her reluctant eyes and thinks, *Telephone*. This time she remembers what a telephone is. But *where* is the telephone? Where is Sophie? A parlor, well appointed. *Her* well-appointed parlor! New York? Head. Oh God, *head*! What's happened to her head? She's having a stroke. Where's the—

Brring-brring.

—telephone?

Sophie rolls to her side and falls unexpectedly from a sofa. A vague memory wafts past: Julie and a bottle of bourbon and not wanting to climb the stairs. Because Father. Because Octavian. Octavian and Mrs. Marshall.

"Julie?" she calls hopefully.

Brring-brring.

The hall. Sophie stumbles to her feet and crashes into a wall. She's still wearing her navy skirt, her untucked blouse. At one point, there was a cigarette. And a phonograph. The rest is silence.

Brring-brring.

Sophie's staggering down the hall now, toward the stairs, wincing in agony. On the half landing, the telephone sits in its cubicle of shame, outlawed from any civilized room. *Brring-brring,* stabbing her temples with a pair of lead pencils. She snatches the earpiece— it's a dreadfully old-fashioned telephone, that's Father for you—and puts her lips to the mouthpiece, and just that same second she realizes she needs to vomit.

"Hello?" (Greenly.)

"Hello? Miss Faninal?" (Crackling.)

Sophie hangs there in confusion, and then she remembers that Faninal is Fortescue. Faninal is Sophie.

"Yes. Speaking."

"This is Mr. Manning."

Sophie is hot and cold and hot. Her tongue is coated in wet flour. A small, succulent rodent seems to have died at the back of her throat. She moves her head—a mistake—and rests it against the plaster wall. "Manning?" she repeats.

There is a slight hesitation on the other end. "Your attorney, Miss Faninal. Your father's counsel. I apologize for the early hour. I'm afraid something's come up . . ."

"I'm sorry. Will you excuse me for a moment?"

"Miss Faninal, this is a *long distance*—"

Sophie sets down the earpiece and bounds up the remaining steps to the bathroom on the second floor, where she bends over the toilet and empties an improbable quantity of poisonous yellow-green bile into the bowl. This takes some time. Every last speck of bile, apparently, must be evacuated, or her stomach won't rest. When she raises her head at last, she doesn't recognize the image in the small mirror above the sink.

She reaches for a square of linen and runs it under the faucet. The coolness helps. Reminds her skin it's alive. When her face is clean and pink, she turns away and walks unsteadily out of the room. There's something pressing downstairs, isn't there? Something she needs to do, and doesn't want to do.

Her father's room lies at the end of the hall, fronting the street. The door is open, a strange thing. Father always closed his door. Even the maid had to ask permission before cleaning it. What time is it? Feels awfully early. There's not much light showing at the edges of the curtains. Sophie's not wearing a watch. Father's room? Father's room has a clock, probably. And if she goes into Father's room, she won't have to do that thing downstairs, that thing she's trying to ignore, even though it's kicking the back of her brain, urgent and unsatisfied.

She walks straight through the doorway into Mr. Faninal's dark and stale-smelling sanctum, but she doesn't look for the clock. (She doesn't know where it is, anyway.) She heads to the first window and pulls back the curtain.

Just past dawn. The sky is an eerie soot blue, streaked with pink above the buildings to the east, and the streetlamps are still lit, a thick and sickly yellow in the morning haze. The street is deserted, except for the milk wagon trundling around the corner, jangling faintly through the glass, and . . .

And a dusty green Ford Model T parked along the curb next to the house.

Sophie's hand crawls upward to her throat and rests against her windpipe. She closes her eyes, opens them, closes them again, and when—slowly—she raises her lids a final time, the car is still miraculously there.

The roof shields the interior from view, and she can't see through the windshield either: the angle is too acute.

But he's there. How long has he been parked there, keeping watch? Her cavalier. After his dinner with Mrs. Marshall? All night?

Sophie starts to breathe again. Her fist curls around the thick damask curtain and drags it to her cheek.

Telephone.

She remembers now. Mr. Manning, her father's defense counsel. Why would he telephone her at this early hour?

She gives her forehead a last damp stroke with the linen cloth and lets the curtain fall. Before she leaves, she catches sight of the clock on her father's small tin mantel:

5:42.

Chapter 20

*There's so much saint in the worst of them, and
so much devil in the best of them, that the woman
who's married to one of them, has nothing to learn
from the rest of them.*

—HELEN ROWLAND

THERESA

The Pickwick Arms, around the same time

At last, the damned telephone stops ringing, but I'm
afraid it's too late. I am irrevocably awake, and it's
not even morning, at least by my standards.

I have slept remarkably well, all things considered.
I don't generally sleep well in someone else's bed, but
the Pickwick people have done themselves proud in the
matter of mattresses, bless them, and at least there's
no one to disturb me. No one to disturb the pattering

of my own brain. The linens are fresh, the furniture painted to harmonize with the flowers on the curtains.

The telephone rests at the side of the other bed. At my bedside perches a neat little white vulture of an alarm clock. I roll to my side and lift it away. My eyes seem to be having a little trouble in this gray light; I can't imagine why. It's either nearly six o'clock or half past ten. Either way, the hour's later than I thought. Those chintz curtains must be thick.

I swing my legs from the bed. My guest will be arriving soon, and I'd like to bathe first.

Though I don't particularly admire the new shapelessness in fashion—the dropped waist, the straight, roomy lines—I suppose I should be grateful. In the bath, the roundness of my belly is obvious enough.

I squeeze a washcloth over the slight and gentle summit and admire the way the soap cascades downward in luxurious runnels. The doctor says late October. I suppose he's right; after all, I was able to provide the date of conception with reasonable precision. *Congratulations, Mrs. Marshall,* he said, without irony. *Couples at your stage of life are seldom successful in conceiving.* I presume he doesn't read the gossip pages.

I suspect it's a girl, though maybe I don't remember the particulars of pregnancy well enough. The differences between them. It's been so long since Billy was born. I've forgotten how sleepy you are, how your veins ache. I've never been that sick, early on, but I've been sick with this one, let me tell you. That's how I knew. First I thought it was a germ of some kind, and then I thought it was the immense strain of everything. When they discharged the Boy from the hospital, he was so distant and distracted. He wouldn't stay the night; he wouldn't go to bed with me at all. Observing the proprieties, he said, until the divorce came through, fair and square, but I knew it wasn't the divorce he was waiting for. It was her. It was the trial, the Faninal trial. The damned Faninals and their love affairs.

Eventually, I put two and two together and went to the doctor. Congratulations, Mrs. Marshall. You now have a trump card, a final surefire piece to play in this little match. If all else fails.

We are required, Sylvo and I, to be separated for a year before a suit for divorce may be launched in court. (You can get it done faster in the state of Nevada, I've heard, but we want to do this in a respectable, dignified fashion.) We've decided I'll be the one to file the lawsuit, citing adultery. Again, very proper and gentlemanly of Sylvo, taking the blame like that, when the facts clamor that we're both adulterers. That's what the Boy called it, anyway, the very morning after I paid my first call upon the van der Wahl guesthouse. He made breakfast, as I said, and sat down at the little table with me, but his face wasn't so gleeful as it seemed during the night. He hardly spoke. I asked him if anything was wrong, had I done anything wrong, and he looked up at me and said—I remember the exact words, the exact miserable tone of voice—*I guess I've committed adultery now.*

I pointed out that *I* was the adulterer, not him; he was merely my accomplice. A garden-variety fornicator. *A fornicator of a married woman,* the Boy said, staring at the crowded surface of his plate, and I set down my coffee and climbed into his lap. I said he wasn't to worry about that; the sin was mine. *Mine, do you hear me? You have nothing to atone for, silly Boy.*

Well, he'd never had a woman in his lap before, that much was obvious, and after a little persuasion he put his hands under my bottom and lifted me up and carried me into the bedroom, before I could explain that the kitchen table might prove even more amusing, for a change. I don't know how he managed, after such a night of dissolution, but he did. Youth, I suppose, and all those years of suppression, and the simple act of turning our bodies to find the mirror on the dresser, exposing the lascivious angle of our joining into perfect view, his flesh disappearing into mine, until we had no choice. No choice but to strive on for the pinnacle, hard and ecstatic and eviscerating.

But the melancholy returned right afterward—it usually does, with the Boy, as I soon learned; I think there's a Latin term for the condition—and he detached himself and lit a customary cigarette and declared that, on the contrary, he had plenty to atone for, that he was now utterly damned. That we would have to get married, that was all there was to it. I said he was crazy. You don't marry your mistress. *Is that what you are?* he asked the ceiling, and *That's what I am,* I confidently replied.

He turned to me and asked what would happen if I became with child.

I won't, I said, and *What if you do?* he insisted.

The possibility seemed so remote. I had miscarried twice after Billy, both early on, and then nothing. Not that I had much opportunity, at the time; Sylvo and I were just reaching that placid, friendly, sterile stage of our marriage when I was occupied with the children and he was . . . well, otherwise occupied. The idea of pregnancy had blurred away into the past, like debutante parties and trousseau fittings. Something that younger women did.

I crawled, naked, to where he sat at the head of the bed, smoking his cigarette, propped up by a crumpled pillow, looking far too sunlit and fresh-cheeked for either activity: sex or cigarettes. But his eyes were old and blue, and his skin reeked marvelously of debauchery. Of me.

Then I guess I'd have to get a divorce, in that case, I said, but I didn't mean it. I had no intention, ever, of ceasing to be Mrs. Theodore Sylvester Marshall of Fifth Avenue. I just said it to please him. The Boy, I thought, would be my little secret, for as long as I needed him. For as long as he still wanted me.

Mrs. Lumley arrives at precisely six forty-five, just as I requested. Her knock is timid, her hat brim wide and low on her forehead. She's dressed respectably, in a neat suit of forest green, and I ask her if she's had breakfast.

She removes the hat with trembling hands and says she isn't hungry.

"Well, I'm famished," I say, and I lift the telephone receiver and ask for room service.

Though terribly nervous, Mrs. Lumley is an attractive woman. Her hair is smooth and dark, not a single gray hair, and her eyes are large and brown. When she was eighteen, and a fresh new housemaid in the Faninal house, she would have looked so appealing, like a young doe. She removes her gloves and places them alongside the hat. I invite her to sit on the sofa, and she obeys me, stroking the wings of her hair with those trembly little fingers.

As she sits, the telephone rings again. Mrs. Lumley darts me a frightened look with her wide brown eyes, and I wave her concern away. "It's not for me. I've taken the room from someone else," I explain.

"From whom?" she asks, suspicious.

"From Mrs. Fitzwilliam. She left yesterday afternoon with her daughter."

"Where's she going?"

"To Florida, I believe. To join her husband. She was terribly eager to be away, not that I blame the poor woman. What a dreadful ordeal for the two of them."

Mrs. Lumley looks into her lap. "Yes."

"However, as I told you yesterday over the telephone, Mrs. Fitzwilliam was good enough to discuss the case with me before she left, inserting a few details she didn't see fit to air in a public courtroom, if you understand my meaning."

"Yes."

"You can speak in perfect confidence, Mrs. Lumley. The case is obviously closed. Mr. Faninal has been convicted, and I understand that no appeal is planned. There's no danger to you, even if I were the sort of person to reveal secrets, which I most assuredly am not." I laugh comfortably. "I have enough secrets of my own, believe me!"

She presses her thumbs together. "I'm sure you do," she whispers.

"Because, if your husband were to find out—"

"No!" Her face flashes up, so white. "You won't say a word to him, will you?"

"Of course not. Husbands should never be privy to one's secrets, I've always thought."

"He simply can't know I'm here."

"Of course not. Of course not." I reach between armchair and sofa and pat her tangled hands. "It's none of his business, is it?"

She's starting to weep. I rise and recover a handkerchief from my pocketbook. "We never did it, I swear," she says, dabbing at her eyes.

"Did what, my dear?"

"You know. We only kissed a few times, that's all. He was a gentleman. I only felt sorry for him, because of—because of—"

"Because of his wife."

"Yes." She takes in a deep breath, collecting herself. "She was always nice to me. I felt awful, what we were doing to her."

"What *you* were doing to her? My goodness, you're generous. She wasn't exactly a saint, herself."

"But it still wasn't right." Mrs. Lumley looks up with her watery eyes. "It's been killing me ever since."

"Secrets have that effect. And now the trial is over, and Mr. Faninal has been convicted and will probably hang in short order, which should spare you any further embarrassment."

"I don't know what to do! I'm going to die of it."

"Calm yourself, my dear. We don't die of guilt." I lean forward and capture those tearful peepers with my own, firm and steely. "Even for adultery."

"Adultery?"

"Yes, adultery." I lift my eyebrows. "Good heavens. Do you mean to say there's *more*?"

Her gaze drops hastily back into her lap. "No! My goodness. Of course not. Just—just that."

"But I thought you said that the two of you didn't actually—oh, what's the phrase—*do* it."

"We didn't! I mean—dear me. I must be going. I shouldn't have come." She jumps from the sofa. "I have—my husband will be wondering—"

A knock strikes the door.

I put one hand on the arm of the chair and rise to my feet.

"Ah! There we are at last. I confess, Mrs. Lumley, I do enjoy a good breakfast."

Now, I don't mean to bore you with all my stories about the Boy. Maybe it's the pregnancy, turning me all sentimental, or maybe I simply want to do him justice. You can skip them all if you like. I don't care.

Except this one. It's too important.

We had been lovers for a few months, I believe. Long enough that we were at ease with each other, attuned to each other's habits. I knew that he liked fish over meat; he knew that I liked the opposite. I knew that he had nightmares, violent ones; he knew that I knew, and that I wasn't going to speak of it. That sort of thing.

At the same time, we preserved a certain frisson between us, by virtue of only seeing each other twice a week, and by harboring our little secret in front of an obsessively secret-mongering society. We would walk along a street in Greenwich Village, or some other neighborhood safely out of the way of my usual crowd, and my attention, as we made our way along the sidewalk, hung utterly on him: his movements, the details of his dress, the few words he could spare.

The Boy, on the other hand, didn't seem to pay me much attention at all. His eyes never roamed my face and figure; they roamed the streets and buildings, the passing vehicles, the nearby men and women: a fact that caused me no end of agony. If I could just get him to notice me. To answer my questions with genuine sentences. Then I would *know* he loved me; I'd have proof of his devotion, wouldn't I?

Until the evening we were walking toward some new club or other, a little joint I'd heard about from certain quarters, in an insalubrious spot near China-town. Chattering on about the day's news, about our plans for the night. An ordinary Tuesday. And a man came up, as men do, and produced a gun and begged that we should do him the favor of relinquishing our money and our jewelry into his keeping.

Rather foolishly, I had on a pair of diamond earrings and a ruby bracelet—well, a lady likes to show off a bit, from time to time, especially when she's in want of a little personal attention—and I'm afraid I disgraced myself. Screamed in terror. The shock, I think.

Not the Boy. Oh, no. Cool as you please, he kicked the gun out of the man's hands, drew back his fist, and delivered our poor thief a piece of chin music that very nearly killed him. I thought it *had* killed him. He crumpled to the ground without a sound, and for a second or two—notwithstanding the blood dripping from his split knuckle—the Boy stood over him, gazing down, like a lion claiming his kill.

Then he turned and held out his elbow. "Come along," he said to me, and I, stunned, just took his arm and stepped around the body. A minute or two later, when I could speak, I asked if the man was dead, and the Boy said no, still breathing, and I asked why we hadn't called the police and the Boy laughed—not a civilized laugh, I assure you—and said because it wouldn't make any difference. The Boy had delivered justice himself; what was the point in summoning the law to finish off the man for good?

We walked a little farther, heels smacking on the pavement. I was going to ask how he learned to fight like that, how he learned to knock a man senseless and not even care, but I already knew the answer to that, didn't I? I already knew the source of the darkness inside him; there was no need to drag it out into the light and dissect it into its endless component pieces, and then oil up the parts and put the Boy back together again, like Humpty Dumpty. Instead, we continued on to the club and got ourselves all pie-eyed, and then we continued on back to his apartment and fucked, splendidly and desperately, for what remained of the night. Voilà! All better again.

But I did ask, a few days later, how he had remained so calm, when I had been paralyzed with fright. I wanted to know the trick, you see; I wanted to know how I could laugh in the face of danger, or at least to deliver danger a solid punch to the kisser.

Well, there were two ways, he said. The first is that you're born cold-blooded. The second is that you learn.

How do I learn? I wanted to know.

(We were lying in bed, nice and snug, listening to the midnight rain batter the window.)

Trust me, said the Boy. You don't want to learn.

Anyway. Back to breakfast, arriving at my door this very instant. But—surprise! It's not breakfast.

Well, to be perfectly fair, the breakfast is there on its tray, all right: coffee-scented, strengthfully borne by a slight, wiry man. Beneath his low-slung cap, however, his face is rather familiar, and not at all servile.

Mrs. Lumley lets out a cry.

"Monty!"

Chapter 21

Some women can be fooled all of the time, and all women can be fooled some of the time, but the same woman can't be fooled by the same man in the same way more than half the time.

—HELEN ROWLAND

SOPHIE

The lobby of the Pickwick Arms, that same instant

Miss Sophie Faninal, poised at the familiar Pickwick front desk, wearing yesterday's navy suit and a fresh pair of white gloves, curls her fingers around her pocketbook and attempts to master a growing sense of panic.

"But I don't understand," she says. "Why hasn't my sister answered her telephone? Hasn't anyone bothered to check on her?"

"We are not in the habit of disturbing our guests unnecessarily, Miss Faninal," says the man behind the desk.

"Except to telephone them."

"That was the police." He glances at the men standing at Sophie's shoulder, dressed in uniform, and then at the man standing quietly at her side. He clears his throat. "In any case, Mrs. Fitzwilliam rang down at approximately six forty-five to order breakfast, so I believe we can rest assured that she is alive and well."

Sophie holds out her hand. "Then you'll be so good as to return my key, won't you? My sister and I *were* sharing the suite, after all."

The man coughs and glances again at the policemen behind her. "Of course. But I'm afraid these gentlemen must wait in the lobby. It is not our policy to disturb our guests—"

"Unnecessarily. Yes. I quite agree." Sophie forms a white cotton fist around the brass key, which is attached to a round brass plate engraved with the number 404, and turns an exact half circle. "Gentlemen? You'll excuse me. I shall return shortly with my sister, and we will put ourselves entirely at your disposal."

She looks each man in the eye, and saves a last confident half smile for the detective in charge, a man named Lieutenant Curtis. Lieutenant Curtis has been unexpectedly kind. From the moment of her arrival, driven out of Manhattan and into the suburbs in Octavian's Ford—driven by Octavian himself at a steady and ripping forty miles an hour, engine whining in disbelief—the lieutenant has taken her shock and dismay at face value, unlike the rest of the squad, who seem to think she has something to do with her father's escape from the Fairfield County Jail, at some point in the middle of the previous night. She wants to tell them that she was drinking bourbon on the kitchen floor with Miss Julie Schuyler at most points in the middle of last night, when she wasn't dancing a mad and unsteady turkey trot to an old ragtime record on her father's Victrola, but that isn't the kind of thing you tell a disapproving arrow-straight police detective, is it?

At least she had Octavian by her side, thank God, tousle-haired and reassuring. He didn't say much, but he wasn't leaving her alone: that much he made clear to everyone concerned, including Sophie. He was popping out of the Ford and onto the sidewalk almost as soon as she opened her front door on Thirty-Second Street, an hour or so earlier, asking if she was all right. "No, I'm not," she told him. "My father's just escaped from jail."

Well, he wasn't expecting that, but he didn't waste any time. "Come along," he said, opening the passenger door, and she didn't have to tell him where to go. He just drove, up Third Avenue all the way to the Bronx, where he picked up the Boston Post Road and plowed straight through, almost without stopping. Like last winter, only faster and warmer and more ominous, and Sophie wasn't sleeping. She was clutching the door handle, clenching her stomach, as if that could make the Ford go faster, make the miles shorten and disappear. Father escaped. Why? He had just submitted to the guilty verdict the day before. He had admitted defeat. He had bowed his head and given in at last.

The question still screams in her mind, but she doesn't let it show. Oh, no. When Lieutenant Curtis nods his approval and turns to direct his squad toward the various entrances and exits of the hotel, she looks at Octavian and smiles bravely. "You'll wait here for me, won't you?"

"Of course. Do you want me to come up with you?"

"I don't think they'll let you. They're suspicious, for some reason."

"Don't worry about that. Just get your sister down here, and I'll speak to the lieutenant. Find out what I can."

Her hands are damp inside her gloves. She rolls the key in her palm. Octavian looks expectant, almost as if he's about to lean down and kiss her good-bye. As if they have the right to kiss each other.

"I meant to ask—" she says hurriedly.

"What?"

"Why weren't you with her? Last night?"

"She wasn't there."

"Oh. I see." The air in the lobby is warm and summerlike; every window is open to catch what morning freshness is available. To her left, the desk clerk is casting curious looks, though he's pretending to write in his ledger. Sophie feels a little sick. As she turns to the elevator, she says, "Could you see if they have anything to eat? I'm famished."

"Of course. Coffee?"

"Yes," she says, over her shoulder.

There is a single elevator at the far end of the lobby, with burnished bronze doors, hidden behind a pair of pillars. As Sophie waits for the car to descend, another guest joins her, a man. A little too close. She makes a half step to the side, and he says, in a low voice, "I beg your pardon. Miss Fortescue?"

"Faninal."

"I beg your pardon. I couldn't help overhearing that you're on your way up to see your sister?"

She doesn't turn her head. She stares up at the slender arrow on the dial above the bronze doors, heart thudding, and says, "I'm afraid it's a private matter, sir, but I appreciate your interest." (Her standard response to a member of the Curious Public.)

The man shifts his feet. She can't see him, but he seems about average: average size, average clothing. His voice has a bit of masculine bite, that edge of roughness that suggests a smoking habit.

The arrow begins to move downward. Three. Two.

The man persists. "I—I understand. It's just . . . well, I believe my wife is upstairs with her, this very minute."

"Your wife?"

"Yes, ma'am." He hesitates. "I think you're acquainted with her. Mrs. Lumley."

The bell dings softly, and the doors open, revealing a delicate metal grille. The attendant opens it and looks at them expectantly from beneath his cap. The car behind him is small and square, upholstered in red, smelling faintly of a woman's stale floral perfume. A narrow bench of red leather runs along the back wall.

Sophie turns to the man beside her. He's shorter than she remembers from the trial, and his eyes are dark and pleading. "Mrs. *Lumley*?" she says. "She's visiting my sister? Right *now*?"

"Yes. She—she left early this morning, and I couldn't help wondering why—she wasn't herself—I followed her here, just to make sure she was all right, and . . . well." He tips his hat. Licks his lips. "I'm sorry. Don't mean to disturb. But I'm awfully worried, and they won't tell me what room it is."

"Sir? Madam?" says the bored attendant.

Sophie recognizes the weight of Mr. Lumley's face, the sick despondency of his eyes. The poor man. Her heart beats a little faster. Her skin itches beneath her clothes. Mrs. Lumley! What in God's name is Mrs. Lumley doing with Virginia?

She reaches out and touches the man's elbow.

"Mr. Lumley. I'm so sorry. I'll send her right down to you, I promise."

She steps forward into the elevator car. Says, *Fourth floor, please.*

The attendant reaches for the grille. Just as he begins to rattle it shut, Mr. Lumley hops forward to join them both in the car.

"If it's all the same to you," he says, staring up at the dial, reaching into his jacket pocket, "I think I'll come along."

He unwraps a piece of candy, pops it in his mouth, and offers another to Sophie.

"Peppermint?"

Chapter 22

There are only two kinds of men: the dead,
and the deadly.

—HELEN ROWLAND

THERESA

The Pickwick Arms, room 404, at the same time

Well. You can imagine my surprise! The murderous Patent King himself, turning up at my hotel room, dressed in a clever red uniform like a monkey and unaccompanied by any visible member of the police force: local, state, or federal.

"Why, Mr. Faninal!" I exclaim, surveying the room for possible weapons. The pistol still lies in my pocketbook, tucked inside the drawer in the bedroom. "What a tremendous surprise. I thought you were in prison."

He closes the door with his foot and sets down the tray on the nearest table. Mrs. Lumley utters a scream and runs for the bedroom.

"Where's Virginia?" he says. "Where are my daughters?"

My gaze alights on the fire irons. I edge a half step toward the hearth. "They're not here, I'm afraid. Miss Faninal is consoling herself in Manhattan with my fiancé, while Mrs. Fitzwilliam and her daughter have taken the train for Florida."

"Florida!"

"Yes. Something to do with that absent husband of hers. She's decided the time is ripe to claim her matrimonial rights, now that her father's been convicted of murdering her mother. But what about—"

There's no point in continuing my sentence, because Faninal's gone and followed Mrs. Lumley into the bedroom. I hover for an instant, torn among fire irons and telephone and door. But I can't leave poor Mrs. Lumley to face the wrath of her onetime lover, can I? Heavens, no. I reach for a poker, nice and heavy, and then dash for the telephone, dragging the poker behind me.

"Put that down!" Faninal says, from the bedroom doorway. He's holding Mrs. Lumley by the arm, and the expression on her face is wide and stiff with terror.

I bring up the earpiece. "Nonsense."

Faninal whips something out of his pocket and holds it to Mrs. Lumley's throat. "Put it down!" he roars, and *click!* The earpiece goes back in the cradle.

If I were the Boy, I think, standing there next to the telephone, cold hand wrapped around my impossibly heavy poker, I would have knocked Faninal to pieces by now. I would have slung my poker into his head and brained him. But something's stopping me. Maybe it's the baby, tiny and fragile and infinitely dear; maybe it's some flaw in my nature, some softness in my upbringing.

Maybe he can tell what I'm thinking. "Stay where you are," he says, more softly, edging into the sitting room with his prize, step by step. He forces her down in an armchair and stands above her with that instrument of his: a kind of knife, except the blade has been sharpened into a point, like an old-fashioned dagger.

"You can't possibly imagine you're going to escape," I say. "The police will come here first."

"The police are already here," he says.

"Then why did you come?"

"I wanted to see my daughters first."

"First before what?"

His lips compress into a thin, pale line. He's not going to tell me, of course. Why should he tell me, a stranger?

"Well, they're not here," I say, "so it's all for nothing. I suggest you surrender yourself to the police at once. I can't imagine what you hoped to accomplish by all this."

Beneath his hands, Mrs. Lumley has begun to shiver. The whites of her eyes begin to show, and I realize her eyes are rolling back in her head. She slumps forward, and Faninal catches her just in time.

"I'll get water!" I exclaim.

"No! Stay where you are."

"My God! Don't you care?"

There is a strange little silence. Around Faninal's eyes, the tense lines soften, and his lips part. The hand holding the knife drops to rest on the back of the chair, and the other hand eases Mrs. Lumley back into the cushion. He turns for the tray on the lamp table, a few feet away, and for some reason I don't press my advantage. I stay right where I am, between the fireplace and the telephone, clutching my iron poker.

Faninal takes a napkin from the tray and wets it with a little water from the pitcher. He comes around to the front of the chair and presses the cloth to Mrs. Lumley's temples, almost tenderly, and I hear him mutter something under his breath, though I can't make out the words.

During the trial, the defense devoted an entire day of testimony to the subject of Mr. Faninal's background.

How he came from an old and respectable (though not precisely *distinguished*) Boston family; how he met Mrs. Faninal at a Cambridge party and fell in love; how they settled in Greenwich because Mrs. Faninal did not like city life, and how her parents—several rungs higher on that implacable Brahmin ladder—weren't all that pleased with Mr. Faninal's unsociable habits and obsession with engineering: his dirty hands, in other words. (The middle-class jury, I expect, was supposed to feel sympathy for his predicament—the man cast away from his wife's blue-blooded family, I mean, for daring to work with his hands for a living.) Better to move elsewhere, then, somewhere away from all that familial friction, and Greenwich was so pretty and newly gentrified, the old farms now splitting up and filling with the country houses of the pedigreed people and their pedigreed horses. Mrs. Faninal fit right into Greenwich society, at first. Most of the seaside houses were occupied only seasonally, but the Faninals were year-round residents, and while the husband was considered a bit eccentric, the wife made friends at the garden club and the ladies' committee at the local Congregational church. And eccentricity is always overlooked among country families; it's almost a badge of pride, isn't it? It's only murder that gets you thrown out of the club, once you're in. Murder and cheating at cards.

Now, I admit, these revelations gave me a new appreciation for Mr. Faninal. I suppose my native snobbery was appeased by the fact that—lo, behold!—he came from decent blood, after all. But you can't quite forget those descriptions of the grisly Greenwich kitchen, the little girl weeping over her mother. Even as I fought to save him from conviction, I felt distaste. I felt the filthiness of what I was doing. I looked at his impassive face and thought maybe he wasn't human; maybe he wasn't worth saving, whatever my fine reasons for saving him.

But humanity isn't so simple, you know. As Faninal sits in front of Mrs. Lumley and presses that linen against her temples, no one could accuse him of a lack of common feeling. And there's the fact that he exists in this room at all. Why not simply disappear, when he had the chance? Almost as if he never actually meant to escape at all. As if he told me the truth, a moment ago: he only wants to see his daughters outside of a prison's four walls, without bars or guards or guilt.

"Mr. Faninal," I say softly, "have you anything to say to me?"

Mrs. Lumley's eyelids move. Faninal's hand falls away, and there is a moment, brief and precious, filled with nothing but a kind of reverent interior silence. A bird whistles through the open window. A car engine roars down the nearby avenue. The morning sun beats and beats against the awning.

"Why, you *didn't* murder her, did you?" I whisper.

He presses his lips together.

"Why don't you say anything? Are you covering for someone?"

"No—"

"Who is it? For whom are you covering, Mr. Faninal?"

"Monty," murmurs Mrs. Lumley, or maybe it's a moan.

The poker drops to the ground, making a soft thump on the Oriental rug. I fumble for the telephone beside me. As my fingers touch the earpiece, a sharp knock rattles the door. "Virginia!" calls a female voice.

Faninal jumps to his feet and lifts the knife. His face turns urgently toward me.

"Who *is* it?" I call, all singsong, like one of the birds near the window.

Muffled by wood: "It's Sophie."

Now. I really don't know Miss Faninal all that well, considering the many bonds that link us together. We've barely spoken to each other, isn't that funny? But I've seen her day after day in court; I've examined, when I thought I could get away with it, all the details of her face and dress and manner. My rival. I've hated her and admired her, and hated that I admired her. I have come to comprehend—wretchedly, agonizingly—why the Boy can't resist her, why my darling Boy has gone and fallen in love with this clean young creature.

But I haven't come any closer to her than that, not even in her time of greatest need, when any woman could use a friend. I suppose, therefore, I'm not the best judge of her inner nature, of her true character. I'm not really in a position to understand the tone of her voice when she says, brightly, through the wooden door of a suburban hotel suite: *It's Sophie!*

So there's no reason at all that I should suspect something's wrong, and yet, as Faninal drops his knife in relief and calls out *Come in!,* I release the earpiece of the telephone and bend down to grip the heavy iron poker with both hands.

The lock rattles; a key clinks loudly. I think—foolishly, since I already know the answer—*Well, now, if she's got a key, why did she knock first?*

Then the door swings open, and Sophie herself appears under the lintel: pink of cheek, creamy of skin, slanted of eyebrow.

Accompanied by a man in a wrinkled brown suit.

Chapter 23

*A husband is what is left of a lover, after
the nerve has been extracted.*

—HELEN ROWLAND

SOPHIE

Just outside room 404, a few seconds earlier

In general, Sophie tries not to think much about that
horrible February night, the night of her engagement party, when the old Sophie broke into pieces and
the new one was unwillingly born.

There was the terror of the firing gun, there was
the moment somebody shouted out *Rofrano's shot!* and
her heart stopped beating. Police and screaming and
confusion, and nobody would let her see Octavian or
Father, nobody would tell her anything. Someone—
was it Jay Ochsner?—physically held her back, carried
her to a bedroom, gave her a drink. A message from

Virgo: *Go home, I'll explain when I return.* Jay drove her home. She remembers that clearly, at least—the horrible silence, the dread that petrified them both. She had forgotten her coat and scarf, and Jay took off his own plush wool overcoat with the velvet lapels and helped her into it, arm by arm. So when she thinks of that night—again, she tries not to do that, but it *will* keep returning to her imagination—she thinks of the smell of tobacco smoke, and Jay's shaving soap, laced with orange blossom.

When Virginia returned to Thirty-Second Street, gray-faced, at three o'clock in the morning, she found Sophie still awake. Of course. How could Sophie sleep? She shivered in her bed while Virginia curled up next to her, under the blanket, and told her what had happened. Explained why, as best she could. And it was too much to understand all at once: too many aspects, too many connecting threads. Octavian taking her to the house in Greenwich that day—ah, so Octavian knew, too. Octavian knew from the beginning, and he hadn't said anything. Virginia knew; her father knew. Everyone she loved had kept this secret from her, because they thought she was too young and innocent and delicate, they thought she needed *protecting*.

Now she was the little girl in the kitchen. *She,* Sophie. *She* was that famous, pitiable little girl, trying to wake her mother, in a scene engraved and reprinted in a thousand daily newspapers across America. And Sophie could not understand that. How could she be that girl, when she didn't remember?

"But what happened?" she whispered to Virginia, too numb for anger. Too numb even to care, at this moment, that her sister had been part of this deception. "Did Father really kill her?"

Virginia didn't know. Virginia never asked. At first, she was too young to ask such a thing, of such a father. After that, she was too afraid of the answer. What would she do if he said yes? He was their father, for heaven's sake.

Sophie had pondered on the enormity of Virginia's burden, how Virginia had taken the weight entirely on her own shoulders, and never asked Sophie to share it with her. She pondered a lot of things, actually, during that dead month between Father's arrest and the official indictment for the crime of capital murder, by a grand jury in Stamford, Connecticut, and all of those things troubled her.

Most of all, she was troubled by this: she, Sophie, is the only one who knows what really happened.

Well, not exactly. Not *her*, not the Sophie who presently exists. But this theoretical child-Sophie, this tiny person who once was Sophie, *she* knows who murdered her mother. Sophie's sure of it. *She* saw what happened, *she* ran to her mother when the killer left, and that's where Mrs. Lumley found her.

Sophie *knows* what happened, somewhere inside the folds of her brain.

And—of course—the killer knows.

At the moment she knocks on Virginia's door, however, Sophie isn't troubled by the elusive contents of her memory. She's trying to fight down the panic choking her throat. The rapid stroke of her heartbeat against the skin of her neck. The sweat prickling the pores of her arms and her brow, warning her of *danger, danger.*

She can't explain why. A moment ago, waiting for the elevator, she was just fine. Calm and collected. Maybe a little anxious on the inside, because Father has absconded from jail, because he might have come here to find her and Virginia, and Virgo hasn't answered her telephone, though she *has* ordered breakfast.

But that's no reason to feel as if she can't breathe, as if the world around her is shivering on the brink of explosion. Cold and hot and cold, her clothes itching madly against her skin, her chest moving in spasms. The reek of peppermint smothering the air in her lungs.

She lifts her hand to knock.

Mr. Lumley stands stiffly by her side. Mr. Lumley, who hasn't said a word, and Sophie doesn't blame him, though there's a heated quality to his silence that feeds the terror inside her skull, the quiet scream inside her throat. The elevator took ages to rise to the fourth floor, and Sophie spent them all trying to think of something to say, trying to dispel the air of impending catastrophe while Mr. Lumley sucked loudly on his peppermint candy, but what did you say to a man like that, in the throes of matrimonial despair? Did you comment on the weather? Chirp: *I'm sure there's an innocent explanation?* Absurd. There is no innocent explanation for Mrs. Lumley's visit, not this morning of all mornings, not to Virginia of all people.

If Virginia's the one Mrs. Lumley is visiting just now.

"Who is it?" calls Virgo, muffled by the wood, far too cheerfully.

"It's Sophie!" she calls back, in the same too-cheerful voice, as if they're both enacting a pantomime. She tries to fit the key into the lock, but her eyes keep blurring. Her fingers keep slipping.

"Allow me," says Mr. Lumley, leaning close, drenching her in peppermint, and his hand covers hers, inserting the key without trouble, turning the lock, opening the door.

Maybe it's her nerves, maybe it's the scourge of the receding bourbon in her system. Maybe it's the series of shocks assailing her over the past few days, or the past few months. Sophie looks down at Mr. Lumley's hand operating the key, bare and pale next to her white cotton glove, and the scream lying in her throat rises and fills her mouth.

You.

The door swings open.

"Father!" Sophie gasps, almost before she realizes it's him, but the word—really a whisper, all she can manage—is swallowed by a female shriek.

Mr. Lumley shuts the door behind them. "There you are, Charlotte," he says to the shrieking woman. "I think we'd better go home, don't you?"

Sophie jolts. Covers her mouth. Is *that* Mrs. Lumley? Hair askew, eyes wet, the muscles of her face slack with terror. She's stopped shrieking. She jumps from an armchair and stands there, wringing her hands, bearing the full force of the morning light from an open window.

And my God! Father stands near her, also rumpled. His gray hair stands out from his head in electric shock. He stares at her, at Mr. Lumley.

"Lumley!" he whispers.

"I've come for my wife, Faninal."

Father looks so pale and stunned, so unlike himself. The way Sophie feels on the inside, right now: terrorized and speechless. He's wearing a gray shirt that must once have been white, and a pair of brown trousers held up by elastic suspenders. No jacket. He wets his lips, steps back, and says, "Of course."

Mrs. Lumley begins to babble. "I didn't say nothing, Fred. I swear I didn't."

"Shut up." Mr. Lumley steps forward and takes her by the arm, not very gently. Mrs. Lumley falls silent. Around the room, for a brittle, teetering instant, nobody moves.

Sophie whispers, "Father, where's Virgo?"

But Father doesn't even notice. He's staring, astonished, at the two of them: the Lumleys, side by side. Mr. Lumley turns his head and returns the stare, and there's nothing desperate or pleading about him now. Just two rigid vertical lines, on either side of his mouth, and a tic at the corner of his eye that Sophie didn't notice before.

"Don't blame her," Father says.

"I don't."

"She didn't come here to see me. She came to visit my daughter."

"Well, now. Is that so?"

"That's so."

"Huh. I'm not so sure about that. I'm not so sure I can take your word for anything, Faninal." With his empty hand, Lumley reaches into his pocket. "I guess, if a man's going to be thorough, he's got to make sure this never happens—"

"No!" Sophie darts forward, and the gun—a small revolver, flashing in the sun—turns toward her.

"I don't want to kill you, miss. I think you've been through enough. But this man here, this father of yours—"

"Don't," she says. "Please, don't. Call the police. They're right downstairs. Please."

"What, and let him die in his own time, after what he did? He deserves killing. He killed your mama, in cold blood—"

"Oh, Fred, no," sobs Mrs. Lumley.

"You shut up. Didn't I tell you?" He shakes her with his left arm, hard and vicious, and she cries out.

"Stop!" Sophie says. "Please stop!"

Mr. Lumley turns a pair of cold, narrow eyes toward her. "What I want, you see, is some kind of assurance that this won't happen again. And the way I see it—"

"Sophie!" Father barks. "Stand still. Don't say anything."

"—the way I see it," Lumley continues, aiming the gun back at Father, "nobody's going to care if a man fires a gun in self-defense, hitting a confessed murderer, saving the state the trouble of carrying out an execution."

Sophie leaps forward. The gun swings back toward her, and in the instant before it fires, she sees those cold, narrow eyes again, deep inside the folds of her brain, and her face opens up in a childlike scream.

You.

BANG.

The gun explodes in her ears. But she doesn't see it coming, because someone jumps before her face, grabs her by the shoulders, jerks mightily, and tosses her backward to the floor.

She opens her eyes and stares at the gray-white ceiling, gasping, trying to move her ribs, but the body slumped upon her chest won't move. Deadweight.

She opens her lips, and her mouth fills with someone's hair. Her father's coarse gray hair, wet with copper blood.

Chapter 24

A man never knows how to say good-bye;
a woman never knows when to say it.

—HELEN ROWLAND

THERESA

On the floor, next to the telephone

You become, I'm afraid, a rather selfish creature when you're expecting a baby. Or maybe it's the baby that's selfish, hoarding all your energy for her own exclusive use, hoarding your vitamins and your sleep and your blood.

So there you are, imagining yourself a courageous and forthright sort of individual, the kind of woman who confronts intruders and fights back against snatchers of pocketbooks. And a suspicious character walks in, wearing a gun-sized bulge in the pocket of his rumpled brown jacket, and you drop the poker in your hands, sink to the ground, and crawl behind the sofa.

Yes, I know. Very commendable.

You sit with your back to the sofa back, hoping no one remembers you're there, praying to God that the small being in your belly survives the next few minutes. Your lips actually move, in supplication to this God that you've railed against, pleaded with, ceased to believe in altogether. Just keep me alive, long enough for the baby to be born. Keep me alive until then, and I'll light you a hundred candles a day, I'll build a church, I'll build a convent, I'll devote my life to the sick and the wretched.

Just keep my baby alive.

But you can't help overhearing the conversation. You can't help hearing that Mrs. Lumley's husband is here, and he's not pleased, for some reason. That you were perhaps right about Mrs. Lumley having something to hide. That you were certainly right about that gun-shaped lump in Mr. Lumley's jacket pocket.

That the sweet little Sophie is a braver woman than you are.

And here you crouch, blood hot and cold, heart rattling beyond control, thinking reprehensibly that she should just let the wrathful husband kill Faninal and leave the rest of you in peace—hating yourself for thinking it, but thinking it anyway—and then! *Then!*

You spot the telephone earpiece dangling from the little table in the space between the sofa and the armchair.

You bite back a gasp. You shut your eyes. You open them again.

You roll on your stomach and crawl across the few yards of plush Oriental carpet, the patch of hot sunlight. You hear a scratchy tin voice: *Hello? Mrs. Fitzwilliam? Hello? Is something the matter?*

You reach one long hand to the table, snatch down the metal base, and whisper in the mouthpiece, terribly hoarse: "Help! Send the police!"

"Mrs. Fitzwilliam! Is something the matter?"

Louder: "Police!"

BANG!

Shriek.

Thump.

SILENCE.

(Stunned and awful.)

You duck for the sofa—again, reprehensible—and an almighty crash fills your ears, a cataclysm of splintering wood, and a familiar voice shouts, *Sophie, my God!*

The Boy! Oh, God. Not the Boy.

BANG!

And this time, you can't even summon the courage to see what's happened.

Until you can, somehow. Until, amid the shouts and confusion, someone spots you on the floor and says, "Hold on, we've got another one."

You think, *That sounds like the police.*

You crawl out from behind the sofa and heave your body upward, bracing each hand, and your brother exclaims, "Holy God! Sisser! What are you doing here?"

You look briefly downward, and there are two dead men on the floor of the parlor of room 404 of the Pickwick Arms, and the police are filing in, issuing orders, swearing, contradicting, taking photos in sudden white explosions of light that hurt your eyes.

You turn your head and vomit into a blue chintz cushion.

Ox. Good God. Ox is standing right there, jumpy and rattled and pretending otherwise, offering me a damp handkerchief. He seems to be paired up somehow with the Boy, who's alive, thank God: alive and talking to the police in a corner of the room. I don't see Miss Faninal, but the bedroom door is open. Police going in and out. My head is still numb and dizzy. I avoid looking at the mess on the floor, on which two sheets have already been placed, white and stained with blood.

Faninal and Lumley. Someone has killed Mr. Lumley, in the nick of time.

I ask my brother.

"Rofrano," he says, staring at the window. The morning sun casts an unkind glare on his face. His skin is pale, the whites of his eyes shot with tiny red threads. "Rofrano shot him."

"How do you know that?"

Ox's gaze shifts to me, not quite focused. "Because I was right behind him, that's why. Saw the fellow hit the ground." He taps his forehead. "Right between the eyes."

"My God."

"You didn't see?"

"I'm afraid I was hiding behind the sofa."

"What, you? Sisser? *Hiding*?"

"Like a bunny in Mr. MacGregor's garden."

He takes my shoulder, a little hard. "Are you all right, then?"

"Perfectly well. A bit shaken."

"Shaken? My God. What were you doing here, anyway?"

"I was paying a social call."

"My God," he says numbly. "A social call. My God."

Well. Shortly after that, a detective approaches me courteously, asks me if I can describe what happened. Someone brings coffee and whisks away the old cold tray, the breakfast tray that started it all. I'm not quite sure what I tell that nice detective. Whether I make any sense at all. He takes copious notes, however, and he screws his face into an expression of utmost concentration as I speak. Eventually he lets me go. I turn to Ox, who's sitting beside me, and ask him where Miss Faninal's gone. Have they taken her away?

"No," he says. "I think she's in the bedroom."

Someone has put a blanket over my shoulders. A blanket, in this heat! Wool, thick, plaid: the kind of garment Scotsmen wrap around their middles to fend off the Highland winter. I remove the thing and fold it neatly, hanging it over the back of the sofa, and I take Ox by the arm and lead him through the door into the peaceful little chamber where I slept last night. The sleep of the unsuspecting.

The light's dim, the chintz curtains drawn. The window faces west, so the sun hasn't arrived yet, and it's much cooler in here than in the living room. I pause at the threshold, allowing my eyes to adjust, and when my sight returns, it falls upon a young female form seated on the bed nearest the window. Her head is bowed, her hands rest together in her lap. Another of those Scotch blankets lies like a shroud around her shoulders. At her feet, kneeling on the rug before her, the Boy holds one large hand clasped around hers. The other hand covers her knee.

Neither notices my presence in the doorway. I can't tell if they're speaking; there's too much noise from the other room. I suppose it doesn't matter, does it? Whether genuine words pass between the two of them. The Boy reaches up and brushes her cheek with his thumb.

"*Sophie?*" Ox exclaims, behind me.

The Boy breaks away and rises to his feet. Sophie gasps and clutches the blanket, just as it slides from her shoulders.

"We were just looking for the lieutenant," I say coldly.

The Boy clears his throat. "I believe he's still in the other room."

"Say—!" begins Ox, tone of outrage.

I snatch my brother's arm. "Don't be a boor, darling. Come with me."

I don't know why he follows me. Possibly my voice contains more authority than I imagine, or else Ox's memory of the bullet between Lumley's eyes is still fresh. He simmers beside me, however, as I steer him past the sheet-draped bodies and the still-dangling telephone in the direction of the nice lieutenant, who stands by the open window, air of command, surveying the scene.

"What the devil was that about?" Ox says. "Sophie and *Rofrano*?"

"*You* were the one who appointed him cavalier, my dear."

"On your recommendation! Aren't you going to do anything about it?"

I stop and turn to him. "Ox, darling, do keep your voice down. Can you not recognize that this is hardly the moment to make a scene?"

"Not make a scene? He's in there making love to my fiancée!"

I place my hand on Ox's chest. "He's consoling her, that's all. Now, do be a gentleman, will you? No medieval outbursts."

"I'll show you outbursts—"

"Ox. Darling. *Grace*."

My poor brother. His chin sinks. He says nothing. The too-harsh sunshine strikes his tarnished hair with a clang.

"Oh, Ox." I pat his heart. "That's better, isn't it? It's always better to behave with dignity in these matters.

Do leave everything to me, won't you? Everything will turn out all right."

I give him a last pat—he sinks, chastened, onto the arm of the sofa—and walk the remaining yards to the lieutenant by myself.

"Mrs. Marshall," he says, pushing back his hat, tucking his notebook into his jacket pocket. "Is there anything I can do for you?"

"You've been very kind. Your men are terribly efficient. It's all so very dreadful."

"I'm sorry you had to be a part of this, that's all."

"Thank you," I say, and just like that, I am *exhausted*. Drained of the very marrow in my bones. The sunlight strokes my arms. I knot my hands together at my middle. "Are we free to leave, Lieutenant Curtis?"

His back holds the window, so the expression of compassion on his face is difficult to fathom. But his voice, I think, contains a measure of kindness. "I'm afraid, Mrs. Marshall, that in matters as serious as this, we would ordinarily escort all the witnesses to the station house for further questioning. Mrs. Lumley's already been taken away."

"But surely—well, Lieutenant Curtis, *surely* this is a clear case of self-defense. You are already acquainted with Mr. Rofrano, and he behaved with such courage and prevented further bloodshed. And we have all been through *such* an ordeal."

The lieutenant hesitates. He lifts his hand and removes his hat, which he holds above the waistband of his trousers, rotating the brim under his fingers until it's just so. "Mrs. Marshall, I don't know if you remember my name. Curtis. I served with your son, in the Thirty-Ninth Infantry."

I fasten my gaze upon a point between the lieutenant's bushy eyebrows.

"Oh! Did you?"

"I'm awfully sorry, Mrs. Marshall. He was a good man, the best officer in the regiment. I was proud to serve under him. A real shame, a damned shame, if you'll excuse me. And now this." He gestures to the scene before them.

"Now this."

The hat returns to his head. "Well, Mrs. Marshall. I guess I always said I'd march through fire for Captain Marshall. Go on home with your friends. I'll let you know if we need you back."

And I'm afraid that's the last I ever see of the Pickwick Arms Hotel.

Chapter 25

There are people whose watch stops at a certain hour and who remain permanently at that age.

—HELEN ROWLAND

SOPHIE

Crossing the Third Avenue Bridge into Manhattan, an hour later

Jay needs a cigarette. He asks Sophie if she minds.

"Not at all," she replies. Who cares about a cigarette, after all? Sophie doesn't. The top is down, the warm draft whips away the smoke.

"You all right?" he asks, after he's put the cigarette case safely back in the inside pocket of his jacket

"Not particularly." Her voice is braver than she expects. That's something, isn't it?

"Poor Sophie. I'm awfully sorry. I suppose he wasn't much of a father to you, but—well, it's an awful way to go, a damned shame that you were there—"

And Sophie begins to laugh, just high hysterical giggles rippling out over the Harlem River, louder and faster and louder. She bends over, clutching her ankles, staring at the floorboards, gasping for air, and each time she thinks she's got herself under control, the giggles bubble back up in her throat.

And that's when she realizes that her shoes don't match.

Because Jay is so absurd. Sophie's not really thinking about her father, is she? Not yet. That's too immense to comprehend, too stunning, the sight of her father flinging himself upon her just as Lumley fired his gun. The little jerk his body made as the bullet penetrated his back and sliced through his heart, stopping the muscle instantly. The police said she was lucky the shot didn't find her, too, but apparently her body crashed to the ground at just the right angle. The spent bullet ended up striking the wall instead.

That her father—her father!—just died, died just now, is no longer alive, has snuffed out his own life to save her life, because Mr. Lumley was going to shoot her: my God, that's too much to think about. There isn't even any pain, just the numb list of Things She Must Do. Find Virginia and communicate this development, before the newspapers generously handle that task on her behalf. (The reporters were already gathering outside the

Pickwick Arms, clamoring for information, and Lieutenant Curtis had to escort the four of them—Sophie and Jay, Octavian and Mrs. Marshall—out through a hidden back door and a dark-shrouded basement that looked suspiciously like an underground saloon.) Make funeral arrangements. (Where on earth did you bury such a man? Greenwich? New York City? Boston, where he was raised and disowned?) Lawyers. Money. Personal effects. All those things, lining up like shocked miniature soldiers at in the center of her mind, while a single question pounds and pounds at the back of her mind: *WHY?*

Why would her father submit to a verdict of guilty in the murder of his wife, when he hadn't committed the crime?

Because he hadn't committed the crime. He didn't murder his wife. Sophie knows that now. She knows that as surely as she now understands the terror that inhabited her body while she ascended the elevator in the company of Mr. Lumley, sucking his peppermint candy in greedy smacks of his tongue and mouth.

But she will never know why, or how, because her father is dead. She will never speak to him again. She'll never know who he really is, who he really was, and it's *that*—the shock of a story cut off in the middle, a life cut off in the middle—which she can't comprehend. Can't stretch her mind to encompass.

It's over. She's safe. And her father is dead.

And the front of her mind? That's occupied, too. Stupidly occupied by another thought entirely, by an image: the image of Octavian, escorting Mrs. Marshall quietly to his green Model T, opening the door for her, settling her inside. His face absolutely still, not even looking her way. Not even a parting glance, as the magazines called it. She heard the motor start, the pistons settle. The smell of exhaust.

The thing about Mrs. Marshall, she's so good at managing everything. The graceful way she extracted Octavian from Sophie's side, the way Sophie found herself being led tenderly away by Jay Ochsner, while Octavian performed the same service for Mrs. Marshall. How had that happened? A few smooth words, a limpid gaze. A strange air of inevitability. Octavian didn't even struggle. Like an animal led to slaughter, except he was doing the leading. He tucked Mrs. Marshall's hand into his elbow and escorted her downstairs like the most delicate creature, which Mrs. Marshall certainly was not. Delicate. My God. Those shoes. How did Sophie come to wear one brown shoe and one black?

The car is pulling over to the side, slowing, stopping. The brake sets with a groan. Jay's arms surround her shoulders. "Poor Sophie," he croons. "Poor little dear. What a shock. No wonder."

His chest is nice and warm. She lets her head rest there for a moment. She thinks of the way Octavian held her hand in the hotel bedroom, the way his palm felt around her fingers. He didn't say anything, just allowed the understanding to flow between them, because he had just killed a man for her sake, hadn't he? He had killed Lumley for her. They were united in a deep and primitive way by this terrible thing. Death. And now Octavian was unspeakably comforting her, and she was comforting him, and in that singular moment she wasn't alone, and everything was going to be all right.

"It's all right, darling," Jay says. "It's going to be all right. I'll take care of you, darling, don't worry about a thing. Jay will take care of you."

Her head's so heavy. Jay's shirt is rumpled and damp, and Sophie realizes she's crying. That her giggles have turned into shameful sobs.

"Jay will take care of you," he says again, stroking her arm, and Sophie closes her eyes and thinks, *No, you won't.*

The traffic's awful, and by the time they turn the corner of Thirty-Second Street, Sophie has recovered her composure. She feels, in fact, quite clearheaded. She will telephone Mr. Manning and schedule a meeting for this afternoon, in the firm's offices down-town, to sort out the events of this morning into some kind of logical order, to solve whatever mysteries can be solved—Mrs. Lumley is still alive, after all, still able to explain some part of the story—and in the meantime she will take a long bath and a nap. She will change clothes. She will summon the servants (surely they will have appeared by now) and explain the situation, or what she understands of it, and Dot will make her some lunch. Once all the practical affairs have been concluded, she will join Virginia in Florida, and they will decide what's to be done. What they will do with their lives. Sophie's not certain what that means, but she does know that it won't include Jay Ochsner. Maybe not even any man at all, ever. She doesn't seem to have much luck with them.

The car rolls to a stop, and Sophie doesn't wait for Jay to set the brake and walk around the fender to open her door. She reaches for the handle and helps herself.

"Sophie! Wait!"

She takes the key from her pocketbook and opens the door. "Come on in," she says, tossing her hat on the stand and the pocketbook on the table. "I won't be a moment."

When she arrives back downstairs, Jay is standing in the parlor, hat between his hands, as if he's not quite sure whether he's been invited to stay. Sophie pauses on the threshold, squinting a little at the polite figure he makes, planted near the window, through which the golden afternoon sun is still pouring. The diffuse light is gentle on his worried forehead.

She steps forward and holds out a square box of navy-blue leather, stamped in gold. "Thank you," she says.

He stares at the box, and then at her face. "*Thank you?*"

"You've been very kind. I appreciate your driving me home. But I can't marry you, and I don't wish to raise your hopes. It's simply impossible."

He stands there, a bit stupid with shock, a few steps away. His hair's all broken up into thin, greasy pieces from the drive, and his eyes squint in the sunshine. His poor suit, all rumpled. He turns his head a few degrees, taking in the decoration of the nearby wall, and says, "You do know that Rofrano's my sister's lover, don't you? They're planning to get married, once she divorces her husband."

"I know that."

"And you don't care? You don't—Look, Sophie." He turns back to her, wearing a look of pathetic appeal, like a dog that doesn't realize it's no longer a puppy. "I know I'm not young and brash, like these bright fellas out there, but I do love you. I've stood by you, all this time."

"You've stood by me? Or my money?"

He winces. "By you. I won't say your money wasn't a part of it, in the beginning. But I really—I came to care for you. It's true. And I've already sowed my oats, Sophie. I'm ready to settle down and be a husband to a nice girl, a sweet loyal girl like you. I think you'll see, when all the shock wears off, that—"

"No, Jay." She says it kindly. "It's not the shock. It's just impossible. You know it is."

He looks down at her hand, which is still out-stretched, containing the navy-blue box. The rose-shaped Ochsner engagement ring.

"Jay. Please. Let's be dignified about this."

He says something, a couple of words she can't hear. He lifts his head, and good gracious! His eyes are actually wet. Wet and blue. But he takes the box anyway, and then holds her hand in his soft, damp palm.

"Then I guess it's good-bye," he says, and he leans forward, kisses her cheek, and walks back down the hallway and out the door, settling his hat on his hair as he goes.

Chapter 26

A man is like a cat; chase him and he will run—sit still and ignore him, and he'll come purring at your feet.

—HELEN ROWLAND

THERESA

Fifth Avenue, the same moment

There's nothing like the scent of your own home, is there? I don't mean how it ordinarily smells, when you're living in it—that smell you don't even notice, because it's always there, and so are you. I mean the peculiar perfume that greets you when you've been away, the delicate balance of wood and paint and plaster and upholstery, stripped of your own living essence: just the substance of the house and nothing else.

Of course, the Marshall apartment on Fifth Avenue is never exactly empty. There's the housekeeper and the cook and the maid, all of whom live in, in the old-fashioned manner; and there used to be Sylvo's valet, too, before my husband moved into his bachelor digs on Lexington Avenue. Moreover, I've only been away for a single night. Since yesterday morning, by my calculation.

Still, that single night has aged me like a lifetime, and the air that rushes through the opening of my own dear front door goes straight to my solar plexus, as if I've embarked on a voyage around the globe since I last stood here. *Home*, it says.

I close my eyes briefly and turn to the Boy.

"Why don't you fetch us both a drink, hmm?"

He obeys me silently, as he always does, measuring tonic and gin in perfect three-to-one proportion. I notice his hands, as he serves me: how large they are, compared to mine, and how they remain rock-steady throughout. To think he killed a man, just this morning.

I sink into my favorite armchair. The Boy remains standing, near the window, the one facing west over Central Park. The shadow of the awning runs across his body in an acute diagonal line from right shoulder to left hip, slashing him into two pieces: light and dark.

"Come sit down," I say. "I can't see your face like that."

"I'm sorry." He moves forward a few steps, but he doesn't sit. Instead he props himself on the arm of the sofa opposite and swishes his drink. The other hand rests on his thigh.

"Ox tells me you shot Lumley between the eyes."

"I didn't have much choice."

"Poor fellow. An awful thing, jealousy. Drives one to the most terrible extremes. In France, I understand, they have a special exculpation for such crimes."

"I suppose so." He opens his mouth, as if he's going to say something more.

"What is it?"

"Nothing, really. Just something Sophie said."

I swallow down the rest of my drink. The tonic is fresh and crisp, the gin pleasantly anesthetic. "Oh? And what did Miss Faninal say? Something clever, I suppose?"

"Not that kind of thing. It's just that she had the feeling, when Lumley turned around to shoot her, that he was involved somehow. In her mother's murder, I mean."

"*Lumley*? My goodness! Did she remember something at last?"

"Not exactly. Just a flash. An intuition, I guess. She was there when it happened, after all, even if she was just a little kid." He shrugs. "I'm not sure that it really matters, anymore. They're both gone."

"No, that's true. But *Mrs.* Lumley remains very much alive, if memory serves, and I suppose that clever Lieutenant Curtis will discover the truth soon enough." I hold out my glass. "Would you mind terribly? I'm parched."

The Boy levers himself from the sofa arm and takes the glass from my fingers. I watch him cross the room, marveling at the economy of his motion, the apparent laziness that disguises his efficiency. No one I know walks quite like the Boy. I wonder, sometimes, if the war turned him into this perfect machine, or whether he was always thus. I find myself wanting to ask how he's feeling, what it's like to kill a man, does he want to talk about it. Instead, I tell him he's looking rather haggard, which is also true.

"I didn't get much sleep last night," he says.

"Why not?"

Clink, clink, goes the ice. The liquor cabinet's always kept in flawless order, according to the season. In June, the ice is changed three or four times a day, whether or not we've used any. Just another of the little luxuries we swells command, up here in our monumental Fifth Avenue apartments.

The Boy answers. "Because I slept in the Ford, outside Sophie's house. She was staying by herself, and I was afraid those damned reporters would find her." *Phisht,* spits the tonic from the siphon.

"Oh, of course. How gallant of you."

He adds lime and returns to me. "I waited for an hour at Delmonico's, but you didn't turn up."

"I was tied up in Connecticut. Didn't they give you my message?"

"Eventually."

I pat the cushion next to me. "Sit."

He sits. He's left his drink on the cabinet, half empty, and he knits his empty fingers in the slight gap between his knees. "Look. I've been a heel, haven't I?"

"I wouldn't say that."

"No, I have. And you've been as patient as a saint. Let's just forget the last few months, all right? We'll go away for a few days, a week or two, and get back to where we were. I'll be the man you deserve, just like I promised. I was thinking we could head out to California right away—"

"Darling. Look at me."

Gracious, he looks haggard. And I'll be damned if it doesn't actually suit him, somehow. When the bloom's off his cheeks, and his unusual seawater eyes have lost their sparkle, there's nothing left to admire but his good solid bones, the admirable heft of his brow and jaw. Yes, he's grown into a man, my Boy, over the past two years. He'll make a strong husband, a dependable father.

There is a slow flutter in my belly, like the wings of a butterfly.

I set down my drink and put my hand on the Boy's cheek.

"Dearest," I say, "I have something to tell you."

Indulge me for a moment. I suppose you might have been wondering about Mrs. Virginia Fitzwilliam, there at the back of your mind, at least until more important matters came along. You might have been wondering exactly how we went from a little confession—a dangerous thing, I'm told—to a pair of train tickets down to Miami. It's really rather simple, and I must say I'm proud of myself. A little maternal advice, it seems, goes a long way.

After Mrs. Fitzwilliam told me about her father's infatuation with the kitchen maid—how she saw them embracing in the library once, how the electricity between them was of such a curious voltage that it caught the notice of a nine-year-old girl—and how she carried this suspicion on her shoulders like one of those old-fashioned farmer's yokes, throughout the entirety of the next sixteen years, I put my arms around her and told her not to worry. At the time, I thought she was right, that her father had kept his silence in order to spare Mrs. Lumley any further questions, and that really it was a generous act, a graceful way for a murderer to pay his debt to society and to his daughters.

"And what about you, my dear?" I then said. "What will you do?"

She was silent, and I thought, *The poor dear.* The poor brave motherless creature.

I said, "Do you still love him?"

She knew I was no longer speaking about her father. "Yes," she said.

"Do you believe he still loves you?"

"Yes." Again. But it was a sob.

I was conscious, as we sat there on the sofa, of little Miss Evelyn Fitzwilliam, drinking her lemonade and eating her cookies in the other room. Who had looked after the girl, all those hours that her mother sat in an overheated courtroom? Some woman from the hotel, perhaps. "At least you have his daughter," I said.

"A daughter he's never even met."

At which point, Miss Evelyn herself toddled through the doorway, crumbling cookie in hand, looking a bit like her mother in her cheeks and hair, but something entirely different around the eyes. Something rather wild and beautiful and promising that raised all kinds of curiosity inside me. She turned her head a few degrees to the side and regarded me, trading my curiosity for hers, and a pair of words floated, uninvited, across my head.

How extraordinary.

So what else could I do, *in loco maternis?* What else could I do, except to give that broken, heavily yoked Mrs. Fitzwilliam an encouraging squeeze about the shoulders, and the best advice available from the vast four decades' store of my experience?

"Well, then, my dear," I said briskly. "I think it's about time you did something about it. Don't you?"

Because, eventually, we all come upon that point of decision. The point at which you must act at last, for good or ill, and I suppose the choice you make, in that instant, represents the true nature of the bargain you have negotiated with your Creator. What sort of person you are. What sort of person you will be. What sort of soul you will, one day, commend to His keeping.

I stroke the Boy's cheek with my thumb, and I notice how wizened the poor digit looks, how sharp the nail, next to his new, clean skin. And we were so happy together, once.

"My precious, precious Boy," I whisper. "I think it's time for you to go."

TIT AND TATTLE, BY PATTY CAKE

Dear readers, for the past two decades I've brought you the latest from the world of the greatest, and today I have the privilege of outdoing even myself. Yes, my dears, your own Patty Cake has scooped them all in the Trial of the Century.

My sources tell me that the dramatic events of two days ago—the conviction of the Patent King on the charge of murder, to the great dismay of the pretty Patent Princesses, followed by the notorious shootout at the Pickwick Arms Hotel that sent both Mr. Faninal and his apparent rival, Mr. Lumley, to their final rewards—have proved a mere cover for the real story, the genuine article, which I now bring to you in all its horrifying certainty.

Far from being an injured party, it seems, Mr. Lumley is the mastermind of all. In a tear-streaked confession to the authorities, Mrs. Lumley revealed that she did not, in fact, first encounter her husband at the Bluebeard Restaurant in Scarsdale, two weeks after the murders, but that he had begun stepping out with her earlier that summer. It was he who conceived a plan by which the kitchen maid would seduce the master, who (Lumley learned from his comely partner) had been left brokenhearted by the easy behavior of his wife in the years following the birth of their second child. Blackmail would then ensue (over which liaison I can't say for certain, since there are so many to choose from), enabling the Lumleys to start off married life on the right foot: that is to say, shod by the affluence of the Faninal family.

But plans went awry, as they so often do, and the soon-to-be-Lumleys were interrupted in a heated discussion one morning by none other than the lady of the house. The kitchen maid, it seems, was developing too great a tendresse for her victim, and wanted to make an honorable retreat. Mr. Lumley, I am sorry to say, was of a different mind, and in the course of the ensuing argument, Mrs. Faninal became unavoidably cognizant of their scheme. Hearing the victim's gasp of outrage, Lumley took the nearest weapon—the famous kitchen knife—and made certain threats. The gallant lady defied him, and for this final act of courage paid the ultimate price, God rest her troubled soul.

In the immediate aftermath of this dreadful act, Mr. Lumley naturally swore his paramour to secrecy, and concocted a scheme by which she would make a false confession to Mr. Faninal, claiming that their guilty affection had been discovered by Mrs. Faninal; that during this violent confrontation the maid had been forced to strike her mistress in order to save herself, and the blow proved fatal. Mr. Faninal, racked with guilt that his lady love should have endured such a horrifying struggle because of his own passion for her, gave the girl sufficient money to start a new life, and then—as the world knows—disappeared with his two daughters, promising to take his kitchen maid's secret to his grave.

And so, it seems, he tried to do.

No doubt you will be hungry for particulars, dear ones—heaven knows I am—and I feel confident that my colleagues in the newsroom will labor day and night to satisfy your appetites. For now, however, I mean to sit back and absorb what we have just learned, and to perhaps spare a prayer or two for the soul of the Patent King, whose character we have all misjudged so grievously.

And lastly, I offer up another prayer for his two surviving daughters, whose whereabouts at the moment are not publicly known. I don't know about you, but I find I cannot blame them for their current seclusion, given this mauling they have both gracefully endured, and I wish them every possible happiness in the years to come.

Chapter 27

Marriage is like twirling a baton, turning handsprings, or eating with chopsticks. It looks easy until you try it.

—HELEN ROWLAND

THERESA

Southampton, Long Island, the fifteenth of June

For some time, I sit straight in my chair, elbows on the desk, and regard those last words on the page before me.

In the absence of the steady clicking of the typewriter keys, the ocean makes itself heard from the open window to my left. The slow, familiar crash of water. It's not quite dawn, and the wind is calm and briny, the gray light just visible on the sky outside. I grasp the knob on the right-hand side of the typewriter and scroll the paper upward, until it falls free from the roller.

Ordinarily I would mail the column to New York, inside a plain brown envelope addressed *NEW YORK HERALD-TIMES, Attn. MR. MIGS BERKELEY,* but this is a special story, a scoop that will appear on the front page of the afternoon edition, and I've got to telephone every last word to Migs by seven o'clock this morning, from this quiet little office on the attic floor of Windermere, of which even Sylvo is unaware.

But for now, it's only four thirty, and I'm not inclined to pick up the receiver and make conversation, though I know poor Migs is standing by, checking his watch, smoking a nervous cigarette. Well, let him wait. It's the least he can do, isn't it? When I'm delivering the scoop of the century straight into his waiting cup, cherry on top.

I lean back and stretch—my God, that feels good, poor old bones and sinews all cramped up—and look out the window. The surf bubbles quietly on the sand, that same stretch of beach on which my children have played, my guests have frolicked, my lovers have made love between the dunes. Every possible joy has been realized there. But you would never know, just now. It's empty and dark, the color of soot, and the sun is just a violet-pink promise to the east.

Outside, the breeze is both stronger and cooler than I expect, and I sit at the edge of the tide and bring my knees up to my chest, cradling the little lump of humanity inside. I think, as I always do, about the Boy. Not about that last dreadful half hour yesterday—I'd rather not think about that, the sight of his disappearing pink neck as I stood nobly next to my Sargent portrait in the foyer—but about those early days. The relief of physical intimacy. January the second, when the Boy was all mine, and we lay in the attic of the old carriage house while the frozen dawn assembled outside.

The Boy is no longer mine, but at least he's left something of himself behind, which—if I still believed in anything, and maybe I just do—I would consider a gift. A kind of earthly reward for my brief moment of nobility, only maybe it's a penance instead. Maybe the Boy's little daughter is my shame. God knows the world will consider her so. God only knows what I'm going to do with her. I suppose, like everything else, I'll find a way.

The sun rises and spreads, and I guess I'd better head back inside and telephone my column to Migs, before he has an apoplexy.

———

But the house is not quite so empty as I left it. The scent of human habitation is thick in the hallway, and as I turn the corner to the back stairs, I catch a glimpse of its source: my husband, sitting on the floor of the morning room, smoking a cigarette.

The sight is so unexpected I'm rooted to the spot. Hand on the newel post, foot on the step. Sylvo looks up, flushed and unsteady.

"My God," I call out softly. "Sylvo? Are you all right?"

He doesn't answer, and I propel myself into motion, across the hallway and the worn rug. The smell of whisky surrounds him, though there's no visible evidence of sin. I lower myself next to his right side, shaking with terror.

"The boys?" I whisper.

"They're fine."

The breath escapes me. I cross my legs, Indian-style, and take the cigarette from his fingers. It's nearly exhausted, but I extract a long draft anyway and hand it back to him. He crushes it out against his shoe and drops the stub atop the rug.

"She's left me," he says.

"Adelaide?"

"Yes. She ran into an old flame, a younger fellow. It seems he's made himself a bit of a fortune since then. Army contracts."

"Oh, Sylvo. I'm so sorry," I tell him, and I mean it. I thread my arm through the crook of his elbow and lean my head against his shoulder.

"Don't be sorry. I don't deserve it. I'm just an old fool, I suppose. Older and more foolish than most."

"Not that old, really."

"I'll be sixty-three next month. My own father would have been dead for two years by now."

"But you're not dead, darling. You're hale and hearty and handsome, with plenty of good years before you. You'll find someone else, I'm sure."

He makes a noise that might be a sigh, but is really more like a snort, buzzing with nasal derision. "No doubt. No doubt I'll be shortly making a fool of myself all over again, won't I?"

"Oh, Sylvo."

"Well, at least you're happy with Rofrano. I suppose that's something. I suppose that's the least I can offer you, after all I've forced you to endure. Which you have, with immeasurable dignity. My dear and long-suffering wife."

"No." I stroke his arm. "That's over, I'm afraid. He's left me."

"What? When?"

"Yesterday. I'm far too old for him, you know. I'm from another age, really. It simply wouldn't work."

"Oh, dear," he says. "Oh, dear. Look at us."

"Isn't it funny?"

The sun, fully risen, turns the window alive. In another moment, it will be too bright to stare out to sea like this, the way we're doing, side by side.

"Forgive me," Sylvo says.

"You were forgiven long ago, darling. We are who we are."

"But I've made you unhappy."

"I've made myself unhappy. And I suppose I've made myself happy, too, from time to time, so I can't really complain. In the great sum of things."

He reaches for my hand. Sylvo's hand, well tended and familiar. The gold signet ring, nothing else. I weave my fingers into his.

"We could still be unhappy together, you know," he says. A light, quiet suggestion.

"Now, that would be even funnier."

"I'm quite serious." He squeezes my hand and turns a bit, so we are just barely looking at each other, married eyeball to married eyeball. Breath to vinous breath.

"You're a little the worse for whisky, darling, but I appreciate the thought all the same."

The sun blisters the glass, too bright. Sylvo draws me back on the rug, and we lie there, staring at the ceiling, for some time. I breathe in the comforting fumes of his drunkenness, the lingering rasp of his cigarette, and I think about the first time we arrived here, after returning home from our obligatory European honeymoon. I was already pregnant with Tommy, and not much inclined for what, in those days, we sometimes delicately called bedsport. Like the gentleman he was, Sylvo didn't insist on what (again, in those days) we called his matrimonial rights. He settled me in his arms instead, and we contemplated the bedroom ceiling together, and I remember how perfectly contented I felt, how perfectly *married:* even more, perhaps, than I had felt in the aftermath of passion.

Sylvo says softly, holding my hand against the rug, "How about it, though?"

I smile at the ceiling, high and white above us, so elegantly finished, and try to imagine my husband saying those exact words a quarter century ago. When we were both so young.

I reply, just as softly: "I suppose that depends."

"Depends on what?"

I lay my other hand on my stomach, and I tell him what.

Chapter 28

Love, like a chicken salad or a restaurant hash,
must be taken with blind faith or it loses its flavor.

—HELEN ROWLAND

SOPHIE

Somewhere in Oklahoma, four weeks later

What Sophie loves most about the open road are the stars. In Manhattan, only the very brightest ones are visible, and those usually turn out—disappointingly, somehow—to be planets. Here, in the middle of Oklahoma, there are millions of miraculous dainty suns, a dazzling array. You can lie back on your blanket, next to your sleeping husband, and count all night.

But you don't. All that open air and exercise means you're usually fast asleep by the time you reach a hundred or so. Still, the plenitude is reassuring. It's good for the imagination.

Tonight, sleep hasn't come so quickly, and not even the stars are helping. That happens, too, and Sophie knows what to do. Another quarter hour of fruitless counting, and she slides out from beneath the blanket—Octavian stirs, but doesn't wake—and finds the notebook in which she keeps the letter she's writing to Virginia.

Letter. It's really more of a diary, since she's received only a single communication from her sister—a postcard sent from Miami three and a half weeks ago, promising to send a forwarding address that hasn't yet arrived. Sophie will send her the letter (forty-six pages and counting) when there's somewhere to send it.

Or maybe she won't.

Sophie lights the kerosene lantern and carries it away from the sheltering hollow in which they've set up their camp, to the boulder that's served as a table, and sometimes a sofa. She takes out a pencil stub and writes: *Still in Oklahoma. We love our little campsite here too much to leave, I guess. There's a lake nearby, where we bathe in the morning, and the weather's been terrific, nice and hot and dry. We haven't put up the tent in days. Of course, we've got to leave sometime, but we don't have to be in Los Angeles until the middle of August, when Octavian's new business partner returns from Europe.*

She pauses, chewing on the pencil, because she's repeating herself, isn't she? Telling Virgo all the facts she already knows. And this letter isn't supposed to be like that. It's not supposed to be about facts.

I miss Father

The pencil hovers. Sophie adds a period.

Isn't that funny? I miss him awfully. I have so many questions he can't answer, so many things I want to tell him. I wish I could tell him that I'm doing fine, that I'm building a brave new future, and I'm not quite happy yet—at least the way I've always understood happy to mean, the way I used to be happy—but I've got something close to it, something maybe even a little better than simple joy. Or at least, it will be. Octavian says

She stops again. She hasn't written for a few days, and she's conscious that her words are stiff, the way words sometimes are when you haven't spoken with a person in some time. She's forgotten how much she already told Virginia, how much she's kept to herself.

And that single word: *Octavian.*

She looks over her shoulder, at the bed they've made for themselves in the grass, covered by a tarpaulin and a blanket and a sheet—that's the mattress—and another blanket to cover them, just one, because it's July. The moon is thin and distant, shedding only the faintest amount of light, and she can't really see her husband.

But she doesn't need eyes to know he's there, does she? His presence is like a magnet, like a gravitational center, communicating itself to her as a current of electricity along some invisible primordial wire. His arm is a faint gray smudge atop the blanket, where Sophie should be. She can almost feel the weight across her breast. That's how connected they are, these days.

She turns back to the notebook on her lap.

Octavian says we'll have plenty of time for walls and roofs when we get to California. (And clothes, ha ha

She scribbles that out.

For now, it's the best honeymoon a girl could ask for. It's just us, getting to know each other, and as far as I'm concerned, I never want to see another human being. (Except you and Evelyn, of course.) No doubt that will wear away in time—wanting him and only him—but right now it's perfect, because I think he's the only one in the world who understands, and that understanding ebbs and flows between us in this beautiful and aston-ishing way, every time we touch each other, every time we speak. What I mean, I guess, is that we both need this freedom at the moment: to kiss and touch and be man and wife whenever we want, without anyone else to see or care or intrude on what we are saying to each

The lead breaks. Sophie's writing too urgently again. She takes the penknife out of her pencil case and sharpens the end, by the oily yellow light of the kerosene lantern. Around her, the peeps and hoots and rustles of the nocturnal world go quietly on, not regarding her at all. The prairie wind has died down, and the air is warm and still, smelling of sweet July grass. When she sets down the pencil case, she writes the word *other* after *each*, and puts a period after it.

Anyway, married life is grand and we are making more plans every day. Octavian works on his airplane designs and I'm learning how to draft, because I want to be a part of this, too: a real partner, and not just a financial one. (Octavian won't have it any other way, really, because he hates the idea that's he's somehow "taking" my money to build his airplanes.) We're going to find ourselves a pretty cottage in the middle of an orange grove. Octavian seems to want about twenty kids and I think I'd be happy with two or three, so I guess we'll have to compromise somewhere, although at the rate we're going

She smudges that out and puts a period after *somewhere.* Smiling to herself.

But I suppose that's the point of all this, these weeks we are taking to get to know each other, in the privacy of the Great Outdoors. If there's one thing we've learned, the two of us, it's that marriage isn't always easy, and there will be times that try us without mercy.

We will sometimes—maybe even often—disagree, and things and people and events will come along that test our courage and resolve, and that's when we will turn to the memory of this precious time together, and the knot we are weaving to bind us into one. This language we are creating that belongs only to the two of us. Sometimes, when we are lying together at night, Octavian whispers in my ear a single word: Wife. *And I know that word doesn't just mean* I love you. *(We hardly ever say that anymore, because it's so small and insufficient and unnecessary.) He means that I am his entire family, the source of his earthly happiness, the object of all the loyalty in his dear and faithful heart. That he will protect and adore me to his last breath. (The strength of his emotions sometimes awes me, and I think how strong I must be to receive and return them. He is not for the faint of heart, my Octavian.) You might say that all of our marriage vows are packed into that one marvelous little word.*

And, in return, I tell him: Husband. *And that's that, really. It's all we need to say before we go to sleep.*

Sophie rests the notebook against her knees and lifts her arms to the night sky, stretching and stretching, linking her fingertips above her head. There is a continuous and friendly ache in her muscles these days—Octavian's not for the faint of frame either—but she doesn't mind that. She relishes this new awareness of her own body, the faint and decadent echoes of physical love. They remind her of her wedding night—or perhaps *elopement* is a better word—eighteen days ago, in an otherwise unremarkable hotel room outside of Philadelphia, and the gentle, patient way by which her new husband coaxed her into the intimacies of marriage. As it turned out, there was nothing at all the matter with her sex-instinct. It was all just a question of honing it properly! What a relief *that* was.

Sophie looks down at the page again, the careful and small-written lines in the light of the kerosene lantern. Does she really mean to send this letter to Virgo, after all? Or is it just for her, for Sophie: an ecstatic diary of her unconventional honeymoon, so she can read it one day and remember what it was like to be newly married, embarking on the open road in a forest-green Model T, starting a life and a business and a family together? Embarking from the abyss of grief, inch by inch, toward a new and promising future.

She puts the pencil back to the paper.

We held another funeral today. I don't think I've mentioned those yet. Actually, I don't know if funeral is really the right word. We did the first one somewhere in western Pennsylvania. Octavian was talking about France and one of his friends who was shot down and died behind enemy lines, the last day of the war, and I could see he was growing more upset, until he stopped talking altogether. So I said, let's hold a service for him, and I got out the Bible from one of the trunks in the car and that's what we did, and it seemed to help a great deal.

Sophie reading the service. Octavian sitting there on a rock with his head bowed, the moonlight spilling over his bare shoulders—it had been awful, though she didn't write that down, my God how silent and upset and shuttered away—and when she closed the book he just took her in his arms and wept, and eventually they crawled under the blanket, into the most beautiful silence in the world, full of pain and joy and intimacy, the most astounding night, and afterward Octavian slept until nine o'clock the next morning, a thing he had never done before.

Tonight we had a funeral for Quentin Roosevelt. Octavian only knew him for a few weeks, but I think they had a kind of sympathy together. I think they were men of the same substance, though Octavian won't have it, because he never believes himself to be nearly so good as he really is. I suppose

"Scribbling again?"

Sophie startles all the way to her feet, pencil flying.

Octavian laughs and hauls her into a bearlike embrace. "Sorry. I thought you heard me coming."

"I usually do," she says, into the skin of his chest, thinking how much she loves the sound of his laugh, and how much more often he's laughing now. How much *freer* his movements now—imagine that bear hug on their careful and tentative wedding night!—and his words, too. "I was writing about the funeral."

"Mmm. Come to bed."

"But I'm not finished yet."

"I can't sleep alone."

"Lies."

He growls in her ear—hungry bear!—and lifts her off her feet.

"The lantern!" she exclaims, and he swoops it up, too, pretending to drop her as he does, and they stagger, laughing, to the blankets, where he drops her right smack in the middle and collapses by her side.

Later, when they're settled in, and Octavian's arms hold her securely in place—*No more running off tonight, now*—she tells him that she was writing to Virgo about the funeral for Quentin Roosevelt.

"We can drive into Tulsa tomorrow, if you like," he says. "See if there's any word from her."

"All right."

"You're not worried, are you?"

"Not yet." She hesitates. "Are you worried?"

"I guess I am, a little bit. She's my sister now, isn't she?"

"Yes, she is," Sophie says firmly, snuggling deeper.

Octavian breathes into her ear, a terribly slow respiration.

"You know, if you want to do one for your father . . ."

"One what?"

"You know. Like we've done for my buddies." (He doesn't like the word *funeral* either.) "So, if you want to do it, I can read the service for you. The way you have for me."

She finds his hand on the wool before her.

"Let's wait for Virginia," she says. "Virginia should be there, too."

"All right." He kisses her temple. Touches the parting of her hair. Adds, quietly: "Wife."

She closes her eyes and tucks his fingers close, right where they belong.

"Husband."

Author's Note

I experienced a weird and probably inappropriate childhood. From the tender age of five, I was regularly exposed to the uncensored lewdness of Shakespeare at the summer festival in Ashland, Oregon, and I distinctly remember watching *Don Giovanni* ("Daddy, what's a mistress?") at the Seattle Opera when I was seven years old. The orchestra was on strike, and a pair of pianos accompanied the singers. When I was eight, a bomb threat interrupted a perfectly good performance of *Lucia di Lammermoor.*

It was all downhill from there, really—social ostracism, a humiliating memory of enacting Desdemona's death scene on the living room sofa for the amusement of dinner guests. If a torrent of sexual passion runs through all my books, you can just blame my parents for that Live from the Met broadcast of *Manon Lescaut* in which a young and exceptionally hot Placido Domingo topples into bed with Renata Scotto. Imprinting starts early, folks.

You can blame them for this book, too. I don't know exactly when it occurred to me that Richard Strauss's *Der Rosenkavalier* might work as a novel set in 1920s Manhattan, but the idea took root and refused to wither. In my defense, there's some logic attached. First performed in 1911, the opera enacts a struggle between old and new—old money and new money, physical maturity and youth—in lyric, bittersweet music that itself clashed with the dissonant modernism then in fashion. Audiences ate up the eighteenth century Viennese setting, the sensual opening scene in the Marschallin's luxurious boudoir, the angsty rivalry between a beautiful young ingénue and a lady of a certain age.

And if the Roaring Twenties were about anything, it was the conflict between youth and age, between tradition and modernism, between old and new.

Of course, I soon realized that Strauss's opera hasn't got enough plot to support a modern full-length novel—the good old Scheming Servants storyline doesn't pack the same punch as it did a hundred years ago—so I had to invent a murder mystery to drive the action along. Purists, I hope, will forgive me for the embroidery.

No need, however, to embroider the wonderful wit of Helen Rowland, a journalist and humorist who—a century ago—wrote a popular column called "Reflections of a Bachelor Girl" for the old *New York World* newspaper. As usually happens, I stumbled across Helen's ironic wisdom while researching something else, and not only did I adore her turn of phrase, I felt as if I'd discovered a clear and sharp-edged window into changing social customs in the early decades of the twentieth century . . . and, for that matter, an insight into how much has remained the same! I have a feeling Helen would find plenty to say about the contemporary state of love and marriage.

As for the horse race that brings Theresa and Octavian together, you can blame my horse-mad daughter, who insisted I write the legendary Man o' War into a novel set at the beginning of the 1920s. I was happy to oblige. The 1920 Dwyer Stakes was one of the great races of the age, and the eighth pole at the old Aqueduct was preserved and dedicated to Man o' War when the new track opened in 1959.

It still stands there today.

Acknowledgments

A *Certain Age* marks a homecoming: to my very first editor, Rachel Kahan, now of William Morrow, who fell in love with the manuscript of *Overseas* several years ago and introduced herself in a memorable phone call that marked the start of my career as a professional writer. I'm so grateful to have her passion and expertise in my corner again, along with the tremendous energy and enthusiasm of her colleagues. And I'm grateful as well to my dear friends at G.P. Putnam's Sons for five books in four fabulous years, and for helping me make the transition with so much grace and goodwill.

The one and only Alexandra Machinist guides my professional affairs with such energy and commitment, I feel like every book rides out the door atop a truckload of thanks to her and to the entire terrific agency team at ICM. I can't imagine my career without you.

I am always humbled by support of family and friends, in-laws and outlaws, and above all my endlessly wonderful husband, Sydney, and our four children. As we up sticks and move along the coast to more rural climes, I want to send out special thanks to all those dear friends in Greenwich who touched our lives in every way: from the Starbucks baristas who let me sit and write for hours in the corner table, to the waitresses at the Putnam Diner who kept my coffee cup filled, to my fellow moms and dads at Julian Curtiss School who cheered me on from the first book, and to everyone in between.

Readers! Booksellers! Bloggers! Author buddies! A final thanks to you, who make it all possible. I love your messages and your tweets, I love meeting you on the road, I love your passion for books and your breathtaking support. Putting a book out in the world is a naked, dangerous journey, and you give me clothes and shoes and shelter. I can't hug you enough.

About the Author

A graduate of Stanford University with an MBA from Columbia, Beatriz Williams spent several years in New York and London hiding her early attempts at fiction, first on company laptops as a communications strategy consultant, and then as an at-home producer of small persons, before her career as a writer took off. She lives with her husband and four children near the Connecticut shore.